The Streets of Babylon:
A London Mystery

Carina Burman

Published in Great Britain and the United States in 2008 by

MARION BOYARS PUBLISHERS LTD
24 Lacy Road London SW15 1NL

www.marionboyars.co.uk

Distributed in Australia and New Zealand by Tower Books Pty Ltd,
Unit 2, 17 Rodborough Road, Frenchs Forest, NSW 2086, Australia.

Printed in 2008
10 9 8 7 6 5 4 3 2 1

First published in Sweden by Albert Bonniers as *Babylons gator: Ett
Londonmysterium* in 2004.

A CIP catalogue record for this book is available from the British Library.

A CIP catalog record for this book is available from the Library of Congress.

ISBN 978-0-7145-3138-0

We would like to thank the Arts Council of England for
assistance in the translation of this book.

We would like to thank the Swedish Arts Council for their support.

Set in Bembo 11/14pt

Printed in England by J. H. Haynes & Co. Ltd., Sparkford

The Streets of Babylon:
A London Mystery

by Carina Burman

Translated from the Swedish by Sarah Death

MARION BOYARS
LONDON • NEW YORK

'Nothing is what it appears to be, dear Euthanasia.
Nothing.'

CONTENTS

CHAPTER ONE

IN WHICH AGNES AND I VISIT THE GREAT EXHIBITION

The sun rose blood red after a terrible, pitch black night. No one could yet imagine what horrors the sea had witnessed. There was more wreckage in the waves than there had been at dusk, but no watchful eye was there to discern it. From her cliff top the fisherman's daughter saw nothing but the flaming hues of the sun, lending both sky and sea traces of blood and horror.

'London! England!'

The cabin door opened, and I hastily stowed away my manuscript in my portmanteau. Agnes was so eager she could hardly keep still. The steamer *Helen McGregor* was docking, and I hurried up the stairway with my book bag in tow. My companion was not the only one feeling over-excited. My own heart, too, was ticking like a demented Swiss watch.

Before me lay buildings familiar from prints and engravings. For the country dwellers in Miss Austen's novels this was a city which represented the height of refinement. From here, the young Queen ruled over an empire on which the sun truly never set. By her charming example, the world would soon see that feminine gentleness and serenity could rule just as well as masculine brutality. In this city, readers sat poring over my novels, learning still more about manners, politeness and the thousands of opportunities open to women. On deck sat a young lady, in fact, so engrossed in my novel *The Manor House* that she had scarcely noticed we were putting in to London. Perhaps in English translation the Swedish province of Sörmland was as exotic as the Tower, St Paul's Cathedral and the Greenwich Observatory.

'Look,' cried Agnes, once we were on deck. She was pointing in all directions – at the grand buildings, at the small boats and other craft, at the Thames dockyards where ships to command the oceans were being built.

For me, too, London was new and virginal. I grew up in a Swedish manor house, and I have seen a good deal of the world. No one would believe Euthanasia Bondeson to be a country girl. Granted, my parents had a taste for peculiar names (I would have preferred them to choose 'Malvina' or 'Ariadne', which they were also considering), but my experiences have not been unvaried. When the great city revealed itself before me, I gasped.

'Look, Aunt Euthanasia! What sort of boat is that? Oh, so many steamers!'

I relayed information and explanation as best I could. The many-masted vessel was a square-rigger and that slender beauty could be nothing other than a clipper, soon to be speeding across the waves to fetch tea and silk from distant China. Alongside her bobbed a row of steamboats, like provincial lasses at a Stockholm ball. Small boats hurried to and fro; there were gentlemen in uniform and sailors in white trousers; there was the singing sound of capstans and masts – the great city went to my head, and all the bridges of London extended before me: London Bridge, Southwark Bridge, Blackfriars Bridge and all those other names. The greatest miracle of all was invisible to our eyes. The Thames Tunnel ran from Wapping to Rotherhithe, linking north and south beneath the waters of the river.

'Isn't it fabulous?' said Agnes, and gave a little jump of delight, making her earrings leap and her gold chains jingle. Her dress rode up several inches, of course, revealing both button boots and well-turned calves. I gave a small sigh, but then smiled and instructed her thoroughly in the geography and customs of the city. The gangplanks were lowered into place, and we stepped onto British soil.

Today was the seventh of September 1851. London was more than ever the centre of the world: it was the year of the Great Exhibition, and the inhabitants not only of the Empire but of the whole world were assembled in Hyde Park, as though they had been summoned there to be taxed.

I cannot deny that the Exhibition was one of the reasons for our own visit to England. It had been a busy year for us both. In the spring we had travelled in France, where I collected material for a novel about the revolution of 1848, and we spent the summer months bathing at the Hälsans Brunn Spa in Skåne, the southernmost province of our homeland. For Agnes it was a tranquil summer, with all the diversions and attentions that a young girl may expect of a spa visit, while I battled with proofs and new manuscripts between my bathing sessions.

In London we knew no one. That was one important reason for going there. My publishers were there, of course, and my translator – but they would not demand friendship. They knew the literary world. Here we would find peace and quiet. I would be spared readers looking at me, first shyly, then with determination, uttering their interminable 'Euthanasia Bondeson? Can it really be my privilege?'

No one met us on the quayside. One gentleman immediately noticed that we were travelling alone and asked if he could help. He seemed to be an honourable man, but I had to think of Agnes, and asked him to summon one of the police officers.

The English police are unlike anything seen in Sweden. When we talk of police officers, the English say 'policemen'. I would almost go a step further and call them 'police gentlemen'. They are a splendid species, the English police: tall, upright, well dressed in close-fitting, dark-blue tailcoats with silver embroidery on the collar, tall black hats and white gloves. One can hardly believe they perform the same task as our surly Swedish police officers, who stink of schnapps and wield their sticks on anything that crosses their path. The English police gentlemen are unarmed, and it is not beneath their dignity to help two unaccompanied ladies with their luggage and find them a cab.

The obliging police gentleman piloted us past the small, light, two-wheeled hansom cabs, the popular choice. They are for passengers only. With all our baggage, we required a slower, more stable, four-wheeled carriage, known as a *growler*, which conveyed us safely towards the centre of London.

A teeming city greeted us. Agnes's jaw dropped, in that rather goose-like way of hers. She is considerably cleverer than one might give her credit for, but young and impressionable. The menfolk of London gawped just as much at her as she did at their city. When we came to a halt in a traffic jam at Temple, they began crowding round our carriage to get a glimpse of the girl, and I heard voices say the name Jenny Lind. Agnes is a very beautiful girl, with the pale blond hair of the Nordic races, blue eyes and a dainty nose, and the seductive freshness of the high mountains, her cheeks as red as a lingonberry. It is an insult to compare her to Miss Lind, whose snub nose is as renowned throughout the world as her voice. I called to the cabbie to get us out of there, and he raised his whip and brought it down everywhere but on the horse. The men dispersed, and we continued at a brisk pace to the Golden Cross, a family hotel in the Strand.

Our police gentleman had recommended the hotel. It was an excellent choice – comfortable without being elegant, homely without being cramped, and affordable without seeming cheap. What is more, the Golden Cross was a name we ought to have been able to remember. We installed ourselves in two rooms with a connecting door – an absolute necessity for my writing – checking ourselves in as Miss E. Bondeson and her companion Agnes Björk. A tree name: she has that much in common with

Miss Lind. Lind means 'linden', and Agnes's surname means 'birch'. The birch, tall, slender and fair, is a most appropriate symbol for her.

Outside, the sun was shining. We had left Skåne on the verge of autumn, but here it was high summer. Agnes was as thrilled as a child, wanting go out and explore at once. There would not be time for the Great Exhibition, of course, as it was already Sunday afternoon, but could we not at least take a little stroll along the streets of the city?

I could understand her impatience. That longing for the unknown can still, after forty years, take a claw-like grip on my stomach regions. A wise mistress can hardly ask a girl to rest and relax, with the whole world clamouring outside the window.

'Very well!' I said, glancing in the mirror and taking up my umbrella – for you never know with the English weather. 'Let us venture forth and conquer London!'

Agnes is taller than I, but we are both strong walkers. We would never think of taking newly purchased boots on our travels, and our everyday skirts are always well bound at the hem to withstand both mud and the filth of the streets. I had already studied my map of the city carefully. I wished to say nothing to Agnes, but I can reveal to my dear readers my difficulties in finding my way in strange cities. Even in Stockholm, my home town, it is not always easy. I am neither inattentive nor stupid, but my surroundings spin like a cogwheel in my head. I presume it is all to do with the rotation of the Earth. Thorough study and a reliable map are the only cures for my affliction. Agnes is even worse, and therefore admires my sense of direction. I chose not to disillusion her as we hurried downstairs and out into the Strand.

Out in the street, Agnes gasped. People of every physiognomy, costume and colour were rushing along the pavements. The streets were thronged with carriages and brightly coloured omnibuses. Stockholm was a backwater compared to London.

'I never knew there were so many people!' whispered Agnes,

and I felt glad I had not taken her to Paris. We walked past St. James's Palace, on through Green Park and into Hyde Park. Then we were thrown from one extreme to the other – from the hurly-burly life of the streets into the lush stillness of the parks – until we saw what we had really come for. Over by the Serpentine lay the Crystal Palace, that glorious construction which housed the World Fair. Even from a distance, the Palace was unlike anything we had ever seen. It was at the same time a shrine to the peaceful intercourse of people, a hothouse for culture and industry and a station for the railway trains of human encounter.

The Crystal Palace was almost 2,000 feet in length and built entirely of iron and glass. The strongest and the frailest of materials had entered into beautiful union, and I felt my heart beat faster with joy. 'What a piece of work is man, how noble in reason,' says Prince Hamlet – and though the melancholy prince may not mean it, I do. At the sight of that gigantic structure, surrounded by a swarm of people and carriages, I was filled with delight at the human race, myself included.

'Aunt Euthanasia, it's wonderful!' whispered Agnes, rolling her blue eyes so much that I was afraid she might swoon. I put my arm about her waist and looked around for somewhere to sit.

In London one is seldom left long in a quandary. A kindly lady came sailing like a Thames barge along the path through the park, and hove-to alongside us.

'Is the poor girl unwell?'

'She just feels a little faint.' Agnes gave a wan smile. Her English is very limited.

'There are cafés everywhere,' said the lady, 'but if the girl is delicate, there are cows in St. James's Park, and fresh milk is available.'

I must have resembled that curved symbol generally used to conclude dubious statements. The lady smiled.

'I expect you are a stranger here,' she said. 'There are cows in the park. Many Londoners would have to go without fresh milk otherwise.'

'Oh, I see!' I said, and explained this to Agnes. The news transformed her.

'Yes! Yes! I want milk!'

She now seemed anything but delicate. We went back the way we had come, and did indeed find a whole row of cows along the edge of St. James's Park. The milkmaid was ready at once to provide Agnes with a mug of milk. While the girl drank, we watched the crowds: the children decked out in their finery, being taken for walks by their nursemaids; and the pretty servant girls being courted by soldiers. Despite the bustle and decadence of the city, I felt a hint of the pleasures of country life. Fortified, we returned to our hotel.

★★★

The sun knew that blood had been spilt during the night. Its gleam spread crimson across the sea, for the sun cared little for the horrifying deed that had been done. The junipers stood like sentries along the coast, tall and slender, but though they might be able to offer protection against the wind and surging seas – they were no defence against Death...

Our second day in London was earmarked for *The Exhibition!* First I wrote a few pages, then Agnes and I ate a substantial breakfast of the British variety. Agnes gorged herself on a steak, while I more cautiously consumed bacon, egg and baked beans. Insipid tea accompanied these; the Golden Cross Hotel could produce no coffee for breakfast. Disconcerted eyebrows were raised at my enquiry. On the British Isles, tea is served at breakfast, coffee mid-morning, and tea again in the afternoon. Perhaps the explanation for this interminable tea drinking is the possession of so many colonies, whose economy one wishes to support. I decided to make further enquiries on this point when the opportunity presented itself – which it did soon enough.

Curiosity prompted us to take an omnibus. These carriages can accommodate twenty-five reasonably compact passengers and are drawn by two strong horses with well-groomed brown coats, docked tails and cropped manes. The omnibus was almost overflowing with passengers, but with Agnes's stateliness and my determination we succeeded in getting on board. We would have liked to ride on the open top and enjoy the view, but the conductor blocked the stairs and explained that this was not for ladies. There was no point in arguing. Instead we squeezed ourselves in by a window and gathered up our skirts.

'All right! All right!' shouted the conductor, and thumped on the ceiling.

London began to move past our window pane. Not for a moment was it quiet. The conductor kept shouting out the next stop, and we found it impossible to have a whispered exchange. Around us sat not only representatives of John Bull's robust race, but also various other foreigners. The Turk in his fez was easily identified, and the blond gentleman at the front must have been Scandinavian, but we had a long, loud debate about where a particular dark, stylish gentleman might have originated.

Everyone was going to the Exhibition, for this, the year of grace, 1851, was the year of the very first World Fair. Outside the Crystal Palace there was a fearful crush. One could scarcely push one's way through the mass of people, carriages and other vehicles. I let Agnes clear a path and followed on her heels through the Prince of Wales entrance.

Today was a 'Shilling Day', a reduced price day when absolutely anybody could visit the Exhibition. Seeing the throng of people, I momentarily regretted that we had not waited until the following day, when the five-shilling entrance charge would limit the visitors to those from the upper classes. Then I looked at the throng again, and felt a warm surge of enthusiasm. Could one hope for a better occasion on which to see the World Fair than today, when the inhabitants of the whole world had made their way here?

'Aunt Euthanasia! Hurry up!' called Agnes, far ahead of me.

The girl had become separated from me in the crush. I made myself smaller still and edged past some solid rural labourers (or that, at least, was what I took them for). I could see the blonde head in front of me.

'Agnes! Wait for me inside the entrance!' I shouted, but there was no girl awaiting me inside. She had already paid her shilling and was disappearing into the distance. Around me I could hear the heady, incomprehensible hubbub of a thousand human voices. There were mostly English sounds, as soft as the rolling landscape, but also the rasp of Frenchmen, the hawking of Germans and Welshmen and an energetic jabber of consonants from Italians and Spaniards.

I stood there, beneath the tall, glass vault of the Crystal Palace, and amidst all the din I was utterly alone. I was still unconcerned. In fact, I felt almost exhilarated, as I used to when I evaded my nursemaid as a child and ran off to make my own discoveries – and when I raised my eyes, I was back there, a little girl in the big conservatory at home. The sun shone through the glass, concentrated and embellished by the refraction, and I could actually smell the scent of orange trees and exotic flowers.

I, Euthanasia Bondeson, was tiny beneath the vast dome of the Great Exhibition. Glass and iron soared all around me. One cannot imagine anything more beautiful – but if my readers allow themselves to be distracted by my memories and imagine that the Crystal Palace was like a greenhouse, I must correct them at once. Glazed it certainly was, but whoever could visualise an ordinary greenhouse longer than the Royal Palace in Stockholm and taller than the crowning arch of Uppsala Cathedral. I stood there in reverential awe, for this was a temple – a temple to mankind, to mankind's great ability. But I am doubtless becoming tedious, and moreover, I had mislaid Agnes.

I have had a good education myself, with early tuition in all the major languages, but Agnes speaks very few words of English. She could say 'Good morning' and 'Good evening', though strangely not 'Good night'. Furthermore, she could inhale through her nose in a manner that makes it even straighter and lovelier than usual, and ask those around her 'whether 'tis nobler in the mind to suffer the slings and arrows of outrageous fortune'. I did not think these linguistic skills would get her far in the Crystal Palace. The only item that could possibly be of any practical use to her was her most recently acquired phrase: 'You are a humbug, sir!'

So I set about looking for her. Agnes is my lady's companion, but it is I who looks after her. She is always getting lost. Apart from beauty, a certain silliness and the occasional bout of good, common sense, it is her most prevalent characteristic. I have lost her in Stockholm and Copenhagen, in Bordeaux and Dresden – and yes, even in the small Swedish town of Åmål.

In the Crystal Palace I forged my way past handicraft displays and tools, between masterpieces produced in France and Outer Mongolia. I came to a place where they were serving ginger ice cream, which Agnes very much likes, but there was no girl to be seen. I found myself trapped near the Swedish spinning wheel, which looked pitiful amidst all the splendour. My companion had not sought it out. I found August Kiss's much-admired sculpture of an Amazon. It was not unlike Agnes in appearance, but she was not there. I turned on my heel with a snort and set off for Hindustan, an exhibition I had long wished to see.

Whereupon I immediately collided with a gentleman.

It took me a moment to extract myself. The collision had been a hard one, and I had managed to entangle myself in the gentleman's watch chain. He unhooked me with extreme *courtoisie*, carefully took hold of my collar and removed my person to a decent distance from his own. Then he looked at me with an expression of surprise such as I had hardly ever seen, even when I was young and forever attending balls. I am not beautiful, but I know my appearance can be fascinating.

'Miss Bondeson? Can it really be my privilege? Is it truly…?'

And I, who had been so happy at the thought of not being recognised, could have embraced that man all over again. He had noticed me, and addressed me by name. I was no longer a stray woman at the Great Exhibition; I was a successful authoress at an exhibition, which, while worthy of esteem, was still only an exhibition.

'I am one of your greatest admirers!' said the man.

My heart melted. Nothing wins a writer's heart as easily as cheap compliments. I raised my eyes from the man's breast pocket – which was most aesthetically filled with an elegant handkerchief, inserted with consummate nonchalance and not the slightest regard for the usefulness of such objects. Above it was a soft collar – truly an aesthete! – and a floppy, lavender-coloured cravat. And finally the face; certainly not a face to be despised, with a straight nose, big, dark eyes and a mouth with a sardonic curl that was by no means repellent. Moreover, it was a dark face, for the man was an Indian. He had touches of grey in his hair, and must have been about my age. His look was as much amused as anything else.

'I am delighted!' I replied, and I really was. After all, this man had recognised me from lithographs and saved me from the predicament of being lost. What was more, he appeared attractive, if not entirely harmless. Such readers are very welcome.

My aesthetic admirer bowed deeply, kissed my hand and introduced himself:

'Professor Devindra Sivaramakrishnan.'

'I beg your pardon?'

The man with the long surname gave an almost imperceptible smile.

'I am an artist by nature and a physician by profession,' he went on, omitting to mention that he was also extremely forbearing. I was doubtless not the first to stumble over his name. 'You can call me Professor Devindra; most people do.'

So he took me to the exhibition of his home country, talking extensively about India, which he had not seen since he was sent to school in England as a boy. I have always dreamt of the East, so I questioned him closely and at length. As I gazed at a stuffed elephant carrying a house on its back that could accommodate a maharajah and several doe-eyed ladies, I finally queried the amount of tea drunk in England.

'The English drink tea because they are a civilised people,' replied Professor Devindra, with a slight elevation of one of his shapely eyebrows. 'Coffee is a low beverage, not unlike Scotch whisky – it stimulates, but such excitation is not wholly desirable.'

Nonplussed, I told him of our incessant Swedish coffee consumption, and how that blessed beverage had increasingly become a substitute for schnapps. Now it was Professor Devindra's turn to be astonished. Deep in contemplation of the differences between England and Sweden, we strolled on past the exhibitions of the Oriental peoples and my guide promised I should meet his artistic friends.

Professor Devindra had a marvellous talent for putting people at their ease. I let him take me out into the Transept, intersecting the main body of the crystal shrine and housing the cafés of the Exhibition, which had been secreted among tall elms, murmuring springs, dwarf trees from Japan and blazing red bushes from America, between English weeping willows and Swedish firs. I sank down on a chair with a sigh, for by now I felt both tired and at a loss. My gentleman at once summoned a waitress and muttered his order without consulting me – and what a surprise! A tray was immediately placed before me, filled with tiny, delicate pastries, not unlike those I had once been served in Turkey, with a pot of the spiciest, most invigorating tea I had ever tasted. I felt as refreshed as if I had just enjoyed a long sleep. All at once I could see the sun shining through the roof, its light splitting into rainbows in the waters of the fountain, see the statues placed among the foliage and hear the pianoforte music, which like the purling water seemed to have been provided solely for the refreshment of an exhausted lady traveller. Something within me took up the thread where I had left it that morning and pondered on the blood-red sun, grim events and sombre junipers. I wondered where my novel was going.

Then Agnes came back into my mind. There were so many things that could happen to a young girl in this crush – alone, vulnerable, with no knowledge of either the language or the *mores*! Imagine what low scoundrels might attempt to seize her gold chain or her most precious treasure! I had met a cultivated admirer, but she had been forbidden to talk to strangers. Beauty is a dangerous attendant, and her Swedish directness might easily be misinterpreted.

'You must meet my friends, Miss Bondeson!' said my gentleman.

'I have a problem, Sir,' I replied. 'I have mislaid my lady's companion.'

Professor Devindra again raised an eyebrow, and again I felt such relief at having found him.

'In that case, we must tell the police,' said Professor Devindra. 'If you will just wait here, I shall be back very soon.' He got hastily to his feet, while I took a few more nibbles of a sweet pastry. People were surging all around me. Here in the refreshment area, their mass was less impenetrable. A little way off sat a young couple, clearly newlyweds, sampling each other's pastries and twittering like caged birds. A group of French people close by were complaining loudly about the coffee, which was far too much like dishwater for their taste. How remarkable that coffee and tea were the subjects to unite all the visitors to the Exhibition. On a bench sat three youths from the country, eating a packed lunch of meat pie and drinking beer from a wooden keg – no doubt provided by their local inn at home, since no country dweller dare rely on the comestibles the city provides. Their banter amused me, though I could not understand the half of it. The peasant lads did not speak Professor Devindra's 'university English'.

All at once I caught sight of Agnes' blonde head. It detached itself from a crowd of people and popped up beside the Swedish firs. It pleased me to see her that way – like a medieval vision of Swedish young womanhood, striding briskly through the fir forest and fearing neither trolls nor devils. But the Cuban hibiscus rapidly became her backdrop, and then she vanished behind England's weeping willow.

'Agnes! Wait!'

Without a thought, I was on my feet and rushing after her. I saw the blonde head sticking up some way off, and followed it. Now and then, a sunbeam came stealing through the transparent dome and made the top of Agnes's head shine like gold, as if she were a Buddhist statue and not an ordinary Swedish girl. There she was in front of me, presumably beside herself with worry, alone at the Great Exhibition.

'Agnes!'

She did not hear me. Suddenly the shimmer of gold was gone and I was alone. Perhaps I had been following a phantom. She was not to be seen, the girl who was my company and my security. Emptiness engulfed me.

Maybe I exaggerate? It undoubtedly felt empty, but that was mostly inside me. Around me, it was as crowded as ever. People were pushing and shoving, so I drew aside and raised my eyes. Perhaps Agnes would appear after all.

But the girl was, and remained, gone. I was surrounded by shining steel. As vast and solemn as the colossi of antiquity, machines towered all about me. Arms and cogs moved to and fro in perpetual mechanical patterns. The metal was burnished to the sheen of a racehorse, yet the cogwheels were a greasy black. The stench of oil and fire hung in the air around me. I had ended up in the Exhibition's machine hall.

Until then I had been searching without the slightest fear. Now panic made a grab for me, like a troll's hand suddenly protruding from the forest to seize hesitant passers-by. I looked around. There were of course people in the machine hall, too, but none I could ask for help. Even if I had shouted, nobody would have heard. Here at the centre of the modern world, I was more isolated than in the wilds, and it was the terror of the wilds that I was experiencing. All around me the machines were in constant motion, and for every piston stroke they made a clunk, a screech or a bellow. Experimentally, I gave a little scream, but not a single head turned in my direction.

Then I broke into a run. The sun was still scorching down through the glass roof, and around me strolled gentlemen and ladies, men and women of every possible kind. None of them were my Agnes, and none were my previous gentleman. Anxiety pursued me. I ran until I came up against another machine. Weights rose and fell before my eyes, and suddenly there was a human being there, talking to me.

'This is the hydraulic press that's to be used on the great railway bridge.'

I turned to the man. My eyes must have been full of madness, for he recoiled. He was a working man, broad-shouldered and undoubtedly rational. I suddenly felt the security of ordinary humanity.

'Is it true that there are plans to run trains underground here in London?'

'That's what they say,' replied the man. 'But if it's the future you're interested in, Ma'am, you should carry on walking north-west – that's where you'll find the electric machines that'll be giving us heat and light in just a few years' time, and link the whole planet together by telegraph. And further on, in the Swedish section, you'll come to a sort of boiler that's going to give us quicker, cheaper boat crossings – to the New World, the Mediterranean, even Oceania!'

The man's words opened the machine hatch and let in the sunlight. It wasn't red, but bright and summery. I felt I had met a soulmate, who happened not to have been born in a manor house and thus had not been able to travel as I had done. I was on the verge of offering him a job on the spot – as a coachman perhaps, or some other superfluous position – to give him the opportunity to take a steamer trip, at least as far as Sweden. But I stopped myself.

'Have you by any chance seen a tall girl, with unusually blonde hair and pale blue skirts?'

'Sorry love.'

I shrugged and headed for the electricity, musing on his way of addressing me as 'love', which certainly had nothing to do with loving. It somehow summed up that lack of respect combined with goodwill, with which the English treated me.

The moment of horror was past, but my anxiety persisted. I tried to make my way north-west to see the electric miracles, but could not work out which way was north-west, or even plain west, for that matter. Even so, I found myself as far west as one can possibly go – in America, where they were displaying Californian dinner services of gold, ploughs from the prairies and Hiram Powers' Greek slave. I respectfully studied the slave girl of marble beneath her canopy, trying to work out whether the naked, fettered figure was there purely for decoration – for she was indeed beautiful – or if she was meant to serve as a reminder of the indignation of subjugated peoples. For she could surely not be a reference to slavery in America? That would seem excessively bold.

I must admit that I grew a little depressed as I stood there, for the more I stared at America's Greek slave girl, the more she reminded me of Agnes. My worries returned. I started thinking like a book. My books always depict dreadful successions of events. In the lonely throng of the Exhibition, I began to fear that novels could rub off on real life and that the blood-red sun of my story augured terrible things.

'*Hr-m!*'

It was the most expressive clearing of a throat. At once I became aware of the slave girl's marble-bound hands, the world of my novel reverted to mere words, and I felt confident that Agnes had had the sense to return to the hotel.

'Miss Bondeson!'

There he was again, my gentleman – Professor Devindra. I rushed forward, clasped his hands and cried:

'Have you found her, Sir?'

'Unfortunately not!' said the Professor. 'But I have spoken to the police and I have spoken to my friends – who have all come to meet you!'

I then realised that the Professor was not alone. Two ladies and a gentleman were ranged behind him, viewing me with interest. I felt a little faint. An authoress earns her own keep, and has no need to be a lady. Writing is best done at one's desk, far from the public gaze. And yet there are those readers who so much want to talk – and to whom I am happy to talk – and of course all those society hostesses eager to show off a famous writer and make her the jewel in their own little crown.

'Sir Edmund Chambers…his wife Lady Margaret Chambers… Miss Ruby Holiday.'

There was a kissing of hands, a bowing and an exchange of the most refined greetings.

'Are you…*the* Chambers?' I asked, studying Sir Edmund more closely. He was a tall man, taller than the Professor and even Agnes. His outward appearance was as aesthetically arranged as Professor Devindra's, but like the reverse side of a textile, light where the Professor was dark. Sir Edmund, too, was dressed in soft, expensive fabrics, which hung so agreeably that I had to stop myself fingering them. He was like a work of art, just as beautiful and just as unreal. His sandy locks reached to his shoulder, draped around his collar. The collar naturally had a lace edging that would have been more in vogue two hundred years ago. His waistcoat was a fanciful creation of scarlet velvet, embroidered with delicate tree motifs and expertly tailored to reveal his slim form. Cool and pale-eyed, Sir Edmund bore more resemblance to a historical prince of Vasa than a modern man. He was as beautiful, not as a young god, but as a portrait. I did wonder whether his exterior would have been quite so striking had it not been for all those silky, artfully woven fabrics.

'At your service, Miss Bondeson!' exclaimed Sir Edmund, bowing anew.

I must admit that my jaw dropped a little. In this company it was not my pen that was most prominent, but Sir Edmund's paintbrush. I had expected many things, but not that I would simply run into the famous Chambers – the man who had revolutionised art, who with his firm, slender hand was attempting to lead the over-idealised, bloodless art of painting back to its medieval origins. And I, poor thing, had only ever seen his work in engravings!

'I am quite overcome,' I said – and truly meant it – before turning to the ladies. Lady Margaret Chambers and Miss Ruby Holiday were as alike as two peas in a pod. They both had the same auburn hair, pale skin and crimson lips, whose colour I suspected owed something to artifice. Both of them were real beauties. Her Ladyship had hair of a slightly lighter shade, kept her chignon in place with a large tortoiseshell comb and seemed a little quieter and more reserved – perhaps simply because she was a married woman – while her junior had a more lively, exuberant air.

'You ladies must be sisters,' I ventured to declare. I was right. Lady Margaret was the elder – albeit younger than I – and Miss Holiday her little sister. Both gentlemen, the dark and the fair, were like me, something over forty. That is a good age. Old enough to have begun to mature, but still young enough to experience the emotions of youth.

They made wonderful company. I loved them at once. Sir Edmund considerately offered me his arm and we strolled together to the medieval section, twittering about Art and Literature as we went. Several of Sir Edmund's most outstanding works hung there: the Madonna and Child, the beautiful Mary

Magdalene and the Maid of Orleans. I recognised them, despite having previously only seen them translated into black and white lines. Largest in scale was his Madonna, her mass of brown hair half hidden by a blue veil and her lips as chaste as a briar rose. Her look was tranquil and misty-eyed as she tenderly watched a baby Jesus, even fatter in oils than he had appeared in the engravings. Her gentleness was in stark contrast to Mary Magdalene's insolent stare from beneath that mane of auburn hair. Beside me stood their prototypes: Lady Margaret had modelled for the Madonna and Miss Holiday for the whore.

'Truly magnificent!' I said, and shifted my gaze to a Saint Joan at the stake, stripped of her armour and almost sickeningly graceful in her semi-nakedness. Here was a woman who knew her place – fair as a lily, yet prepared to die.

'I must carry on looking for my companion. No one knows what has become of her; she is such a scatterbrain!'

Edmund Chambers bowed again – he was almost irritatingly chivalrous – and said something very fast, which I failed to catch. He really was a handsome fellow.

'Pardon?'

'I wonder if that was the young lady we encountered. Meg, my dear – could she have been the blonde girl we saw in the Russian section? Dressed in blue, tall and fair-haired? She gave the impression of being Scandinavian – she had something of that *je ne sais quoi*…that Jenny Lind quality, perhaps one might say.'

'She did not answer when addressed,' said Lady Margaret.

'But nor did she run when I spoke to her,' added Sir Edmund.

'But she did as soon as you had finished!' said Miss Holiday, quite sharply I felt.

'That was my Agnes,' I said. 'Although she is a great deal prettier than Jenny Lind!'

'We must tell the police!' announced Professor Devindra. I turned swiftly away from the artist. Eminent he may have been, but he lacked the practical disposition of my Professor, who was always ready to help me.

'I shall accompany you, Miss Bondeson!'

I took the arm he offered me, bade the rest of the company *au revoir* and allowed myself to be taken to the Exhibition's police headquarters.

There sat a row of policemen, all dressed in identical uniforms and virtually all extremely friendly. But one of them rushed up to us, grabbed my arm and shouted:

'There you are at last!'

'What?' I said, lapsing into Swedish in my confusion.

'There must be some mistake!' Professor Devindra burst out, grabbing my other arm, so for a moment I felt like the child at King Solomon's court. The policeman relaxed his grip, thank goodness. The Professor, while admittedly looking like a foreigner, spoke like an English gentleman. In this country it is the language that counts.

'This is a famous Swedish novelist,' said the Professor. Now being Swedish does not count for much in England, I could see that in the policeman's look, but when the Professor whispered a few titles to him, from *The Young Ladies of Söderbärke* to *Count Rudolf*, he at once showed greater sympathy. The policeman, too, must be one of my readers. As I mentioned, I am not totally insignificant, even though I am short in height and come from a small country.

'The café bill,' mumbled the policeman discreetly, and the Professor and I looked at one another, nonplussed. It was all too true! Neither of us had thought of the bill as we rushed off in our separate directions in the hunt for Agnes. I blushed deeply. I do not deny that I have my eccentricities, but I have never yet run away to avoid paying a bill. I at once took up my reticule, but the Professor stopped me and promised to settle the matter.

That pleased me. Gentlemen are very welcome to pay the bill. But then the next incident erupted. The telegraph bell rang, and policemen hurried off to the entrances. Visitor numbers had risen to fifty thousand, and the doors must be closed before any more could flood in.

The figure astounded me. Over half the population of Stockholm would fit into the Exhibition at one and the same time. And as if that were not enough, another policeman entered, with an unruly woman clamped under his arm. She swore, and most emphatically.

'*Je vous en prie, mademoiselle!*' begged the policeman, who had clearly learnt a thing or two about dealing with foreigners.

'*Släpp mig. Ushliga karlslok!*' screamed the woman, which roughly translated meant that she wanted the wretched fellow to let go of her. Her hair had come loose and was hanging down over her shoulders, as blonde as a field of rye on a summer's day, whitening towards harvest. She was taller than the policeman, as stately as a Valkyrie but with a softness of line one would not associate with armour or warlike deeds. Yet it was clear that she was very angry.

'This woman insulted a gentleman visitor. She is alleged to have said: "You are a humbug, sir!"'

'But Agnes dear,' I said. 'What in Heaven's name possessed you to say something like that?'

At that she fell into my arms, dear girl, and began to weep.

We were together again, emerged unscathed from the Exhibition and were denied neither food nor slumber that day, after all. Whom she had insulted, I never discovered. But the day ended, and with it this chapter.

CHAPTER TWO

IN WHICH AGNES AND I SEE SOMETHING WORSE

Our third day in London had just begun. As usual I had risen early and devoted the first hours of daylight to my novel. I always begin work by reading through yesterday's chapter, frowning and making so many crossings out that a fair copy really ought to be done at once. On this morning I found myself lingering over yesterday's sentence: 'The junipers stood like sentries along the coast, tall and slender, but though they might be able to offer protection against the wind and surging seas – they were no defence against Death.' It was an impressive sentence, but there was something wrong. All at once it came to me: the novel was not set on the Swedish coast, but in *the south*. I exchanged my junipers for cypresses, just as tall and considerably more menacing, and could at last move on to my writing for the day:

> *The solitary shapes lay still on the pale sand. They took no pleasure at all in the wild beauty of the coast. Their figures were contorted. No sooner had the sun risen than a procession of people crept forth from the village. Each one walked as if he were alone – as if he or she were alone, for there were also many women and small children among them – and bent over the dead as if to honour them. But the villagers' custom was of a different kind. The church bells were tolling for the lost ship, as in the weak morning sun the village dwellers collected*

their dishonest profits from the dead.

When I, too, had plundered the fictitious corpses – albeit in a more literary manner than the villagers – Agnes and I sat down to a peaceful breakfast. The day before, we had scarcely had a chance to talk. She was utterly exhausted when we got home from the Exhibition, poor girl, and sought her bed after a few drops of laudanum. She slept well on those extracts of poppy. As for me, I had – I admit it – abandoned the sleeping girl and left the hotel again. I could not sit indoors with London seething outside my window. I walked along the streets in the failing light, listened to the clatter of cabs and carriages and admired the city's gaslight. It was a huge improvement on the stinking oil lamps of Stockholm, so much lighter and brighter.

Among my idiosyncrasies is the fact that whenever I have experienced anything, it does not become real for me until I have written it down, or at least spoken of it. Words are a necessity for my comprehension of the world. That is why I talk a lot, and why I like writing letters. That was how I became a writer of novels. Now I felt an urgent need to tell Agnes all about my evening, since its events were scarcely suitable for my letters to my sisters. Hazardous exploits are not to their taste, whereas the thirst for adventure is one of the things my companion and I have in common.

'So you abandoned me, Aunt Euthanasia? While I was sleeping?' said Agnes reproachfully, helping herself to the beef.

'But you were completely safe in the hotel!' I assured her. 'I made sure to lock the door. I could scarcely lose you in here.'

'Do tell me about your evening, then,' said Agnes. Perhaps her conscience was pricked by thoughts of the previous day. She often gets lost, but seldom as thoroughly as yesterday.

'Well, Agnes,' I began, 'Not even the gaslight of London reveals every murky deed, you know.'

The girl gave a shiver. My audience was primed. I could begin the tale of my London escapade.

'I went out with no particular plan and set off walking in the same direction as we went the day before yesterday. Then I turned up to the right and back along Piccadilly. What a wonderful street! Tall buildings, illuminated shops, radiant architecture...you will see, Agnes! But all at once I was aware that not everything was so fair, so radiant, as I had been imagining. I suddenly saw figures huddled in the side streets. You know how seldom I take fright...'

Agnes nodded her agreement, just as I had hoped she would. I went on with my tale.

'Even so, I began to walk faster. It was as if the city had secrets that were to be concealed from me – that it would perhaps be undesirable for me to discover. In the doorways lay objects that looked like piles of rag rugs, but which must have been human beings. You may shiver, my girl, but you should have seen it! I, a woman all alone out there, and you in your bed, slumbering on your poppy pillow.'

'Ugh, Aunt Euthanasia!' shuddered Agnes. 'How shocking, the very thought of it!'

Poverty scared Agnes, and the slums alarmed her even more. Yet I could not help being drawn to them. I had seen so much of beauty in my life. I can give inside descriptions of grand balls at the Exchange without even thinking. I have also seen a good deal of destitution, but from the outside. Yet still I want to see those wretches over and over again, to encounter people who are suffering and tormented. Of course I want to do good works – and perhaps have done, on occasion – but there is more to my appetite for the slums than that. I am disgusted yet fascinated. I am filled with righteous indignation and the desire to help – and with the writer's unpalatable urge to note it all down.

'You should have seen it! Men looked out to see if I was pretty, and used to the business, but turned away...'

There was a burst of laughter from Agnes. She is young, tall, slender and attractive, and in her worst moments terms me 'rococo' – I am so old fashioned, so antiquated at barely forty. But I am good to have as a friend. In fact, it must be said that I am still slim and quick, admittedly small in stature and a little bent, but with big blue eyes and a great deal more stamina than my twenty-two-year-old companion. But Agnes has to laugh. I expect no less.

'Now, now, Agnes! Not all of us carry our beauty so outwardly visible. Are you listening or not?' She nodded. 'Well! I was beginning to accustom myself to all those figures huddling in the alleyways. I decided that the more briskly I walked, the sooner I would be home. Then some great rats ran over my feet – or what I at first took for rats, until I saw that they were tiny, thin children. They were so small, so spindly and pitiful! My heart was touched. All one could see of them was rags, and I thought of them growing up in rags and remaining poor all their lives…'

Agnes was tearful now, and even I had to blow my nose.

'Then a man stepped forward from the shadows and spoke to me.'

'No!'

'Yes, he spoke to me – very amiably, like a gentleman who happened to have been born into the worst circles instead of the best. 'Ma'am,' he said, as the folk here do. 'Ma'am, it is not safe for a lady to be out this late.' I answered, 'Indeed?' or some other remark intended as a snub. Naturally I was poised for him to attack me, stab me, or beg from me at the very least. Then a little boy crept up beside us and looked at me, wide-eyed. 'What lovely eyes that lady has, Father,' he said. So I felt for my purse to give him a coin, but my purse was gone – and the boy, and his father.'

'They stole your purse, Aunt? What… scum!'

'Yes, but since I am a sensible woman, I had only taken a few shillings with me. After all, I knew it might be dangerous. And that was that, nothing more happened – I hurried home.'

'You must be careful, Aunt!'

'*You* must be careful. What actually happened at the Exhibition?'

Agnes kept me in suspense while she hesitated between mustard and horseradish for her beef.

'I don't really know what happened – suddenly you were gone, Aunt, that's all!' said Agnes, cutting off a bit of meat and putting it onto her mouth with her fingers. I cleared my throat. She took no notice and began talking and chewing at the same time.

'*An-I-wor-a-wor…*'

I interrupted the girl with another cough. It simply was not done, speaking with one's mouth full of food. She chewed and swallowed before continuing – but not without irritation.

'I said I walked and walked – round the Exhibition. I even called out, but no Aunt Euthanasia.'

'We should probably have arranged a place to meet. Did it never occur to you to go back to the hotel?'

Agnes chewed another mouthful or two, and thought. I meanwhile tackled my sausage, which was small and pale, but spicy and full of green herbs. While Agnes thought about the Exhibition, I thought about the herbs and determined their species. Sage and rosemary. I really should publish a cookery book one day.

Then Agnes began to speak.

'Yes, I thought of that, but I couldn't recall the name of the place. I know I should have taken note, and I *know* I've done this before… it just went out of my mind. And you *know* how bad my English is, Aunt!'

I gave a nod of assent. Agnes naturally could not help her dreadful sense of direction. She could, on the other hand, try to avoid losing me all the time.

'I met lots of people, of course I did, but what was I to do? I can't speak English.'

'You could have tried French,' I said. 'It is a world fair. People expect foreigners.'

'Some of them talked to me. Most of them were very kind, in fact. I suppose they could see I was lost. A long-haired gentleman and two ladies came along. You should have seen them, Aunt! I don't know what sort of people they can have been. The women were pale, but with red lips, almost as if they made their living as – you know what I mean, Aunt Euthanasia – and long, flowing hair. I really wondered how they got to look like that. I have an idea the man was an artist, because he sounded the way they do when they want to paint you – but I tossed my head and ran off – though he was handsome, that's for sure. And a long while later another man, an ugly fellow, came up and grabbed hold of me. So I glared at him and looked as angry as I could... and it seemed right to say, 'You are a humbug, Sir!' – but then the police officer came along...'

'It was all sorted out in the end, anyway,' I interrupted her. By this time the beef had vanished from Agnes's plate. All that remained was a patch of grease and two dabs of mustard and horseradish like little eyes. I ate the last bit of my egg and spread marmalade on my toast. Agnes made haste to pour me a cup of tea, with milk but no sugar, and I was surprised how good it tasted. Perhaps Professor Devindra was right, and it is a beverage both beneficial and stimulating.

'Don't forget the post!' said Agnes, pushing a few letters across the table. I prised off the sealing wax with the back of my spoon and glanced through a letter from my publishers in Stockholm. They were asking for the finished manuscript and proposing to print 2,000 copies and pay me 100 *riksdaler* per sheet. I found a pencil and made a note in the margin to ask the size of the sheet.

'Weren't you frightened at all?' I asked her.

'No ... well yes, in fact I was! When I found myself in some sort of square with crosses and dark colours ...'

'The medieval section?'

'Yes, it might have been. But apart from that, it was all quite fun.'

I gave a little sigh. There was I, worrying myself to death, and she thought it was fun. This is what always happens.

The second letter was from my youngest sister, Thomasine, who had just had her fourth child – a little boy, Torkild. We all did gymnastics under Professor Ling, with his fascination for the past, but Thomasine became quite obsessed with all things Old Norse.

The third letter was from Mrs Russell, the translator who puts my novels into English.

Southwold, 8th September 1851

Dearest Miss Bondeson,

It is such a delight to welcome you to England, but it causes me distress that I cannot be in London to greet you myself. My husband and I, with our daughter, are renting a cottage just outside the seaside resort of Southwold in Suffolk. It is quite enchanting here and we are greatly enjoying the summer. It is very hot, but there is always a stiff breeze by the sea – bracing! Refreshing!

My husband brings reports from the social life of the resort, my daughter THOROUGHLY enjoys the bathing, and as for me, I am writing short stories – mere bagatelles you understand – about the lives of the common people in these parts. The sea is wild here, but sublime, one might even say divine. We live like kings, or at least like those of yore, savouring the MILK, BREAD AND FRESHLY CHURNED BUTTER! What more can any person wish for?

As soon as the summer starts drawing to a close, we will return to London, where we hope to have the opportunity of meeting you, Miss Bondeson. It would be so nice to see you. You know how highly I esteem your books, and what a pure

*pleasure it is to read them! I LONG to discover if you are as
I imagine you. NATURALLY I have seen your portrait, but
to descry the life in your eyes, the spark in your soul would
mean so much more!!! Have you also had your photograph
taken? The sun is a DIVINE portraitist! But merciful he is
not, the rogue...*

Your affectionate translator

Amanda Russell

I folded the letter and decided to answer it that evening. Now
it was morning, and Agnes and I were to devote ourselves to
tourism.

'What are we doing today?'

'Today, we are free to look around. I thought we might walk
for a while, and then – why not? – sample the omnibus again...
Perhaps you would care to visit the Zoological Gardens?'

'Didn't you want to go to the British Museum, Aunt?'

I shook my head. 'Tomorrow,' I said. 'Professor Devindra has
promised that he and his artistic friends will show us round the
Museum. I believe they are displaying a new acquisition from
Nineve.'

'Will there be giraffes?'

'I should think so,' I said. At that moment there came a firm rap
at the door, and a serving girl looked in.

'There's a gentleman here asking to see you, Ma'am... Miss.'

'A gentleman? What sort of gentleman?'

'Just a gentleman, Ma'am...Miss. I'm sure I can say no more.
He looks like a gentleman – but he speaks like a Welshman, so it's
true he can't be a proper gentleman. Here's his card.'

I took the visiting card she held out.

Owain Evans
Chief Inspector
Detective Department
Metropolitan Police
Scotland Yard

'Ask him to wait a moment!' I said, fixing Agnes with a look. The serving girl left the room with our empty plates. I could not remember having ever made the acquaintance of an inspector in the London police force. I might conceivably have forgotten a John Smith, but not an Owain Evans. I looked up again with a sigh, and stared at Agnes.

'What have you been up to now, my girl?'

'Nothing! Nothing at all, Aunt Euthanasia!'

I drained my teacup, put my head in my hands and visualised Agnes running amok at the Great Exhibition. In my mind's eye I can see her overturning the Russian vacuum boiler, stabbing her parasol through Sir Edmund's ecclesiastical paintings or knocking one of the chains off the Greek slave girl. All by accident, undoubtedly, but my imagination was running riot and would not be stopped. I saw Agnes rushing through the main entrance to the Exhibition and throwing herself onto the horse behind August Kiss's beautiful Amazon sculpture, digging her dainty boots into the horse's flanks and galloping away – out through the Transept, scattering little old ladies in all directions, breaking – oh heavens! – a pianoforte in the shape of an artichoke, and finally dispensing with exits and other such trifles altogether and exploding straight through the wall of glass. It shattered with a most noble crunch, and the entire Crystal Palace slowly gave way.

'Is that the truth?' I enquired. 'Are you sure you haven't done anything? It was just the humbug episode, nothing more?'

'But what about you, Aunt, going off without paying the bill?'

'That was quite unintentional,' I said. 'What is more, I consider it part of a gentleman's duties to pay.'

There came another knock at the door, this time a more cautious one.

'Come in!'

The door opened, and there really was a male personage standing there. When I read the word 'police' I had visualised a policeman in a blue tailcoat and a top hat, but this one was not in uniform and did indeed appear to be a real gentleman. It was only when he opened his mouth that I realised why our hostess had labelled him 'a Welshman'.

'Miss Bondeson?' He had a thick accent, which could be difficult to comprehend. It was as unlike Sir Edmund's and Professor Devindra's well-schooled English as the hardy mountain sheep of Wales are unlike their kempt English relations. But he gave me an unwavering look, and he had lovely dark eyes, a moustache and a glossy beard. The thought ran through my mind that the Welsh were Celts, and remarkable tales are told of the Celts.

I stood up and offered him my hand. It counts in his favour that he kissed it without hesitation – I noticed a moment too late that I had marmalade on my knuckles.

'To what do we owe the honour?'

'Miss Bondeson? I am quite overcome!'

'For goodness sake! Sit down! A cup of tea, perhaps?'

He accepted immediately, and I rang for service. The extra cup arrived instantly – I would not be the least surprised if the serving girl had been eavesdropping outside the door.

As behoves a good woman, I poured the Inspector his tea, and he sugared it generously before he began to speak.

'It came to my notice that you were in London, Miss Bondeson… I could not imagine anything more wonderful than meeting the woman, whose hand has written all my favourite novels …'

Oh no! Not all that again!

Now clearly I love praise. Clearly I get very excited when people admire me, and there is *nothing* wrong with an attractive, dark-haired gentleman declaring that he adores my work. For that was precisely what Inspector Evans was doing. This was my second admirer in two days – upon my word, there was no danger of feeling forgotten here in London.

The Inspector would not have made so bold as to come to the Golden Cross, had it not been for our little incident at the Exhibition yesterday. He begged my pardon a thousand times over.

'You have to understand, Miss Bondeson. The Exhibition is full of villains of assorted calibre. The staff have to be constantly vigilant. You cannot imagine how many people slink off without paying – and I must say I admire you. I have never heard of anyone who avoided settling their bill for as long as you!'

I begged the Inspector's pardon at least as many times in return. It had not been my intention to run away. I had had the money to pay, after all. I therefore told him the whole story, and as I spoke, I found myself taking a remarkable pleasure in talking English – it flowed so well, sounding so lovely, and I was truly impressed by my ability to put my thoughts into words. Agnes, on the other hand, remained silent, but I hope she was listening intently and learning from the conversation.

'It is undeniably easy to get lost at the Exhibition,' said the Inspector. 'But we do have police officers there – in uniform, and also a number of detectives in plain clothes.'

'Are you a detective yourself, Inspector?'

'Yes.'

I was actually silent for a moment. Our Swedish police are frighteningly underdeveloped, and we have no detectives. But I had heard that they existed in other countries, and I had sometimes thought that the police working on a crime might be a productive and saleable subject for the lighter sort of novel.

'So crime is your concern, Police Inspector Evans?'

The policeman gave a laugh. His whole face lit up – perhaps like the sun breaking through the clouds in the Welsh mountains – displaying even and attractive teeth. There came into his eyes, too, a sudden, sunny glint. They were almost as dark as Professor Devindra's, and in spite of his obvious British lightness of skin, Inspector Evans seemed in many ways darker, as if more weighed down by his thoughts than the Professor. Maybe it was because he devoted his life to the fight against crime rather than to medicine and modern painting.

'Yes indeed, Miss Bondeson. Terrible crimes, the like of which you have never seen in Sörmland.' He actually knew how to pronounce the 'ö' sound, which was enough to warm a Swedish heart. 'I am in the violent crime section. All police officers solve and prevent crimes, but I devote my days to the worst outrages – to murder, or at best manslaughter, and to abduction.'

'Then you see much of the world!' I exclaimed, watching the rose-patterned teacup being raised towards the dark eyes, the flash of sunshine in them and the cup being lowered once more. Presumably what I should have said was 'Ugh!'

'Probably all too much. I see such things as ladies should beware of.'

'I may be a lady. But I am also an authoress.'

'And I admire you as such, Miss Bondeson – your flights of imagination, the sunshine at haymaking, the glittering surfaces of Swedish lakes. All light, all innocence!'

'Well then, Inspector, perhaps you could show us the slums of London? We have today free for an excursion.'

The sun retreated behind a cloud over those mountains to the west that I had never seen. The hardy Welsh sheep lifted their muzzles and there was a feeling of rain on the way.

'I had in fact intended offering myself as your guide to the city – but not that part of the city! I thought you would want to see Westminster, the parks, the Chinese junk, the Hippodrome or Wyld's Monster Globe.'

'Wyld's Monster Globe! Oh yes!' cried Agnes suddenly, but in Swedish. 'I want to see that!'

'You will no doubt see it all in good time!' I said. News had spread as far as Sweden of the model Earth that had been erected in Leicester Square. Everything was coloured – the oceans blue, the snow of the North Pole white, the deserts khaki – and one could climb about in the centre of the Earth by means of staircases. 'For now, we shall do something more useful.'

Agnes seemed disappointed, but there is a limit to what a sensible woman should assent to for a capricious young girl's sake. It was after all she who was companion to me, not the other way round! The slum I had already seen had aroused my curiosity. I wanted to see more.

'Well, Mr Evans, we can see the great globe on another occasion, if we care for it at all; we have already seen the parks, and we find Chinese junks of no great interest. But the London underworld – I should like to acquaint myself with that!'

The Inspector's visage was still clouded and bore a look verging on disappointment, so I made haste to say:

'And naturally the charitable works of the better classes in the slums!'

The sun peeked forth again.

'For being permitted to show you something as beautiful as that, Miss Bondeson, I can be persuaded to show you the worst of London, too. You no doubt saw Prince Albert's model homes for workers while you were at the Exhibition ...?'

I mumbled that I had sadly not had time, since our visit to the Exhibition had turned out more eventful than we had hoped. But we were planning to stay several more weeks – maybe even until the Exhibition closed in October – and would certainly find time for them eventually.

'Here in London, much has been done for the poor – it is a vast city, a cruel city, but there are also good people here. In recent years, new areas of housing have been built for the workers, in line with the latest principles, and cooperative associations have been set up by the workers. I have a friend who is a vicar in one of the worst slum districts … '

'I should like to meet him!' I interjected. 'I have still not met a single clergyman of the Church of England.'

Then I stood up, and we were ready in a trice – the serving girl came and cleared the table, the Inspector withdrew to the hotel lounge, and Agnes and I made ourselves ready for a day in the slums. I knew our role was to be that of do-gooders and anonymous observers, but even so I made sure that Agnes exchanged her blue dress for a quieter grey, took off her jewellery and concealed most of her blonde locks beneath a bonnet. She made a deal of fuss about having to abandon her earrings, both gold chains, the large pendant crafted from all the treasures of Bergslagen and the considerably smaller, less skilfully made brooch that she had woven herself from flattened gold braid. As for me, I attired myself in black – not merely a serious colour, but also one that suits me – with a lilac shawl in case it grew chilly and a matching parasol in case the sun came out. I dabbed a touch of lavender oil on my wrists, and we proceeded from the room.

The Inspector bowed wordlessly, and I was pleased that he neither commended our appearances nor commented on our transformation.

We opened the front door of the hotel to find ourselves in bright sunshine, and Agnes and I simultaneously put up our parasols. The Inspector looked about for a cab, but the street was empty. All the cabs had presumably been hired to take visitors to the Exhibition, which by now was open for the day.

'I shall have to pick up a cab at the station,' said Mr Evans.

'We will come with you.'

'But your shoes…?'

'Do not concern yourself. You see, Inspector, Swedish women are sturdily made. They are not afraid of walking a few steps.'

The Inspector maintained that my novels had already revealed all the superior qualities of Swedish womanhood, though I had a feeling he was looking more at Agnes than at me.

We soon came upon a cab rank, where a horse and cabbie were dozing in the shade, and before we knew it we were *en route* to the least desirable part of the city. Inspector Evans pointed out that it was advisable for ladies to visit the slums in the mornings. As if we would have been so stupid as to venture there at night!

'London is a whole world in itself,' said the Inspector, launching into his lecture. 'The poor, the orphaned, the crippled, maimed and blind are sufficient in numbers to populate an average British town. There are more Irish people in London than in Dublin, and more Catholics here than in Rome. No doubt you have your poor in Stockholm, too, Miss Bondeson?'

'Undeniably!' I replied. 'And we have small children who speak only the language of thieves, youths bent by disease into old men and little girls obliged to sell the only asset they have.'

The Inspector looked at me in consternation, perhaps because at that moment the cab lurched to avoid running over a beggar. Owain Evans was thrown off balance, narrowly missed landing in my lap, grabbed the edge of the seat and gave me a long look – so long, that I realised it had been prompted by my words. I sometimes find it hard to remain polished and rose-tinted.

'That is not the kind of unvarnished truth one is accustomed to hearing from women, Miss Bondeson.'

'Maybe not. My lot is a fortunate one, Inspector. I am the eighth of ten daughters, but I was born into money. Now I am too old to attend balls, and needlework does not interest me. Practical philanthropy, on the other hand – visiting the poor – I believe that does some good.'

'I am touched to hear you say so...'

'At least *some* good,' I snapped. 'But I call a thief a thief when I see one!'

The pleasure I take in being admired goes hand in hand with the anxiety that someone might fall in love with me. Police

Inspector Evans seemed far too nice for me to want to fob him off. There was something about Britannia's men that made me feel attractive — stronger, more decisive and vigorous than usual. But Agnes kept her counsel. Perhaps that was just as well.

The cab took us on across London. There really were some disreputable areas I could not have imagined in my worst nightmares — and I can assure my readers that things I have seen in the back streets of Stockholm around the Royal Palace have made many a lady do-gooder go weak and hysterical. This was worse.

Our destination was the slums of the East End. From the Strand we steered our course down Fleet Street to Houndsditch, Whitechapel and Spitalfields. That is where the *noblesse* of the slums are to be found, although palaces can be seen all over London, as can poverty and decay. The evening before, I had seen for myself the hungry eyes, sunken chests and greedy fingers of people who rarely get a meal. Hungry children peeped out between the tall buildings along the Strand, and if I had dared venture further from Agnes and the Golden Cross Hotel I would have seen the same sights in St. Giles, a few streets away from the modern British Museum. The poor districts always lie cheek by jowl with the rich, hovels alongside grand houses. As if in mockery, fate has distributed its resources in such a manner that the poor of London are never out of sight of excess and elegance.

But here we turned into Spitalfields: dilapidated houses, houses that had lost their plaster or never had their floor boards completed, houses with cracks and holes, houses with missing windows, the openings stuffed with rags. In short: houses that were themselves in shreds, collapsing, half-built shanties along the boulevards of the kingdom of rags, where all the subjects wore the same uniform and banners waved from the windows — all in the kingdom's very own glorious colour. Grey. Dirty grey.

In the city centre one could perhaps stop, raise one's eyes to the facades of the buildings and say: 'Here is evidence of faded grandeur! See that crumbling stucco! Look at the magnificence of the friezes – cracked and half worn away, yet still very much in their element in the capital of the Empire!' Nothing like that could be said here. London was so vast – this one city had almost as many inhabitants as the whole of Sweden – and for me it has always seemed a kind of Rome. Whereas the roads of ancient times led to the capital of the Roman Empire, our steamer routes lead to England's great city. For me, London represented modernity – not Parisian frivolity, but a rational life, filled with thoughts of good literature and dazzling theatre, yet also of trade and shipping. Alighting from the cab in Spitalfields, I saw another metropolis. It was no Rome. My boot stepped down onto the streets of Babylon, and through its thin leather sole I could feel the whole city vibrating with poverty, want and vice. So Agnes and I followed our Inspector out into that place of perfidy and decay.

Though it was barely ten o'clock in the morning, the streets were full of people. They looked out of doors and studied us closely. They raised their eyes from their begging bowls and immediately lowered them again. Eyes all around us. Terrified eyes. Terrifying eyes. Eyes pointed at us to beg – for money, for sympathy, for affection. It was hard to look at them, even for a woman as hardened as myself. I thought of my own breakfast and felt ashamed.

Worst were the eyes I did not see. Wherever we went, people turned away. Young girls turned their faces to the wall. Little children buried their noses in their mothers' skirts, staring into the grey fabric and breathing in the grey smell of poverty. Agnes whimpered at my side and quickly drew closer. I took her hand, as if she were a child, and held her firmly beside me.

'It is an upsetting sight,' mumbled the Inspector behind us.

'And does a detective such as yourself have much cause to come here, Inspector?'

'I'm afraid so,' declared Mr Evans. 'In London there are thousands of women who can only live by their own degradation. There are also thousands of men who cannot make a living by labour and have to turn to crime. Most of it is...oh, just the petty kind. The sort of thing our police constables clear up – theft of small items, half-empty purses and those pretty silk handkerchiefs like the one you seem to have in your coat pocket, Miss Bondeson.'

I hastily stuffed the handkerchief out of sight, for it was a present from my sister.

'But when people get hungry enough, they get desperate. We recently found a girl murdered and tossed carelessly aside, against a wall. The perpetrators hadn't even bothered to hide her. And do you know why she died, Miss Bondeson?'

'No,' I replied. I felt for a moment as if I did not want to know.

'The lass was wearing a little gold trinket – a cross someone had given her as a present. It was no bigger than this –' he used his thumb and forefinger to indicate half an inch, 'but for two starving fourteen year old lads, it was enough to strangle her for.'

'Ugh!' I said, squeezing Agnes's hand. She cowered closer to me, like a frightened little dog, and I thought of her gold earrings and thick gold chains. Thank goodness I had insisted she leave them all at the hotel. She was so young and trusting there beside me, and I would not have had her scared for the world. So I said no more, keeping to myself the horrific images that were forming in my mind. At first I saw only figures, human but more frightening than either beasts of prey or ghosts, arranged in scenes on a well-crafted tapestry. There were no beautiful virgins dancing here, no bold hunters riding to hounds – here the lowest of the low gathered in scenes of crime and murder. Then it was as if I had gone too close and could only see individual sections of the fabric. Claw-like hands fumbled at my neck. I felt pressure on my windpipe, and when I told myself I was silly and over-impressionable, I sensed instead the faint tickle of a knife or the cold sensation of a pistol barrel at my temple. I was obliged to take out my handkerchief and blow my nose loudly to banish these images of evil. On the thin, violet silk I saw traces of black – of coal dust, or of sins and crimes.

Police Inspector Evans naturally had no inkling of what was going on inside me. He was still talking about himself and the slums.

'So I certainly do have cause to come here, Miss Bondeson. When I was a constable, this was my beat. And before that...'

I sensed a confession might be on its way. As an authoress, I love confessions. They inspire; they provide insight into character. If I am in the mood, they may find their way into a novel, in time. But that is the awful thing about us writers – everything that moves us, everything that drives us to laughter or tears, can be remoulded and used in *The Wrecker's Revenge* or some other book.

I therefore gave an encouraging, 'Yes?'

'You can hear, Miss Bondeson, that I have not always lived in London. I was born on a Welsh mountainside. It was a beautiful place, but very poor. One day I left, and at length reached London. My home was here in Spitalfields – a hovel a few streets away from here – and I made my living as best I could, before joining the Navy. I did well, advanced to coxswain and was put to studying as a cadet. Then our ship went down – it wasn't a battle, just an ordinary storm – and I suddenly found myself a peeler, an honest policeman patrolling the streets I knew from before.'

'So you are a self-made man, Inspector?' I asked, at once wondering, of course, whether this man had a criminal history. He seemed hardened enough. Those features which were represented in Evans the policeman; firmness and strength of character, could once have been hallmarks of lawlessness and brutality – or at least I, in my constant romancing, imagined they could.

'Yes,' came his answer to my question.

'That is both honest and honourable.'

We stopped by a building that seemed to be a darker shade of grey than its surroundings. The Inspector knocked at the door, which was opened by a physiognomy I would not have liked to encounter unaccompanied. I could not even tell if it was a man or a woman – it had long hair matted with dirt, thin hands and bare arms, and a stomach distended by hunger, or repeated pregnancies. I squeezed Agnes's soft hand once more.

The building we entered was a so-called lodging house. It was a sort of inn, but that gives too cosy an impression. There were no individual rooms here. Some were lucky enough to get a bed; others lay on heaps of rags. Though it was broad daylight, many were still sleeping. I could see two small children, as innocent and rosebud-mouthed as the Princes in the Tower, a few old women and a number of men – all in the same room, with no regard for privacy or what one might call decency. I whispered words of solace to Agnes. She, sensitive soul, was already suffering with those poor people, and I suffered with her. She was trembling, and I found it hard to keep hold of her hand. In the gloom she was as light as an image of a saint, as the innocent St. Agnes.

A man sat at a table, cutting out cardboard. He seemed oblivious to us.

'Good day to you, Three Fingers John!' said our police escort.

'Well, well!' cried the man. 'If it isn't the Inspector!'

They greeted one another warmly. Mr Evans took a seat opposite the man, and they began to talk. They made a strange couple. I could not imagine Three Fingers John ever having been in contact with water, for either internal or external use, and his clothes were well past the stage of being whole enough to identify. I could not make out whether his outer garment was a coat or a jersey, and whether it was a waistcoat or a vest he was wearing over the fabric that must have been a shirt or blouse. There was something protruding at his neck that might have been a bit of old lace, though from some angles it looked more like wire. Inspector Evans was by no means as polished as Sir Edmund Chambers and his ilk, but in this company his rough tweed suit seemed a miracle of the tailor's art. And yet they were alike, he and Three Fingers John. Perhaps they had been bound together by common experience; or perhaps it was just the good policeman's empathy with those less fortunate than himself. In the course of the conversation, the Welshman slipped into the same cockney idiom as the other man. I could scarcely understand them.

Three Fingers John showed us what he was doing. The cardboard was to be assembled into railway carriages, which he sold as toys.

'A new invention,' I remarked. Three Fingers John regarded me earnestly.

'That's right, lady! Children today, see, they don't want to play with pasteboard stagecoaches. They hardly know what they are. So I started making these railway carriages, and they sell like hot cakes!'

'Have you any completed ones that I could buy for my nephews and nieces?' I asked. He did, so we left the house with two railway carriages under our arms, destined for my favourite niece and nephew – two little children who had never travelled by railway train, as their parents had hitherto only holidayed at Swedish bathing resorts. In Sweden we still lack even the tiniest snippet of a railway.

'Have you seen enough of the worst aspects?' the Inspector asked.

I felt I could visualise even worse things, but Agnes nodded in relief. She was beginning to understand what people were saying – apparently even Inspector Evans, who was not always easy to follow. We walked on to the district where the sun was beginning to penetrate. This was where our companion's friend did his good works.

In London, efforts are being made to help the poor in many different ways. It is said that poverty must exist in every prosperous town. But more recently, voices have begun to dispute this: it need not be so. For that reason, model homes have been built – in the hope that all working people may soon be able to live that way – and for that reason, the workers have begun to organise themselves. They have formed cooperatives, workers' societies and trade associations. We visited some of the model accommodation, with clean rooms, small individual flats and big laundry rooms. They were tasteful and modern, and all the wives we met seemed content. There were communal laundries and bathhouses; there was running water from kitchen taps. It all bore witness to great benevolence and was a world away from the slum we had seen – but even the brightest rooms were darker than any room I have ever lived in, and five children would still be living with their mother and father in one or two rooms. Amidst all the goodwill, I was aware of a chill in the ideal homes. Maybe the benefactors felt too much and understood too little, or maybe they thought more than they examined their feelings. I observed everything and was extremely polite. Yet my existing conviction was strengthened: only when poverty has been eradicated can all humanity be happy.

In the sky, the sun had reached its zenith, and I found myself intermittently contemplating our midday meal. Now that we had emerged from the worst slums, it was very easy to think about food, and I speculated as to whether it would be a piece of meat – possibly the roast beef of old England – or whether we might be able to find some hitherto unsampled style of refreshment. Then Inspector Evans led us south through Spitalfields and did not stop until we stood before a tall green door with a round window and a brass doorknocker. It was a most imposing doorknocker: a magnificent, shiny yellow and in the shape of a pelican bending its head to bite its own breast. The walls on either side of the door were made of brick – originally red, one supposed, but now blackened at the edges, like everything else in this city. Turning my head, I could see the silhouetted skyline, with London Bridge and the Tower nearest to us. We had reached streets where there was a view, where the buildings were not clambering all over each other. I took a deep breath. It was as if I had forgotten to breathe all the time we were in the slums, even in the estimable model homes. Now I could feel new life in my body.

'Over there,' said the Inspector, pointing, 'are the remains of the old city walls.'

I scanned the walls of the London houses before me, searching in vain for anything that looked 'old', assuming the walls were medieval, if not older. London had, after all, once been one of the furthest outposts of the Roman Empire. But I could see nothing, and Mr Evans grasped the pelican by the neck and knocked.

The door was opened by a trim maidservant, who curtseyed to the Inspector and greeted him by name. She would fetch her master at once.

We were shown into a bare drawing room, with the day's newspapers laid out on the table. The walls were not much to look at – there were no pictures, just an unornamented wall clock and a neat little cupboard with a brass handle. The Inspector sat with his hands resting on his knees and looked in the direction of the cupboard, but I could not resist picking up the *Illustrated London News* and flicking through it. There are no illustrated papers in Sweden, and I am always childishly fascinated by the pictures. There was naturally a good sprinkling of impassive old codgers who had rendered some service to the Empire, but there were also large lithographs on the front cover. Today there was a report on the new Assyrian friezes in the British Museum. You could see every detail in the pictures – men swimming across a river to escape their enemies, some of them hugging what looked like cushions, presumably for added buoyancy.

The Inspector leant over the newspaper to see what we were looking at. I was aware of his presence, slightly too close.

'Those are sheepskins,' he said. 'That's how we learnt to swim in Wales – we bobbed around on an inflated sheepskin.'

'Oh!' I said, unable to suppress my fascination. 'I cannot swim, but I love bathing. Sheepskins would certainly be a help.'

That made the Inspector laugh, perhaps at the thought of a

middle-aged woman bobbing around on a shaggy sheepskin bag at some fashionable bathing resort. The idea was so ridiculous that I began to laugh, too, and whenever I am amused, Agnes laughs as well. She is familiar, moreover, with my frilled bathing cap in a shade of old rose, and thus had all the more cause for mirth.

In the midst of our merriment, the clergyman came into the room. I have met many men of the cloth, and a fair number of them have enjoyed a joke. My cousin, who even in adulthood would not hesitate to balance a bucket of water on top of a door, is a highly respected dean — perhaps I had better not name the diocese.

Inspector Evans' friend was no prankster. I could see that at once. Yet I could not stop laughing.

'I see you are enjoying yourselves.'

I hastily folded the newspaper and avoided catching Agnes's eye. I had clearly behaved inappropriately — but the Inspector was still chuckling. I gave the priest a hard stare. He was somewhat under average height, not fat and jovial like my cousin but thin and emaciated, with the unspoilt skin of one who spends most of his time indoors, as pallid as a private tutor's. His hair was straight and blond, his eyes were big and clear, as if open wide to see the light of Heaven. It was an ascetic face. His mouth, on the other hand, was full and red and profoundly sensual. Even so, it was pursed in disapproval. Could lips unwilling to smile ever entice kisses?

Since none of us could stop laughing, the priest smiled — a wan smile, of the sort that claims to be a cream sauce but is only made with milk.

Police Inspector Evans rose from his armchair to greet the priest. They gave each other a friendly nod, but neither shook hands nor embraced. Then he introduced us, and I offered him my hand. George Amis was the man's name, Rector his title, and the slums his domain. He briefly brushed the tips of my fingers, but his kissing of my hand amounted to no more than a stiff, abortive bow. There was something unsubstantial about his form, as if he were half way to canonisation. And yet there was something that entirely contradicted this impression – something impassioned, not to say improper. His mouth could have been attractive, but never his hands. They were so limp, so cold against my own. Such hands did not seem created to be clasped in prayer. For some disturbing reason, I found myself thinking of Owain Evans' tale of the murdered girl with the gold cross. I shivered and forced my mind to turn to healthier subjects – to food, to be precise. Although it was dinnertime, there was no smell of cooking wafting from the kitchen. The preparation of the meal could not be very well advanced.

'So you work in the slums?' I asked, looking up into the priest's pale eyes.

He sat himself in an armchair, and we began to talk. I felt somewhat dubious. The Reverend Amis was too much of an idealist for my taste – I find it hard to have confidence in such people.

Funnily enough, Agnes was overcome with enthusiasm. Her eyes brightened to a vivid blue, and the joy of living burst forth in her face. She looked delightful, just the way one would wish to see a young girl; and moreover she began nudging me and whispering.

'Is this a real life benefactor, Aunt Euthanasia?'

'Why certainly, he is a minister of the slums, who helps the poor and so on.'

'How tremendous! Can you help me to ask him some questions, Aunt?'

'How could I refuse?' Agnes asked, and I translated. The Rector looked from Agnes to me, and the girl's questions rattled from my lips:

'Are you involved in the workers' organisations?'

'How do cooperative stores work?'

'Is it like the Inspector says, that your sermons deal not only with God, but also with the welfare of humanity on earth – and the question of workers' rights?'

Every question prompted a minor lecture, and by the time the lectures were at an end, my pocket watch was showing two o'clock. I was beginning to feel light-headed and could feel ill temper creeping up on me, as it always does when I am hungry. Agnes does not react in the same way at all. She rises above her hunger, and so was now able to go on calmly asking her questions. The Reverend Amis softened as she did so, becoming somehow more substantial when his eyes were upon her. He was resting his hands on his knees, but leaning forward with great interest, far too close to the girl.

'If we can arrange a cab, perhaps I could take you two ladies to the cooperative stores?' the Reverend Amis said.

'These ladies can walk,' answered Inspector Evans, not without a modicum of pride, I thought. But perhaps it was my imagination. As we were walking to the stores, I began to prepare my starved self for hallucinations. The cooperative stores looked like any other shop and sold all the usual staples – flour, sugar and other groceries – to its members. There were no tempting steaks or sausages, but I could see jars of dried apricots and prunes, which would serve perfectly well to restore my flagging spirits. But no one said anything about making purchases, so I refrained. Perhaps outsiders were not permitted to buy. I praised the cooperative movement instead.

'Excellent!' said the Reverend Amis. 'So now that you have seen what we can achieve – you must excuse me. I have a sermon to write.'

He bowed stiffly, and Agnes gave an exclamation.

'No! Is he leaving?'

'He has to write his sermon, Agnes,' I explained in Swedish.

'But couldn't they come to the museum with us tomorrow? The Reverend seems much nicer than your Professor, Aunt!'

Involuntarily, I pursed my lips. Really, she had seen very little of the Professor! But I did translate her question.

'No, I'm afraid not,' said the Reverend. 'I will be busy all morning.'

'It would hardly be possible,' said Mr Evans.

So the Reverend Amis departed. Agnes's farewell radiated warmth, and she sadly watched him go. Clearly she detected qualities in him that were not apparent to me.

'Tell me,' I asked the Inspector, 'is there anywhere round here we could get a bite to eat?'

Owain Evans laughed. He had a big laugh, as rumbling as London itself, and not merely sunny, like the western slopes.

'The Reverend Amis is a little unworldly. Hunger is not in his nature.'

'Is there no Mrs Amis?'

'No. He could really do with a vicar's wife, but...'

This utterance was followed by a shrug, and the Inspector began scanning the street. I realised he was looking for a cab. He signalled with his glove to a four-wheeled growler some way off. His hand was without rings.

'You are not married either, are you Inspector?' So where do you usually take lunch?'

'Here and there.'

He indicated the next street corner, where a male figure was standing – respectably dressed in a coat and tall hat, with a white apron around his stomach and a kind of tin box beside him in the street, We had emerged from the depths of the slums. We were standing opposite George Amis's church, with the cooperative stores behind us. I slowly became aware of my surroundings. The fellow on the corner was selling something, and I could hear his cry:

'Pies! Penny pies! Get your lovely pies! Toss the pieman!'

'Toss the pieman?'

'All Londoners are gamblers. You toss a coin – heads or tails. If the pieman wins, you pay your penny and get no pie; if you win, you get your pie for nothing. It's a popular sport here.'

'Are the pies for sale as well?'

'Oh yes. They nearly always have meat pies and eel pies. I like eel pie best myself, but then I was born and bred on the coast. Sometimes they have apple pies and cherry pies, too.

The man's cry rang out again:

'Pies! Lovely 'ot pies! Come and get 'em! Toss the pieman!'

'There's just one thing,' said Owain Evans. 'Ladies don't usually buy from piemen. That may be why there are so many pie shops now.'

'I am sure we can disregard that,' I said. 'As long as you promise not to tell on us, Mr Evans.'

He laughed again, and then was so familiar as to take both Agnes and I by the arm and advance on the pieman. I won two pies, because I have always been lucky in games of chance, and found that eel pie was much tastier than one might imagine. And having now got my own way and had not only lunch but also a tour of the slums, I readily acceded to the Inspector's offer to show us the Zoological Gardens.

The afternoon and evening were more like those of the average London visitor. At the Zoo we saw the giraffes and the newly arrived hippopotamus, a fat and contented beast that the naturalists call a river horse. What a delightful combination they made: the giraffes slim and thin-necked, the hippopotamus portly and sluggish. It made me think of myself and Agnes, and perhaps the Inspector suspected as much, for he told us that the hippopotamus is in reality quick and agile, in actual fact far more dangerous than the two-horned rhinoceros. I am the same, of course – quick and agile, and actually much younger than I pretend to be.

In the Zoo, we were like children. We went from creature to creature, suffered for a while with the lion, took tea and cucumber sandwiches, and finally moved on to the Diorama. There we let the Inspector choose the destination, and he took us on a journey from London to Calcutta. We sat in comfort, while before us the sights moved as if travelling past us in a boat. It was all simply unbelievable. It felt utterly prosaic to step out into Piccadilly once more, despite its being a thoroughfare of impressive elegance. It was late by then, and we were far too tired to go to a restaurant. Instead we ordered a little beef tea at the hotel, and were soon asleep. London is well known for leaving its visitors in a state of permanent exhaustion.

CHAPTER THREE

IN WHICH I STUDY ANCIENT BABYLON

The horse's head writhed in pain. Whether it was the horse of the sun, which had sunk its whole body in the sea after the hard day's journey across the sky, or that of the moon, which had been working just as hard all night, I could not recall, though Sir Edmund had undoubtedly told me. Yes, the ground-breaking artist Sir Edmund Chambers had condescended to show two such insignificant persons as Agnes and me round the British Museum. Lady Margaret Chambers, Miss Ruby Holiday and Professor Devindra were also members of the party. It was Wednesday, and our fourth day in London. Just now it was the frieze from the Parthenon on which the artist was volubly holding forth.

'The frieze conveys all the grandeur of antiquity...the whiteness and simplicity that was a sign of spiritual purity...'

I took pains to adopt an interested expression and then closed my ears to Sir Edmund's flow of words. I felt the horse's suffering quite well enough as it was.

I am a traveller of some experience. I have seen art before. The Parthenon frieze was among the most beautiful works of art I had ever seen. It was enticing, drawing me in. Sir Edmund Chambers did his best to destroy that feeling.

Like so many eminent men, Sir Edmund believed only he had read learned books and thought important thoughts. His wife and Miss Holiday stood nodding their agreement. Maybe he had managed to tame them; maybe their thoughts were as far away as mine. Though I admire Sir Edmund's art, I can think for myself. My great-uncle's best friend was with Gustaf III on his Italian cultural pilgrimage, and as a little girl I used to play with the pieces of marble he brought home. They were mere fragments, but they were cool and smooth and rested so nicely in my hand. I imagined so many stories about them as I sat in the silence of the library turning them one after another – one lump of stone with egg-and-dart and one with a Greek key motif; a jagged fragment that must once have jutted from a Corinthian column; and a rounded, well-shaped human ear. Those stones were like the jigsaw puzzles that I had seen in French and English shops. I turned them over and over, allowing shape and sensation to tell me where they had come from and what their function had been.

Sir Edmund was not a good cicerone. It was of no consequence to him whether Agnes and I learned anything – he wanted to show off his erudition and good taste. And Agnes, of course, was easily impressed! She stood with Lady Margaret and Miss Holiday, tall and blonde beside the curvaceous, curly-haired sisters, staring rapt at Sir Edmund's face. The impression he made on me, rather, was one of unreality. He was a handsome man, all too sculptural for my taste, but wiser girls than Agnes have swooned over a pair of bright eyes and a persuasive way with words. She gradually edged closer to him, and the two sisters did likewise. Now she was standing so close to him that their locks were almost mingling, his sandy, hers Nordic and fair. Both types of beauty had a treacherous coolness, which like the shade of the tropics could be banished by relentless sunshine. And yet – Lady Margaret seemed merely bored.

I decided to have a word with Agnes later. A young girl really ought to think carefully, even when she has an 'aunt' with her as a chaperone and keeper. We were both still tired from the previous day, and those who are tired may easily do stupid things.

'Miss Bondeson, what do you think of the Elgin marbles?'

Professor Devindra may well be a worse artist than Sir Edmund – at any rate, he had none of his work in the Great Exhibition – but he seemed to me a better human being. I would have liked to introduce him into the salons of Stockholm. It would have amused me enormously to see my lady friends' reaction to his deliberately wayward cravat, his dark skin and lordly, melodious English.

'The frieze is beautiful,' I replied. 'But the lecture is too long.'

Professor Devindra smiled. He was no doubt aware of his friend's bad habits. He caught Sir Edmund's eye.

'I say, old fruit,' he said, leaving me astonished at the remarkable ways Englishmen address one another, 'Shall we go and have a look at the Nineveh marble?'

'Certainly! Unless Miss Bondeson would find it too shocking?'

'I enjoy being shocked. It reminds me I am not dead.'

Sir Edmund laughed awkwardly at my joke. Presumably he found it inappropriate.

We were standing at one end of an exhibition gallery, and as long as we had the Parthenon frieze in front of us, all was harmony. As soon as one looked away from the Greek figures, one saw the place was swarming. We were not alone. We were not the only visitors to London in the late summer of 1851 – and a mass of people was moving among the statues and friezes. One almost felt the whole world was strolling here, the living world and the world of the dead, one of flesh and blood and the other of stone.

Our artist led us out through a narrow passage, where classical sculptures almost crowded out the visitors. I elbowed Agnes gently in the side, but she did not seem to feel it. She still had that doglike expression.

'Whatever you do,' whispered Professor Devindra, 'don't let him show you the illuminated Madonnas! Then we'll never get any lunch, or afternoon tea either.'

That man knew which arguments would sway me. I nodded,

but kept my mouth shut, so as not to say anything foolish. We squeezed past a party of Portuguese gentlemen, passed a mixed group of English people and came to a halt in front of the sculptures of Egypt. Here we were treated to a further lecture, more gaping from Agnes and more bored looks from Lady Margaret and Miss Holiday. Professor Devindra was hailed by two dark gentlemen in dazzling Oriental finery. They conversed quietly, but I would not have understood anything, even if I had been able to make out the words. Presumably they were his countrymen and asking the way to the reading room or the Asiatic Gallery. I looked about for the mummies, but there was nothing around me except sculptures – sharp noses, stiff clothes and almond-shaped eyes. Sir Edmund drew our attention to the Egyptians' remarkable conventions for portraying the human form in the bas-reliefs. A few men, not unlike those we had observed in the slum the previous day, came up and listened with interest. Then Sir Edmund recollected himself and ended his lecture abruptly.

'That was Egypt. Let us now proceed to Babylon.'

'How many miles to Babylon, do you think, Miss Bondeson?' asked the Professor, back at my side after taking leave of his countrymen.

'I fancied it might be at the other end of this gallery.'

Then the Professor hummed me a little song, once we had both agreed that the sculptures and reliefs came not from Babylon but from Assyria and Nineveh – but Sir Edmund perhaps cared little for the distinctions between the cities of antiquity, as long as their works of art were aesthetic.

> *How many miles to Babylon?*
> *Three score miles and ten.*
> *Can I get there by candlelight?*
> *Aye, and back again.*
> *If your heels are nimble and light,*
> *You may get there by candlelight.*

It was a London nursery rhyme, and perhaps a rhyme about London as the modern Babylon. Professor Devindra was one of those people, I was coming to realise, who very easily learnt things by heart and could declaim poetry or reel off nursery rhymes at the drop of a hat.

'How fortunate that Edmund takes no interest in jewellery,' Professor Devindra whispered to me. 'That pendant Miss Björk is wearing – it must be Swedish workmanship?'

'Yes,' I whispered back, 'made of gold, silver and copper from Bergslagen and rock crystal from our brother nation, Norway. But is it not a little tasteless?'

'It would fetch a considerable sum here in London,' said the Professor knowledgeably. I nodded. In Stockholm it had cost a large portion of my advance before last. Agnes likes jewellery that hangs heavily round her neck.

Sir Edmund was not looking at Agnes's gewgaws. His gaze shifted to and fro between the antique sculptures and the girl's eager face.

'In Nineveh,' began Sir Edmund.

'Pardon me, Sir Edmund. Nineveh, *is* it Babylon?'

This from Agnes! Blessings upon her. Sir Edmund was discernibly put out. If I had objected he would probably have been annoyed, but when a young beauty looked at him with blue eyes as clear as the springs of the Assyrian oases, he could neither snap her head off nor make excuses.

'Nineveh!' he now declared, as clearly as one might when addressing children or the feeble-minded. 'I – meant – Nineveh!'

'But what about Babylon?' asked Agnes. She was exploiting her vocabulary to the very limit. I supposed she would shortly be asking whether Babylon was a humbug. I was torn between delight at seeing Sir Edmund nonplussed – albeit extremely handsome and nonplussed – and my education, which called on me to rebuke Agnes.

'I meant *Babylon*, Miss Björk – no, I mean I meant *Nineveh*. It was a slip of the tongue. I meant *Nineveh*. They are very close to each other in location.'

'Like London and Rome,' the Professor murmured at my side. His eyes glinted, and I suspected I had found a kindred spirit. But I am a sensible woman. I moved away from the Professor, from Sir Edmund and the entire party, ignored the ancient Assyrians piling up their enemies and instead viewed their king hunting lions – with his bow drawn and aimed at a roaring animal that had already been pierced by various arrows. The people of the reliefs averted their eyes. They lived in their own world, like characters in a novel, and paid no attention to me. I went from picture to picture, studying these people who had slept in the desert sands for two thousand years. They were almost all men, imposing gentlemen with curly hair and long, elaborate beards. Among the prisoners in a triumphal procession I finally identified some women. Either the women of Assyria were very broad-shouldered, or the sculptors seldom saw any ladies, for only their lack of beards and the curve of their chests distinguished them from the men.

The Assyrians looked away from me with large, bright eyes. They were beautiful, but intimidating. The gods who protected them were fearsome half-beasts that could tear apart their enemies with sharp beaks. I recognised the swimming warriors from the newspaper – vulnerable in their nakedness, and anatomically more precise than the engraver had wished to show. And yet I felt no sense of fellow feeling with them, as I had with the Greeks: the gods, heroes and goddesses – yes, even their horses. I would not have wished to encounter in the narrow lanes of London any of those I now saw on the bas-reliefs – neither man, woman or lion.

All around me people were talking, jostling and jabbering. But in all the din there was one sound missing. When I looked up from the relief in front of me, Sir Edmund had fallen silent. He caught my eye. I stood still, as if held captive, and he came hurrying over.

'Forgive me, Miss Bondeson. I must say *adieu*. Time has moved on, and the pleasure of your company has almost made me forget another appointment. But please say you can attend our salon one day?'

I assured him I could, and Sir Edmund waxed lyrical about all the great literary and artistic figures he assembled there. He left his wife and sister-in-law in each other's care, asked the Professor to show us the bulls of Nineveh, and went off 'to see some of the fellows at my club'.

'Have you worked your way round all the reliefs, Miss Bondeson?' asked the Professor.

'I think so,' I said. 'Did I miss anything?'

'Hardly.'

We proceeded together to the bulls. Behind us I could hear the rustle of the other ladies, the sound of silk against stockings and skirt hems against button boots.

'Do you want a lecture?' the Professor asked. 'I have actually read several articles about the human-headed bulls of Nineveh.'

'No thank you!' I said. 'I prefer to do the talking myself.'

The Professor and I halted in front of the first bull and stared him in the face. We had to crane our necks well back, and even so we were unable to look him fully in the eye. It may have been just as well, for I felt alarmed that his look could turn me to stone. The creature filled me with terror and respect. The bull had the visage of a man, with the same curly hair and beard as the king in the bas-reliefs; he had strong, muscular legs; curly, manly hair covering his stomach, back and the tuft at the end of his tail; and a majestic pair of wings neatly folded on his back. He bore no resemblance to the big Blue Måns on the estate at home. Moreover, he had five legs. Seen from the front he was perfect, and equally so when viewed from the side.

'You are silent, Miss Bondeson,' said the Professor.

'He is so beautiful – and he frightens me.'

'The articles I read referred to the noble, kindly expression in the bull's eyes – do you find that frightening?'

'That one is not kindly. He despises me. He despises us all as the bloodless people of the present age.'

Having uttered those words, I lost myself in a gaze – not that of Nineveh's winged bull, who still cared nothing for me, but in the Professor's, and his eyes were at least as big and dark as those of the Assyrians. Miss Holiday whispered something to her sister, and I wrenched myself away.

'The feathers in the bull's wings are truly an impressive work of art!' I exclaimed, to divert attention from my activities. 'Don't you think, Agnes?'

This last was in Swedish – but when I turned round it was not Agnes's eyes that met mine but Ruby Holiday's. The girl was gone – again!

'I beg your pardon?'

'No, I thought Agnes...: What do you think yourself, Miss Holiday, as an artist, of the sculptor's work on the wings?'

We proceeded to talk art for a good while, until I began to wonder where Agnes was. The Museum, as I have mentioned, was full of visitors, and as the dinner hour approached, even more had arrived – perhaps to swallow down a little cultivation before their pie. They tacked like Thames barges between the cats and Pharaohs of Egypt, and ambled among the virtually naked, simple white statues of Greece. It would not be at all difficult to get lost here.

I tried to recall when I had last seen Agnes. She had been with us when we went from Egypt to Assyria, because she had argued about Babylon and Nineveh. But after that? She had definitely been standing right beside Sir Edmund when he began his oration on the reliefs, just as I tired of it and went off by myself. Was she there when we moved on to the bulls? My attention had been focused on other things.

'When did you last see Agnes? Agnes Björk, my companion?'

Neither Miss Holiday nor Lady Margaret could answer – 'Of course', I am tempted to say. Ruby Holiday, it is true, did not think Agnes had been with us on the way to the bulls, but she was not certain. Her sister had no idea.

'But what about you, Professor Devindra? A man of science must be a keen observer, surely?'

'Indeed – but I was engrossed in the art, Miss Bondeson.'

He gave me a knowing look, which I decided to ignore. I was at ease with the Professor and these ladies, but I suddenly felt myself transported to the Exhibition, to glass walls and cast iron columns, and could see people of all nationalities and classes thronging in good-natured curiosity. Only I was on my own. Agnes was gone. I felt an unwarranted fear of losing the one of whom I was fond, of being alone in the world.

'There was no sign of her as we walked over to the bulls.'

The Professor's words summoned me back to the Museum. I was surrounded by those divine works of art, in which I could revel for days on end. I pulled myself together and returned to the bas-reliefs. No Agnes there. I called out, but the sound did not carry in the tumult. The ladies and the Professor asked questions of kindly concern.

'It is nothing,' I said, thinking once again of the Exhibition. Everything had turned out well there, after all – just as it had in Copenhagen, Dresden and Åmål. 'She is bound to turn up,' I went on. It always worried me when she went missing, but I was starting to get used to it. Parents of small children presumably feel the same way.

'Then let us view these fragments in the meantime,' Ruby Holiday suggested.

So we did, devoting our full attention to them for some time. Then we took another stroll through Assyria, Egypt and Greece, but without finding Agnes. In actual fact I was rather anxious. We had agreed to meet back at the hotel if we became separated, and by now even Agnes ought to know that it was called the Golden

Cross. On further reflection, I even thought it likely she would have a few sheets of the hotel's headed notepaper in her reticule, for she had a reprehensible habit of collecting such items. It was as if the orphaned girl longed for someone to write to, someone else to depend on besides her Aunt Euthanasia. Maybe she dreamt of men and marriage. Maybe I would soon lose her for good.

We began to feel we had had enough, and I let the Professor take us to a pleasant tavern close by, where Lady Margaret dined on poached fish while the rest of us had roast beef, roast potatoes and Yorkshire pudding – a little like Swedish dumpling, but roasted instead of boiled.

It was a cheerful meal. The Professor ordered wine. There are few comestibles as fortifying as red wine and a decent piece of meat. Here, the meat was reasonably well done, the carrots a little overcooked and the savoury puddings crisp outside, doughy inside and surprisingly appealing. I discovered the English word 'horseradish', and embarked on a merry, slightly odd discussion of life in ancient Assyria.

'Do you think they went around feeling scared of those gods of theirs? Or did they find them reassuring? I mean – devils who turned on their enemies...'

'...but were on your side?' supplied Miss Holiday.

'Perhaps.'

'In India, everyone is terror-struck by the goddess Kali – even those who worship her.'

'Is she not merely one of the goddess's many incarnations?' asked Lady Margaret, who had been sitting in silence for some time. 'I seem to think my friend Amanda Russell told me...'

'Oh! Is that my Amanda Russell?' I cried, and bit my lip. She is 'my' translator of course, but whether she is 'my' Mrs Russell is much more open to question.

'Do you two *know* each other?' exclaimed the two sisters, and then for a moment we were all talking at once. They knew my translator very well. London is vast, admittedly, but the artistic world is more contained.

'Do you remember when we were at her house, Meg?' said Ruby Holiday. 'She showed us all those idols...her husband is extremely interested in cults and suchlike...is writing a book about it, if I'm not much mistaken.'

'I thought he wrote society columns of some sort.'

'Well, one has to live. Even Edmund has had to produce paintings he would rather not have put his name to.'

'He is a strange man!' said Ruby Holiday. 'Mr Russell, that is – not Edmund, sweet man! – assuredly most kind-hearted inside, but as ugly as sin and as white as a sheet, though Mrs Russell is a real *dear*...'

Her intonation reminded me of Mrs Russell's italic-strewn letters. Maybe it was typically English. Thus we chatted on, no doubt sounding like typical women. Professor Devindra listened politely, putting in an occasional comment.

We calmed down when the dessert came, for all our energies were devoted to chasing the fruit pie around in its pool of *crème anglaise*, or custard as they say here. After that we made so bold as to muse on the role of the king in Assyrian society and try to answer the Nineveh-Babylon question.

I have not had so enjoyable a meal since my last visit to my friend and fellow authoress Mrs Carlén. The sisters were the sort of ladies who find it easier to socialise when the man of the house is absent. Lady Margaret is a woman of few words, and it struck me during the meal that she looked somewhat haggard. Perhaps museum visits exhaust her. Ruby Holiday is all the more voluble by comparison. I have seldom met anyone with such a fitting name – she really did put one in mind of gemstones, deep colours and carefree, work-free days. Nor was Miss Holiday lacking in opinions about anything in English society, or in the Empire for that matter, or probably in the whole world.

'Oh,' said Miss Holiday when asked, 'but the Empire encompasses the whole world, you know.'

'Well,' I replied, 'some countries have still not been subjugated. Sweden, of course, with Norway pressed up against it the way a little girl cuddles her doll, Prussia, France, Spain – and then there is the trifling matter of Russia, which we must not forget.'

At that, Miss Holiday laughed heartily, showing all her teeth. They were very white and strong, and made me think of the roaring lionesses of Nineveh.

The Professor poured me another half glass of wine. I protested, but weakly, all too weakly. I liked Professor Devindra. There was a time when I was intended for marriage, but I became an authoress and made my own way. My family has been roused to indignation on several occasions, but I could never bring myself to compromise over the question of marriage. I realised early on that it is asking a lot of a man to expect him to put up with a writer for a wife. Looking into the Professor's eyes, I felt maybe such men existed after all. It was a short, delicious moment – and then I turned my eyes to the other ladies, pushed aside the fat I had cut off my beef and took a resolute gulp of wine.

Ah yes! That really was quite a meal!

The ladies had a thousand suggestions for the afternoon – we could go shopping together: they knew where one could find the prettiest trinkets; the most select gifts; the best afternoon tea; ice cream with preserved ginger such as one had never tasted... that made me think all at once of Agnes. I declined all these amusements, pleading fatigue, and allowed the Professor to escort me to my hotel.

I was like a mother trying to ignore her uneasiness and convince herself all is well.

When Agnes was not to be found at the hotel, I was more annoyed than anxious. That girl is a scatterbrain, and her English is abysmal – but she is not stupid. One can easily be deceived by those blonde tresses, but Agnes has her head screwed on – as long as she remembers that is where it should be. So I read the daily paper and started a letter to my next eldest sister. With eight of my nine sisters still in this world, I could have sat composing missives until dusk, but after the first my conscience pricked me and I turned to my novel. Recent days had proved so eventful that I had almost forgotten how I make a living. Now I returned to the deserted beach, where the plunderers in my latest chapter had left the corpses washed up on the shore and rowed out to the wreck.

The storm had abated. The cypresses were no longer lashing in the violent wind, but standing still and straight. As the boat put out toward the larger vessel, there was a moan from the beach. Those who showed compassion were now approaching from the village – the priest, a few good-hearted fishermen and Miss Giovanna, ceaselessly concerned for the wellbeing of her fellow men. Little did they imagine that among the dead bodies lay a man in whom life still faintly flickered... Miss Giovanna noticed his chest rising and falling – she gave a scream, and the priest hurried over. Could it be that a survivor would bear witness to the villagers' plundering? Could the village's dark mystery finally be solved?

I spent several hours weaving ingenious plots for my plunderers, my surviving sailor and the most kind-hearted inhabitants of the village. Then anxiety gripped me again.

Agnes should have been home by now. Even if she had wandered off to another part of the Museum and been staring in fascination at some mummy or harp, hunger should have brought her to her senses. Then she would have taken out her little pocket watch, looked at it and cried in consternation: 'Blow it! Whatever will Aunt Euthanasia say!'

I could picture her, stumbling around among tall sculptures and calling my name. The image brought the odd tear to my eye. It was past five o'clock. The British Museum must have closed. I rang for a member of the hotel staff.

'What is the postal service like in this city?'

'We have eight deliveries a day.'

'Upon my word!' I said, thinking of the postbag at the manor house. Here, my letter would be in the post the moment I had written it. That was a relief, but anxiety was still gnawing at me. I ordered a hot bath.

After my bath, I felt a momentary calm. Then I dressed, went downstairs and asked if any answer had arrived. Nothing. Back upstairs. My room was dark and empty. I rang for service, was provided with candles and heard myself, to my surprise, ordering a cup of tea. The tea was good, but further attempts to work on my novel were fruitless. The figures were dead. They moved like automata and spoke hollow words. I threw down my pen in anger. At that moment there came a knock at the door.

I had felt ready to embrace Professor Devindra over dinner, and felt just as ready to fall into the arms of the man who now stepped into the room.

'Inspector Evans! I am so glad to see you!'

In fact, I was up and halfway across the floor before I knew it. I took his hand – warmly – and looked him deep in the eyes. He was so much more rigid and of rougher material than the artists. His necktie was dark and simple, and not one of his garments was made of velvet.

Inspector Evans cleared his throat.

'Agnes, my companion, has vanished!' I went on.

'Your note indicated as much, Miss Bondeson. Tell me what has happened.'

So I told him. It was a relief to be able to speak, to tell him about the day and about Agnes. I started with breakfast and went on to the Museum, listing our whole party at the Inspector's request and ending with a full description of Agnes. This last was the most difficult. It felt like identifying a dead body.

I had feared that the Inspector would laugh at me, call me a mother hen with an over-fertile imagination, say Agnes had probably met some gentleman and gone off with him. Nothing of the kind. On the contrary, he was very worried.

'London is a dangerous city, Miss Bondeson. Surely you saw that yesterday?'

Then he frowned so deeply that I suggested some tea and rang the bell again. The tea arrived in a pot, accompanied by rich, finger-shaped biscuits. Mr Evans said they were Scottish shortbread. Since I could hardly take out my notebook – the Inspector currently enjoyed the privilege of being the note-taker – I made sure to memorise the name. If I were ever to write anything set in England – I undoubtedly would – I would need details of this kind.

As I was taking a bite of shortbread and finding it pleasantly buttery, the Inspector continued:

'Did anyone make contact with the girl at the Museum?'

'Not that I saw. I would have seen, surely?'

Mr Evans gave a shrug, and I knew what it implied – I had not even noticed when Agnes disappeared from under my nose at the Museum. My head had been full of Assyrians.

'I was wondering whether someone had seen her and thought she looked valuable... Was she wearing jewellery today?'

I nodded.

'You see, Miss Bondeson – we do get cases of kidnapping. There could be various reasons for abducting a lovely young girl of – what is she? Seventeen?'

'No, no! We northern races last longer than southerners. Agnes is over twenty. Twenty-two.'

'To British eyes she would seem significantly younger. But she might also simply have gone out, you know – left the Museum for some reason – and got into difficulties.'

I swallowed. Then I took a sip of tea and swallowed again. The Inspector went off on a new tack.

'Violence, robbery – we have already mentioned those.'

'And other, dreadful fates.'

The Inspector smiled.

'Sometimes it's helpful to be dealing with authoresses. You have an imagination, Miss Bondeson.'

'Ye gods, yes! We saw those Assyrians – they were so beautiful – and so terrifying! If they could have come back to life, I dread to think what they might have done to a young girl.'

'And you saw the swimmers?'

'They were floating very nicely on their sheepskins. If I had been able to get a word in edgeways, I would have told Sir Edmund Chambers about them.'

'What is he like, Sir Edmund? I only know him by name – he's a famous man, a great artist. Knighted on merit, I daresay, and what's more, for his merit at the easel!'

I gave him my account. I described the artist, his female colleague, and her Ladyship. The Inspector nodded and made notes. Then he finished his cup of tea, brushed a few crumbs from his waistcoat and stood up.

'Tomorrow I will start my investigation, Miss Bondeson. If she turns up before then – let me know! If you have any questions, send a note or a telegram. Scotland Yard is connected to the telegraph network' – here I saw him swell with pride at the modernity of the police – 'and you will find a telegraph office out in the Strand. I shall put some men onto making enquiries in the meantime. It may all be a storm in a teacup.'

I thanked him, bade him farewell, and after the tea things were cleared away I stood there with my eyes still fixed to the closed door. A storm in a teacup? My instinct told me otherwise.

★★★

I went to sleep without company and I awoke alone. Agnes had never been gone this long. Everything suddenly felt desolate, dark and cold.

But I made myself sit down at my writing desk and dip my pen in the ink. There was nothing else to do, and anyway, writing usually helped. If I was cheerful, work made me more so; if I was sad, it distracted me from my cares.

'No! No! Do not kill me!'
The compassionate priest bent over the wounded man and whispered his reassurance:
'Do not despair! We are your friends!'
The cries of the man who had survived the shipwreck ceased. His face grew calm and untroubled, and he awoke.
'The dark stranger...was he just a dream?'
'You are delirious,' whispered the priest, worried that he might disturb the wounded man if he spoke at his normal, clerical volume.
The sailor put his head in his hand. The panic slowly evaporated from his eyes. Never! Never had he experienced such terror as he had that night. Every moment had felt as if it would be his last. A sailor grows accustomed to mortal terror. That night he had known he would be smashed against the rocks and sucked down into the watery depths.
'I am alive!' whispered the man, amazed at hearing his own voice. It sounded the same as ever.

I toyed with my food at breakfast, leaving my sausage half-eaten. Today it had a musty taste. Only the eggs slipped down without difficulty – pale, insipid and congealed, they reminded me of myself. Armed with two triangles of toast and my final cup of tea, I sat down at my desk and went on with my day's work. Today we were to have gone back to the Exhibition, Agnes and I, and put right everything that had gone wrong.

I had seen the Exhibition. I had seen the Zoological Gardens, the Diorama and the British Museum. I did not want to venture back alone to any of them. Perhaps I should have steeled myself and gone to the Tower or Madame Tussaud's, but the very notion reminded me of how much Agnes liked such places. No one had ever taken her to visit waxworks or castles when she was little. I always go with her gladly. Maybe I am childish, maybe I have simply retained the curiosity required by an author.

So I wrote instead. One reason for books about authors always being so dull is the difficulty of portraying someone writing. I sat there at my desk, opposite the window where Craven Street opened down to the Thames. I could read the signs opposite, if I allowed myself to become distracted. *Whistler. Silversmith. Jeweller. Guns, Pistols & c.; E. Lodge & Co. Shirtmakers, Hosiers and Outfitters...* So I pulled myself together, dipped my pen, sipped my tea and wrote, wrote, wrote.

My reader can see what I mean. A story of activities such as these would turn out no longer than a religious pamphlet. But matters gradually resolved themselves, at least on the writing front. My novel made great strides. It would be a lie to say I kept writing all the time, but the manuscript pile kept growing. What else was I to do? Cry until the ink ran? My heart was aching, my stomach was griping, and I had no appetite even for English cheeses.

It was not the world that was wrong. The error lay in me. People were all very kind, doing their best to look after me. The Inspector often came up to report on developments in the case – or lack of them – and tried to cheer me up with little anecdotes from his life. One day he was called out urgently to the Exhibition, where there were reports of rioting and abduction. To his chagrin he found nothing more remarkable than two deft French pickpockets, Jean Legros and Arsène Petit, whom he arrested with the same distaste as a wine expert might force down the slops served at a tavern by the docks. The Inspector's simile, not mine.

My translator Mrs Russell sent a kind letter, which I answered in tearful terms. Lady Margaret and Miss Holiday invited me to the Chinese junk, where I ruined everything by regaling them with tales of my visit to the Dowager Empress of China. I have travelled far, but never as far as China. Not that anyone dares call me a liar, but sometimes I am a little incautious with the truth. Perhaps it is because my every waking hour is devoted to making up stories.

By Saturday, six days had passed since our arrival in the capital and three since Agnes's disappearance. Then a note arrived from Professor Devindra, whose surname I had still not learnt. He and his friends certainly had no intention of allowing me to sit moping in my hotel all weekend. Now I was to see what London had to offer! We would go first to Wyld's Monster Globe and then on to the theatre. I hesitated, but accepted. It was just as easy to be mournful in company.

The evening was as warm as it might have been in July, when we – Professor Devindra, Sir Edmund, Lady Margaret, Miss Holiday and I – took Sir Edmund's carriage the short distance from the Golden Cross to Leicester Square. There towered the Globe itself, beautifully disguised in cool, classical style. The top of the dome was visible, apparently trying to break free from its shackles.

'Look Miss Bondeson, what a sight!' said Professor Devindra. 'Wyld, a Member of Parliament, lining his pocket at the tourists' expense.'

'But you cannot deny that the globe has an educational value for the masses,' objected Sir Edmund. The Professor gave a derisive snort.

'I do wonder,' I said, 'what this lovely creation can teach us any better than a standard globe.'

'Now do not encourage their bickering, Miss Bondeson,' said Lady Margaret gently. 'My husband and the Professor hardly ever disagree, it merely sounds that way.' She herself was so quiet, so self-controlled – perhaps not classical in her manner, but almost. Lady Margaret did not argue, oh no. She even looked pale, despite her hair being of the same red shade as her sister's. Perhaps this was how a woman ought to be, not talkative like me or colourful like Miss Holiday. The latter was dressed for the theatre in flaming red, with elaborate ruby earrings dangling down to her shoulders.

'Well then,' I said, 'let us see what is inside the Earth!'

Of the four entrances, my English friends considerately chose the most northerly – it took us straight to those parts I knew best, though we had to round the globe first.

I knew well enough that the Earth was densely populated, but had never imagined there was room for so many people inside it! The globe we now entered had in fact been turned inside out. It was like twisting a cap inside out, so the wrong side shows and old hairs suddenly protrude from the outside, while the inside is smooth. Inside the Earth, we could see the continents high over our heads. Four flights above me I could make out the Scandinavian peninsula, with a poorly delineated Denmark beside it and Finland slumped against Russia like a punctured balloon.

Within the sphere, sound was amplified. Human beings, so insignificant on Earth, were here large and inflated, confined within the miniature globe. Giant feet scraped above me, Olympian gods coughed on the stairs.

'Good gracious!' I cried without thinking. 'I take back what I said about the standard globe...'

'...and maintain the opposite?' asked Professor Devindra, offering me his arm. We set off up the stairs. Way above us lay Sweden, and finally we were standing before its lion-shaped form. I showed them Sörmland, where I grew up, and the little dot that was Stockholm. Professor Devindra took a step back, as if to get a better view, and then engaged Miss Holiday in conversation. I cautiously moved closer to Sir Edmund.

'You live near the capital, Miss Bondeson,' he said.

'Barely a day's journey away,' I said, 'if one travels swiftly.'

'And you do,' he supplied. 'I can see that you travel at the speed of light.'

Lady Margaret admonished him, as if he had said something improper. I could hear her discreet reproofs while I was trying to remember the thick woodland and rolling fields around the manor house of my childhood. Though I had the whole world at my feet, I could not summon up the scents of midsummer in the pasture back home.

'Miss Bondeson – I would like to show you my native land.'

Professor Devindra was at my side once more. He was a thoughtful escort, and I liked him very well. But I felt a slight hesitance. He was unlike the general run of men. Somewhere around the Black Sea I had a vague feeling that his admiration extended beyond my books. Such vain notions sometimes strike one, even when one is old enough to know better.

So we descended to India, where the Professor told us of his childhood years and his longing for his homeland. He did not speak for long, but I looked up into his eyes and thought of countries where the heat never ends. Then Sir Edmund took over and instructed us – in the geography of India, I think, or the differences between Asia and Europe.

The same thing happened as at the British Museum. Sir Edmund's torrent of words became an empty droning in my ears, and I raised my eyes. Above me towered India and the immensity of Russia; beneath my feet extended the body of water. This was the Monster Globe, Agnes's British sightseeing dream. She had never come here, and now she was gone. Nowhere in the whole world could I find my Agnes.

I was filled with melancholy again, moved apart from the group and stood on my own. Beside me was the dot indicating Bombay. The whole world felt fragile. The kings of Assyria raised bulls and friezes to mark their power, but everything was hidden in the sand and only discovered two thousand years later. A young, radiant woman disappeared from a museum. In a drab, grey London square, a greedy businessman built a model of the world, and we saw it in our own imagination. But Wyld's globe, too, would fall into decay and be pulled down. All is transient. I was aware of tears in my eyes. I thought that perhaps I should begin grieving for a dead friend. Perhaps I was naive still to have hope.

The Professor touched my arm, tucked it under his and accompanied me out into Leicester Square.

'I am going home now,' I said like a sulky little girl. 'I don't want to go to the theatre.'

Sir Edmund and his ladies came out of the globe behind us.
They looked like little figures in an engraving.

'I shall accompany you,' said the Professor.

'Very well,' I said, pulled myself together, said farewell and set
off for the hotel. The Professor left me at the door and no doubt
went back to the theatrical performance.

In the hotel foyer, my next gentleman was awaiting me. There
sat Inspector Evans, reading a volume of fiction. I wondered if it
was one of my novels.

'Miss Bondeson!' he exclaimed, getting to his feet. 'How
fortunate that you are here!'

'I was going to the theatre,' I said. 'But I decided not to bother.
Vanity, vanity, all is vanity! What was there at the theatre for me?
Nothing happens! Presumably you have got no further with the
case?'

He shook his head slowly.

'There has been no response to our enquiries. You would think
Miss Björk dissolved into atoms before she even left the museum.
But I have had an idea. Did you notice her talking to anyone in
Spitalfields?'

'No. Why should she do that?'

'She got along so well with the Rector. Maybe she felt a feminine
urge to do good, to care for the most wretched in society...'

'I hardly think so,' I said, and held out my hand. 'You must
excuse me, Inspector! I am tired and must get to bed.'

'Good night, Miss Bondeson,' Inspector Evans said and gave
a stiff bow, clicking his heels together in a quietly military way,
which I felt appropriate for a naval man.

'Good night,' I sniffed, perhaps more haughtily than I had really
intended. Thus I left Owain Evans and mounted the stairs. I had
little faith in his new theory. There were reasons for Agnes to stick
close to her Aunt Euthanasia. She would never visit the slums of
her own volition.

CHAPTER FOUR

IN WHICH A GIRL MEETS WITH MISFORTUNE

I slept badly that night and awoke on Sunday morning full of foreboding. Writing did not feel at all agreeable. Perhaps my own feelings added to the sense of alarm in the novel, as I spent twelve pages describing the surviving sailor's gradual realisation that the plunderers were hunting him down. The dark stranger was naturally among the suspects — readers love the lure of the exotic.

The tender-hearted Miss Giovanna felt sorry for the sailor, who was still far too weak to leave the village by the sea. She listened closely to the story he whispered forth in his weak, broken voice.

'You cannot imagine, Miss,' said the sailor, and Giovanna leaned forward. It moved her to see the strong young man, who seemed wholly made for the swift flight of a ship across the ocean. Now his wings had been clipped and he had been broken down, mentally and physically, by the shipwreck and the looting. She dabbed her handkerchief to the corner of her eye, concerned not to reveal her emotions.

'The shipwreck must have been terrible,' she said — whispering, like him.

'It was horrific. But worse still was waking up on the beach — when I thought those people were coming to deliver me

— and they tried to kill me.'

She lowered her eyes and contemplated the golden yellow, silk bedcover in which his lacerated body was swathed.

'My good fellow, many coastal dwellers live by wrecking.'

'This was no usual looting of a wreck, Miss! They had a chief, a leader. I saw him with my own eyes. It was he who stabbed me, with his knife — here!'

Miss Giovanna averted her eyes. She still caught a glimpse of the gaping wound in the man's side. She had never seen such a thing before.

'What did he look like?'

'He was dark...very dark, with black hair and black eyes.'

'I know no one who looks like that,' said Miss Giovanna, getting to her feet. For she was telling an untruth. She knew him. She knew him only too well.

The heroine of the novel was not obliged to wait for something to happen. When I wrote, the action rattled along like a steam locomotive on rails. Only my life was devoid of action.

At breakfast I contemplated my day of rest and wondered whether I should write at all. London was full of churches. St. Martin's was just next door, and I knew the city even had a Swedish church. I ate all my bacon and took a bite of sausage. It tasted better today.

A knock came at the door.

'Come in!'

There stood a complete stranger — a proper peeler in a blue tailcoat with a row of shiny buttons and a substantial top hat.

On the railway platform, the sight of a peeler had inspired me with confidence. Here, in the peace of the hotel, it made me nervous. I watched anxiously as he looked at me, looked away, and fumbled with a piece of paper. It had been hastily folded, and was addressed in a rather childish-looking hand.

'A message from the Inspector, Ma'am.'

Inspector Owain Evans' note was extremely brief. Might I be able accompany the officer to police headquarters for a discussion of Agnes's disappearance?

Close to Whitehall stands an imposing building with large windows and tall doorways, which breathes power and importance. One entrance is from Whitehall Place, the other from a narrow street called Great Scotland Yard. This lane has given its name to the police station that is home to the detectives of London.

Inspector Evans received me in his office in Scotland Yard, safely barricaded behind a wide desk and with a steel-nib pen in his hand – as though he employed the same weapon as I did. The room was hot and stuffy, with the sun shining in at the window. As I entered, the Inspector laid aside his pen, stood up and bowed. I installed myself in the visitor's armchair, and he sat down again. He had a sombre look about him. His hair seemed greyer and more unkempt. His eyes were tired and lustreless, quite without their usual sunshine.

I sat upright on the padded seat, folded my hands in my lap and tried to appear unconcerned. The Inspector said nothing, and I shifted my feet uneasily. I could feel something sharp. A tack must have worked its way loose from my left boot. I would have to deal with it once the day of rest was over. I rearranged my feet once more. The Inspector was observing me, and a sense of powerlessness descended on me.

Something must have happened. Admittedly the London police were on duty round the clock, but that hardly applied to a Scotland Yard inspector – and certainly not on a Sunday, before morning service.

'Miss Bondeson...I...'

'Yes, Inspector?' I said, as politely as I could. 'Out with it!' I felt like saying. 'Let us get it over with, so we need be tortured no longer!'

'Do you know what a mudlark is?'

'No. A bird from Australia, perhaps?'

'No, not that. Mudlarks are part of the family *Londinii*. They come in both sexes and all ages. They are people who spend their lives in the Thames mud. And you see, Miss Bondeson, among all the remarkable creatures of London, they are among the least valued. While the sewer rats pick their way along the sewers looking for objects of value – and sometimes actually find a lost pocket watch or an earring that has fallen off – the mudlarks seldom find anything of any worth. They scavenge on the shores of the Thames, spaced as far apart as possible, and not talking to each other. They make their finds. Mainly lumps of coal, bones, stumps of rope and, if they are lucky, copper nails. Many of them are children – little children, who should be out minding the sheep or sitting at home on Mother's lap, listening to stories – who are obliged to earn what they can and know only one way of doing it. For now, I should say...'

'It must be a dreadful life!' I burst out, much affected by his story.

'I know one little girl like that. She is maybe five or six – she does not know herself, because her mother forgot to tell her before she died. The girl is too small to make the big finds, but last week she found something no one else had found, or seen as their business. She thought it a real prize, and did not tell anyone. Are you feeling quite well, Miss Bondeson?'

'Fine, thank you.'

'The girl found a woman who reminded her of her mother. She was lying totally still in the mud, but she had long, blonde hair, which the girl would sometimes sit and play with. The girl we are speaking of is rather slow-witted, but eventually even she became suspicious, as the woman never moved. She was lying in the same place every day. What is more, the woman started to smell disgusting, and one day the girl frightened off a big rat when she arrived. She screamed – the rat was huge even by a slum girl's standards – and other mudlarks rushed over to her. An old woman, physically decrepit but mentally alert, realised the girl had found a corpse and went to fetch a constable.'

As Owain Evans was telling me this, I began to feel all the symptoms of hysteria. The tears welled up, my head spun and I would have liked to slump back and call for the smelling salts. But another feeling was surfacing at the same time. The tears had already begun to flow. I shed them involuntarily, and although I could feel my already sniffing nose starting to run, I thought nothing of it. I took out a handkerchief and blew my nose. The sensation I had was no mild, soft feeling of the kind one might expect of a lady. I wanted to know the truth!

'So the woman was Agnes?' I asked, regarding Mr Evans with a clear eye through my tears – or so I hoped.

'We believe so. The face is not intact, and the body must of course be examined...'

'And who is the perpetrator? Was she *murdered*?'

'Why? She is dead.'

'It would be just as well for you to tell me the whole truth. I want to see her.'

'It is not a pretty sight, Miss Bondeson. I wonder what must be going on in that little girl's mind...it is so hard for those people, so terribly hard...'

'I asked: '*Was she murdered?*'

'Yes. She was stabbed with a knife – at least I assume it was a knife – just below her left breast. It must have pierced her heart or come very close. The examination will reveal which. She has been killed, or murdered. Moreover, she has been... I mean...'

'Thank you,' I said. 'I understand. I have been involved in charity work in the slums of Stockholm, Mr Evans. Do not forget that. I know what can befall women.'

'I know, but I forget. I remember the heart-rending scene in *The Manor House* when Angelina and Lieutenant Bertram find themselves alone in the cave...'

'When am I permitted to see the body?'

'You are not permitted to see the body.'

A moment of sullen silence followed, with me glaring at the Inspector while he started to write – presumably continuing some report or other, unless it was a letter to his old mother by the Dyfi.

'Agnes was my companion. She and I were really very close. You cannot deny me the chance of rendering her a service now she is dead.'

The Inspector put down his pen and sighed.

'You can no longer save her body. Her soul is with the Redeemer, who receives the souls of the innocent. The best thing you can do is to assist me in my hunt for her murderer.'

I could no longer look at the Inspector. A veil seemed to be laid over his face, and I had to lower my eyes. I finally wept in earnest. I wept for Agnes. The swell of my tears was like a stormy sea. I sobbed, blubbered and whimpered. Every time my thoughts came back to Agnes, another huge wave broke, and then I thought of the poor mudlark, of all the poverty and misery of London – and of Agnes again.

Owain Evans let me cry. I slumped back in the visitor's chair, snivelling; I blew my nose and cried some more. My cheeks were smarting with the tears. Far away I heard the Inspector moving, shuffling his papers, going out and coming in again. A cough made me look up. There stood a peeler with a cup of tea, which I gratefully accepted. Tea relieves mental agitation – so the British believe, and it is actually true. I sipped the milky drink, dried my eyes and gave my nose two good blows. I drank the tea and smoothed my hair.

'Better now?' enquired the Inspector, putting down his pen. I nodded. My eyes were swollen and sore, but my heart felt better. In the midst of the darkness I discerned light. Whatever had happened to my Agnes, perhaps I could still help her. Instead of inventing plots of novels, I could hunt down real-life conspiracies. Instead of studying the sights of London, I could interrogate suspected ruffians. I was not aware of it at the time, but it struck me later: when Agnes disappeared, I grew ten years younger. It was like when my sisters and I were let loose without our mother and somehow revived, although we loved her. Without Agnes at my side, I grew young myself – I became less sensible, more reckless, less well-mannered and more outspoken. It was as if a bit of Agnes had taken up residence inside me.

'Mr Evans? That last thing you said? Was it an invitation? Do you want me as a detective?'

'No, no! Not in that way – I meant give a thorough witness statement, seriously consider where you last saw her...'

But he had already set me on the trail, and with my terrier-like instinct I had picked up the scent and was now following it at a furious pace, my nose to the ground and my tail in the air. I wondered if he had initially intended asking me for help and then changed his mind; if his natural sympathy for me – reinforced by his unreflective reading of my books – had made him temporarily forget I was a woman.

'How many people do you have at your disposal? Surely the Exhibition swallows up a large proportion of your resources?'

'Indeed it does. Admittedly the Exhibition is a police district of its own, but it makes demands on us all. It requires more than a thousand men to patrol it – without counting the extra forces we have borrowed from all over England, from France, Germany and Belgium.'

'So an assistant would come in useful?'

'I have a deputy...and there are the constables of course. I cannot send you to Spitalfields, Miss Bondeson...'

'No. But with me at your side, people might think you were showing a Swedish lady writer round, as you actually did on one occasion. And that writer can be a little curious about people seen of late. Naive questions can be productive, Inspector. Perhaps I really can help with a few things. Unlike your little mudlark, I am very quick-witted, you know.'

The Inspector rocked in his seat and regarded me with an

expression that was both amused and irritated.

'Do you leave me any choice, Miss Bondeson?'

'Not really,' I said – and then began to laugh, as I had not laughed for many days. The Inspector joined in, but restrained himself and grew grave. I thought of the dead woman and beseeched all the higher powers I could summon to mind to let it not be Agnes.

'My idea is to begin with my friend Amis, the clergyman of the slums. He seemed to get on so well with your companion, so I think you should give him another chance. Oh yes, I saw what you thought of him!'

'I object to self-satisfied men.'

'The Reverend Amis is not self-satisfied. You misinterpret him! Whatever his drawbacks, that is not one of them. He is impulsive by nature, and sometimes over-hasty, but not in any way that has a bearing on you. What's more, he is genuinely devout – more so than almost anyone I have known – and keeps his nephews at boarding school out of his meagre stipend. Reverend Amis knows this district; he knows people of all sexes and classes. He may have heard something. But we must make haste – it is already past nine, and he should be home from the early morning service.'

I was rendered speechless by this unwarranted oratory – or was it a scolding? – but nodded and got to my feet. In spite of our recent laughter, the mood was hardly light. Inspector Evans was gritting his teeth and exuding determination. We hurried down the stairs and took a hansom cab to the rectory. On the way we stopped at a coffee barrow and the Inspector leapt out to get us a cup of coffee and a slice of fruitcake each.

'There's no way of telling when we will get our next meal,' he explained.

'How much do I owe you?' I asked, the situation not being one in which I could assume he would pay.

'A penny ha'penny. But don't trouble yourself.'

Having sampled English coffee, I now know why the British live on tea. The answer was as simple as that. The beans must have been boiled up a fair few times, and the drink was a pale, transparent brown. Furthermore it had an unpleasant, bitter aftertaste. The Inspector saw my expression and explained that the coffee would probably have been blended with chicory and burnt sugar. If the British cannot do something about their coffee habits they will have lost the Empire within a hundred years, mark my words! The cake, on the other hand, was excellent – sweet, moist and full of firm little currants. I licked my fingers and resolved to stick to tea in England, as far as was humanly possible.

So we found ourselves once more in front of the green door with the brass knocker, and the Inspector knocked with the self-sacrificing, long-suffering pelican. Today, the Rector himself opened the door. The maid no doubt had Sundays off.

George Amis was as thin and virtually transparent as last time, but he greeted us with more warmth, giving the Inspector a manly thump on the back and almost touching the back of my hand with his lips. I concentrated on liking him, trying not to forget those little nephews and his good works in the slums.

Before we could say anything, the clergyman began to speak. We stood in his living room and he told us excitedly about the latest meeting of the Tailors' Association. Their group had been formed almost two years before, on the initiative of Amis, several benefactors and a couple of master tailors.

'And now,' explained Amis, 'the tailors are working to support themselves, not for others' gain.'

He went on to tell us how the cooperative's representatives would be meeting other gentlemen of the cooperative movement from all over England, and from Scotland and Wales. He had mentioned this important question in his intercessions at the early service, and in the main morning service…

'Are there no associations for women?' I interrupted.

'Well, it is the men who are the family breadwinners…' began the Reverend Amis.

'I know many women who are family breadwinners,' I said.

'Husbands can die or disappear, too.'

'There is an association of seamstresses, actually,' said the Inspector, and that prompted George Amis into a detailed discourse about their organisation, the shop where one could purchase their products and the poverty and oppression that prevailed in the so-called 'sweatshops'. I would not know how to translate that word into Swedish. Modern factories are still so rare in our country, and I hope we will avoid letting in any sweatshops. They are sewing workshops or manufactories of a sort, in which poor girls and women work for starvation wages.

'Have you seen my photographs?' asked the Rector, as if he thought I was becoming tiresome – as though I might be on the verge of making some remark about it being quite obvious that a poor girl would rather go on the street than work in a sweatshop.

His question really did sound like an evasion tactic, but when I raised my eyes I saw that the parlour had changed since last time. The walls were still quite bare, but between the clock and the cupboard hung several photographs, clearly taken by some enthusiast inspired by modernity. They were portraits, which to judge by appearances were Biblical figures in highly physical incarnations, muscular and handsome. I could make out a David, with slingshot and loincloth, and a long-haired, surprisingly attired Mary Magdalene. There were also photographs of modern street scenes. I had never seen such things before.

'These are really wonderful!' I said. 'Where did you buy them?'

'I take photographs myself.'

The Rector rose somewhat in my estimation. There was the door of his church, and next to it a morning shot of a slum street – the former empty of people, the foreground of the latter full of figures.

'How did you get the people so clear? Does it not take a long time to have one's photographic likeness taken?'

The wide mouth smiled.

'The exposure time is quite long. That is true. But I mounted some portrait pictures against the background afterwards.'

'And made the people as small as that?'

Now he was laughing openly at me, that priest. And I had thought him incapable of laughter!

'I shall show you. Owain, will you come with me? There is quite a lot of equipment to carry.'

'Of course.'

'If you will excuse us, Miss Bondeson?'

I did, even though it meant a delay in our investigation. When the gentlemen had gone I studied all the photographs again, with great admiration. It really was time to have my picture taken by the sun. Perhaps I could persuade the Rector to take a portrait photograph. But even I had to admit that such a thing would be inappropriate.

As the gentlemen had still not returned, I began to inspect the wall cupboard. It reminded me of my father's schnapps cabinet. One might wonder what sort of spirits an English clergyman kept in his house – our Dean at home in Sörmland always drinks schnapps flavoured with St John's wort, and is very particular about which slope the plants are to be picked from and how long they are to infuse in the spirits.

The longer I waited, the more bored I became, and my *tristesse* made my curiosity worse. I gave the little handle an experimental tug: nothing happened. But it was only a little cupboard, and I was not born yesterday. I pulled a hairpin from my bun and picked the lock. It worked exactly the same as the lock on father's cabinet back home.

The Rector's cupboard contained not a single bottle. It was full of pieces of paper. I took out a pile of them. They were photographs. Portraits, you might say if you were being generous – but full-length, and in a greater state of dishabille than the Biblical subjects. There was an intimacy, there were details such as I had never seen so explicitly before. The bodies were naked, powerful and shapely. They were shown in relationships of a kind I had never reflected on.

Then I heard the men's voices outside. I threw the photographs back in and shut the door, peered short-sightedly at Mary Magdalene's mane of hair and hoped my flushed look would be attributed to my earlier tears.

The camera and equipment were truly impressive. The Rector was as eloquent about photography as he had been about charitable works. He perceived them as linked - if one documented people's living conditions, the world would come to know of the unsatisfactory state of affairs and things would instantly improve. I nodded. He told me of the very latest wet collodion method, which employed glass instead of paper, but on the other hand had to be developed while the negative was still wet. This obliged the photographer to carry his developing materials with him wherever he went. Reverend Amis took out his bottles of chemicals and explained them. He sat me in an armchair with the cupboard as a backdrop, adjusted in a kind and most fraternal manner the hairpin I had hastily stuffed back into my bun, and told me not to move from the spot.

'But I have just been crying!'

'You look charming, Miss Bondeson!'

And then he photographed me.

During the exposure I sat unmoving, staring unblinkingly into the camera with a fixed smile on my lips. The Inspector, meanwhile, came to the point at last.

'George, old friend. You recall my previous visit here with Miss Bondeson? Do you remember her companion?'

'That pleasant girl? Yes, of course.'

'Do you remember my telling you she had vanished? We suspect now that she has been murdered. We've found a body down by the Thames. We presume it to be her.'

'Was she wearing the same clothes?'

'There were no clothes. No jewellery either. The earrings had been torn off.'

I felt suddenly sick. He had forgotten to tell me that part. But I had to remain still.

'Robbery with murder?'

'And rape.'

'Goodness!' said the Rector, looking uneasily in my direction.

'Miss Bondeson will be all right. She is made of strong, Nordic oak!'

I stared hard into the eye of George Amis's camera, so he would not think me a namby-pamby woman.

'Have you heard any whispers from your parish or the associations? Any shady types? New women? Fights and screams?'

'There are fights and screams virtually all the time. But many of the slum folk are decent and honest. Some of them are too old and sick to work...'

I could no longer sit silent. The photograph would have to take its chances.

'Well, they could hardly strike down and rape a healthy girl of twenty and a bit. Agnes is taller than most English men.'

The Rector gave me a quizzical look. I knew very well that I sounded angry, that my anger seemed both misplaced and unfeminine and that I was, moreover, talking about Agnes as if she were still alive. But she was my girl. I wanted to see the body and send the culprit to the gallows. Then I could grieve.

'I expect that was a long enough exposure. But you see, Miss Bondeson, it is sometimes easier to steal than to work. There are whole gangs of small children, brought up by thieves. And there are those who kill for gain. And there are men who – forgive me, Miss Bondeson – enjoy a fallen woman more if they can stick a knife in her afterwards – or maybe during. It's horrific. We in the Church are doing all we can to prevent such things...'

'So are we in the police – though not so much with Bible

classes as with prison.'

'God knows which is most effective!' retorted Amis. It struck me that this was the first time I had heard him speak of the Lord, and so emphatically that even an old cynic such as myself was moved. But then, it was Sunday. 'I think the portrait can be saved, if I develop it at once.'

'What we are wondering is whether any other girls have disappeared. Miss Bondeson's companion was no prostitute, and it was not here she went missing but in the British Museum.'

'Kidnapped? And then murdered?'

The Inspector gave a shrug. He did not know, and I did not know, but it seemed plausible.

'The two of you got along so well,' I said – and had intended saying more, but had to stop. Reverend Amis was frowning, deep in thought. It would have been improper to interrupt such meditation. His weak profile took on a determined look. Seen alongside the Inspector's coarser features, his head with its wavy hair and neat beard looked like that of some Roman statesman. I sensed his brain leafing through gossip and confidences, until the right page suddenly opened and he looked up.

'Something odd happened at our Bible group the other day.'

The Inspector and I leant forward, raised our eyebrows and showed every sign of interest. And the Rector told us about the Bible group for fallen women, where they devoted themselves particularly to discussions of Mary Magdalene and the sinner's path to the Lord. I was somewhat frustrated by his volubility, but he finally got to the point. A few days before – the day after Agnes vanished – there had been an argument at the Bible group. It was one thing, maintained one of the more established members, for new girls to turn up on the street. It happened all the time. They came and went, fell sick or died or managed to move on. A few made decent marriages or decided they preferred the starvation wages of a seamstress. But that day they had been highly indignant. A new girl had turned up without the faintest idea how to behave;

she did not hesitate to appropriate the others' street corners and poach their clients. George Amis admitted he had been put on the spot. How was a servant of the Lord to react? Should he warn the girls against jealousy and exhort them to share what they had, or should he condemn their profession?

I could see his dilemma. I was also alarmed. Heavens! Did I not know that rogues could drug girls and force them to do all manner of things? Oh yes, I knew. I just didn't want to think about it.

'It was a tall, blonde, quiet girl,' the Rector went on. 'She spoke to no one.'

Because she could hardly speak English. Because all she could do was cite the slings and arrows of outrageous fortune or accuse those around her of being humbugs.

I felt suddenly weak. It was as if I were bleeding to death, as if my life's blood were leaking out — life pumped rapidly away, leaving me pale and robbed of all strength. Euthanasia Bondeson seldom allows her feelings to get the better of her. But I could no longer be strong. I gave a whimper, rose swiftly as if to flee, tripped over backwards and caught the edge of the cupboard of photographs as I fell in an elegant arc, straight into the arms of Owain Evans.

It is lucky policemen have such quick reactions. He caught me and held me with a firmness and softness that again made me look up.

'It must have been Agnes,' I said. 'She speaks extremely little English.'

The Inspector smiled at that, in spite of the mess we were in. It was a blessed sun, a sun that warmed without being too hot, a sun quite different from the one which had been plaguing London for several weeks.

'I know,' he said, smiling at my refusal to believe Agnes was dead.

In an instant I saw two things. Behind the camera stood

George Amis, mouth open, eyes staring. Turning my head, I saw the cupboard door swing open, and a pile of photographs that had been roughly thrust into it floated slowly to the floor. Naked bodies fluttered like summer butterflies about my head. I swiftly shut my eyes and pretended I had swooned.

The Rector rang for the maid...and after that, my recollections are blurred. I was made to lie down on a chaise-longue and sip a decoction of lavender. I could hear the mumble of male voices outside, Owain Evans raised his voice from time to time, but not enough for me to make out the words. No one had said anything about the photographs. Could it be that the Rector had not noticed? Or didn't he care? It pained me to be excluded, but I felt so incredibly tired.

I may have slept a while before the Inspector popped his head round the door.

'I am going with Amis to morning service. I shall come and fetch you afterwards, Miss Bondeson.'

'Do not trouble yourself,' I said – and heard my voice, sounding as hollow as a megaphone. 'I shall take a cab home.'

'Are you quite sure?'

I nodded, and my neck felt as stiff as that of a jointed wooden doll. The door closed and I laughed silently to myself at the thought of the doll, which could be bent to and fro and have its arms, legs and head put into poses. Perhaps I had such a doll, once. I no longer recall...no, I had seen it in a studio somewhere. It was used as a model for sketches of the human form. It moved so much more easily than us, weighed down as we are by flesh and blood. We humans are so heavy and tired. I felt it so intensely. I could hardly turn my head when I tried to lie on my side...such tiredness was strange. And it was only morning... I thought that it must be the grief.

***

When I awoke, fear overtook me. My slumber must have been deep and long. I felt refreshed, but alarmed. The room was dark and smelt strange. It was a smell of dust, not found at the hotel, but there were also other unfamiliar smells: coal, as everywhere in England – but also a faint scent of perfume that put me in mind of Oriental rites, of India and the East, of Venice and Rome... Incense. That was it.

I groped for a candle and found it beside the bed. A box of lucifer-matches was lying beside it, and I struck one of them on the sole of my boot – whatever had happened, at least I still had my boots – and lit the candle.

I was lying in a cosy boudoir with a red chaise-longue and thick curtains of the same red. For a split-second I thought myself in a brothel, but then I spied the big book on the table. George Amis had considerately provided me with a Bible to sustain me when I awoke. That also explained the smell. Accustomed as I was to fastidious Lutheran services, I had at first not recognised the scent of incense, which had spread from the church to the rectory. Such Papist trappings are also used in some English church services.

I sat up and flicked through the Bible for a bit, as it was the only book to hand. Then I took heart and looked at my watch. It had stopped at five. It felt later. I did not feel well, and my head ached. My tongue was dry and swollen. I picked up the cup, which still contained the blue dregs of the lavender drink, and sniffed the contents. Here, too, there was something different, foreign – not incense, but a smell better known among the women of our time. Some kindly soul – I hoped – had put drops of laudanum in the lavender. No wonder I had a hangover. I had slept well on opium. I got up, took the candle and ventured forth

The house was dark. I stood still outside the boudoir, trying to look about me in the thin light of the candle flame. There was not a soul to be seen. Not a sound to be heard. The candle illuminated nothing but dark walls, without pictures or lamps.

I had never been further than the rectory's reception rooms

before. I had no idea what the house looked like. Everything about the Reverend Amis seemed so thin and bloodless, and when I emerged from the little room there were no smells other than my own scent of lavender and the faint burning smell of the candle. There were not even any kitchen odours to follow, since the Rector did not seem to have any taste for cooked food.

This was my first visit to an English home. In a Swedish house I would have felt my way around, guessed the layout of the rooms and found the exit with comparative ease. This house was constructed differently, and the candle showed me scarcely more than my own hand and a bit of wall beside it.

It was a sensation of depth that saved me. I felt as if I was on the brink of an abyss, and I knew I was going to fall before I tripped down the first step. I grabbed the banister with both hands. The light fell like a star down the stairs and went out. I was left sitting on the step, trying to catch my breath, as if I had run a long way. I was still feeling the effects of the opium. I was less coordinated than usual, and I am generally quite clumsy enough.

Like a petrified child on a sledging hill, I began to shuffle down the stairs. One step at a time – thud – thud – thud. Just at that moment, there seemed no better way of descending. Finally I was sitting on the last step but one, my feet on a solid stone floor and firmly supported with both hands. Now I could stand up.

I groped my way across the room. It was large, hall-like, and wherever my fingers felt they found the same wallpaper – dark, with a pattern of medallions and a faint whiff of wallpaper paste. There in the gloom, I slowly caught up with myself. The effects of the opium were receding. It was still dark, but I broke out of that drunken, listless acceptance. I was suddenly myself again. Once more I became Euthanasia Bondeson, and Euthanasia is prone to being scared and mutinous at the same time. The same happened now. I listened in terror for any sound. My exaggerated sense of smell began to fade. I smelt nothing and heard nothing. I was alone in the rectory, and ice ran down my spine.

In the darkness of the hall, I recalled the Reverend Amis looking at Agnes. She had been so taken with him. She had appreciated his wordy idealism, while I had merely sniffed and disliked the man. The girl's appreciation was utterly innocent, but what had I seen in his eyes? Admiration of a beautiful person, of God's goodness in creating Agnes? Or had I sensed desire? Who knows what an ascetic clergyman might do if he once let loose his urges. He had that sensual mouth, after all.

I shivered. Foot by foot I edged forward, keeping my hand flat against the wall. I came across a cupboard. It must be the schnapps cabinet. All at once I remembered the photographs. I fumbled at the lock. The door opened without resistance. There was nothing inside. My hands made out that the walls were as bare as they had been on my first visit to the Rector. No photographs, no David or Mary Magdalene, no slum street and no church. Beneath my hands was nothing but medallion-patterned wallpaper and emptiness.

At that point I tripped over some piece of dining room furniture. I thought the kitchen must be somewhere close by, and the kitchen must have a door. That would also be the safest way out. Whatever the Rector's inclinations, I could not imagine they ever led him to the kitchen.

I was suddenly feeling about in thin air. Though I managed to stop myself crying out, a little sigh did escape me. My feet were still firmly on the ground. I moved my hands sideways and upward, and realised I had put them through the serving hatch. This was the way to the kitchen – not a door, as in our Swedish manor houses and town apartments, where the servants run in and out of the dining room. Here in England, the food was sent to the dining room and entrusted to staff of another calibre, formally dressed men in dark coats and white stockings, and silent, pretty girls who served the sauce without raising their eyes.

I peered about me in the darkness. There was no one there. In my gymnastics lessons with Professor Ling I had proved myself very athletic. Beneath my skirts, I was still slender and agile. I opened the hatch wide, felt about to check there were no sauce boats lurking on the other side, and pulled myself up – as Professor Ling had once taught me to do on the parallel bars.

It was not difficult to crawl through the hatch. I was slightly uneasy about ending up in a pudding, but I was much more uneasy about remaining in the house and being forced to meet the Rector eye to eye. And if he was a villain, what about the Inspector? Ouch! I do not know what hurt most, that thought or the carving fork stabbing into my hand. I pulled it free, thought a curse I dared not say aloud, and licked my palm. It tasted salty with sweat, but had only a slight metallic tang of blood. Evidently I was not seriously injured.

I jumped down lightly to the floor, made my way round the table and opened the kitchen door. It was night time, but the outlines of the Tower and London Bridge were visible on the horizon. I took a deep breath and stepped out through the door. Someone grabbed me hard about the waist. A hand was clapped over my mouth. I didn't even have time to scream.

CHAPTER FIVE

IN WHICH I VISIT MODERN BABYLON

The man held me fast, and no stretch of the imagination was required to guess his intentions. I could already visualise the knife in his hand and see myself naked, tossed onto the shores of the Thames. But there was a tack sticking out of the sole of my left boot, and since it was a day of rest – and other things had got in the way – I had not had it mended. I kicked out at the man's ankles with all my might, and registered the nail puncturing his leg.

'*Ow*, damn you!'

He cried out, but did not release his grip. Instead he pulled me closer, so I could feel his face close to mine. My assailant had a silky, well-groomed beard. I stopped kicking and tried to speak, but produced only a mumble.

'Well! What have you pilfered this time, you slattern?'

The man raised his hand and turned towards me. It was the moment at which I would have feared the knife, had my mind not already been set at rest.

'Inspector Evans!'

'Miss Bondeson! What are you doing here?'

Owain Evans instantly became less rough – in his language, pronunciation and actions. His grip was hard, but he cautiously released me, as if I were a hare that might hurt itself on the cobblestones. I twisted round to shake off the unpleasant sensation.

'Your friend put laudanum in my lavender tea.'

'What? Surely that must have been a mistake?'

I gave a snort of derision – and then a suspicion crept over me. What was the Inspector himself doing there? Was he perhaps implicated?

'You think not? But to calm you...?'

'Does that seem likely, Inspector? Wasn't it rather because I unearthed his dubious photographs?'

'Photographs? What photographs?'

'The pictures that fell out of the cupboard – definitely not something *I* would want an unmarried lady to see!'

'I don't know what you're talking about.'

'What of the photographs on the wall, then? And all the equipment?'

Inspector Evans gently shook his head.

'It must have been an opium dream, Miss Bondeson. Photography is a difficult art, nothing a hard-working clergyman would have time for.'

'But...?' I began, then stopped short. What if he were right? Or – what if the photographs had signified something I did not understand? Perhaps I had been too distracted by the naked bodies to notice something else, something that needed to be concealed? And what if – the worst thought of all – my nice Police Inspector had been involved in the murder?'

'Incidentally, what are you doing here yourself?' I enquired. 'And where is the Rector?'

'I don't know where Amis is at the moment. As for me, I was in Whitechapel – for professional reasons – and was just passing. Then I spied a shadow coming out of the rectory, suspected burglary – and you know the rest.'

It did not seem the likeliest time of day for detective work. If it had been to do with Agnes's disappearance, he would surely have mentioned it? Though I was no doubt too ignorant of the finer points of police work. There was probably a perfectly reasonable explanation. For anyone of a less suspicious disposition.

There was nothing else for it. I had to put my trust in the Inspector, and I so badly wanted to. There was no one else to rely on here.

We went in silence out into the street and along several dark alleys until we had left the outlines of the Tower and the bridge behind us. A hansom cab happened by, and Mr Evans hailed it.

'The Golden Cross Hotel in the Strand! And make it snappy!'

We sank back into the soft seat.

'Tell me the whole story!' the Inspector said, and I did – how I had woken up, and the various thoughts I had had about the Rector and the preceding day. It had still been morning when we got to the rectory, and just before I fell asleep, Mr Evans and the Reverend Amis had gone off to morning service. When I awoke it was dark, and Mr Evans's watch said it was midnight. I wound my own and put it to the same time as his. I had slept for over twelve hours.

'I do not understand,' said the Inspector (which it was very decent of him, as a police officer, to admit). 'How are you feeling?'

'I'm quite awfully hungry!' I said, as it suddenly hit me. We had had morning coffee so it would not matter if our dinner was late, and then I had gone and slept through dinner, afternoon tea and supper!

'Lucky there are piemen, then' said Owain Evans, who called to the coachmen to stop and jumped out. He did not bother to toss this time but bought us two eel pies apiece. We had demolished them by the time we reached the hotel. There he dismissed the cab and came with me into the lounge. I called first for water, for my thirst, and then for wine, for I needed something kind and gentle to drink. Then we sat with our glasses beside us and it was my turn to listen and his to narrate.

'I parted from George Amis after the service and nosed

round Spitalfields and Whitechapel. I know the thought pains you, as someone close to her, but although Miss Björk moved in other social circles, many things point to the murder having been committed there. And the body was found nearby, too, of course.'

'And?'

'I spoke to some pimps – and some girls – there is a certain peace even in areas like that on Sundays. Several of them told me a new girl turned up sometime last week. No one seems to have known her. She came one day and was gone the next, and behaved like a novice in every respect. It's the same on the street as in the drawing room – there are rules of behaviour. The girl seemed not to know them.'

'Are you saying, Inspector, that Agnes walked straight out of the British Museum, went to the slums, prostituted herself and was murdered? It does not really sound very plausible, does it?'

Inspector Evans gave me a look, uttered a faint sigh and poured out more wine. I raised my glass and watched the deep red liquid trembling, like an ocean halfway to a storm.

'I completely agree. But we must follow up all our leads. Maybe someone lured her away. Maybe someone drugged her and forced her to do things she would never do otherwise.'

Here I grew somewhat sombre. Then I thought of Agnes, and hope returned. In my mind's eye she stood before me, fair and tall, pure and invincible like her saintly namesake.

'But how can the perpetrators be found in London – in this immense city? You know Inspector, almost as many people live here as in all of Sweden!'

'And more than in all of Wales. Where there are people, there is not only danger – there is also hope. There is always someone who has seen something. Witnesses may keep their mouths shut, but eventually they can be persuaded to talk – by threats worse than the murderer's knife, by bribes...even if they only amount to a few decent meals and a new set of warm clothes, now winter's coming on.'

'I feel sorry for the human race,' I said, 'but now it is way past my bedtime. Let me know if you discover anything!'

'I shall telegraph!' said the Inspector, brought his heels together with a military click and kissed my hand.

I slept well that night, despite having lost the whole day to sleep. I awoke round six and sat down to write.

Miss Giovanna awoke with a start. The soft feather bolsters of her bed felt prickly and repellent. Beneath her thin nightgown she was échaufée, and she wondered if she had been dreaming. Then she opened her eyes. She was instantly gripped by the dreadful realisation that she was not alone...

It was the murderer! Miss Giovanna could hear the man moving in the room. His movements were quiet and cautious, but each step wafted the smell of the man's body to the girl in the bed. Miss Giovanna lay as stiff as a board, not even daring to shut her eyes, and inhaled the smell of salt water, tar, sweat and chewing tobacco. There was a man in her room. Did she dare to scream? Had he already killed the poor survivor? The steps came closer. Now he was standing beside her bed. Her scream rent the air.

When breakfast was served at about nine, I had produced fifteen pages and threw my famished self on the selection offered that day. As well as my usual egg, bacon and sausage, I helped myself to kidneys, a fish and rice dish and a little cup of potted shrimps. After breakfast I read the day's post. Two of my sisters had written accounts of their married lives and offspring; an admirer had heard I was in England and wanted me to visit Norfolk; and Professor Devindra had invited me to supper that evening.

As soon as the table had been cleared, I sent an amiable refusal to Norfolk and an equally cordial acceptance to Professor Devindra. I pondered a while whether it was appropriate for me to meet a strange man without a chaperone. I would normally have taken Agnes with me. But I was a grown woman, and it would be absurd to pretend I was scared when I was not. I set my seal on the envelope and telegraphed the Inspector for news. Then I continued work on my novel for a few hours, received confirmation from the Professor that he would pick me up at six-thirty that evening and a message from the Inspector that there had been no new developments. He would be returning with his deputy that morning to Whitechapel, the slum district adjacent to George Amis's rectory. Once again I wondered what he had really been doing on Sunday evening, and if the Rector had indeed spent the whole day on church business, on pastoral visits and administering the last rites.

By then I had writer's cramp and made a solitary detour to the Exhibition, where I took the opportunity of looking at Prince Albert's model homes for workers. I somehow owed it to the Inspector. Shortly before half past six I was ready and waiting at the Golden Cross, neatly dressed in violet and with my hair unusually well coiffed.

Professor Devindra was more elegant than ever. He kissed my hand, complimented me on my choice of colour – I am one of the few people whom violet really suits – and helped me up into a hansom cab.

'Now we have seen the Exhibition, the British Museum and Wyld's globe together, Miss Bondeson. Today I shall show you something unusual, but very much of the Empire.'

'The pie stalls?' I asked, and the Professor gave a start beside me. They were not part of his world, for sure. 'Sorry,' I said, 'I was only joking.'

'You'll see,' beamed the Professor. 'Have you heard anything of your companion?'

'Sadly not.'

I was a little short at that point, but before the cab reached its destination I had begun interrogating him, little by little. Agnes's disappearance had been so sudden, so abrupt, that I suspected the whole world and simultaneously expected it to help me. Hadn't the Professor seemed remarkably interested in her huge pieces of jewellery? As soon as the opportunity arose, I started asking questions. Had he noticed anything, at about the time she vanished? Had he heard any rumours? Was he aware of any known villains being in these parts? Maybe I thought he would tell me of murderous Indian sects who sacrificed the hearts of blonde girls to evil gods. When I got a chance, I would ask the Inspector if the heart had still been in the body.

The Professor knew nothing of murderers and had not noticed anything. His profession was medicine, but he preferred talking about art. So we embarked on a discussion of the Pre-Raphaelites, and the cab came to a halt.

We were in a rather disreputable looking area. Yet there was something familiar about it. From the cab I could see the same silhouette as the previous night: the Tower and London Bridge – but from a different angle than I was used to. We were further east in the city than I had ever been before.

'Where are we?'

'Whitechapel. What is known as the East End. The docks are just down there.'

It was the third time that day I had heard mention of Whitechapel, a place I had been told not to go after dark. Between us and the Tower was a mass of masts, reminding us that England was a seafaring nation. I felt the importance of the Empire, for here were as many types of boat as I could imagine. Only the largest anchored farther out. A haze clung round the masts, and I thought of the vessels' distant origins and distant destinations. Boats appeal to me. Unlike the junk to which Lady Margaret and Miss Holiday had dragged me, these were real ships that sailed between foreign lands disseminating goods and knowledge. Paddle-steamers and clippers were waiting down there to waltz across the dance floor of the waves, returning at length with silk, tea and spices from the

Orient.

There was an autumn nip in the air. That's how it is in England – changes in the weather happen instantaneously, without warning. I felt the chill on my face and realised the air was damp – not with proper rain, but with drops that hung hesitantly, considering whether to fall. It was the same haze as around the ships' masts. This was not a pleasant district, and I wondered whether I had misjudged both myself and the Professor. He took my hand and helped me out, and a faint, unfamiliar scent came from him – perhaps of perfume, pomade or spices. The street was dark, and Professor Devindra was a glimmering silken silhouette against the night. Perhaps he was someone other than he made himself out to be? Perhaps it was he who wielded the ritual blade and abducted young women?

'Where are we going?'

He bent down towards me and laughed, and then pointed up at the sign above my head.

CURRY HOUSE

'You are about to taste a real Indian meal, Miss Bondeson. I have read so much in your books about Swedish food: your cakes and buns, your roast meats and fish and jellies and boiled potatoes, steaming hot and newly dug from the loamy soil of Sörmland... it must all be delicious, but now you are to sample what India has to offer.'

He gave me his arm, and together we stepped from the poor street into the rich Orient. There was the gleam of beaten brass tables, there were draped fabrics on the walls, and the guests sat in throne-like seats. At the sight of Professor Devindra, the head waiter rushed forward to welcome him – not in English, but in a language I did not understand. There was such crackle and laughter in that language that I forgot the anxiety I had been feeling. Maybe it was precisely that Oriental, semi-incomprehensible element that appealed to me about the Professor. He was a genuine Englishman, and yet he was a foreigner.

At a time when I was permanently walking in the forest of fear, that evening was like a joyously illuminated glade, in which you can see the fairies dancing. I very rapidly stopped believing the Professor could do anything bad as I sat at the table sipping *lassi* – an Indian fruit drink like a more liquid version of our thick, soured milk.

Indian cuisine was a little like the food I had been fed as a girl. Under King Gustaf, the better sort of people favoured spices that had arrived at our shores in the age of travellers, with Vikings and medieval merchants. Our cook carried on preparing such food even after the Fersen murder in 1810, before a more French style of cooking was introduced at our manor house. The spices of older times survived in food for high days and holidays: in our mulled wine at Christmas, our saffron buns and cinnamon bun rings. Perhaps it was even the case – I mused, licking a cinnamon stick – that the lasciviousness of the Gustavians was in some way associated with the spices. A clove had such a deliciously full flavour as I bit it. Their food was strong and sweet, with rich sauces like the taste of my childhood.

'This is a good place,' explained the Professor. 'But the very best thing of all is eating in the street – from a cone of paper or a pot, with all the people around you. London is pale and tame in comparison with Bombay. It is so drab and grey here, and there is such a display of vibrant colour there. Saffron yellow, all manner of reds from purple to scarlet...and the food! You must go there, Miss Bondeson!'

Our food had still not arrived, so we sat nibbling on a variety of peculiar little dishes: roasted nuts shaped like half moons; worms of deep-fried dough; diminutive pies; small, elongated meatballs; prawns on skewers; crunchy bread made of a flour totally unfamiliar to me.

'The food in the bazaar back home in Bombay, Miss Bondeson... you simply have to taste it! Little pieces of grilled meat...crisp, golden *samosas* – these are actually not too bad – and then *khatte chhole*! Even if they had *khatte chhole* here, one would be foolish to eat it – a trained chef could never produce the right, sour taste that you get from ginger, lemon and spices. It is as if the taste is something emanating from the land, the air, the walls of the houses. Bazaar food is strong, sour and sweet – just like India.'

I suddenly realised why the Professor had looked so unappreciative when I mentioned pies. Anyone raised on spicy, tasty street food could not but seek to avoid London pies. I listened eagerly to the Professor's stories of the food of his Bombay childhood – gaped, listened, ate and was amazed – and dreamt of going to India some day. It must be a wonderland.

'Do you never long to go home?' I asked, though I felt sure that he must.

'Yes, often. It is not always easy being an Indian in England – I am altogether too black, though an English education, good birth and a wealthy family help a great deal. For money matters to them, the English.'

'Why do you not go back? Surely India has need of an artistic doctor?'

The Professor smiled and crunched through a piece of deep-fried bread before answering. 'Ah, that is the difficulty. Here I am too Indian – anyone can see that at a glance – and there I am too English. And that is much worse, because they only realise it when I open my mouth.'

I wanted to say something comforting, but did not know what. He regarded me across the table with his black eyes, and the waiters took away our empty dishes and gave us warmed plates.

Like the food of my childhood, in Indian cuisine many dishes were laid out at once. Everything was steaming hot and tasted excellent. The Professor wrote down the names of the dishes, and

I can still spell my way through them from that smeary scrap of paper. That, too, is aromatic with the freshness of coriander and the warmth of cumin: *masaledar basmati* (that was the kind of rice, more like a pudding than ordinary rice); *baigan achari* (the vegetables, a strong stew of aubergines); *dum gosht* (a delicious braise of spiced meat); *murghi tikka* (baked chicken, spicy but not too strong); *naan* (tasty unleavened bread); *kheere ka raita* (a soured milk dish fortified with herbs) – and even then, I realised as I read that the Professor did not make a note of all those things we nibbled while we were waiting and he was busy talking.

I ate more than I had ever thought I could – I had, after all, missed several meals the day before – and I felt perfectly happy. A sensual pleasure spread through my body. The spices intoxicated me. Agnes was so far away I scarcely remembered her, and when the Professor walked me to the door of the hotel I was no more than twenty-years-old. He leant down to take his leave, and I knew that if he kissed me I would not be able to bring myself to slap him. But he remained a gentleman. His lips touched my cheek fraternally, and we said good night.

Once I was safely in my room, I felt very aware that I had recently slept around the clock. My bed did not tempt me – not like this, not alone. Less than twenty-four hours had passed since I awoke from the influence of the opium, and I felt the same lack of responsibility for my actions – but wide awake rather than sleepy, bold rather than frightened, enterprising rather than cautious. I opened my trunk and took out my emergency kit. Every sensible female traveller should follow George Sand's example and keep a jacket and tie, a pair of men's trousers and naturally the most indispensable item – a top hat, to hide all your hair.

It did not take me long to get out of my dress and into my man's attire. Very soon an unknown gentleman was creeping out of the Golden Cross Hotel and taking a hansom cab back to East London. I stopped the cab just east of the Tower, alighted and slipped through the streets.

The visitors to the Exhibition were peacefully asleep in their beds. Here in the slums, things were still in full swing, though it was nearly midnight. Men were walking several abreast, talking loudly. Some were staggering. Intoxication was desirable in these parts. Perhaps it was the only way to get through an ordinary evening. I am no supporter of strict temperance, but being here made me feel lemonade would be preferable. Sober at the drunkards' feast, I looked around me, quickly closed my eyes and opened them anew.

Someone had collapsed against the wall of a house. A man was lying there in a bundle, snoring loudly. That meant he was not dead. The house, too, was ramshackle – as if the human being and the house were holding each other up, and the old man had fallen first. People were passing by. Nobody saw him. How could the Inspector imagine anybody would have noticed a murder?

The women of easy virtue at their lampposts had a look that aroused my pity. I suddenly noticed how foul the lamps smelt. Here there was not gaslight, as in the Strand, but the same reeking oil lamps as in Stockholm. I was aware of the surrounding stench, as if all my senses had again become exaggeratedly heightened. All around me were the usual odours of London: coal smoke, horse droppings, cooking smells – but beyond the stink of the lamps there were smells I could not readily identify. Some of them were presumably odours of unwashed humanity, but others were harder to recognise. Was it pure dirt, I wonder? Filth, ingrained in people who never washed? Dirt, overflowing privies, bad gin, opium fumes – and all intermingled with the smells of the Thames – seaweed, sludge, tar.

I could not linger here. I decided to begin my investigation.

'Hrrmph,' I went, clearing my voice in a manly fashion. At the next lamppost, a girl raised her head. I went over and looked her in the eyes. Superficially she looked a little like Agnes – slim, blonde and tall – but she had tired eyes that I did not want to see on Agnes ever again.

'Business, Sir?'

'I am looking for particulars.'

'And which particulars would Sir like me to perform?'

She had a slightly insolent manner of speaking, with her head on one side and her blonde hair partially tumbling down. I ignored her retort and took a step nearer. There was something ancient yet childish and vulnerable in her gaze.

The smell of perfume was like a wall between us – a defence of her virtue in the midst of everything. In her cleavage hung a small cross, to give her a little more protection. It was so unlike the sort young girls usually wear – this was no confirmation cross, carefully crafted by a skilled goldsmith. It was stamped from some base metal – tin, perhaps – and put me in mind of the early Christians. Maybe it was the girl's age-old profession, maybe the simplicity of the cross, maybe just something about its shape that led me to such associations.

'Have you seen a new girl in the district – tall, blonde – who came one day and then was gone again?'

'When would that have been, Sir? My memory's a short one.'

The slums of London think the same way as those of Stockholm. I slipped her a few coins, and she looked satisfied.

'Four or five days ago.'

She seemed to be thinking. Since the city was full of Exhibition visitors, she too must have been seeing a lot of foreigners. That meant it mattered less that I seemed odd, unusually short for a man and with no wish or capacity to disguise my voice. I am a pleasantly deep alto, so perhaps it was not necessary anyway. My clothes were bought in France, and the English know so little of foreigners that we are all Frenchmen to them. I have a governess, a native Englishwoman, to thank for my good English, but I still always have trouble with the fricative – especially when I have to say 'three', and my tongue rather stumbles between the strange sound and the 'r'.

'Yes I did, Sir. She looked a bit like me, didn't she?'

Was this a witness statement or a ploy to make me more interested in her lacklustre appearance?

'You had better tell me the whole story.'

'Well, this girl turned up here...never seen her before. She seemed to be asking more than the rest of us...had no manners. Stood in front of the entrance there, like she was selling puddings. When I asked her to move, she went and took my lamppost. What a cheek!'

'Did she stand there long?'

'No. A kerb crawler come along almost straight away and picked her up, and then I got a customer myself, and when I come back she was gone.'

'How long did she stand here? Minutes? Hours?'

'I can't really say... Miss.'

'Damn! My cover completely blown! But nobody had heard, and I slipped the girl a few more pennies before I moved on. At the very next corner, I remembered what I had forgotten. I ran back, took the girl by the arm and whispered insinuatingly in her ear:

'What did he look like?'

'He?'

'The girl's client. The kerb crawler.'

She thought about it. I waited breathlessly. Was it anyone I knew? Would he be dark-skinned and refined, tweed-clad and soft-bearded – or simply an ascetic clergyman?

'Sort of pale. I thought how pale he was, all over. Seemed to me' – here she giggled – 'it was new for a ghost to need that sort of thing. But maybe he just wasn't used to it.'

I thanked her, fished out a few more coppers and hurried off. It was lucky I always seemed to end up with so much loose change. I would need it tonight.

Just then, the bells of London chimed twelve deep chimes, and I went on my way through the dark and disreputable streets. I had soon made it my habit to accost fallen women. It was not at all difficult, once you knew how. You just grabbed hold of them, the way we used to catch our playmates when we were young, leant close and started a conversation. That was what their real clients did, I noticed. Presumably they were discussing their specific tastes, the ones neither wives nor compliant maidservants were willing to indulge. I grew really rather curious about these erotic variations – but they were not the object of my search, Agnes was. In any case, I could not write about such things. My readers would never buy such risqué books.

The witnesses all agreed. Just as the Inspector had heard, a girl had popped up here and then vanished. I was onto my fifth girl before any more details emerged.

'It was a bit odd, you see Sir...' she drawled, leaning back against her lamppost and fiddling with her watch ribbon. I wondered vaguely whether the ribbon ended in a watch or was just for decoration.

'Yes?' I said with interest.

'They took 'er into that place over there – and that's a molly house!'

They? Just now there had only been one seducer, but I had followed in the footsteps of the girl who might be Agnes, and more had materialised.

'How many men?'

'Two – one pale and one big. The big one was coal-hauler Claire, for sure.'

As far as I could recall, Claire was a woman's name, and I fancied the duties of the coal-hauler were heavy and unsuitable for women. But I said none of this, so the girl had to go on with her story.

'And they went in there. But it's a molly house, d'you see, Sir!'

She spoke in the same delighted, semi-indignant tone as before. And I was as uncomprehending as ever.

'Pardon me, but what is a molly house?'

That made her laugh at me openly.

'You're a foreign gentleman, ain't you Sir? Go in and find out!'

This girl, too, received her coin, and then I crossed the road and entered the strange building. I was filled with the thrill of the hunt. I was not in any way frightened, despite being the only respectable woman in this part of town. That was strictly speaking an irrelevance. Decency is always a relative concept. And anyway, I had my walking stick with me, in case anything untoward happened.

I do not know what I was expecting – a meagre place, perhaps, as crude in its furnishing as in its practices. I could well imagine what a molly house was, you see.

I was wrong on all counts. I have never encountered such a warm, feminine house. Everything you would associate with a woman's apartments was to be found in each and every room: draped fabrics, soft upholstery, pieces of needlework in progress, twelve-volume novels, the smell of freshly baked bread and even the sound of children's laughter. Only one element was jarring. I was the only woman there, and I was one of few dressed in men's clothes.

I had dressed to blend in. Now I was the one who stuck out. I decided to take off my hat and reveal my chignon, and then proceeded to converse with the occupants of the house. They were sitting about in dainty dresses that looked incongruous alongside their rough chins and the hairy chests revealed by their necklines. For mollies are men in women's clothing. Many of them would have liked to live bourgeois lives, but as the world is, they had no option but to hide away in the slums. Some of them could live on what they produced – like the *pauvres honteuses* they made a living by the sewing they had learnt in their youth – but most of them had only that one way of earning their daily bread that is the easiest and most lucrative for women in the slums.

The most astounding thing of all was how normal it all seemed. No doubt the middle-class ladies of London lived just like this, though without so many shaving mirrors and all those unwarranted visits by gentlemen. Many of the rooms were light, not unlike the apartments of my manorial home. Others were more darkly sophisticated, with red velvet such as that I had seen at the Reverend Amis's. I felt perfectly safe, just as normal and just as odd as all the rest.

Wherever I went in the molly house, I was warmly received. Those men who were there moved cautiously, as if ashamed of their unusual proclivities. I would not call mollies men. They all denied they were – they were women, they had children (rescued from the streets), and they wanted nothing better than to live quiet, domesticated lives We could speak as women together, and I wish my readers both male and female to know that I liked them very much. It pained me particularly that I was here with hostile intent. I believed Agnes had been brought here – if it really was Agnes.

I was particularly drawn to a molly called Dolores, a rather attractive person with delicate features and thin hands, about the same age as me. She would never have done as a labourer. She responded tirelessly to my questions, brought tea and biscuits from the kitchen and was not in the least shy in the face of my inquisitiveness. For I cannot deny that although I was playing the policeman, I was still an authoress, and everything that happens in my life can be put to use in my writing. I asked her about coal-hauler Claire, and soon we were joined at the tea table by a youth in male clothes. He could not have been more than twenty, and under his shirt I could discern a figure that would have looked very well in a Michelangelo sculpture. Dolores whispered that Claire was far too broad and tall to be able to wear women's clothes.

I questioned them both as we drank our tea. Our conversation was general at first, but then I began asking my questions. It was a most peculiar interrogation – if such it could be called – as Claire refused throughout to talk to me, addressing himself to Dolores.

He mostly spoke English to her, but from time to time went over to a language I did not understand. It was the second time that evening I had been excluded from the discussion, though this language seemed less foreign than the Hindi at the restaurant.

'Did you see a young girl passing through the house five days or so ago?'

'Yes, I saw the girl,' said Dolores. 'But I was busy with something else, so all I saw was some fair hair and a couple of men.'

'Was Claire one of them? Were you, Claire?'

Claire stared sullenly straight ahead. He was strikingly beautiful – if such a word can be used of a man of his size. This was no Apollonian figure, more a Titan. The young man could pass for a work of art. Only his head was slightly less well proportioned. That great, handsome body could only accommodate the brain of a child.

'I *vada nanti*,' muttered Claire.

'He didn't see anything.'

'But several people saw Claire with the girl.'

Claire looked down, twisting and turning a teaspoon and looking like an overgrown schoolboy made to stand in the corner.

'What have you done, Claire?' I asked.

The coal-hauler shook his head and screwed up his eyes. Dolores sighed, as agitated as a mother whose child is getting a scolding.

'Come on Claire, please answer!' she said.

'I had *nanti dinarly. Nix mungarlee!*'

'That's still no excuse for being dishonest!' cried Dolores. 'What will people say about us?'

I smiled, but hastily raised my teacup to hide my expression. It might not be a laughing matter. A molly's life was probably not very different from a normal woman's. Most women live confined lives, with home as their whole world, and their family and social circle as their missions in life. Any woman who gets a dubious reputation is lost. If your entire life depends on people, what do you do if those people desert you? For mollies it was possibly even worse. If the house came into ill repute, its inhabitants might lose not only their income, but also their position as women.

Dolores and Claire were talking quietly in the strange language, which must be some kind of English argot. '*Nanti*' presumably meant 'nobody' or 'none', and '*nix*' was much the same. But '*dinarly*'? Could that be 'money'?

Dolores looked up.

'Claire says she had no money and had had nothing to eat for days. A man promised her money for giving a whore a fright – and what was poor Claire to do? That big body of hers needs a lot of food. She went with him, the man picked up the girl and Claire took them through here. In the backyard she was paid her money and left the two of them there.'

'What did the girl look like?'

'A *filly palone*...,' Claire began.

'Talk properly, Claire!'

'A pretty woman with a blonde mop, almost as tall as yours truly, big brown...hazel eyes, I think.

'Hazel? Are you sure?'

Dolores and Claire conferred again. It was Dolores who answered.

'No, she isn't sure. But her eyes weren't blue or grey. Claire thought the girl's blue dress went well with her hair, but with that eye colour she'd have chosen a lime green dress, herself.'

I could only defer to this expert knowledge. There was just one problem – Agnes has cornflower-blue eyes. Once again I dared to hope she was alive.

Night was on its way towards morning, and the children of the molly house had gone to bed. I thanked my informants for their help, and Claire made it his business to slip swiftly away. No matter. Someone his size would scarcely be able to remain concealed if Inspector Evans wanted to interview him.

In the big drawing room, Dolores showed me with a laugh how her friends were flagging over their needlework. One molly was winding wool, but dropped the ball and concealed a yawn with her hand.

'Nearly beddybyes time,' said Dolores. 'That means our guests have to leave. We aren't as casual with our opening hours as the brothels.'

'What are the guests actually doing?' I asked.

'Providing for us,' laughed Dolores. 'Come on, it's time to be guardians of morality!'

With my hat under my arm, I followed Dolores around the house. She seemed to know where the visitors were to be found – she knocked on doors here and there and called 'Time's up!' and the answer came from within: 'Right!' or 'Just coming!' Both the reminder and the answer came so smoothly that I realised whatever else one may say about molly houses, both the inhabitants and the visitors are highly civilised people.

As we made our way back to the drawing room, the guests were emerging. They were gentlemen of a perfectly ordinary kind – men in men's clothing – who paused in front of the many mirrors in the house to adjust their ties, hair and moustaches. In the drawing room they bowed to the mollies who were still up and took their leave. I did likewise.

By the hall mirror I stopped, pulled down my trouser legs to cover my thin, women's boots and put my hat on. A guest on his way out came up behind me – I could see he had been visiting the mollies for some purpose of his own, as he had that awkward, half-dressed demeanour that men seem to acquire *post festum* (to put it delicately). Presumably he took me for a fellow guest, since he came to a halt behind me and looked over my head into the mirror to comb his light hair and straighten his stiff collar.

My gaze caught his in the mirror. His eyes grew bigger and he seemed all at once paler and more emaciated than before. Only his mouth seemed natural in this situation – wide, red and full, as befits a sensualist. He had come here incognito, but I recognised him.

'What a coincidence, Rector!' I said, ramming my hat more firmly onto my head.

He, too, put on his hat, but I noted that he glanced down, as if to check that his clothes were buttoned and not in disarray.

'I come across you in all manner of places, do I not?'

I was gratified to see that he looked shocked. I was eager to get my own back for that spiked lavender concoction.

'Miss Bondeson? What are you doing here?'

'I am trying to track down my missing companion. The last I heard was that a young, blonde girl had been led through this house by a couple of men. One of them was strikingly pale. Do you know anything about that?'

'Certainly not! Whatever gives you the impression...?'

'That drink, maybe? Or the fact that you kept out of the way on Sunday?'

'Come, let us leave now.'

'No, thank you. I prefer not to go anywhere with you. It feels quite safe here.'

'Then let us go back in.'

We returned to the drawing room and took an easy chair each. Most of the mollies had retired, but Dolores was still up, and came to sit with us.

'Can you tell me why you gave me lavender tea with laudanum?'

'You seemed agitated.'

'Perhaps because we were discussing my companion, who may have been raped and murdered? Or was it because I found your photographs?'

'Photographs? You are mistaken!'

'It must have been an opium dream, you mean? Have you and the Inspector agreed on a story? Why did you take your fine pictures off the walls? Was it so you could dupe me? So I wouldn't tell tales about the naked boys? Very attractive boys too, I must say, but doing a few things I was quite unaware one could do... and that dainty titbit in his corset, with women's boots the size of schooners – it was coal-hauler Claire, was it not?'

The Rector looked away. Dolores gave a twitch of the eyebrows and sent me a meaningful wink. I smiled back.

'Can't you speak, man? I thought the clergy were supposed to have the gift of the gab.'

The Reverend Amis looked at me with his big eyes.

'You frighten me, Miss Bondeson. You suspect me. You believe me to be a criminal and a murderer, just because I have contrary tendencies...'

'Contrary? Dash it all, your habits are positively Greek, man!'

'Sodomy is not unusual, Miss Bondeson. You need not think it is easy for a man in my position. I could give you a lecture, I could explain everything – but I am sure you would not listen. At least try not to condemn me!'

'Now it is you who are mistaken, Rector. I do not condemn. Just the opposite. Why should people not be free to find pleasure wherever they will? Now it might be a spinster's prejudice, but... your photographs are a different and much less reputable matter.'

When it came to it, I could tolerate the Rector's pictures. They certainly seemed to me perverse, but they were also quite educational. I decided to be conciliatory.

'Forgive me, Reverend Amis! I should not have picked the lock of your photographic chastity belt! But duping me, putting me to sleep...'

'Forgive me, too,' said the Rector, getting to his feet. 'I hoped the opium drops would make you forget. I felt you were trying to trap me, trying to turn my oldest friend against me. Owain Evans has done so much for me, you have no idea. He did not know I had put you to sleep, but he did help me clear the photographs out of sight. You can imagine what a rush it was to get to morning service. Then I hid myself here, until late at night – when I got home you were gone.'

'And your sermon?'

'Went down very well. But there is one more thing!' He sat down again. 'I drugged you and behaved badly – but I did not dupe you. What I told you about the quiet girl – was false, but also true.'

'May I hear the whole truth?'

'Of course. I make a habit of talking to the girls on the street. The one I told you about really *is* a member of the Bible group, and it is true that I try to teach them about salvation. We talk about how religion is the same for everyone, about the love of Jesus even for those who have fallen furthest... But I saw the girl in here with my own eyes. She did look like your companion – the same slim, blonde beauty. I called out to her, because Agnes – is that her name, Agnes? – had seemed so favourably disposed to me and to fighting the good fight, but she did not turn round. I never saw her face.'

'You could have rescued her. Have you thought of that, vicar?'

'I am neither strong nor brave. I am a man of the church.'

'Hypocrite!' I cried, forgetting the sympathy I had been feeling.

'Wait! This is yours!'

He passed me an envelope, but I was unmoved. I put it away in my inside jacket pocket and gave a manly snort of derision. There was only one thing left to add: 'You are a humbug, Sir!'

Then I stormed out of the nearest door, with my top hat crooked and anger choking me – abusive and unwomanly. I was perhaps over-hasty in my exit. I was expecting a gloomy back street, not the pitch darkness that met me.

It was quite apparent I ought to turn round, go back through the drawing room, possibly passing the Rector, and come out on the right side of the molly house. Any rational person would have done so. But I sometimes wonder quite how rational I am. The girl, who might be Agnes, had been brought out here. I took a few steps, leaving the door of the molly house ajar. It shed such a cosy gleam, like a cottage in a wintry forest. Before me I still had nothing but darkness. Undaunted, I felt my way forward.

There were buildings on all sides, just as in a back courtyard in Sweden. They ought to be outhouses: conveniences, stables and store sheds, or maybe a back building housing the poor. And yes, here was the privy – I could tell by the smell, so I changed direction – and here was some kind of dwelling house, with old curtains at the windows and ladies' boots put out on the step. Perhaps some mollies lived there. But the third building, straight ahead of me, was something else entirely. It was built of stone, like the kitchens or library of an old castle, and was in total darkness. Darkest of all was the rectangle that must be the door. It was locked. I tried the windows, but they did not budge.

How long I stood there, I do not know. I stood stock still, listening for sounds. It being night, London was quieter, but even so I could hear noise from all directions. Down at the docks, the rigging of the ships clacked in the wind; out in the street, some roisterers sang the same lines of a comic song over and over again – just two lines, no more, and so slurred that I could not hear the words. A police whistle blew at a distance, and a steamer whistled, too. Somewhere, a woman screamed – half a scream, cut off in mid-flow. From the top floor of the molly house, teasing feminine laughter in dark voices could be heard. I put my ear to the door and listened. The surface was cold, and when I ran my hand over it, I could feel the bolts. It was as solid and secure as a church door. It struck me as strange for a small building like this.

I turned my head to check that the door of the molly house was still open. I had no wish to be marooned in the yard. Yet curiosity kept me there. Light was what I needed! The last time I had worn my gentleman's outfit, I had walked home through the streets of Paris with a cigar between my teeth. Presumably I had done as a man does – popped the matches into my pocket and forgotten about them. But which pocket? It took a while to find, but at last I had my box of matches.

The door was as black in the sudden glare of light as in the darkness. I held up the match and examined the doorposts – two smooth, formal pilasters, topped with the strictest capitals I have ever seen. And above them...then the match went out. I struck another. Now I could see clearly. Set in the stonework above the door was a relief that had been carved in another time and another country. Its main characteristic was utter harmony. The figures were beautiful and seemed as innocent as the marble from which they had been sculpted. There were three of them: a man, a woman and a girl. The man was a soldier, with breastplate and helmet. The girl was wearing a flowing garment, its folds so real that the coolness of the linen was palpable. She was lying down, with the man in front of her and the woman behind her. Beside the girl, the woman looked skimpily clad, in a short *chiton* that left her legs bare. Over her shoulder she carried a quiver, and I felt she was standing ready to rush forward and seize the child. The man – who looked like a soldier – carried no other weapon than a knife, which he held raised over the girl.

There the artist had stayed his hand. There the moment had been frozen and preserved for posterity. Over two thousand years later, I stood in London and looked at the relief, just as I had viewed the Parthenon frieze at the Museum, a few days before. Agamemnon had his knife eternally poised over his daughter Iphigenia, the sacrifice demanded for the Hellenic fleet to get a fair wind to Troy. The goddess Artemis was waiting to rescue the girl – or not. If my memory served me correctly, the myth was somewhat hazy on that point.

It was a beautiful relief. As I vaguely wondered how it had ended up there, I burnt my fingers and dropped the match. I turned quickly and saw the door of the molly house slowly closing.

'Wait!' I cried, and sprinted back through the darkness. I got through the door in the nick of time.

'Thank you,' I said to the molly inside. It was Claire.

'You don't happen to know anything about that stone building in the yard?'

She shook her head and put her hand over her mouth. Mute, as she chose to be at that moment.

'Say goodbye to Dolores for me. She is a good person!'

I came out onto the street that had earlier seemed so shady, but now felt almost homely by contrast with the strange, dark courtyard. The nightlife was still in full swing. A swarthy man was playing the barrel organ, children with no manners or schooling still played in the gutters, the street girls kept an apathetic eye out from the lampposts. There was something particular about people's eyes here in the slums. Whether they were big or small, dark or light, they had the same inscrutable look as the Assyrians at the Museum.

Soon the first messengers of morning would make their entrance: the bakers, milkmen and a sea bird or two. But for now it was still night. I looked about me for a cab, but there were none to be seen. Undaunted, I pulled my hat well down over my brow, swung my walking stick and set off along the Thames. As I went I saw boats putting out into the river. Perhaps they were river folk, scavenging like the mudlarks, but for finds that float rather than those that sink into the mud. I went on past vessels and docks, past the outlines of the Tower and the bridge that now felt so familiar. The walk lightened my heart, and suddenly I heard myself humming:

> *How many miles to Babylon?*
> *Three score miles and ten.*
> *Can I get there by candlelight?*
> *Aye, and back again.*
> *If your heels are nimble and light,*
> *You may get there by candlelight.*

The song was pretty much right. So I went on up Lower and Upper Thames Street, found Fleet Street and at length arrived at the Golden Cross. And inside it was my soft, warm bed.

CHAPTER SIX

IN WHICH DISAGREEABLE TRUTHS ARE UNCOVERED

The following morning – my tenth in London – I awoke late. My bed had been as soft as I had hoped, the hot water bottle like a trusty spaniel at my feet. I remained oblivious to my surroundings until the room attendant knocked on my door at nine and served an excellent breakfast.

I had squandered my first writing period of the day on sleep, but once I tasted the game pie I felt myself so invigorated that I completely forgot my guilty conscience. I had achieved something as the Inspector's assistant after all, and entirely on my own. I had succeeded in tracking down the blonde girl – whose eyes were presumably not cornflower blue – and learnt something of life in the molly house. Moreover, I had solved the mystery of the Rector's photographs and laudanum lavender drink, and found time for a pleasant evening in Professor Devindra's company. I seemed to have lived six months in a few hours. But there was something else – something that felt disagreeable. The feeling was centred on my feet and had nothing to do with my hot water bottle. I rang for room service and sent my boots out to be mended.

I took a large bite of the herb sausage. It was truly heavenly. London resembled the sausage – grey, perplexing, with flecks of green (Hyde Park and St. James's Park), and yet totally bewitching.

I laughed out loud at my own ridiculous simile, finished off the sausage and helped myself to egg, bacon and some beans. Steak had not been served for breakfast since Agnes disappeared.

I have seen a good many cities. Berlin is indeed a charming conglomeration of small villages, while Paris is truly urbane. London surpasses them both. One can never quite make out London and the Londoners. It is a city of contrasts, the capital of England, Great Britain and the British Empire, and has borrowed inhabitants and customs from all corners. Everything is here.

Here is the world of beauty, ennobled and elegant like Sir Edmund Chambers. Beneath it a bourgeois city, like Miss Holiday, though less pretty. London is in point of fact quite ugly, but one does not notice. The city has its aesthetes nonetheless, some of them as plain as the Georgian houses (like my translator Mrs Russell and her husband), others elegant. Sir Edmund again. It is poor, too, like Three Fingers John and the whore by the lamppost; yet also good hearted and helpful, like Professor Devindra, the Reverend Amis and of course the servants of the law, represented by Police Inspector Evans. It is a young and lively city, like Agnes – but also mature and arrogant, like Sir Edmund. Always this artist! Could it possibly be that he typifies the people of London?

Perhaps the city is both male and female. Perhaps it is a molly, a man dressed as a woman, like Dolores, or a woman dressed as a man, like me, or even a man who desires other men, like the poor Rector. But no, London is most certainly a woman at heart – a woman of a better class, shut into herself, her home and position, and constantly at the beck and call of others, of men and duties. If she finds life tedious, she can play the seductress. Perhaps that is why I like London. She resembles many women I know.

I am, of course, generally in the habit of opening my correspondence over breakfast. A number of letters had arrived that morning – among them an eagerly anticipated one from my favourite sister Aurora – and I conscientiously replied to all the invitations, enclosing my visiting card wherever appropriate.

I still had not had time to pay my social calls. I would be obliged to do so that afternoon. My professional contacts were not to be neglected.

Among the letters was a bluish envelope, addressed in an unusually bold and illegible hand. I saved it until last, for it had an air of adventure and smelt quite different from my sisters' daily letters. Handwriting like that was certainly not learnt at one of England's public schools. I had already recognised it as belonging to Police Inspector Evans.

The letter opened with a brusque, 'Miss Bondeson!' – no 'Dear' was deemed necessary – and continued, 'There have been further developments in the case. Can you come and see me at 11 o'clock this morning?'

I looked at the clock, and my next cup of tea was scarcely half-drunk before I had scribbled a telegram and rung for service.

'Please have this cabled to Inspector Evans at Scotland Yard.'

I finished my tea, decided against the toast and put up my hair. It is so awkward without Agnes – if only I had eyes in the back of my neck and arms on my shoulder blades. I made do as best I could. I splashed my face with water and added a few drops of rosewater. My eyes were as clear as Lake Mälaren. And so to the choice between the black and the bottle green. My boots had come back – thank goodness! And tooth powder! It was quite disgusting. I decided to change to another brand as soon as possible. Finally, I spent a couple of seconds in front of the looking glass. Agnes's disappearance really had made me years younger. And of course, green is such a becoming colour.

By twenty minutes to eleven I was bobbing on London's ocean, not unlike a letter in a bottle, thrown out by children on the summer estate, pretending to be shipwrecked. The city is never empty of people. At dinnertime the streets are teeming with hansom cabs and omnibuses, as they are at the beginning and end of the working day. If going to the theatre, one must beware of the traffic and equally so if going to church. As if this molten mass of horses and carriages, people, dogs and cats were not enough, there were signs everywhere exhorting me to do something other than the activity on which I was engaged. 'Find Health with Liver Pills!' 'Drink Nestlé Milk!' 'Take our Omnibus to the Hippodrome – to the Great Exhibition – to St. James's Park!' Every building bore a message – not merely that I should favour a particular tavern or shop with my custom, but also that I should improve my life in some way, naturally with the help of some expensive product. A man dressed in yellow was carrying aloft a placard, which on the front had a picture of a sullen bull, and on the back declared Colman's mustard to be the best. Small boys in rags thrust slips of paper at me suggesting I should advertise for a husband, enhance my breath with mint pastilles and read the *Morning Chronicle*.

I turned down past Charing Cross and out into Whitehall, where a hansom cab had just overturned. I paused for a moment, watched the passengers extricate themselves and noted the coachman's manner of cursing. Then I cupped my hand over my mouth and nose, breathed out to assure myself that my tooth powder had achieved the desired effect so there was no need for pastilles, and almost broke into a run as I made my way down to police headquarters. I had allowed the city to detain me. I was almost late.

The Inspector rose from his desk as I was shown in.

'Miss Bondeson!'

A bow, a kiss of the hand – he was starting to be a very civil fellow. I took a seat in the visitor's chair, but he remained standing, leaning against his desk with his eyes fixed upon me. His look was reminiscent of a bird's: sharp and cold. His beard was as well groomed as ever and his moustache newly waxed.

'Yes, Inspector Evans!'

He really did look attractive. Would I dare to reveal the Rector's hobby? But could I conceal it? The Inspector had undoubtedly seen a great many things, but would perhaps be alarmed, even so.

'The murder case, Miss Bondeson. New facts have emerged.'

'What facts are those?'

'Another girl was found murdered last night, in Whitechapel.'

'In Whitechapel? Indeed?'

I was aware of a sudden shiver and felt suddenly as cold as ice. In the district where I had spent half the night. It was only with some effort that I forced myself to ask where she was found and how long she had been dead. The answer was as I had feared. She was found at about three in the morning, and had by then been dead no more than a few hours.

'Do they know who she is?'

The police officer nodded.

'A prostitute – quite a newcomer, but well known. She was about seventeen years old.'

'Mr Evans,' I said. 'I too have some revelations to make. But first, I demand to see the two bodies.'

'That I cannot allow.'

'Nonsense!' I said. 'I know very well that they will not be a pretty sight, but I am also quite sure you can scarcely have had time to bury them yet. No doubt they are in the ice cellar?'

'You could put it like that,' said the Inspector.

He gave me a long look, straight in the eye. I did not avert my gaze. Then we set off to the mortuary.

It is by no means an enjoyable experience, visiting a mortuary. Like all women of my standing, I have ministered to the dead, washed and dressed them, put hands together in devout prayer, even those of the atheist, and closed eyelids over malicious, gazing eyes. I do not like it. I imagine them to be somehow transformed. Even the most kindly of people appear evil to me after death. The most good-natured of my sisters was torn from us in untimely fashion in childbirth. I was convinced that her soul was in blessed repose with the Redeemer, just as our clergyman assured me, but as I sat watching over her body, I was seized with terror nonetheless. Perhaps she detested me and wished to avenge herself, now I was living and she dead. It was not that I believed Adalvia had become wicked, but I sensed that her dead body harboured feelings other than those she had in her lifetime.

All these are but passing fancies which must be banished from our minds.

The two girls were lying side by side, like two sisters in the night. I recognised one of them, though she lay there naked. Her perfume had evaporated, and the crucifix which had dangled on her breast was gone. Yet she still looked the same. The girl who had died the previous night was the whore to whom I had spoken the evening before — and who had said herself that she looked like Agnes.

Only it had not been Agnes she had seen. It was not Agnes they had found in the mud. The other girl's face was covered, but I knew it was not my companion.

'It is not her, Inspector.'

'How can you know that, Miss Bondeson? Her whole face has been eaten away by rats.'

I vaguely wondered whether he was trying to disgust me. Well, two could play at that game.

'Because this girl has brown nipples and Agnes's are pink. Moreover, Agnes has a birthmark low down on her stomach, just above her pudenda. As you see, this girl does not.'

And I turned on my heel and went, leaving behind the dead, leaving behind their ill will to the living. It struck me that it might well be justified. What we saw on display here were young girls, admittedly no modest rosebuds but with their dignity and honour intact. Then they were shown to strangers, men who looked dispassionately at those cold bodies and drew their detective conclusions. The mortuary attendants were procurers for dead whores.

The Inspector caught up with me outside the building. It was truly autumnal now, and I realised I should have brought my shawl. The mortuary had been so cold.

'Miss Bondeson?'

'Yes.'

'I wish you had not had to see that.'

I would very gladly have been spared it myself, but there are times when one has no choice. At any event, I did not intend to betray my vulnerability by rushing off to vomit in the gutter.

'There was no other way we could be sure, was there? And let me tell you another thing: if that girl in there had had any face left, you would have seen that her eyes were hazel, not Swedish blue.'

I was beginning to feel as giddy as I had in the Rector's drawing room. My head was swimming, so I stopped and leant against a wall for a moment. I was freezing cold. Eugh, how cold I was! The skin on my arms turned to gooseflesh, and all the little hairs stood on end like a dog's, to repel the cold. I knew it was not just the autumn, or even the mortuary, that was chilling me so. My encounter with the dead girls had frightened me. They were just like me, only dead.

It was not an appropriate time for weakness. I could give way on some other occasion, when everything was resolved and Agnes restored to me. I took slow breaths and tugged at my sleeves, so at least my wrists grew warmer. The Inspector was standing so close that I could feel his warmth. He was stock still, like a toy someone has forgotten to wind up. Perhaps it was a habit he acquired when standing watch on board ship. His body was there, and his eyes were alert, but he was as immobile as a hunted animal. He gave not the slightest sign of having noticed my weakness. Then he glanced at my face. Its colour must have returned, for he broke the silence.

'We must talk further. Perhaps it is almost time for lunch?'

The thought of food was uncommonly nauseating to me. I swallowed hard, several times, and tried to concentrate on life. I was actually alive. I had hopes that Agnes was, as well. I had to be strong and energetic; I must not fail her. Admittedly I had breakfasted late, but I must not deceive myself and start missing meals. For a really elegant lady, food is the great threat, which destroys the figure and thus all prospect of success. I am not as elegant as that. In the Swedish provinces, the young ladies of the country manor houses learn the importance of eating, to keep up their strength for balls and sleigh rides. The same applies for hunting English criminals.

'Do you usually have pie for lunch as well?'

'Hardly. This time we shall go to a restaurant.'

So the Inspector took me to an agreeable hostelry nearby, where we ate cold meats with green salad, pickled vegetables and *sauce aristocratique*, this last presumably neither made with, nor made by, leftover aristocrats from the latest revolution, but named thus for its refined flavour and expensive ingredients.

During our main course we conversed about all manner of everyday topics, such as the weather, politics, Prince Albert's sudden popularity, the gold in Australia, the Great Exhibition, and of course my novels. For dessert we had *charlotte russe*, and I felt I could no longer postpone my story. I told him everything, without censoring the slightest detail – all about the mollies, their home, the dead prostitute, and finally, the Rector's confession. I was reluctant to lower the parish priest in his friend's estimation, but the truth must out, and George Amis's excesses were a part of that truth. The only item I omitted was my own detour into the inner courtyard. In the light of day it seemed confused and irrelevant.

Inspector Evans listened at length without interrupting me, and when I had finished he merely nodded.

'Does this upset you, Mr Evans?'

He smiled, shrugging his shoulders.

'Not particularly. You forget that I have lived in Spitalfields. I have seen many things.'

'Even in clergymen?'

'In almost everyone. And George is a loyal friend – he is no murderer or villain, though you appear to suspect him of it.'

'Even if the Rector were my best friend, I would be suspicious of him for having behaved so strangely. He is a coward. He could have prevented a crime, and he failed to act.'

'But I am a police officer, Miss Bondeson, and you are an authoress. I cannot put together a coherent story...'

'...and I cannot solve a mystery? Well, we shall see. Neither of us is yet old enough to cease being surprised!'

In the middle of autumn gloom the sun came peeping through, that sun which illuminates the hillsides far off in the west, and I could make out the grey, perilously alluring sea beyond them. The Inspector took my hand and squeezed it – in a most comradely way, I might add – and waxed lyrical about how alike we were, he and I, and what good friends we could be.

'For a woman, you are one hell of a fellow, Miss Bondeson!'

'And you are a very fine girl, Inspector!'

We went together to Scotland Yard, and from there it was not far to the Golden Cross Hotel. I paused for a while in Trafalgar Square before the equestrian statue by the Strand, then took a walk round the square. It was as crowded as ever. People were now on their way back from their dinner to their homes or their work, and I mused on what they had been eating, and talking about. How many of them had discussed two murdered girls, whose conduct and profession had been far from exemplary? Where was the man who had bribed coal-hauler Claire to manhandle a young girl through the molly house in the East End a few days ago? Which of them had returned yesterday evening and perhaps gone through that very same molly house with another girl, who today was rigid and dead? I cast a glance up at Lord Nelson as he stood there so stylish and sterling, like a victorious god of war. I had been in Whitechapel when the fallen woman was murdered. I might well have been closer than I imagined.

My thoughts returned to the building in the back courtyard. It no longer seemed inconsequential. The building had been dark, locked and unlit, but had it been silent? Could one be sure it was empty? The more I thought about it, the more suspect the building seemed. Had there not been sounds from inside? Sounds I had not reflected on at the time, sounds that had been masked by all the cries and shouts of the slums, the whistle of steamers and the blast of police whistles, the creak of carriages? I had heard a scream. What if it had come from the building? I suddenly recalled a scraping sound, a rattle of chains, possibly the sound of metal on metal as a knife was unsheathed.

I shivered. The building in the courtyard would be an excellent location for murder. Were I going to murder somebody myself – which of course would never occur to me in real life, but possibly in a novel – I would choose a place like that.

I would in fact be very much a suspect myself, had I been capable of committing the deed. Could I stab a person? It would be entirely out of character, of course, but it was a physical possibility. If the victim were unprepared – but there my speculations ended. I lacked the physical qualifications for committing rape. On the other hand, I knew two men who had been near the site of the murder the night before – the likable Professor Devindra and the strange Reverend Amis. I knew which I would suspect, given the choice. Furthermore, the Professor had actually left Whitechapel – but then so had I, only to return almost immediately.

The bas-relief suddenly came into my mind, with deep shadows as in the light of a Lucifer. It was an exquisite piece of art. The facial features, the garments, the tense bodies... Agamemnon about to strike, Artemis on the verge of leaping in – and the girl Iphigenia, instinctively cowering from her father's knife.

There was an autumnal chill, but insight flared like a burning brand in my mind. Certainly the relief was a superb piece of work, chiselled several hundred years before the birth of Christ in the most harmonious of styles – but it showed a girl about to be stabbed to death. Agamemnon and our unknown murderer had something in common. Like her sisters in the mortuary, Iphigenia was to be sacrificed.

I realised I was standing staring at a huge lion, raising its head to the skies in a roar from the top of a noble palace on one side of the square. This was a creature that had been provoked, and like Nelson at Trafalgar was rising to fight. Admittedly it was most clearly a male lion, with a curly shock of mane like Sir Edmund Chambers' artist's locks, but I felt much like that lion. Upon my word, Euthanasia Bondeson can also be provoked. I did not know what had befallen my Agnes, but I surmised she had not been violated, nor stabbed just beneath her left breast. Yet still my unruly mind was not calmed. Somewhere there was a monster who killed innocent girls – for they were innocent, whatever they had done. They must have suffered severely, in life and in death. They had experienced the same anguish as Iphigenia. I clenched my fist and entered into a compact with the lion. I would find Agnes and avenge the death of the street girls. The Inspector would have to become my trusty ally. There was nothing for it but to return to Scotland Yard.

The police constable guarding the entrance let me in without demur, though he looked slightly confused to see a woman practically running in through the tall gateway.

'Inspector Evans!' I panted. 'I've thought of something.'

Owain Evans looked up from his paperwork – that blessed paperwork, to which he had returned in the blink of an eye, instead of getting out to snoop round the slums.

'How lucky I caught you!' I went on, seating myself in the visitor's chair and giving him a long look. It was meant to come across as a penetrating stare, but in fact just gave me a chance to get my breath back.

'The building in the inner courtyard, Inspector! I saw a building in the yard! There must have been something hidden there... What if the girl was murdered there...? A relief... from classical antiquity, showing the sacrifice of Iphigenia... There were sounds coming from it, chains and... The knife, Inspector. The sacrifice of the young girl! What if she was murdered in there while I...?'

I reeled off these last words without thinking, but they did at least have the effect of making the Inspector look up in agitation.

'God damn it! Why didn't you say so right away? You're not making this up?'

His oaths really were quite different from the Rector's. I sensed that Inspector Evans could hardly be from the more devout Welsh circles.

'And Claire,' I went on. It pained me in fact to set the police onto Claire, for I was convinced he had his good sides, even if they were well hidden. But the Truth demanded sacrifices. I could make no exception for Claire.

'Claire melted away,' I said. 'After I had questioned her – him – Claire took care to melt away. Then he was standing at the back door when I wanted to leave.'

'Have you any idea what time that was, Miss Bondeson?'

I took out my watch and looked at it, as if the timepiece could offer me evidence. Then I remembered that I had not even had the watch with me. It is a typical ladies' watch, inlaid with semi-precious stones and engraved with a monogram. Hardly an object for a man's pocket. But surely I must have seen a clock somewhere in the course of the night? I tried to think.

'When I had been in Whitechapel for a time, I heard the bells chime...that would have been midnight. Then several hours must have gone by before Dolores said it was time to go to bed, and after that I had my conversation with the Rector. It was just starting to get light as I was walking home.'

'The girl was found at three – not by the river, like the first girl, but in an alley not far from the molly house.'

'I believe it was striking twelve as I left her.'

'So she was alive at midnight. You are right, Miss Bondeson – she must have died either just before you went into the molly house or while you were inside.'

'Poor Dolores!' I sighed. 'I thought they were such lovely

people.'

The Inspector shook his head slowly.

'My dear little lady!' he said. 'You are a great writer, and I admire you immensely – but there are many things you do not understand at all.'

I contemplated taking offence, and felt my self-confidence taking a little knock. But then it struck me that he was certainly right. The slums are always an alien country, but London is a foreign capital, and the poor quarters are even more incomprehensible than Stockholm's. Perhaps I did not understand. I think myself sharp, but that does not mean I comprehend how people such as the prostitute, Claire and Dolores really think. I took it for granted that Dolores was thinking the way I do, simply because she looked and behaved like a middle-class lady. I realised that I may well have been more stupid than I thought.

'That may be,' I said, 'But it feels wrong, you know.'

'We shall investigate the building in the yard. And however reluctant you are for us to do it, we will have to interview Claire, your lady friend Dolores and all the other mollies we find.'

'Just try not to scare the children.'

'Don't you think those children have seen enough for it to take more than a couple of peelers to disturb their peace of mind?'

The thought pained me, but of course I could see that the Inspector was right. This was his field. If we were to discuss chapter construction and dialogue writing, I would have the upper hand. But it still made me feel a little sad. I thanked him, got to my feet and was on my way out. I paused at the door.

'What was her name?'

Owain Evans looked up.

'Who?'

'The girl who died last night.'

'Mary. Mary Smith.'

Could there be a more common name? As I left Scotland Yard, I thought of the girl as one of us. She was the woman who had descended into the kingdom of the dead as our messenger. I found myself thinking about her life, how it had been, why she had ended up on the street and the fact that her eyes had grown so tired and hard before their light went out for good. She was about seventeen, but had looked well over twenty. What was I doing when I was seventeen?

Still lost in thought, I reached my hotel. I clattered up the stairs, entered my room and remembered how it was, long ago.

I was seventeen, once. I was allowed to spend the whole winter in Stockholm for the first time. It was a time when the old King had still not grown old but was able to make us think of young revolutionaries; when the princes were beautiful boys and Stockholm like a winter's bride beneath her snow-white quilt. The scent of the Gustavian era still hung in the air. Old men still wore knee breeches with metal buckles, and male courtiers were sometimes known to powder their hair. I was seventeen, and trembled at the thought of being grown up. I trembled with cold, too, as I stood at my first New Year's ball at the Exchange – in much the same state of undress as the dead prostitute, except my thin frock had cost a fortune and been bought in Paris. I was not to suffer because I was daughter number eight! I was to have a proper ball gown at least once in my life, not one that had been altered to fit, a hand-me-down from plump Eudoxia who is number seven...and what a ball gown it was! What a ball! Thin, shimmering fabrics, pearls in the girls' hair, radiant looks all around me. I was young and happy. When I made a full curtsey, the whalebones stuck so far into my midriff I thought I would swoon.

It was wonderful being seventeen. An instant before I had been fifteen and everything was horrible and hard, but it was as glorious to be seventeen as to be eight, eleven or twenty-two. I was to live among people, dance and laugh and go the opera, for ten years. Then I began to write.

I closed the door of my room behind me, and the bare-shouldered girl at the ball vanished into the past. The day came back to me – the social calls I had failed to make, the novel that had been lying fallow since the previous day. I was getting on with it quite well. How many pages could Miss Giovanna endure in her room with the murderer creeping about? I sighed, dropped my reticule on the floor and got out the manuscript. The plot really was dramatic. Yet I felt it was time to bring matters to a head. Real life may be cruel, but that does not mean fiction has to be.

The dark man leant over Miss Giovanna. In the pale moonlight coming in through the curtains, she could distinguish the glinting weapon in his hand. She gave a desperate scream, a scream of anguish and mortal terror. 'Never!' she thought. 'Never will I allow my life to be taken without resistance!'

The feeble body of a girl would be easy prey for an assailant. He was bringing his knife down, the man who had tried to kill the sailor – the man who did not want to reveal his murderous act to others.

Miss Giovanna's frail breast housed a brave heart. She was thinking frantically. There were no weapons to hand. She snatched up the book beside her and rammed it into the knife. With a clink and a thud, both knife and book fell to the floor.

I dropped my pen. Should the book be a Bible or something more worldly? Should Miss Giovanna's reading reflect her personality?

My late night was beginning to take its toll. Manuscript in hand, I threw myself on the bed, and unlaced and removed my boots whilst in a recumbent position. My intention, of course, was to look through the manuscript and judge the character of my slender heroine, but I had not even picked up the first page before I fell hopelessly asleep.

I awoke in the middle of the afternoon and simply lay there for some time. There were some interesting cracks in the ceiling plaster, where a chandelier ought to have hung. The cracks made me think of maps and continents, of the Exhibition and the monster globe, Agnes and Professor Devindra. I could almost make out the triangular shape of India up there. I thought of London, the metropolis that could accommodate the whole world. I had been here long enough to see all manner of things – some I should never have imagined. Think of my return to Sweden and my sisters asking: 'What did you see, Euthanasia dear?', and I would begin listing them: the Great Exhibition; the British Museum, the Diorama, the Zoo, Wyld's monster globe, the slums, police headquarters, a house for men in women's clothes, the mortuary... Heavens, they would be dumbfounded! 'You never learn, Euthanasia,' one of the eldest would say, and I would smile my smallest, most sisterly smile that made it look as though I were as level-headed an individual as them.

There came a knock at the door. I leapt up, patted my hand over my hairpins and pushed them in. Ouch! A little too far, perhaps.

'One moment!'

This hotel let absolutely anybody up to the room. It might be the maid with the afternoon post, of course, but it could equally well be Inspector Evans with news of the investigation or Professor Devindra with an invitation to try some new, exotic pastime. I thrust my feet into my boots and laced them as quickly as I possibly could.

'Come in!'

I was looking presentable now. I ran my hand over the bed to smooth it and tucked the manuscript under the pillow. The door opened to admit Miss Ruby Holiday, without either her sister or her brother-in-law. Did the girl actually dare to go about the city without a chaperone? She was rising a little in my estimation.

Great delight ensued. We exclaimed, kissed one other on the cheek and were the best of friends. We installed ourselves on the sofas and I rang for tea, which came with tiny slices of toast and an iced cake that made me very happy. For twenty minutes we both talked eagerly, about nothing of note.

I liked Miss Holiday and her sister well enough. They were in fact the only ladies I had met in London who were not either dead or men in women's costume. And yet I felt a distance. We have our society in Stockholm, and I, too, have a place there, but the memory of myself as a seventeen-year-old suddenly resurfaced. I had loved the high life for a few years. Then I came to loathe it. Not that an artist must of necessity starve in a garret in Paris, but Sir Edmund's well-groomed and aesthetic exterior got my back up, nonetheless. His two ladies were as well dressed as he was – his wife a little pale and withdrawn, his sister-in-law exuberant and highly coloured – but I did not doubt Sir Edmund was a great artist. Ruby Holiday and her sister were indistinctly outlined, as artists are not. Sir Edmund and Professor Devindra are not like this, and nor am I.

'What news of your companion, Miss Bondeson? Is she back?'

Ruby Holiday looked about her as if expecting to see Agnes peep out from behind the chest of drawers and shout 'Peep-bo!'

'I'm afraid not,' I said. 'And I have no idea where she is.'

That was true, at least. I watched Miss Holiday as I said it, as I had a feeling she knew something – she was there when Agnes went missing, after all – would her face reveal anything; would she look shifty or do anything else suspicious?

'I do wish we had noticed when she vanished,' I said. 'The police suspect she has been abducted.'

Here I hoped for a reaction, but nothing happened. Ruby Holiday studied the bed I had tidied and wiped her nose with a handkerchief.

'I have a message from my sister,' was all she said. 'She wonders if you would like to come to Edmund's salon this evening.'

Were we not to go on talking about Agnes?

'Salon,' I said hazily. 'that would be nice.'

'And maybe read from one of your works? Do I glimpse...' Miss Holiday craned her neck and stared at the bed 'a hurriedly secreted manuscript?'

'Indeed you do. But I write in Swedish, so there is little you would understand. But perhaps from one of the translations...'

We came to an agreement that I would read that evening. The salon started about seven, and a light supper would be served. I wondered whether that really meant a light supper, or whether I was expected to have eaten something substantial before I arrived. As my reader will have realised, I love food, but I hate eating before readings. There are limits to what an author can stand.

'Well, Miss Bondeson...' continued Miss Holiday, just as I was expecting her to get to her feet and go. With her head tilted girlishly to one side, she regarded me with her dark eyes – not blue like Agnes's or hazel like the dead girl's, but as black as you would see on a dog or a horse.

'How is your sister? Is anything wrong?'

'No, no, not at all!'

She gave me a quizzical, uneasy look. I looked back. I am not the sort of person to flinch.

'Miss Bondeson, I must talk to you. That is why I came here alone. Meg wanted to come too, of course, but I persuaded her to lie down and rest for a while instead. She is getting so delicate... Meg is the elder of the two of us, you see, and she tries to look after me all the time. But I wonder how *she* is feeling. An unmarried woman is not necessarily a fragile flower, no more fragile than a married one. I am not a child...'

'I know,' I said. 'And I have several married sisters.'

'We are only two. Our parents died prematurely, in a cab accident, and Meg has in many ways been a mother to me. When she married Edmund, they let me move in with them – not every newlywed couple would want a little sister in the house! – and I still live there, though I am a self-supporting artist. It is hard for you, of course, to even notice me alongside Edmund – he shines as brilliantly as a sun and I know he dazzles everyone – but I have actually started to make my mark lately, and my works sell quite briskly...'

'That's excellent!' I said, wondering where all this was leading. Had she sought me out to discuss her artistic career or the problems of being a younger sister? As I mentioned, I am number eight of ten. I know everything there is to know about siblings. Miss Holiday was surely not so concerned with business that she had come to sell me a picture? Such things happen when one gets involved with artists. That is how I have managed to acquire both a lovely Adlersparre and a rather bad Herrlin.

'Sometimes I really am childish... I liked your companion so well. I felt you were to her what Meg is to me, and she was in your shadow as I am in Meg's. It didn't occur to me that of course you are not related, and you had no doubt helped a poor girl, Miss Bondeson, by taking her on.'

Had Miss Holiday stirred up Agnes to mutiny against me? Was that what she was trying to say?

'I spoke to her a few times. The first time, she was lost. I immediately noticed that Edmund was interested. My brother-in-law, you know...'

She hesitated, and there was a distinct silence in the hotel room. Outside, the cabs rattled their way down the Strand. A cabbie yelled at someone to get out of the way, and a street crier shouted, 'Buy Newmarket sausages! First-rate sausages from Newmarket!' Ruby Holiday shifted uneasily. A shiny little boot protruded under the hem of her skirt. I raised my eyebrows encouragingly and leant closer.

'Perhaps you have noticed: Edmund is very fond of women. I do not know everything my sister has to tolerate, but I know a good deal. My sister and I often model for him, but sometimes he uses other women, and...'

'I thought the eye of the true artist was able to view scantily clad female bodies from a loftier, more artistic plane. Like Plato, and that sort of thing.'

'You might think so, might you not? But Edmund is not like that. And he flirts with every bit of skirt he meets!'

Here I felt the safety of age. He had never tried it with me. At the age of forty plus – his own age – I had become sexually uninteresting to a rake such as that great artist. I felt simultaneously offended, jealous and relieved. Despite his attractive exterior, he was not one of those men whose close acquaintance I would wish to make.

'That is a pity,' I said. 'And it must be very hard for your sister.'

'Yes. And I saw at once he had taken a liking to your companion – when we came across her at the Exhibition, he began chatting to her, being friendly, flattering her and asking if he could paint her. There was just one thing he overlooked.'

'Agnes doesn't speak English.'

The girl's ignorance had saved her from the seducer. How fortunate that he had not tried French, which she speaks extremely well.

'So when we were at the Museum, she and I started to talk. I saw how impressed she was by Edmund's lecture, and I saw him showing off to her. I am sure he thought she would be an easy conquest. A little girl from the country, from a small country, what is more, from a country far away – she would be bound to fall for Sir Edmund's good looks and smooth tongue!'

'So you warned her?'

'Carefully, sort of. I could tell she was starting to grasp more English, but I have had a thorough education. French worked extremely well.'

'And?'

'She paid attention. I thought... I felt my words were having an effect. Later I was frightened. What if they had tempted her instead? What if she had felt the longing of youth and innocence for the depravity of a man like my brother-in-law?'

'I shouldn't think so,' I said in my most dismissive manner. It sounded as if I was envious.

'Then we got to the Babylonian section.'

'Nineveh. It was Nineveh, actually.'

'Well anyway, somewhere down there – in Biblical lands. We all got there, and Edmund started to speak. The girl was at the front beside him, like a willing lamb to the slaughter.'

Here she fell silent. Perhaps her fancies were beginning to upset her. Yet she knew nothing about the dead women.

'...but when he took us on to the next relief, she lingered, as if it was the art and not my brother-in-law that fascinated her. I turned round to call her – it would have been nice to talk for a while, and you were with the Professor all the time – but suddenly I could not see her. I went back, and thought I caught sight of her blue dress disappearing out of the Nimrod gallery and into the Egyptian room...'

'Didn't you call out?'

'Of course. And she turned, I swear it. I let her be. I decided she might well be just as tired of Edmund as I was, and maybe she wanted to shake me off and look round in peace. So I stayed where I was and listened. But Edmund was talking such drivel – I admire you for showing that total lack of interest and concentrating on the Professor and the exhibits instead, despite the Professor being so black!'

'Black!' I interjected. 'He surely looks more or less like a sunburnt Frenchman!'

'You know what I mean,' said Miss Holiday, screwing up her nose slightly. I knew, but I did not agree. But we all have our little idiosyncrasies, be they prejudice, conceit or debauchery. I let her go on.

'But I soon got bored again,' Ruby Holiday said. 'I went into the Egyptian gallery. We had already seen all that, so I could not imagine what she would be doing there. And indeed, she was not there.'

I sat in silence, thinking. I couldn't for the life of me fathom what had happened, nor was I quite sure why Miss Holiday was telling me this. Scotland Yard would surely have been the appropriate place to report it, and I knew the Inspector had interviewed the sisters, Sir Edmund and the Professor. Ruby Holiday sat there, all loveliness and curls, with her artificially black eyelashes and pouting red mouth. She was a true artist in that sense. That face must have taken a long time to paint into being.

'So you mean Agnes vanished of her own accord?'

Ruby Holiday gave a shrug and a gesture, which for an artist of her kind was no doubt intended to mean: 'I don't know. How should I know?'

'That is what I think,' she said, after a pause. 'And I wondered whether she and Edmund...had agreed something.'

'Agnes has never let me down before. And she has been with me for five years.'

'Well, I don't know, as I said,' replied Miss Holiday.

I thanked her. I did not say: 'Why didn't you tell me at once?' This was presumably a question of appetites that an unmarried woman was not expected to understand. I kissed her on both cheeks as she was leaving, but my lips touched only thin air. I did not want any actual contact. Her story was scarcely credible. Agnes has never deserted me. It would not surprise me if the girl had become enamoured of Sir Edmund. She was young, and young hearts readily yearn for men. But would she have left me and run off with him? She is not stupid, and he is married.

Maybe for some reason Ruby Holiday wanted me to suspect her brother-in-law. Had he done something to her sister that Ruby could not forgive? Women's business was one thing, but could there be more to it? My thoughts ran on, to blackmail, bigamy and criminal abortion, none of it amounting to more than speculation. Nowhere could I find any proof or even circumstantial evidence. But one thought did occur to me. Would Sir Edmund really have dared to steal the girl from me, someone whom he might not respect, but who could still make him uncomfortable as an enemy? I would be wise to keep my eyes open at the salon.

CHAPTER SEVEN

IN WHICH GREAT NAMES FIGURE

Prepared to find myself weighed in the balance, I set off for the great artist's home as evening drew in. London was drooping in the autumn rain, and I had a long wait for a cab in the hotel lobby. Gaslight shimmered on wet pavements, and the road sweeper boys struggled to clear away all the leaves that had suddenly fallen from the trees in the avenues. The city had changed over the ten days I had been there. September, which for us in Sweden is the first month of autumn, is the last of the summer months in Europe. In the resorts of the Mediterranean coast, it is still the high season, and the outdoor cafés still have their parasols up. England, as ever, takes the middle way between north and south. This country has been occupied by Romans, Norsemen and Frenchmen – and upon my word, it shows! From the Romans they have order and regular street patterns, from the Norsemen's organisation, and from the French a wonderfully southern *laissez faire* that one might not expect in the fog and foul weather.

As I alighted from the cab, I had a book under my arm. It was the English translation of *The Manor House*, which I had borrowed from Owain Evans. The Inspector apparently liked it best among my books, perhaps for its blend of idyll, conflict and grisliness. The book had a neat but hardly showy half-calf binding, better suited to the owner than the content. As for me, I was feeling strong, well-dressed and well-prepared as I raised my eyes to the

Chambers residence in the fashionable district of Belgravia.

It was a house designed to make an impact, and I duly allowed myself to be impressed – by the tall, white facade, the thick carpets inside, the bowing footman, who relieved me of my coat and umbrella, folded himself in half and uttered his 'Welcome' from somewhere near the floor. With my book under my arm, I walked into the entrance hall. The buzz of the literary salon issued from two doors to my left.

I have seen a good deal of social life. The eminent writer Bernhard von Beskow is an almost daily guest in my home, my fellow novelists Miss Bremer, Mrs Carlén and Mrs Burén are more like friends than rivals, and as a girl I even resisted advances from the poet Tegnér. It was hardly a serious threat to my virtue – he was old, fat and not particularly good-looking. Not at all like Sir Edmund Chambers – it struck me as he came towards me – who in some respects reminded me of Tegnér. He had the same ruddy look, but was cast in a slim British mould rather than a plump, Swedish one from Värmland. The artist kissed my hand, and I could understand that girls found him attractive. There was something over-refined about him, a streak of pure Apollonian beauty. Now, I prefer men who have been polished with sandpaper rather than a silken cloth. Despite my exclamations of delight, I was happier when Professor Devindra made his appearance.

'Good evening, Miss Bondeson!'

'Good evening, Professor Devindra! And thank you for that curry!'

He kept hold of my hand, and I felt the touch of his lips on the back of my hand. In this case it was neither a moustache nor a breath that I felt on my skin, but a proper kiss. When he stood up, I was wide-eyed and warm, affected by male proximity and charm even in the midst of the literary throng.

My female reader is probably yawning. Literary sex can be so trying. My male reader may perhaps stretch and say an old maid with thoughts of love is simply ridiculous. All my readers are free to think what they like of me and my story. I was feeling a glow that was not to be despised. I have never had a husband, but that does not make me a pillar of ice. When the Professor looked up, I thought what a good person he must be – not just an artist, doing so much for people's souls, but also a skilled doctor, working to save our bodies.

There we stood, absorbed in one another, talking quietly. Sir Edmund's salon – the physical salon, not the literary one – was a very large hall, divided in the middle by a huge set of double doors, with two standard-sized doors to enter by. I stood at the far door with the Professor, Sir Edmund having disappeared into the crowd. A waiter emerged from the kitchens bearing a tray, and I helped myself to a canapé. The lobster tasted superb, but the bread was a touch dry.

Behind the waiter came a big man – bigger than any man I had seen – in the livery of a footman. I have never set eyes on anything like it! Coal-hauler Claire was a delicate lily by comparison with this giant. His chest was as broad as the double doors, the expanse of his shoulders pulled his gold braid out of shape, and his breeches seemed ready to burst under the pressure of his enormous thighs. His face was coarse and looked hastily painted on by a worse artist than Sir Edmund – the nose was askew, the eyes too small, the mouth barely delineated and almost lipless. Beside Professor Devindra, the man resembled nothing so much as an orang-utan.

'Madam?' he asked, looking at me.

'Yes?'

'Letter for the gentleman...for the Sir, that is. Sir Edmund.'

I took the note, and before I had time to thank him, the man backed away into the kitchen regions again, gave a sniff and disappeared from view. There came a shout. It sounded as though the chef was protesting at the man's presence.

'What sort of apparition was that?' I exclaimed as I broke the seal on the letter. This had not been my intention – believe me!

My thoughts were elsewhere, between Professor Devindra's dark eyes and the giant's unlikely appearance.

It was a letter of few lines, and the handwriting was not very legible. I only had time to register one word: 'nine'. The Professor leaned forward as if to read over my shoulder, and suddenly Sir Edmund was back.

'Was that letter not addressed to me?'

'Oh yes!' I said. 'I do beg your pardon – I thought he was looking for me!'

As quickly as he had materialised, the artist was gone again, and I was left crestfallen with my transparent excuse.

'I think I have seen that fellow somewhere before,' said Professor Devindra. 'But where?'

More guests had arrived, and we joined the flow into the salon. It was crowded inside, and I was suddenly pressed tightly against the Professor. Thus I did not at first see the bearded gentleman who was waiting to take my hand. His waistcoat was gaudier than either the Professor's or Sir Edmund's, and he distinguished himself by a smooth beard of considerable length. I told him *David Copperfield* was one of my favourite books, whereas *Oliver Twist* could have been shorter. He gave a slight bow and expressed his envy of my print runs and my talent, both of which exceeded his own. Then we conversed awhile about America, which we had both visited, before Collins – the young man he had taken under his wing – took my book from me, put it on the mantelpiece and suggested I warm myself by the fire. I could only see Professor Devindra's back now. He was leaning forward, engaged in sudden, intense conversation with a lady with a gleaming pearl necklace. I was introduced to a series of faces – publishers, published authors, self-publicists and public nuisances. Most of the greats were there, and all the minor players. The semi-anonymous sisters from Yorkshire were absent, but Mrs Gaskell was in attendance. Mr and Mrs S.C. Hall immediately asked me to contribute material to their latest magazine enterprise, and Mr Chapman the publisher introduced a young protégée, who pursed her lips. I would have pursed mine too, had I been an aspiring authoress and not myself. There were in addition a number of literary and artistic lords, a bunch of Pre-Raphaelites and finally Paxton himself, the genius behind the divine creation that was the Crystal Palace.

'Oh Miss Bondeson! How simply lovely to see you!'

By that stage I had grown accustomed to the extravagantly French style of the greetings. The salon guests were not happy to see me, they were overwhelmed; the encounter transformed their whole life and existence; it was as if a magic spell had been cast on them. I felt the solidarity and disgust of cultural life. They all wanted to be my friend, but also to scratch my eyes out. Few of them would greet me if we ran into each other at the Exhibition tomorrow. Ruby Holiday was in that respect different from the rest. Her greeting contained a warmth that I perceived to be genuine. Miss Holiday seated herself on a stool beside me and made sure I was served some champagne. It was first-rate, an excellent vintage. She behaved, in short, like an obliging younger friend of my sex – as Agnes should have done.

'I am glad you came to see me today, Miss Holiday,' I whispered, in hope of unearthing some clue to her behaviour. It did not work. The reason for the visit remained obscure.

Ruby Holiday sat there at my feet, as if she were my protégée or lapdog, and Sir Edmund clapped his hands and commanded silence. There was an extensive programme for the evening: piano and harp recitals, singing and the performance of a Scottish dance, and finally the famous authoress Euthanasia Bondeson from Sweden would read a passage from one of her novels.

Culture. Refinement. Warmth from the fire and the champagne. Reclining in my armchair, I experienced what Englishmen call comfort, which I myself would categorise as drowsiness. The warmth was on a par with that of the molly house, but otherwise I saw nothing to link this evening with the previous one. Last night the people and buildings were degenerating, vice reigned and the art that existed was crude in its beauty. Here, I was in brilliant company. Ahead of me lay an evening of music, dance and literature, and around me thronged people who would never set foot in Whitechapel. Undoubtedly all the women in the salon were virtuous and the men kept their vices at levels to add just enough spice, but I could not imagine that Dickens or his young, novel-writing ward would spend much time walking in the stench of the rape-oil lamps. Miss Holiday sat at my feet, the image of chaste girlhood, innocent of the dark recesses of the human soul. The young gentleman playing Chopin on the pianoforte was at home in a world of soft fabrics, warm fires and noble feelings.

I have never been enthralled by Chopin. The rendition was stunningly skilful, but I was aware of having to arrange my features to express the correct appreciation. I spent the time looking unobtrusively around at the guests. They could have been ranged on a shelf marked 'artists and authors of Victoria's reign'. Many of them were seated, but some of the gentlemen were still standing. I could see one figure over there that looked familiar, without my being able to put a name to him. His face was narrow and almost feminine, framed by artistically long locks above a clearly masculine coat and waistcoat.

Suddenly it was as if I were viewing the whole company in a mirror. Where I had recently perceived virtue, I now sensed vice; where facial features had appeared noble, they now looked distorted and dissolute. Even here, I was incapable of judging who was good, degenerate or evil. What did I know of where these prominent men spent their nights? How could I allow myself to think that not one among them kept a mistress or three? Where did their fortunes come from? How many of them owned sweatshops in the slums? Whose blood was sugaring our tea? When I knew that at least half the better world of Stockholm is in constant contact with half the worst, it was naive to think London any different. Was I just trying to delude myself?

Then the picture changed again, and I thought what a beautiful piece of work a human being was. Here were eyes shining with aesthetic enjoyment; here were downy cheeks resting on sofa cushions as thoughts strayed far, far away. But that face over there – so unknown yet so familiar – continued to disturb me even after the harp began to play. Beautiful hands caressed the strings and slim, sensitive arms danced gracefully over the harp. We all gaped in admiration at the beauty and melodiousness. I always used to be a little on the chubby side myself, and was therefore not considered worthy to learn the harp. I am, on the other hand, an absolute wizard on any type of piano.

The singing and dancing were quite stimulating, but once the Scots had finished their scampering, I began to wish the reading were over. Presumably it was an attack of stage fright, unless it was simply light-headedness. The waiters were slipping between the guests as freely as street urchins, and the champagne flutes were playing a concert of a virtuosity that would have astounded even Mozart.

Then it was my turn. I got to my feet, drew myself up to my full height and began to read. It is the strangest feeling, reading one's own work. In selecting the extracts I felt a mixture of appreciation ('I really am a pretty good writer, when it comes to it'), astonishment ('Did I really write that? However did I think of it?') and self-contempt ('Oh dear, this chapter is not only dreadful, it is embarrassing. What if anyone were to remind me of the fact?'). In this case, moreover, my book had been translated into a foreign language. Now Mrs Russell is, thank goodness, a very competent translator – she very rarely misinterprets things, and I had naturally not chosen those passages.

It surprised me during the reading how many fricatives had crept into the English translation of *The Manor House* – particularly in the touching scene between the girl and the Lieutenant (the same Lieutenant, incidentally, who later loses his head in the cave), where the word 'three' occurred no less than three times, leaving me no choice but to pronounce its difficult combination of sounds.

I rounded my performance off with an account of how I had come to start writing, which other writers had inspired me (something audiences always unaccountably want to know) and my way of working.

'Miss Bondeson! Are you working on anything at present?'

That is the constant question, not only at readings but even in general conversation. It can be extremely trying at times.

'Yes, I am writing a new novel.'

'What is it about?'

That was the next most common question, which received the next most common answer.

'I'm afraid it is too early for me to say anything about that.'

'Are you ever going to write a novel set in England?'

Then they let me go. Ruby Holiday's hand signals summoned a waiter with more champagne for me, and all of a sudden I had a plate of tongue, salad and pie in my hand. It tasted heavenly. As I took a bite of tongue, a lady came and sat down beside me.

She was a formidable lady. I had never seen her like before. Her grey hair was piled high on her head, but though it seemed permanently on the point of tumbling down, she was handsome and imposing – I am almost tempted to say majestic. When she spoke, it made me think of Queen Victoria. Admittedly, this fine figure of a woman bore little resemblance to the sweet little monarch, but if anyone had asked me to point out the Queen of England among all the people of London, I would have opted for the lady at my side, not the charming, slightly sulky young woman who sat on the Imperial throne.

'Miss Bondeson! How lovely to meet you!'

'Oh, I think the pleasure is on my side, Mrs..?'

'Russell. I am Amanda Russell.'

Niceties and exclamations of delight gushed from my lips. So this was my translator, the Englishwoman I had known longest yet hitherto never met. Recently she had begun to feel like a friend, almost a confidante. Lady Margaret could not fill that role, and Ruby Holiday – who nodded and withdrew when we switched to Swedish – was not up to it either. Amanda Russell felt like a very close acquaintance. No one else in England has been so understanding. Nor has anybody else read my books as thoroughly as she has. The translator is always the most scrupulous reader.

I should have realised Amanda Russell would look like a queen. There was something about the way she conducted herself, the way she lived her life. She was married early to a good-for-nothing, bore three children in swift succession and had the good fortune to be widowed before she was twenty-five. Then she began writing novels, but it did not bring in sufficient income. She sent her children to private boarding school and became governess to an Anglophile family in Gothenburg. There she learnt to speak excellent Swedish, with a slight West Coast accent, and then she tried her hand as a translator. Now she is one of the leading practitioners, and has a fair reputation as a writer, too.

There we sat, Amanda Russell and I, a Swedish island in the English salon. It was wonderful to be able to speak one's mother tongue again. I had not uttered a word of Swedish since Agnes disappeared, and at times my mouth had felt as if it were rusting up. As a Scandinavian, one has to open one's mouth properly and speak up, pronounce a proper 'A', gently coax forth a 'Y' and laugh and grimace over a 'tj' sound. I grew quite elated. My English is not bad, but one is always a little more stupid in foreign languages. There had been so many things I had wanted to say, but not been able to express. It may even be that some subjects do not even exist when I am speaking English. There are green glades in my mental world, which only the language of glory and heroes can reach.

I told Mrs Russell about everything that was preying on my mind: about Agnes's disappearance; about the dead girls in Whitechapel; and of course about Professor Devindra and

Inspector Evans. She understood everything perfectly. She is that sort of person, you see – not one of those people who nods and says, 'I understand', while wondering if there is any pie left, but someone who really *understands*.

By the time we had been talking for a while, I began to see Mrs Russell more clearly. We were discussing me so keenly, but she steadfastly avoided her own life. Inevitably I grew curious and asked. She paled a little, and it struck me that queens, too, have their troubles. I asked about her children. Her sons were grown up and away at university; her only daughter was unmarried and lived at home. She was a good girl, Mrs Russell said, and in fact she was here at the salon.

'But you know what girls are like, Miss Bondeson, she has slipped away and is no doubt enjoying a conversation somewhere.'

'Doubtless three times as brilliant for being heard by young ears,' I said. 'How old is she?'

'Grace? She will be eighteen in November.'

'It is an excellent age. And what of your husband?'

Mrs Russell had until that point exuded light and warmth to rival the fire behind us. Now it seemed to me that the flame died down, flickered and was reduced to the dim glow of a lamp.

'Russell? He is a good man.'

Her hasty assurance aroused my suspicions. Methinks the lady did protest too much. So I asked a few questions. How had they actually first come to meet? Had it not been in Gothenburg?

'No, not at all. We met on the steamer from the Continent.'

In John Bull's eyes, there is something fishy about an Englishman who abandons his homeland and goes abroad. For my part, I see the urge to travel as indicative of a more open personality, a less insular frame of mind than is common among Britons. I tried to recall what the Holiday sisters had said about Amanda Russell's husband. 'Ugly as sin,' was it not? But 'assuredly kind-hearted inside'.

'And you married at once?'

'More or less. The children were younger, you know, and it was good to have a father for them.'

'I can see that,' I said. 'It must be hard to be a mother in sole charge of a family.'

She nodded, and I noticed she was rocking back and forth, as if trying to drive away something unpleasant. The motion did not dispel the majestic impression, but it did make me think of all the monarchs who have wanted to achieve things and not been able to, something we have often seen in our Nordic countries. Rocking is not that uncommon. Even as a girl I was aware that certain women sometimes started swaying, and I gradually came to associate that motion with misfortune – not the sort of misfortune that can befall an overly sensual girl, but the misfortune that poisons the world. The rocking reveals a neglected, desperate woman as plainly as a bronze horse is the hallmark of a monument to a general.

'Tell me truly, are you happy?' I asked swiftly, and wished at once I had kept quiet.

'Of course. Why should I not be?'

I remembered how mother would always take aside my sisters when they were newly wed and earnestly whisper – albeit so loud that all but their husbands could hear – those very words: 'Tell me truly, are you happy?' What can a new wife reply to that but 'Yes'? And what can a married woman reply to a spinster whose works are her livelihood other than the very same 'Yes'? What had I expected Mrs Russell to say? Had I hoped for an exposition on the cramping nature of women's lives? She was, after all, translating my novels and not the campaigning Miss Bremer's.

I could happily have sat there all evening talking Swedish to Amanda Russell. But the lady in question was not so diverted. I had displayed my usual lack of tact, and the Swedish language was only restful for one of us. Mrs Russell soon rose, saying she had to find her daughter and get home. Her husband was having guests to supper, and she was already late. I embraced her, and we determined to meet the next day at her London house – once I had made my overdue social calls. On her way out she would introduce her daughter to me, if they could find their way back to me in the crowd. Needless to say, they did not appear.

When I got up from my comfortable armchair, I felt that I had drunk more champagne than was good for me. I hid my champagne flute behind some portrait miniatures on the mantelpiece and mingled with the crowd, addressing someone here and someone there, discussing the development of the novel as a genre with someone else, the Chartists and socialism with yet another person and (of course) the Exhibition with at least three more. Everybody asked what I thought of England. 'I utterly *love* this country!' I replied, over and over again. It was utterly true. Apart from the fact that Agnes was missing.

Messrs Dickens and Ruskin were engrossed in an interesting discussion that seemed to be half about the duties of the rich toward the poor, half about the superiority of medieval art. That was how I knew it was Ruskin. I stopped to listen, a little curious about the great men, despite myself. A waiter offered them cigars. I took one as well, bit off the top as women do in Sweden – the cigar-cutter always seems to be shut away with the gentlemen – and lit it.

'You smoke, Miss Bondeson?' asked the great sketcher of London, whilst his more poetically disposed companion regarded me in puzzlement.

'I always find it invigorating after a meal,' I said. 'And that was a frightfully good champagne.'

'This Havana is not bad either,' said Ruskin.

'By no means,' I said. Admittedly it was not a Havana, but sometimes one has to exercise discretion and not reveal one's superior taste. Men are so easily offended.

I took a step back and allowed the gentlemen to resume their debate. Cigar in hand, I wove my way through the company. After my reading, the food and the champagne, I felt in need of somewhere where I could check myself in a mirror and get my breath back.

The salon was large, and I had smoked half my cigar by the time I reached the other side. In the doorway stood our hostess, one hand on the doorpost, gazing into the distance. As I greeted her and asked if there was anywhere with a mirror where I could perhaps also wash my hands, I could not remember having seen her at all during the evening. Lady Margaret accompanied me into the silence of the house and showed me to a suitable room. It was badly needed. When I emerged, my hair was back in place, and my cheeks and lips were their usual colour.

Lady Margaret – slumped and lacklustre after all the socialising – sat waiting in an upholstered, golden chair. For evening wear she had exchanged the tortoiseshell comb in her hair for a special coiffure, her curls dressed with shiny, black ribbons. The effect was strange – to me, her head seemed to be wilting like a withered flower. What was the matter with Lady Margaret? She aroused no warm feelings in me – scarcely any feelings at all, in fact. Why did I not want to have her as a friend, though both she and her sister would have been eminently suitable? Why did I feel more at home with the Police Inspector or Dolores the molly?

Then it dawned on me. Lady Margaret was certainly beautiful, somewhere beneath the fatigue, but she was not bold. I believe in courageous people, the sort I write about. Giovanna in my book did battle with the murderer, and Mrs Russell met setbacks with a brave face. Such behaviour was not in Lady Margaret's nature. She was docile. Myself, I am a free female who – unlike a married woman – can do as she pleases. My books support me, and I have petitioned the King and been granted my legal majority. Most women are not in that position. Shut in their homes, they live through their husbands and their social circles, and nothing in the world is exclusively theirs. Lady Margaret was one such. She was not like an artist. She was just a wife.

I did not breathe a word of all this, of course, but sat down on the chair next to hers, which was also gold but less comfortable. The whole artist's residence was sumptuously furnished, mostly with items that looked as if they had been passed down from earlier generations. And yet I knew that Sir Edmund had been knighted for services to art and none of it could have been inherited.

'How is everything, Lady Margaret?'

'Hateful.'

It was not really the answer I had expected of a salon hostess in London, but sometimes I manage to keep my face under control. I cannot help my curiosity. It earns this spinster her daily bread.

'Why?'

It seemed the natural question to ask next. There was a mystery to be solved here, after all.

But Lady Margaret shook her head, clearly concerned that she had said too much. Once she had begun her confidences, she would have to go on. I was agog. A bottle of champagne stood at hand, and I filled her empty glass. She downed it in one.

'Is it your husband?'

Lady Margaret made a snuffling sound.

'I am so worried about him.'

The last I saw of Sir Edmund, he was caught up in some great artistic discussion, punctuated by flowery gestures. He had seemed hale and hearty. But I did not protest.

'Tell me!'

And Lady Margaret began to do so. It was like when a Cossack raises his sabre and slices the neck off a vodka bottle in one fell swoop – everything came gushing out, often so fast that I had no time to lap up the fiery liquid. First came the anxieties about her husband's affairs with women. She quite understood the temptations that the female sex laid in the successful artist's path, but she did sometimes think her husband could be a little more constant. When they met they had both been poverty-stricken artists, and she had welcomed his success in every respect. She had never been jealous. Not even when she had to lay down her own brush had she grumbled. Not about the children, either, the children they had never had. Lady Margaret appeared to admire him in every way.

Then she buried her face in her hands and began to cry. Thank goodness I had a handkerchief in my reticule. It took Lady Margaret a good while to calm herself, and while she was snivelling I managed to waylay a footman and request two cups of tea. There was still an excessive amount of champagne available, but my conscience told me Lady Margaret had already had enough. So had I, when I came to think of it.

'The worst of it is...' whispered Lady Margaret, pouring the tea and indicating I should help myself to milk. She was moving like a mechanical figure, an automatic Turk or dancing doll. 'The worst of it is, I think he has seduced my sister Ruby.'

'Really?' I asked, and could hear how sensation-seeking I sounded. It was actually just my usual curiosity, of course. Meanwhile, I tried to recall what Ruby Holiday had said earlier that day, but the champagne had turned my brain to bubbles, and it was hard to remember. I took a last puff of my cigar and extinguished it in the champagne glass.

'Yes! Ruby is ten years younger than me, you know. She was only a little girl when Edmund and I met – it was natural for her to come and live with us, even when home was just a couple of rickety beds in an attic. But for him to go that far, to steal not only my virginity but my sister's, too...'

I began to feel uncomfortable. Accepting confidences is one thing, but it is something else when they grow too intimate. I was not sure that I wished to hear details of the Holiday sisters' sexual exploits.

But had I imagined Lady Margaret would spare me? Stupid of me, if so. Once started, she was not to be stopped. Admittedly she repeatedly implied that I as a single woman naturally could not know, but she counterbalanced that with insinuations that artistic women always have more knowledge of such things than one might expect, be it from practical experience (like her sister) or from the great artist's knowledge of the true nature of human character. She was drunk – no doubt about it. I had had too much champagne myself, but Lady Margaret seemed to have abandoned all moderation in the number of glasses she had taken.

'Is that so?' I began, but her Ladyship went over me like a roller. I was given every detail of how Sir Edmund had seduced her, and it was a tale of easels, brushes and tubes of squirting oil paint We do tend to think of artists as licentious, but this was a lack of inhibition I would never have credited. I could merely nod, say '*Mm*' and look interested.

The tea was a relief. It was hot, milky and refreshing. I slowly began to sober up.

'And I think he is doing the same with Ruby now!'

'Lady Margaret, do you mean that he...is engaging in physical intercourse with your sister?'

'Yes. I saw them from the attic!'

I could not stop my eyes straying to the grand staircase that ascended to the floor above. This was a house in which one could scarcely imagine attics – such phenomena seemed as out of place as kitchens, servants' quarters and stables. But of course there were things here that had to be hidden, swept under the carpet as it were.

'How?'

'Because they were in the studio, of course!'

Here I gave a scarcely perceptible sigh, stirred my tea and then turned to Lady Margaret with look of avid attention. The studio was an extension of the back of the house and had huge skylights in the roof, letting in a flood of daylight. An architectural quirk meant that it was possible to look directly down from the attic windows onto the artistic work in progress – and naturally anything else that might be in progress at the easel.

'I had gone up to fetch extra blankets for the autumn when I saw... I saw Edmund, so I paused...and then I saw my sister...'

'Perhaps you were mistaken, your Ladyship.'

'No. No – and do not tell me to talk to her, because I have no intention of doing so! It is a worse betrayal than you could imagine – on both parts.'

So I said the only thing there was to say:

'Drink your tea!'

Lady Margaret drank. I gave her a brief lecture about all men being blackguards, even the best of them, and all thinking of only one thing. A good woman must rise above such things, I maintained (feeling deeply dishonest as I did so) and try to lead men in the path of virtue. And a great artist like Sir Edmund, ought he not to be able to channel his desire into his art?

'Maybe...' sighed Lady Margaret. 'He is not painting as much as before, actually. Sometimes...'

A hiccough interrupted her. It was not alone; more followed. When she was telling me about her sister in her husband's arms, she had seemed for a moment entirely sober. But she was drifting into her haze again. I was torn between distaste for her story and suspense at what was to come.

'Yes?'

'You will probably think I am saying terrible things, Miss Bondeson, in revealing all this. It sometimes seems to me that Edmund has stopped painting. Since that Mary Magdalene I have not seen any new work from him – only things he started several years ago, before the fame and the knighthood...'

'I have heard that great painters' creative vein can run dry. And when an artist is as exalted as Sir Edmund, it cannot be that easy to produce anything new. Why, I have experienced it myself. Public expectations can stifle a...you can have no idea, Lady Margaret. Readers complaining that the new book is different from the last one. Readers wondering why you did not explain what happened to every minor character. The only salvation is to begin every book as if it is the first. Art is like sex – as surprising and bewitching every time.'

I stopped myself after that last simile, wondering what Lady Margaret would say. She was still caught up in her own world, a world of champagne and marital distress.

'You see,' she said. 'It sometimes seems to me that Ruby has been doing his painting this last year. The fact that he has not embarked on anything new...that the brushwork seems weaker... that she has stopped modelling for him...'

'It could be because of the other distraction. Perhaps your husband is feeling guilty about the liaison?'

'Edmund? Guilty? No, I assure you! And what is more...A wife should not interfere in her husband's business.'

She hiccoughed again, and I leant forward with an expectant expression.

'Are there financial worries, too?'

'You see, Miss Bondeson, I come from a completely different background. Ruby and I were born into the middle classes, where the wife has to help with savings. Before my mother died, she had secretly started taking in sewing – it was the only way she could keep the family at a respectable level. She was the one who always took care of the finances. And Edmund has always had poor business sense. He is like a child – he would give away his last sweet. It is not long since we were struggling artists. Occasionally he would sell something, occasionally I would. It was real cause for celebration if we sold a painting; usually it was drawings for the illustrated papers. We put every penny in an old cake tin, and every day I would count up how much we had. I was always involved. As I still am...'

'Very sensible,' I said supportively. 'Far too many wives let their husbands spend the money.'

'But I fear that is what Edmund has done. You have seen our house – you can imagine what it costs. Since Edmund was knighted, we can no longer live as artists – we have to live as nobility, although we are so new to it. We have had to take out loans. The Queen paid us well for the pictures she bought

– including an enormous painting of the prodigal son, which had to be hoisted out through the studio window – but it is still not enough. As soon as we are on our own, we have to watch every penny. And even at other times, as much as we can. Did you notice that my dress is last year's fashion that I have had altered?'

I had not done so. I was not hugely interested in Lady Margaret's appearance.

'But the awful thing is, Miss Bondeson…that the money has started coming in again.'

'Is the cake tin full?'

Lady Margaret looked nonplussed, then gave a hint of a smile.

'The cake tin is long gone. These days we have a bank account. I have full access. And I do not know whether Edmund is so stupid that he thinks I have not noticed, or if he thinks I am so naïve that I do not think – but surely even the silliest goose would be surprised at a bank balance multiplying in the course of a couple of months – without a single painting being sold?'

'Might he not have found some well-heeled patrons?' I asked. It was a far-fetched idea, of course. The era of the patron was past and we lived in the age of the buyer. 'But what about loans? You told me the two of you had borrowed money. Might not Sir Edmund have borrowed more?'

She shook her head and asked why on earth he would need to borrow.

'From what you have told me of your finances, one might rather ask why *not*. Could you try to live more modestly?'

Lady Margaret looked about, as if her surroundings were new to her. Her hair was glistening with gold and purple. She could have been stunningly beautiful, if only she had not looked so wretched. I took in her appearance properly for the first time. Fatigue had left its mark on her face. She did not have many wrinkles, just lines at the corners of her eyes that could have been mistaken for laughter lines, but her skin was sad and tired. Her eyebrows and lashes were shiny black, but her eyes were indifferent and dull.

'Anyone who has been a poor artist will find extravagance agrees with them.'

'Initially, perhaps.'

'Edmund so much wants to live as an aristocrat. He so enjoys moving in those circles...'

'Have you never thought how little the really rich spend? That is the way to keep a family fortune.'

I had certainly seen evidence of that in Stockholm. I had a friend – heavens! I had not thought of her for twenty years – who was from one of our oldest families. They had a mansion for every child, and there were as many siblings as in my own family. There was no question of dresses from Paris until they got married. The seamstress came to them and made their dresses. On ordinary days, the daughters were always most informally dressed – not for comfort, but because it was so much cheaper to wear out housecoats than their best finery. Sir Edmund and Lady Margaret's home would have given their *cher Papa* a fit.

'But it could always be that he and Ruby have made it into a kind of artistic industry.'

'Possibly dubious from an artistic point of view, but hardly dishonest. And as long as you can share the proceeds...'

I sounded cynical. Perhaps Lady Margaret was getting on my nerves.

'But what else earns that sort of money, Miss Bondeson? I wonder if he is doing something illegal...or at the very least immoral, like getting involved in the opium or slave trades...'

'Might he not be speculating, though? Property or cargoes from the Empire or suchlike?'

Against my will, my interest was aroused. Money in itself has never interested me, but I have discovered that where there is a jingle of coins there is often vice and crime, as well. I questioned Lady Margaret more closely about my speculation idea, but she denied it emphatically. Sir Edmund would never sink to such philistinism.

'But it makes me anxious, you see, Miss Bondeson. First there was too little money, now there is too much...that is not how it should be. You are such a sensible woman, with your feet firmly on the ground.'

'No, indeed.'

'And things keep happening! The money, and your companion going missing...' Lady Margaret gave a laugh – an unwarranted, startling laugh – and went on speaking. She had stopped hiccoughing. She giggled instead. 'It was really funny, by the way. My lady's maid disappeared too.'

'They run away sometimes,' I said, somewhat less amused.

'Not this one. The cook is her aunt. And she left everything behind. It was just like your companion – one minute she was in the room with me, dusting the table centrepiece, the next she was gone. Nobody knew a thing; there was no trace of her. It was as if the ground had simply swallowed her up.'

'Attractive?'

'Very. It is the attractive ones that get taken on as lady's maids.

'But it could have been a man!' I said. 'The girl suddenly gets bored of it all, so she runs off with the sweep or the baker or the butcher's boy. Have you told the police?'

Lady Margaret shook her head.

'Maybe I should tell Inspector Evans,' I said.

'That Welshman? That parvenu? That...yokel? You should have heard how he interrogated us!'

A voice inside me asked what she was herself, with the materialism of her house and her faith in money. But I did not pass comment.

'The Inspector is a fine man,' I said instead.

'I do not really think...' Lady Margaret said, presumably intending to swear me to silence. That would have been bad – after all, it was in my own interest to follow up this lead. The Emperor Vespasian was wrong. Money does smell. It leaves a distinct scent. I was hoping, of course, that Sir Edmund, to whom I had never really reconciled myself, had been guilty of irregularities.

Before I had time to ask more, and before Lady Margaret managed to swear me to secrecy, Ruby Holiday came hurrying from the salon.

'How is Meg? Is she poorly? I can take over. Miss Bondeson! In the salon they are calling for Swedish songs!'

I nodded silently and hurried in. The illustrious company really had been seized by an exotic desire and was demanding that I play something on the pianoforte. So I accompanied myself and sang a few ballads: '*Kristallen den fina*', 'Beautiful Värmeland' and several Lindblad romances. My voice is not entirely pure, but has a good range. In this company it was ideal. As I played, I surveyed the scene, hoping to discover something suspect. Nothing came to light. People stood chatting, some listened and others seemed bored to death. It was just what one would have expected in a literary salon.

When the last notes of my song had died away, the long-haired man with the weak features I had noticed on arrival came up and took my hand.

'It is nice to see you again, Miss Bondeson.'

I must have looked bewildered, because he smiled and whispered:

'My name is Payne, but you know me as Dolores. I couldn't resist coming to hear you.'

'Dolores, I am enchanted! You made a great impression on me.'

And as I shuffled down from the piano stool, I held fast to Dolores's arm, then steered her (or should I say him, in this context?) to a quiet corner.

'Have the police been to your house?'

He nodded.

'A bunch of peelers. They took Claire.'

'What a shame!' I said, though I had never really been captivated by Claire's charms. But they were not brutal or anything, I hope?'

Dolores gave a grim smile. I wished I had had the sense to hold my tongue.

'Anyway, it's over now. Claire has been arrested, but the rest of us are free. Though there was still a constable on guard outside the building in the yard when I left.'

'There is something odd about that place.'

'Quite possibly. It isn't ours. Someone else rents it. The police seem to think that's where the murder was committed. It's always seemed a bit strange. The window panes are blackened, but some of the kids climbed up and looked in through the top windows. They say there were pictures.'

Blackened panes? That at least explained why the house had seemed in such utter darkness when I had tried looking in. At night and in my confusion, I had not noticed.

'What sort of pictures?'

'Gaping gods, they said. Naked ladies. I'm pretty sure it was worse than they realised, or were willing to say.'

'Do you ever hear noises from inside?' I asked, still unsure about the memory that was coming back to me.

'Don't know. Maybe. At any rate, our house has been cleared – metaphorically I mean – because the constables searched every inch: beds, cubbyholes, wardrobes. The worst they found was half a pound of sausages somebody had overlooked, rotting away in the larder.'

I thought of Claire, driven to crime by hunger. It was one of those ironies of fate. But I said nothing. Agnes was not at the molly house. It seemed increasingly apparent that the trail leading to the slums had been a red herring, as they say in this country – something that threw us off the scent, either by deliberate plan or by pure coincidence. The latter was probably the more likely. However much Agnes means to me, I found it hard to believe even the most hardened criminal would murder two other women just to stop me finding her. This was something else.

'But I still hope they catch the murderer.'

'And your companion?'

'I shall find her. I shall not rest. I am not the kind to give up.'

Dolores smiled her warm, feminine smile. It was peculiar seeing her in men's clothes.

'I am sure you will succeed, Miss Bondeson. I am convinced no criminal would be able to stand up to you.'

'Thank you,' I said. 'So am I.'

It was getting late. Dolores and I hesitated over whether we should kiss one another on the cheek, like two ladies, or she should kiss my hand, like a man. Convention won, she bowed and I smiled my most courteous smile. Then she was gone. I took my leave of Sir Edmund and asked him to give my compliments to Lady Margaret, who had retired. I embraced Ruby Holiday and allowed Professor Devindra to escort me out into the hall.

'Farewell, Miss Bondeson! I saw far too little of you this evening.'

'Yes, I know...occasions like these...so many people...'

I stood facing him, and the front door was open to the street. I could hear the footman trying to hail a cab outside, and above his cries the sound of the pouring rain.

'Farewell, Professor Devindra.'

I bent my neck and looked up. Though the Professor is not a tall man, he is still taller than me.

'Farewell...' he began, and then fell silent. The entrance hall around us was deserted. As if by some agreement, I stretched up at the same time as the Professor bent down, and I felt his lips on mine – soft, champagne-cooled, without the aroma of cigar that I knew came from me. For a moment I experienced that heady feeling, and then we were standing apart once more, while the footman entered and announced the cab was waiting. The Professor kissed my hand, and our eyes met. Then I was out in the cab, and back at the hotel. I parcelled up Inspector Evans's book with a brief note, in which I told him about Sir Edmund and suggested a meeting the next morning. The member of staff I summoned promised to send a delivery boy with the package.

I was tired, exhausted by revelations and champagne, and looked longingly at my bed. But there was a world beyond London. My sister Aurora would be anxious if she did not receive an answer before long.

I sat down at my desk, dipped my pen in the ink and commenced my letter. Aurora is my most beloved sister. Our names may be different – hers stands for the dawning day, while I bear a darkness in mine – but our souls are alike. I could tell her about my adventures in London. She would never reveal anything about the molly house to our more prudish sisters!

So it was that the letter became an overview of what had happened, and thus it seemed natural for its conclusion to summarise my suspicions. When I read through what I had written afterwards, it seemed full of wisdom:

So you see, Aurora dear, it is all a great tangle. Presumably the street girls' murders are NOT IN THE LEAST linked to little Agnes's disappearance, but you never know. This has all been going on so long that I will soon consider EVERY SINGLE PERSON A SUSPECT! The prime suspects are of course those who were there when Agnes vanished. That means me, and I naturally turned my back and noticed nothing – but you know, dear child, that little Agnes is <u>forever</u> going missing, so I had no cause to be on my guard. Moreover, I know I am not the guilty party.

Then we have the four artists.

Sir Edmund Chambers is a <u>handsome</u> gentleman, with such a noble physiognomy that I believe it would make your heart <u>beat faster</u>. He has something of Tegnér about him, though he is slim and more aristocratic (perhaps because he has been raised to the peerage). For some reason I do not like him, even so, and both his wife and his sister-in-law claim he is a <u>lecher</u>. That *may be. He has tried nothing with me – he thinks me too <u>old</u>, you may be sure!*

Then we have his wife and her sister. Lady Margaret is a pale, cowed figure, who this evening was totally pickled from too much champagne. There are worse things to get pickled in, but it DOES arouse one's suspicions. Her sister Ruby Holiday is a COLOURFUL lady, as voluble as her sister is silent, more temperate in her drinking but more EFFUSIVE. She has testified against her brother-in-law, but I cannot fathom why. Lady Margaret, by contrast, claims that Ruby and Sir Edmund are engaged in sexual relations. Perhaps there is some jealousy at work that I do not understand, maiden as I am.

I find Professor Devindra a most congenial man. That immediately arouses my suspicions. Furthermore, he is a foreigner, and all foreigners should be suspects.

Here I lifted my pen from the paper, put it in the inkwell and thought about the Professor for a moment. I could not believe anything bad of him. And it suddenly hit me that I am a foreigner, too! We truly have much in common!

The Professor is also an educated man, some kind of PHYSICIAN (he never speaks of his profession), apparently an authority on the goldsmith's art and, incidentally, a great gourmet.

To this elegant quartet I have to add a less honourable trio: George Amis, priest of the slums, who seems attracted to young men, who on one occasion PUT ME TO SLEEP with laudanum and, moreover, is a LIAR! I do not like the fellow at all. Yet I suspect he is innocent. He is also a skilful photographer – a man of the new age, in other words.

Next we come to Dolores, who sometimes calls herself Payne. This is a man who prefers to wear women's clothes! – unlike anything we have seen in Stockholm. Perhaps we have been kept from those parts of town! I like her (or him) very much, and the Police Inspector does not seem to consider her a suspect on any count. Her friend Claire, on the other hand, an ATHLETIC young man with some extremely Greek inclinations, is implicated in the carrying off of the two prostitutes. ACCESSORY TO MURDER in other words! Very crooked. They say he is under arrest.

Perhaps I should make this trio a quartet. We should include Inspector Owain Evans, a man who has aroused my AFFECTION. But he, too, has CONTACTS IN THE MOST DISREPUTABLE AREAS – he claims to have lived there and worked as a constable on those streets – but he is also a friend of the priest. A policeman cannot be a villain, of course. Yet still I HAVE MY SUSPICIONS. What I wrote about foreigners applies to him, too, incidentally, as he is a Welshman and self-made man.

I do not rightly recall having met any other people, apart of course from Charles Dickens, John Ruskin, Mrs Gaskell, Paxton and quite a few other VASTLY well-known writers and artists. Had this been a different kind of letter, I would have gone on about them at some length. I also met my translator, Amanda Russell. She does not seem entirely happy with her husband, whom others however describe as honest. Hmm! No one is honest in my eyes until it has been proven. She has three children: the boys at Oxford or Cambridge (I forgot to ask which) and her daughter Grace at home. The girl is obviously old enough to marry and CAPTIVATED by literary salons.

I hope you will be at least a little captivated by my letter, my sweet! As for me, I feel like Blue Måns. Ready for the slaughter. Awake or asleep, I remain ever your loving sister

Euthanasia

I applied the blotting paper and then re-read the letter before sealing it. I was as generous in my use of capital letters as Mrs Russell these days. Maybe I had been influenced by all this English around me. I went straight to bed, exhausted by everything I had been doing. Halfway to sleep, I was struck by a thought. I had not said a single word to Aurora about the kiss. So I am not entirely honest myself, it seems.

CHAPTER EIGHT

IN WHICH A MAN MEETS WITH MISFORTUNE

I awoke aching, as if it had been a taxing evening. My head hurt, and I made sure to eat plenty of smoked bacon for breakfast. In my experience, the saltiness of smoked meat works well against physical dehydration and headache. Plenty of fluids were necessary, too. Three cups of tea. There was nothing of interest in the post except a letter from my publisher, Mr Sweet, enclosing his and his wife's visiting cards. In the right-hand corner were the letters P.P.C. – *pour prendre congé* – which meant the couple were about to leave London. And before I had had time to pay my call! This called for immediate action. I would just write a little of my novel first.

Then I forgot the real world. Social calls did not exist in the little village on the shores of the Mediterranean. I walked along the streets I knew so well. They were my own creation. The characters' emotions surged within me. Miss Giovanna fought off the murderer with the aid of an unusually stiffly bound volume of Sue's *Mysteries of Paris*, revealed herself to be an energetic dreamer and threw caution to the winds.

> *'Father!' cried Miss Giovanna. She regarded the lined face of the old estate owner with an expression that was filial yet bold.*
> *'Yes, daughter?'*

'Father, I am leaving.'

'But you cannot...sweet Giovanna, you are to give your hand to young Fernando.'

'It is not to be, Father dear.'

The old man launched forth about the youth of today, the revolution that had destroyed all honour, the bluestockings of Florence and Paris who were tearing down everything their fathers had built up. Giovanna was impervious to his words. As a daughter, she owed her father respect, but as a woman she heeded other commands. She interrupted him with a revelation. Fernando, the dark son of the neighbouring estate, whom she had been taught to love from childhood, was not the virtuous young man her father thought him.

'Dearest Father,' said Giovanna. 'It is Fernando who is the robber chief. Last night he tried to murder me. While you were sleeping, the kitchen maid and I shut him up in the food cellar.'

The writing went so easily that I began to feel the novel drawing to its close. And what is more, with a happy ending, apparently. It could well be time to start discussing the translation with Mrs Russell, while we were in a position to talk it over face to face.

For dinner I had lamb cutlets, green beans that had been very well cooked, and roast potatoes. Ordinary boiled potatoes such as we have in Sweden were never served here. I missed them a little. On the other hand, there was always a dessert. It was generally pie. Today's had a filling of berries and was sweet yet sour.

After the midday meal it is the hour for social calls in London. English etiquette calls for a visit the day after any large event, so my cab ride took me first to the large house in Belgravia. The footman who had bowed so deeply the evening before hurried out to inform me that her ladyship was not at home. That was hardly surprising – I assumed 'not at home' was a polite way of saying that Lady Margaret was not receiving guests. But no mention was made of that! I left my card and continued to Mr Sweet's. This splendid man has, with his son, set up the publishing house Sweet & Sweet, with which my Amanda Russell helped me make contact.

It was a small publishing house. I went to its premises, inspected my publisher in the flesh – all six feet ten inches of it – and then allowed myself to be persuaded to meet his wife. They lived on the floor above. There, I became a very ordinary woman – perched on an armchair, keeping my shawl and bonnet on (as I understand one does) – and was introduced to Mrs Sweet, a soft, loveable little thing who came up to her husband's elbow.

The couple were indeed about to leave town. They were to set sail for the Mediterranean that Friday. The fresh sea air of Nice would be beneficial to Mrs Sweet's weak lungs, and it would be good experience for their son to be left in charge of the business. I promised to continue my negotiations by letter with the younger Mr Sweet, politely took my leave and found myself another cab.

The next four or five calls were wholly uninteresting, both while they were in progress and also for the purposes of my narrative. But finally I was able to take a cab to the outskirts of the capital and find a breathing space at Amanda Russell's. I was longing for a little friendly company, and to escape the chill outside. London was actually warmer than Stockholm in September, but the fog had come down and the moisture hung like pearls in the air. It was hard to decide whether it was raining or not, whether my umbrella should be up or down – the droplets were there, as rain and fog at one and the same time.

Mrs Russell's home was as cosy as I had hoped it would be, warm and inviting, with the scents of floor polish, baking and dried rose petals. The chairs were sagging and comfortable, but gave the impression of having ended up there largely by chance. Their upholstery must have been threadbare in several places, because shawls and blankets had been thrown over the arms and seat cushions. It all had such a pleasing nonchalance, being both practical and homely. Here lived people who felt comfortable in their home and cared nothing for details. The walls were lined with bookshelves, filled with volumes of all kinds – French poetry in full-calf bindings and soft covers, duodecimo novels (both bound and unbound), learned tomes, cloth-bound dictionaries and finally a whole shelf of works of Swedish literature. It warmed my heart to encounter old friends: Kellgren, Geijer, Bremer, in fact the whole Swedish Helicon, right back to Stiernhielm and Mrs Brenner. But there were more of my books than of anyone else's.

The fire crackled invitingly, and as I stepped into the room, Amanda Russell vacated the warmest seat for me. She took my hands and bade me a heartfelt welcome.

'What a horrible day, isn't it?'

'It is the strangest weather,' I replied as I sat down. 'I have nothing against rain, but this permanent damp!'

'We are in London, Miss Bondeson!' said my translator, taking my hands.

'Oh, my dear Mrs Russell! Can you not call me Euthanasia?' I asked, though I was the younger and had no idea of the etiquette by which Englishwomen dispense with formal titles.

'It would be a great pleasure. And my name is Amanda.'

I accepted Amanda's offer of tea with pleasure. On my three previous calls I had declined to take any refreshment. Sufficient time had also elapsed since lunch to allow me to partake of several slices of toasted teacake with a clear conscience.

This time we avoided the question of Amanda's happiness or lack of it, chatting instead about what we had observed at the salon. There was no shortage of items to discuss. My armchair commanded a good view of the room, and as we talked I allowed my eyes to wander. Mrs Russell hastily stooped to retrieve a tea leaf from the carpet. Clearly she and her maid had been cleaning and tidying in preparation for my arrival, and had sprinkled wet tea leaves on the carpet to absorb the dust before brushing it.

The bookshelves must have been made to measure for a different room, as they did not go right up to the ceiling. The stucco work around the top of the walls did its zealous best to stretch down to meet the books but the flower garlands failed to extend far enough. The space between the ceiling and the top of the bookshelves was filled with a collection of statues. They were ranged high up in the gloom, and were not easy to make out. Yet there was something about their physiognomies that made me shiver. Every one of them was human, or not far from it. For some reason, thoughts of Agnes on the day she disappeared and of the winged bulls of Assyria came into my mind. But none of these figures looked Assyrian. There was a dancing Kali and a goddess from Carthage, but apart from those, their mystical connections were entirely unknown to me. I hoped they would remain so. They were hideous in the extreme. The worst of them all was a skeletal-looking figure. He was leaning forward, and under his ribs, his intestines hung in bunches. He undeniably detracted from the homely atmosphere. Were they not the very sorts of gods we had spoken of at luncheon, after we had been to the British Museum?

'Who is that dreadful apparition standing up there?'

Amanda Russell turned her head and gave a laugh. Perhaps I was being over-sensitive, but it sounded like a nervous laugh to me.

'A god of death, my dear! From America, or was it Africa? Do you find him repulsive?'

'He makes the Assyrian gods feel like nursery characters.'

'Russell is fascinated by such things, you know. He has a large collection. We do not have room to keep them all here at home.'

'But it is good for a man to have interests,' I said. 'One of my brothers-in-law collects punchbowls. It creates an awful lot of washing up, my sister says.'

'These are no great bother. We tend to dust them whenever we change the curtains.'

The conversation turned to household matters and servant trouble, and then by some convoluted route we arrived at the business we were really meant to be discussing. The statues continued to unnerve me. They seemed as familiar as old enemies, who make your stomach churn if you happen to glimpse them at the Norrbro Bazaar. With the whole collection staring down at us, Mrs Russell and I resolved to continue our collaboration in the manner that had worked so well up to now.

'So I shall instruct my Swedish publisher to send you the printed sheets as soon as each one is ready, all right?'

'And you will make sure your contract with the English publisher specifies that both editions will be published at the same time?'

'Of course. But you for your part will translate with all due expediency, so my Swedish readers do not have to wait too long?'

We shook hands on it. So that was agreed. Back at the hotel I would write to the publishers in Germany and come to the same arrangement with them. Legislation may move on, but there are no laws to protect a literary work abroad.

A lady writer is fond of likening her book to a woman, confident in her own home. As soon as the woman – or the book – ventures further afield, she is inevitably a target, and can easily be molested. If the woman is going outside her home, she therefore takes precautions. Sensible authoresses (and presumably even an author or two) do the same, ensuring that the translations appear at the same time as the Swedish edition. The worst thing we can imagine is that someone may come too close and give our book a pinch on the leg. Or – to speak plainly – imagine someone getting hold of the manuscript and publishing an unauthorised and presumably bad translation before the original even goes on sale! Such liberties taken with the book would bring shame on me as a writer and, incidentally, put the payment in the wrong purse.

. Once we had concluded our business, we continued our conversation on the most amiable terms. Amanda wondered if we might visit the Exhibition together one day. A splendid idea! I had still not had enough of its wonders. Moreover, I enjoyed Amanda's company. Sir Edmund and his wife and sister–in–law – if that is what I should call her – were no longer congenial to me, and with the Professor there was always that tension, which was not unpleasant but did not really leave much space for other things. Inspector Evans was an excellent fellow, but with all the murders and abductions he had no time to devote to my amusement, however highly he esteemed my writing. Amanda, on the other hand, I could view as a female friend. I think I perceived her as a sort of English sister.

As we were finishing our tea, we heard the sound of the front door, and Amanda brightened visibly. Was she fond of her husband after all? Were my assumptions misplaced?

'That must be my husband!'

Feet ran up the stairs, and a young girl popped her head into the room.

'Mama! Russell is back!'

'So I heard, Grace. Euthanasia – allow me to introduce my daughter.'

The girl was tall and slim, with her hair in a simple coil on her head. She had that waiflike, almost disembodied English beauty. Though she gave me a broad smile, its warmth was faint, like the heat of a fire from a distance.

'Good day,' said Grace. 'You played beautifully yesterday, Miss Bondeson.'

'Good day, Miss Russell. It was a shame there was no time for us to meet at the salon.'

'No, the company of all those young, single gentlemen turned Grace's head and she completely forgot Art and Literature.'

'Oh, Mama!' said the girl reproachfully. I saw then that she was younger than she had first seemed – of marriageable age, but still half a child.

'We have all been girls,' I said, and smiled. The young lady smiled and withdrew, presumably to leave us undisturbed. Her stepfather entered the room almost at once. The amiable atmosphere evaporated.

Mr Russell was a brute. I could see it even in his external appearance, and had I closed my eyes, I would have felt it in the air. His presence was as offensive as unwanted intimacy, and I felt a shiver down my spine. We were colleagues. As an author – or at any rate one who earned a living by his pen – he was one of my own circle. Whilst I embraced and esteemed his wife, I did not want to be near Mr Russell. I would rather have gone without bread than admitted myself a colleague of his. Literature was too beautiful a virgin for his white-haired fingers.

The sense of unease was palpable. In other respects, Mr Russell was a very indistinct figure. His clothes were light brown, in a shade somewhere between sand and the yellow of manor house plaster, and seemed designed for the summer that had until recently plagued London. His hair and side-whiskers were neither fair nor dark, his eyes were an indeterminate bluey-grey green and topped by bushy eyebrows, which strangely enough lent him a characterless look. They drooped, to put it simply. The man was as pale as a corpse.

'Pleased to meet you,' I said, steeling myself to have my hand kissed. I was sure he had not used tooth powder.

'Miss Bondeson! Enchanted!' The words came quickly and indistinctly, as if it were a quite unnecessary to make himself understood. When Mr Russell spoke, I saw that his lips, too, were pallid – as white as those of the girls at the mortuary. I would never have wanted to encounter that man in a dark alley! The Holiday sisters had not seemed impressed either, though they had claimed he was assuredly a reasonable man. I might find Sir Edmund's over-aesthetic, self-satisfied manner annoying, but even though I knew him to be a philanderer, it did not make my flesh creep to stand next to him. I hardly dare say it, but – Mr Russell frightened me. All the charm in the family lay with the wife, the loveable Amanda. I was convinced she could not be happy.

A memory surfaced in my mind. I raised my eyes from Mr Russell's face, thought for a moment of Ancient Greece and looked down again. It took all my willpower for me to sit back down by the fire, chat pleasantly about literature and the growth of the Press, nod at Mr Russell's comments and stare fixedly in his direction.

'With so many commissions you must have lots to do,' I ventured cautiously.

'Masses!' said Mr Russell. His voice squeaked like stirrups on leather. Had I been expecting well-modulated tones?

'Just think!' I said, thinking feverishly myself. What day was it today? Wednesday. It was a week to the day since Agnes went missing and since the first girl was murdered in Whitechapel. 'I often find that the days of the week blur into one. Like today, which happens to be Wednesday. Wednesdays are such good days, in the middle of the week and in the middle of my work. If I had been at home, I would have spent all morning writing, then taken my midday meal at the house of a married sister before going to the lending library and then home to write some more.'

'What do you usually do on Wednesday evenings, Miss Bondeson?'

'I often go to the opera. We have a fine old opera house in Stockholm, built by King Gustaf – who arranged to be murdered there, incidentally. And how do you fill your days? Do yours all look the same?'

'Almost every day is the same. I work from early morning until late at night. Is that not so, Amanda?'

Mrs Russell nodded in agreement.

'Yes indeed,' she said. 'I too. Translating does take such a time, and as you know, Euthanasia, we are very poorly remunerated. The rewards of literature are very unevenly distributed...'

'I know, and it is a great shame.'

'Wednesdays are solitary days for me,' she went on. 'I wish I had a sister to call in on. I take luncheon alone, because Russell goes to his club and Grace usually meets some friends. Then Russell is out all day, and in the evening he is like you, and goes to the theatre.'

'I was at home last week,' said Mr Russell, somewhat gratuitously. There was a moment's silence. A horned god leant forward from the top of the bookcase and studied us with interest. Could it be Baal? And was not he related to Beelzebub himself? Had Mr Russell realised I was interrogating him?

'You were in a bad mood when you came home,' said Amanda Russell. 'And you said the pie tasted stale.'

'I declare I did no such thing! I think I said I was still full after the roast beef I had at the club.'

'Did you? Well, I expect you are right. But you did go to the theatre.'

I could see the anxiety in Amanda Russell's eyes. The fellow really did torment his wife. Cruel, there was no doubting that. Did he beat her as well? I leant forward to take a better look in the dim light, but Mrs Russell was carefully encased in fabric from top to toe. An experienced wife-batterer presumably knows where to land his blows so they will not be seen.

'Not last week.'

Amanda did not allow herself to be put down – she appeared incurably stubborn and seemed to have neither the sense nor the inclination to control herself. Yet I could see she was scared of her husband.

'Russell writes theatre reviews for the *Morning Chronicle*, and they appear on Thursdays. Last week, the review did not go in until Friday, and he was so *cross*!'

'Quite understandable.'

It was the newspaper I had seen advertised on the streets. It seemed as readable and full of material as our Swedish *Aftonbladet*.

Mr and Mrs Russell gave me the uncomfortable sensation of being stranded in a marital dispute, the source and final goal of which were unknown to me. I had heard enough. Mr Russell did not want to admit having left the house the previous Wednesday. Had I been truly suspicious by nature, I might have concluded that he had not seen the play until Thursday – but that might be taking it too far. He would certainly have had time for the theatre, too. The nights are long in Whitechapel. His pallor, his lies, his murderous gods – there were various grounds for believing Mr Russell had been there.

Amanda Russell stood up and looked round. Clearly the papers were usually left lying about. She lifted a sofa cushion to reveal a flattened copy of the *Morning Chronicle*. Yesterday's. Someone had to put a stop to this. This man could do absolutely anything.

'Do you have time to write anything more substantial, Mr Russell? Or do you only write for the papers?'

That was the way to loosen a man's tongue. I leant back and felt the monologue hit me, as hot as the desert sands.

'I am working on a major book...epoch-making...a comparative study of cults among Celts, Cimbrians, Germanic tribes, Semites, Slavs, Indians...'

'Fascinating! Are those...gentlemen...involved?'

I indicated the statues above us, and hey presto! I had their names: Baal, Kali, Molok, Zalmoxis, Jarilo, Mictlantecuhtli, Darago, Brigo. I was unfamiliar with most of them. Thank goodness! None of the gentlemen – or ladies – seemed possessed of that urbane charm I prefer in both my fellow human beings and my divinities.

Heathen gods and their practices were Mr Russell's great passion. He told me eagerly of them, but I was unable to follow his ramblings very closely. I have encountered this sort of mania for one's own interests before, in Uppsala. This is the way glassy-eyed professors talk of their obsessions, describing how the toes of the horse have shrivelled away; the pistils of a flower; the language of the Etruscans; or Quintilian's thoughts on education.

And they all say as Mr Russell does:

'There is not much of the book left to write. I shall soon be finished.'

I shall take that with a large pinch of salt.

Once the niceties had been observed, I excused myself. I had to move on. With a 'Dearest Amanda!' I promised her in Swedish that we would soon meet again.

'Just we ladies, don't you agree? You and I, and perhaps little Grace – and we will go to the Exhibition and view only the things that are diverting, not those dull machines!'

We laughed, like two young girls, and bade each other a tender farewell. Stepping out into the street, I felt liberated. Once I had walked far enough to be out of sight of the house, I jumped in the air and brought my heels together – a trick of mine since I was a girl. I am a free woman! I admit I sometimes feel the lack of a home, a corner that is my own, with a man who loves me. But marriage, as I perceive it to be, is not an example I feel tempted to follow. The self-supporting spinster need never answer to anyone.

There was no cab to be seen, of course. The water droplets in the fog had gradually concentrated into rain. I put up my umbrella and started walking. I was in a hurry now. In the next road I broke into a trot, and spied a bright red omnibus with a destination sign saying: 'Hyde Park. The Great Exhibition.' At least that would take me half way. It would be easy to find my way from there. Ten minutes squashed in with twenty-four other foreigners, eager to view the Exhibition in thirteen different languages – my reticule jammed against my chest – a top hat in my face – and then the cry: 'Great Exhibition! Alight here for the Prince of Wales Entrance!'

I still had some way to walk. But there was air! I could breathe again. Naturally there was still no cab to be had, so I continued along the road bordering Hyde Park, and came to Green Park. There I unfolded my map and orientated myself. My quickest option would be to cut across the park. It was dusk. London is full of dangers for unaccompanied women. Nobody knew that as well as I. But I gave a shrug, turned my umbrella against the gale and plodded on. There are times when personal security is not important. Out in Pall Mall, I thought of my vengeance: I owed it to Agnes and had promised it to the murdered girls. They might have been fallen women, but my vengeance would make them stand tall again.

At Charing Cross I headed into Whitehall, turned into Great Scotland Yard, walked through the front door and loudly demanded to see Inspector Owain Evans.

'I'm not sure he's receiving visitors, Ma'am,' said the constable on the door, tilting his tall hat, possibly as a gesture of politeness.

'He will receive me,' I said. '*I* am Euthanasia Bondeson.'

The name meant nothing to the constable, that much was plain, but he sent word upstairs, and I was immediately shown into the Inspector's office.

In that room I had learnt that a blonde girl had been found murdered in the Thames mud. It had been summer then. The room had been suffocating in full sun. Three days had passed. It was autumn now, and the fog was trying to force an entrance through the sash windows. Then as now, the Inspector sat at his desk, poring over a sheet of paper, steel-nib pen in hand. He looked less tired, and I thought he seemed pleased to see me.

'Miss Bondeson!'

'Inspector!'

He clasped my hand in both of his and smiled behind his moustache. I smiled back, for I really was pleased to see him. The more I saw of the other men of London, the more I esteemed Inspector Evans.

'Did you get the book parcel?' I asked, sitting down in the well-padded visitor's chair without waiting to be asked.

He nodded, and I added my verbal thanks for the loan of the book. It had been a successful reading.

'If I could only have been there!'

'And if I could only have been there when you searched the molly house! Tell me all about it!'

The Inspector grew grave.

'We have much to talk about, Miss Bondeson. You are a woman who notices things. But I must just... No, let us leave that for later. You were right about the building in the yard. Criminal activities have taken place there.'

'Really?'

'The forces of evil reside in that building, Miss Bondeson. A cruel death awaited those two girls.'

He told me it all. A large contingent of peelers had searched the molly house under the direction of Inspector Evans's deputy. They had found what they expected: men, women's clothes, domestic paraphernalia, plentiful supplies of embroidery, wool and canvas – and of course the putrefying sausages. In the inner courtyard they found the homes of other mollies, as surprisingly bourgeois as the rest. And then there was the yard building.

The Inspector fell silent, as if decency had put a gag on him.

'I do not know how to say this.'

'Say it anyway. Say it as if the Reverend Amis were sitting here instead of me. That will be feminine enough for me.'

Indignation glinted momentarily in his eyes but then was gone, as if he could no longer allow himself to worry about his friend. Then he went on with his report. He told me how the peelers had completed their search of the molly house and the deputy had directed some strong officers out into the yard. The building was not massive, but it was built of solid stone. The window panes were blackened, as if the occupants had been expecting an eclipse of the sun. One can observe such astronomical phenomena through smoked glass. We did so in my childhood. But it was darkness, rather than the sun, that smothered the yard building. A constable forced open the door, and Inspector Evans's deputy stepped inside. Then he turned on his heel and hurriedly sent for the Inspector. Not even a hardened deputy inspector, army-trained and used to cannon-fire and explosions, would want to enter that place without his superior. How fortunate that I had not found a way in! If the door had been unlocked, and I had stumbled in, in the dark...

The very thought sent ice into my veins.

He had never seen anything as ghastly, said Inspector Evans. He had hailed a hansom cab and made all haste to get there. At first he had thought the place was a stable, and that his deputy had gone mad. Then he took up a lantern and went inside. The space certainly was partitioned, but into cells rather than stalls. Human beings had been held captive there. Chains hung slack against the walls, with foot irons and neck irons dangling loosely down to the floor. All round the walls stood sculptures, staring like hideous masks, with wide eyes and sharp teeth. All were embodiments of violence.

I was not entirely unprepared. I had, after all, drawn my own conclusions from the Iphigenia relief and Dolores had hinted at more. I could easily imagine the rest. Gaping mouths, tongues hanging out. Divine figures, flaunting themselves without shame or restraint. Naked goddesses – not naked like Artemis or Hera, but shamelessly naked and covered in sweat, without shifts or corsets, their bosoms hanging free. Equally naked gods, engorged and ready. On one relief, a girl was being sacrificed. The knife was poised in the executioner's hand. A Molok stretched out his bronze arms to seize firstborns and consume them. Iphigenia lay on the altar, black on a red pitcher, and by contrast with the relief above the door, she was already screaming, as her father's sacrificial knife plunged into her heart. A dead body lifted its flayed skin, exposing the arteries and layers of fat.

'I would not have told you any of this, if you had not expressly bidden me.'

The Inspector looked quite pale himself. I gripped the arms of the chair and breathed as calmly as I could. He went on with his account.

The building was equipped for violence and orgies – for orgies of violence. The window wall was hung with weapons. They were all edged weapons. No pistols, no firearms to kill quickly and mercifully. Scimitars. Daggers. Medieval poniards and curved blades from the East. Sturdy working knifes. Carving knifes. Heavy knives alongside the lightest of blades. Death and Sex reigned here in ultimate union – and over it all hung that smell... that stench. The smell of old, dried blood.

There were some light-coloured hairs caught in the neck irons, wrenched out in the final struggle. They could have come from any of the girls. There was no doubt. It was here they had been murdered.

'And Agnes? Have you found anything to indicate that Agnes...?'

'No. We've found clothing. But it could hardly have belonged to a well-kept lady's companion. There are details missing: jewellery, adornment, undergarments...you can imagine.'

'I am not so sure I can.'

'But there were a number of victims, Miss Bondeson. We have found hair from at least four women.'

He stopped and we both stood silent, looking at the ground, as if to honour their memory for a moment.

'Not Agnes?'

'No. At least two blondes and two brunettes. No one ever reports prostitutes missing. If nobody happens to trip over them, they...'

If the rats are quick enough. If no slow-witted little girl protects their dead bodies. If they are not casually tossed out into some well-frequented alley. The pain of it overcame me. I felt the girls' suffering. I got swiftly to my feet, as if to flee, then sank back down into the chair again.

'Here, drink this!'

The last time I had swooned and drunk 'this', I had been

unconscious for twelve hours. But this was Inspector Evans at my side, and I trusted him.

The drink tasted repulsive. George Amis's laudanum lavender had been considerably more palatable.

'Ugh! What is it?'

'Welsh whisky.'

'I did not know such a thing existed.'

'Nor did the man who made it, I don't think.'

'The Inspector took a dram himself – screwed up his face, but coughed and spluttered less than I had.

'The murderer is getting careless,' I said. 'You will have him before long.'

'How do you know?'

'There is more to tell you. Just one thing first – Claire?'

'Under arrest. There's no doubt he is an accessory to murder. We have several witnesses – not just the ones you ferreted out, Miss Bondeson, but Dolores and others in the molly house have testified too.'

It grieved me. Claire was without doubt an unfortunate individual, forced into the path of crime by Want and Destitution. He might otherwise have turned out a dependable young man. But there were far worse criminals than he. I could no longer hold my tongue.

'I have found the murderer.'

The Inspector sighed – a short sigh, of the sort usually reserved for children and subordinates.

'My dear Miss Bondeson! You really have been a great help in this case. But sometimes I wonder if you see more than there is to see. You have a fertile imagination, and that is as it should be. You are an artist, after all. And you know how much I admire your novels. They really are formidable. But the note you sent last night. You maintain Sir Edmund is involved in shady dealings... Did he murder the whores as well? Fifty witnesses report seeing him at a ball at the time the latest murder was committed. Are you sure it is not the author in you transforming the dry skeleton of reality by setting it like some holy relic in the shimmering casket of literature?'

'What on earth do you mean by that?

'That the Queen adores him!'

'But his wife has told me...'

And then I related the whole story, in greater detail than in my note. Lady Margaret's revelations, the questions of money and of the proper attribution of the new canvases – I brought them all up. I even mentioned the accusations of fornication, though I avoided Lady Margaret's frank descriptions. As I spoke, the Inspector's suspicious expression faded, and when I had finished he put his fingertips together and gave me a searching look.

'If Sir Edmund is up to some trick to make money – do you really think it has anything to do with the murders? Or with your companion's disappearance?'

'Money smells, Inspector! Now we know there is money involved, we will soon be able to sniff out the trail.'

'Forgive me, Miss Bondeson. I am just a simple, ordinary policeman. Was it Sir Edmund who killed the street girls?'

'No!' I sighed. How can men be so slow? Did I really have to spell it all out? It was as plain as a pikestaff to me.

'They are two separate cases, Inspector.' The more I heard and the more I thought about it, the more obvious it became: nothing had been found to link Agnes's disappearance to the murdered girls. The similarity lay in their beauty and youth, gifts that the gods distribute in equal measure to rich and poor, to the virtuous and the frivolous. In that respect, the three girls – Mary, the nameless girl and Agnes – had been alike, though their lives had in many ways been so different. Their deaths too, I hoped. Chance had lured us onto the wrong track. I put it plainly to Inspector Evans this time, and he listened with interest.

'The *first* mystery is Agnes's disappearance, and possibly that of Lady Margaret's lady's maid, too. The *second* is the murders in the yard building.'

The two sets of disappearances had occurred in circles as disparate as the women involved. The murderer of the yard building had never been admitted to the salons in which Agnes moved – his wife possibly, but not the man himself. I suspected all crimes were to do with depravity, but perversion, too, is rooted in class. In the filth of Whitechapel, depravity was a witch, black and deadly. In better circles she was a Cassandra, surrounded by misfortune perhaps, but also by beauty, by the sweet oblivion of opium and the allure of sensuality.

'And you think the crimes have nothing to do with each other, Miss Bondeson?'

'I believe not. I am increasingly convinced that Agnes's disappearance is linked to the artists' circle. And today I visited the man who has the prostitute's lives on his conscience.'

'What?'

Mr Evans spat out the word. He threw down his pen, got up from his desk and looked out of the window – straight into the fog, which hung like a pale grey roller blind outside, preventing him from seeing anything at all of Whitehall Place. He stood silent for a moment, presumably torn between his admiration for my books and his fury at my interference in his work.

'Do you remember that I was talking to Mary the harlot just before she was murdered?' I asked. The Inspector turned, which of course was the aim of my choice of words.

'You spoke of a blonde girl...'

'And she had seen the first girl vanish. She went off with a man, who was as pale as a corpse. I saw him just now.'

'There must be hundreds of pale men in London. The English sun...'

'Do you believe in female intuition, Inspector? I am convinced that man is a villain.'

'You don't seem to like Sir Edmund, either, and he is a man for whom I have the utmost respect.'

'Now listen to me, Inspector!' I commanded. And told him what I knew. Mr Russell's unpleasant appearance was one matter. Naturally London must be full of pale men. But while the Inspector was giving his account, the pieces of the puzzle had fallen into place. What they showed was a face. The almost ritual murders; the Babylonian prison of the yard building; the black, fanatical dreams of a cult that demanded sacrifice – the sacrifice of women and perhaps children, as with Molok. Somebody was twisted enough to want to kill others to make himself as strong as Baal, Jarilo, Zalmoxis and the rest. We were looking for a man, who could no longer distinguish between our time and the past, between present acts and history.

'*Hm!*' exclaimed the Inspector loudly, and sat down at his desk. 'This is what worries me about you, Miss Bondeson. I so much like what you write – I feel touchingly honoured when you borrow a book from me – but I suspect you are not as reliable in the role of detective.'

'Reliable?' I snorted. 'What a ridiculous word! I am right about Mr Russell, do not doubt it. He will not even say what he was doing the night of the first murder. He is an evil person, Inspector. I know people. I know. What is more, he collects statues, ancient cult figures. There is no room to keep them all at home, his wife says. The collection in the yard building must be his.'

'It takes more than that to hang a murderer. Proof, among other things.'

'Can you not at least interview Mr Russell? Everyone says he is strange!'

It looked as though the beautiful friendship between the Police Inspector and me was about to end as suddenly as it had started. Neither of us was prepared to give way. We were both convinced we were right. We stared obstinately at one another across the desk.

It was Owain Evans who softened. His black eyes mellowed, he stroked his beard and gave me a hint of a smile.

'You may laugh at me, Miss Bondeson. Do you remember what I said at the outset? About you not being a detective and my not being able to write a page?'

'All too well,' I said – perhaps a little more brusquely than the situation warranted.

'I don't know what got into me yesterday. I had an idea for a story – not a lovely, lofty tale like yours, but a slum story, from the world I know.'

'So you wrote?'

'Seven whole pages. Imagine that, Miss Bondeson.'

I walked round the desk and kissed the Inspector on the cheek.

'My brother,' I said. 'I knew we were birds of a feather, you and I.' And since I had already put myself on first name terms with one person that day, I saw no harm in continuing. 'I do not know the etiquette here in England. But since we think alike and work so well together – can you not call me Euthanasia?'

'That would be a very great honour,' said Owain, and we took each other's hands in a most friendly and informal way before drinking a fraternal toast in Welsh whisky. It tasted a little less foul this time. The fact was, it had a strong bouquet of cough medicine.

'The Queen is very fond of whisky.'

'Not the Welsh variety, I assume?'

Owain Evans drained his glass with an appreciative 'Ah!' Just then there was a knock at the door. I turned my attention to the greyness outside, pondering the expression about the fog being thick enough to cut with a knife. It certainly was developing a very strange consistency, though it reminded me more of beer froth than of a soufflé.

Behind me, Owain Evans accepted a telegram and read it hastily.

'I shall go there at once!' he cried. 'Two constables are to accompany me!'

I turned round again. A peeler was just disappearing out of the door.

'What is it?'

'You have accused a broken man, Miss Bondeson!'

'Euthanasia, you mean. You must tell me more!'

The Inspector sat down. The telegram had at a stroke increased his doubts about my conclusion. Like me, he made the mistake of believing other people thought the same way he did. If Owain Evans had had a daughter – even a stepdaughter – he would have been shocked if anything happened to her. The message was from Amanda Russell. Her daughter Grace had vanished. Owain Evans was full of sympathy for Mr Russell.

It was an unexpected blow for me. There I was, claiming we faced two separate mysteries, one involving bestial murder in a slum setting, the other a series of abductions of girls from the salons of the upper classes. Suddenly my theories collapsed, just as the Crystal Palace would descend in a thousand tinkling shards if a horde of elephants charged it. I had been convinced that Mr Russell was the murderer – he was not only disagreeable and full of half-digested notions about cults of antiquity, but also a wife-beater – and then his daughter was suddenly stolen away. This did not add up! Or – did it? What was the link between Mr Russell's modest scribbler's milieu and the life of affluence lived by one such as Sir Edmund? And – since I had now begun questioning my assumptions – what did the great artist have to do with the matter? Maybe nothing at all. Maybe someone else was guilty.

'Amanda Russell is my friend and translator. Shall I come with you?'

'It would not be appropriate. You know how vital it us for us in the police not to reveal anything, even when... I shall be in touch this evening.'

'Be careful, Owain,' I begged. 'Bear in mind that Mr Russell is most definitely not above suspicion, and be careful what you say!'

The Inspector informed me he was well able to take care of himself, and we parted. Thus our story divides into two once more. My half is very quiet. I went up Whitehall to Trafalgar Square, and then the short distance to the Golden Cross Hotel, where I once more wrote a little, dealt with my correspondence – remembering among other things to write to the German publisher – and read an altogether absurd novel of young love, demonic men and haunted houses up in Yorkshire. It was written by one of the sisters who had been absent from yesterday's salon. It was strange, if compelling, but altogether too old-fashioned in its passions. I find it hard to believe it will have anything to say to later, less romantic generations. Then it was evening, I dined at the hotel – the meal was so dull that I have actually forgotten what I ate – and prepared for an early night.

The Inspector meanwhile steered a more eventful course. He took two constables and hailed a cab, which conveyed them to the Russells' house in the suburbs. What happened next was related to me by him at our next meeting, and I reproduce it for my reader here.

It was not yet teatime when Inspector Evans rang at the Russells' door and was admitted by the maid, their only servant. Like me, he was shown into the homely sitting room – which he described in his report as 'shabby' – to meet a tearful Mrs Russell and a pacing Mr Russell.

Their daughter Grace had vanished. It all seemed to have happened more or less as it had when Agnes and Lady Margaret's lady's maid went missing – one moment the girl was at home, the next she was gone. According to the maid, Grace herself seemed implicated in her disappearance – she had hung around the front door, as if expecting somebody to come. Just like Agnes – and perhaps the same was true of the lady's maid. She had probably been ready for some time. Owain Evans (who had listened attentively to my account) thought of the way she had come running when there was a sound from the front door.

'It is not unusual for young girls to be easily taken in,' Inspector Evans told Grace's mother.

'Young people are always gullible,' sobbed Amanda Russell, who was as well versed in the novel genre as the Inspector.

'When did she disappear?'

'Just after Miss Bondeson had left and my husband had come home.'

Here I assume the Inspector replied with a '*Hm!*' – I think I might even have suspected me myself. I had, after all, been in the vicinity of two mysterious disappearances and a brutal murder. But Owain Evans was my friend, and said no more on the matter. Instead, he asked his constables to search the girl's room. Whereas Agnes's belongings consisted of a few items of clothing in a trunk, here there was a real and very lived-in girl's bedroom to scrutinise. It might well yield information.

No next of kin cares to have their home searched by the police, not even if they are worthy peelers. Mrs Russell, too, protested. Was it absolutely necessary? Were they going in there to rummage amongst her daughter's innocent possessions? How could they think that poor Grace had taken the decision to absent herself?

'You see, Mrs Russell, all the evidence is that those who abduct young women do not use only violence. Perhaps none at all. Certainly they can drag off their prey, but the clever ones realise there is more profit to be had if the girls are unharmed. In today's novel-reading society, almost everyone knows young women harbour feelings that might have been beyond our parents' comprehension. I have heard of many a girl who dreamt of being carried off on a Sunday morning.'

Had I been there, I would have tugged at the Inspector's sleeve and pointed out that his source for this was *The Young Ladies of Söderbärke*, where Miss Charlotte dreams of a mysterious stranger who comes galloping over the field of rye, sending the cornflowers flying, to carry her off from the tedium of manor life. What he failed to mention is that Miss Charlotte's dreams come true in a more extreme manner than she could ever have anticipated – she is captured by a whole band of robbers, who hide her in a cave and give her a very rough time.

The constables went up to Grace's room and went through all her possessions. Her dresses were pored over one by one, pockets and reticules were turned out, dressing tables and drawers were searched. They found thousands of letters and notes, but not a single one indicating anything untoward. There was also a notebook, bound in pale mauve silk. It was clearly used as a diary, and the Inspector took charge of both that and the letters. The girl's jewellery was undisturbed. Apart from Grace, everything was in its proper place. No clues came to light.

The investigation of the house could have ended there, had it not been for one of the constables, who slipped on the newly polished hall floor and tried to stop himself falling. As he toppled helplessly backwards, his hands flailed at doorposts and coat hangers, but to no avail. Just before he hit the floor, he grabbed hold of an overcoat, which broke his fall a little, bringing both the coat and its hanger down on top of him.

Somehow, the constable's hand caught in the pocket of the coat, which ripped as he fell. Mr and Mrs Russell, the other constable, the Inspector and the maid found themselves staring down at the figure sprawled on the floor.

'What happened?' cried Amanda Russell, and at the same moment her husband blurted out:

'How did such a clumsy dolt get into the police force? I demand compensation for damage to my property!'

The constable lay still, but he was most definitely fully conscious. In his hand he held a chain, with a little cross attached. It had been in the coat pocket. The Inspector knelt down beside him.

'Jones! Jones! Are you all right?'

'I think so,' said the constable. 'My back hurts, but I reckon I'm just winded.'

'What have you got there?'

The constable passed the trinket to his superior. Owain Evans turned it this way and that. Unlike Grace's jewellery, it was not of precious metal. It bore no relation to Agnes's magnificent pendant. It had been stamped from a sheet of tin and was no doubt one of many. There was some small lettering imprinted in the back. The Inspector recognised that cross – it had been described to him, and he had often seen others of similar, simple design. Only the day before, he had noted it was not among the items found in the yard building.

'By Heaven!' he whispered – a surprisingly mild reaction for Owain Evans – and got to his feet. 'Mr Russell. I arrest you. You are not obliged to say anything, but whatever you do say will be taken down and may be used in evidence...'

The Inspector got no further. Mr Russell had been poised as soon as he saw the cross, and at the Inspector's words he stepped over the recumbent policeman, wrenched an umbrella from the hall stand and made for the door. Owain Evans hurled himself after him – he was a former sailor, after all, and quick on his feet – but Mr Russell jabbed his arm with the spike of the umbrella and rushed to the door. The other constable took up the chase. The door slammed back against the wall, the front gate squeaked and steel-capped police boots pounded out into the street.

'It's lucky I'm not one of those aesthetes!' the Inspector said to me later. 'The wool of my jacket stopped the spike, and the only damage he inflicted was a large bruise.'

Back at Mrs Russell's, Owain Evans had leapt up and run out of the house. Too late. His quarry was out of sight. Only his ears enabled him to track Mr Russell's flight, and the constable's pursuit. A startled woman's voice: 'Stop thief!' The squeal of a cab, swerving to avoid the constable. The whinny of the horse as the bit dug into its mouth. The police whistle, loud and shrill. 'Stop him! Stop him!' The constable had a strong, deep voice. 'Out of the way, ma'am!' At this point, Russell jumped over some barrier. Much clattering of dustbin lids. They were in an alleyway.

Someone trod on a dog's tail. More shouting. More horses: a riding school outing, in neat formation. And there, at last: an omnibus on its way to the Exhibition. Mr Russell jumped aboard, took a seat on the top deck and purchased a ticket. The constable returned crestfallen to the house.

Inspector Evans turned to Amanda Russell.

'Do you by any chance recognise this cross, Mrs Russell?'

She looked at it, and I presume she went through the same torture as every good wife would do in such a situation.

'No,' she replied. 'I have never seen it before. What sort of cross is it?'

'A Celtic cross,' said our Welshman. The cross itself was nothing remarkable. It was one of those the Reverend Amis handed out to the girls in his Bible group. Owain Evans told Amanda Russell about the girl to whom it had belonged – about her death, and its not being found among her effects, though not even the most bungling thief would steal it for money. The priest of the slums had had his reasons for choosing that particular raw material.

'Whoever took the cross presumably murdered the girl. And in a most cruel way, I must add.'

'No!' cried Mrs Russell, staggering backwards. If only I could have been there then! If only I could have aided my friend, supported her, pulled the painful hairpins out of her hair and made sure she had a refreshing cup of tea! She had reached the stage at which a woman almost has a right to faint. But not my friend. She is a redoubtable woman, Amanda. She took a deep breath, swallowed the tears that were welling up inside her and said calmly:

'All right, Inspector. We might as well go back in and continue the search of the house.'

And that is what happened. While the constables were going through Mr Russell's possessions, Mrs Russell and Mr Evans had that cup of tea – the maid had had the good sense to make it – and when the search was complete, the good lady was ready to make a statement.

The finds from Mr Russell's bedroom and study were not enough to convict him. But they were sufficient to prove that however good his conduct, his morals were reprehensible. Receipts and notes revealed him to be a constant frequenter of suspect premises. There was also a diary, written in code. The tin cross told its own story, as did the pale suspect's flight.

From Mrs Russell's armchair, Inspector Evans surveyed the room. If he had been in any doubt, its decor had convinced him. He had seen the images in the yard building. The grim works of art here went together with those like hammer and anvil, like axe and block, like gallows and noose. They were elements of a hobby that had turned into bloody reality.

Inspector Evans left Mrs Russell, robbed of her daughter and her husband, alone with the maid, but he posted a constable outside, in case the master of the house returned. The other constable was despatched to Scotland Yard with the task of assembling a force to hunt down Mr Russell. Owain Evans went straight to the Strand, where he entered the Golden Cross Hotel and told me everything – or as much as he knew at that point – and showed me the cross. It was the same one the dead prostitute had been wearing when she was still beautiful and alive.

I did not say 'I told you so,' though I would very much have liked to. He knew I was right, anyway.

'What does the lettering say?' I asked.

'Mary – and the name of the church.'

I laughed. Inappropriate, I know. The Virgin Mary, as the mother of God is called in English. I thought of the girl under the street lamp, of her impudence and attractive face. Piteous woman! Piteous people!

'I think my duty takes me elsewhere now,' said the Inspector. 'Perhaps then we will have solved half the mystery, at least.'

So we set off in different directions – I in a cab to the suburbs, to find my poor translator, and the Inspector to Scotland Yard, to prepare to apprehend his man.

My activities were of no great interest. I consoled Amanda Russell and listened to her speak of her spouse and daughter. Her husband had always been good to her, she said. Oh no, he had never been mean or suspicious. He had never been cruel! Poor fool. I helped her get undressed, and I actually saw the bruises. I could not believe her claim that she had fallen downstairs!

Amanda Russell loved her husband. Love is blind, of course, but dependence is deaf and dumb. She spoke of her husband's handsome face, of the impression he had once made on her – and she complained about that dreadful police inspector, that yokel who had forced his way in and destroyed her whole world. She even spoke indulgently of her husband's interest in cults. She listed ancient religions as if they were nothing but cultural history, without realising they could be taken out, infused with life and used as an excuse for absolutely anything. In an ancient religion, any person deranged enough could find a justification for murdering and violating girls whose only crime was poverty. But I soothed her and kept my counsel.

However much I liked Amanda Russell, it was a difficult evening. I did not leave her until she was asleep, and by then I had – God forgive me – followed the priest's example and tricked her into taking a few calming drops of laudanum.

The Inspector was meanwhile preparing for the arrest of Mr Russell by studying his diary. It revealed an unhealthy fascination with death and sacrifice. Dates were marked here and there, dates that experts in antiquity would have been able to identify as ritually important – not for one particular ritual, but for a large number of archaic rites, which in a sufficiently deranged mind might merge into one. Greece and Rome, Assyria and Egypt, Persia and Sumeria, India and America, the Teutonic lands and Russia coexisted in Mr Russell's pages. All of history had melted into a great hotchpotch, as if a tangle of gold and barbed wire had been thrown on the fire and fused into a single mass, noble and evil all mixed up together.

Finally they had him. The Inspector had grown increasingly impatient as the afternoon went by. There was too much waiting, too much preparation. A description of Mr Russell was issued and telegraphed all over London. It was so late that the Exhibition had closed. From there and other places, constables were conscripted into the search for the fugitive. One might turn poetic and say that the Inspector was finally able to rig his vessel to pursue his enemy.

The police combed slums and dens of vice, shoulder to blue-coated shoulder, and among them walked Owain Evans in his speckled green tweed. They crept through gateways and narrow passages and searched suspect buildings for the guilty man.

Then − all at once − they find him. No, that is wrong. It is not the police cordon that smoothly surrounds Mr Russell and carries him off to jail. It is Mr Russell who emerges from the darkness in an unguarded moment and grabs the first constable he finds. A terrible sound − then silence.

Inspector Evans turns. His peeler is sprawled lifeless in the road and the figure of a man is climbing up onto the nearest roof. The Welshman gives a shout. The officers see what has happened, but it is Owain Evans who charges after the perpetrator. Foolhardy man! The Inspector is up on the roof in a trice, running after the other man − jumping between the low buildings, sliding down drainpipes, getting caught on protruding nails and tearing himself free. This former sailor was used to heights. He had played in the hills as a child, he had climbed masts en route from Ushant to the West Indies, and he soon caught up with the bloodless Mr Russell.

On a roof in Whitechapel, the pair of them fought man to man. Peelers were catching up with them, but they were way below and could not aid their superior. As Mr Russell drew a knife and the moon glinted on the long blade, they could do nothing but stare in horror.

The combat on the roof was now a matter of life and death. The pallid Russell grasped the Inspector and they waltzed round like a music hall pair. The knife was aimed at the tweed. A blow. Owain Evans slipped aside and tried to get to his pistol. In vain. Mr Russell was kicking and striking repeatedly – and then Owain Evans suddenly found himself at the right angle to land a punch, hitting his opponent square on the jaw.

The pale man staggered. The Inspector took out his pistol and aimed. A shot. A scream. Then Mr Russell was attacking Mr Evans again. They both seemed badly knocked about. A constable began to pick his way into the tumbledown building. Another scream was heard, and the constable lost his grip as a tweed-clad shape fell past him into the road. Another shot rang out. For a moment, all was quiet in the slums.

CHAPTER NINE

IN WHICH I REVEAL A SECRET

'Oh well,' I said. 'It could have been worse.'

'Thank you for that vote of confidence!' said Owain Evans, turning gingerly on the chaise longue. 'It damn well hurt, I can tell you.'

'Should a gentleman swear in front of a lady?' I asked. 'That will be all, thank you.'

A member of the hotel staff had just brought in the ingredients for the mustard compress. I mixed them in a teacup and could not help taking a certain pleasure in the Inspector's grimaces. The extract of lead I had dabbed on his wound was stinging, presumably. His eyes were abnormally black.

'I am no gentleman,' he said. 'And you should know that by now.'

I could not but agree with him on that point – but I said nothing, and began applying the mustard compress to his brow. 'Lie still.'

'This is confoundedly unpleasant – and it smells disgusting.'

'Stop fussing and tell me the rest of the story,' I said. 'Otherwise I know an excellent plaster that cures stuttering and dumbness – but you have to open a fistula in the top of the arm, first.'

'Women are tyrants,' muttered the Inspector, but went on with the account that I gave my reader in the previous chapter. He had had a nasty fall, but his joints were supple and he had managed not to land too awkwardly. The only damage was a scratch on his arm from the knife – on which the extract of lead was already doing its work – and a swelling on his brow, where he had caught the edge of a broken gutter on the way down. He had wisely and dutifully come straight to me to report, but telegrams had gone off to Scotland Yard with promises of a more detailed report the next day.

'Unfortunately we won't be able to try Russell for murder,' the Inspector went on.

'Is he dead?' I asked. Owain Evans nodded. He had shot his opponent as he fell and his aim had been so bad – or good, depending how you see it – that the man was dead before he hit the ground. The constable was dead as well. Mr Russell had cut his throat. The pale villain had claimed his final sacrificial victim.

'I hope my deputy will be able to break the news to the constable's family!'

'I am sure he will do it well,' I said. Worry is not good for invalids, and Owain had been fretting enough about the constable's fate already. Now I began to worry. The wound was not dangerous, but a surge of strong emotion could worsen the infection. Back home in Sörmland, I have seen men get gangrene from shaving cuts.'

'But surely the case of the murdered *filles de joie* is still not entirely solved?'

'More or less. We know Russell committed the murders. The sculptures in the yard building were his, and the prison fittings seem to have come from Newgate...'

'Did he *steal* them?'

'No, but they sold off some of the old shackles a few years ago, when Newgate was turned into a place of execution. I expect they subsequently passed through various shady hands.'

'But wasn't it expensive? I imagine it must have cost a fortune to set up such a... Babylonian prison!'

'Not particularly. Mr and Mrs Russell really were the

impoverished literary types one might have expected. She was probably the more successful...'

'... and I know what she earns as a translator. It is considerably more than a Swedish translator, but *I* could not live on it.'

'Rents are low in Whitechapel, and manpower in London is dirt cheap.'

'So Mr Russell acted alone?'

Inspector Evans tried to shrug as he lay there. I put a hand on his chest to hold him down, so he would not try to sit up in his excitement.

'There is nothing to indicate any accomplices apart from Claire. He will be going on trial, of course. Our Mr Writer seems to have committed the foul deeds all by himself – rape, murder and theft. We've no real way of knowing what else the girls were subjected to. The doctors' skill does not extend that far as yet.'

'And what we know of Agnes's fate is equally limited?'

'Yes. But there is always tomorrow.'

The Inspector freed himself from my grip, turned on the chaise longue and gave a large yawn.

'A successful case, on the whole!' he observed as he put his hand under his pillow and rested his cheek on it. It was like watching a child lie down to sleep, apart from the beard. It had been a hard day. Owain Evans was soon sound asleep.

A successful case? Undoubtedly – for everyone but Mary, the nameless prostitute and their two brown-haired sisters in misfortune; for everyone but the constable, Mr Russell himself and of course for his wife, who had been fond of him in spite of everything.

'Poor Amanda,' I said to myself, and spread a blanket over the Inspector. The hotel staff would presumably be surprised to find a sleeping man in my room, but I would have to put up with that inconvenience. Owain Evans had been so eager to tell me the truth that he had quite forgotten his injuries, and that was indeed kind of him.

The Inspector slept, and it was night. For me, the day's work was not over. One half of our mystery was successfully solved. The other half remained. Agnes must be somewhere. I was still convinced she was alive. But where was the key to her disappearance?

I retreated to Agnes's room, as if to get closer to her, put my notebook on her desk and rang for service.

'A cigar, please – genuine Cuban, not some imitation. And coffee!'

'Black or white, Miss?'

'Black! And so strong that the spoon stands up in it!'

'*Café noir?*'

This cheered me to a point where I could only nod. Occasionally the English can prove themselves wondrously civilised.

I had paid off one debt. The girls in the mortuary had had their revenge. The murderer was dead. It was just a shame he had perished so easily and neatly, shot in the heat of battle as though he were an honourable man. I would have liked to see him on the scaffold. But he was gone, and Mary Smith could have a Christian burial.

I had incurred another debt. Wherever I went, people died. Some girls were murdered, others abducted. First Agnes went missing, then the lady's maid, and now Grace Russell. I could not help feeling guilty. It was my fault Grace's stepfather was dead, so it was I who had to help Amanda get the girl back. Once again, two or three young women were demanding that I transform myself – that I mentally (and perhaps physically) step out of my long skirts and turn detective.

At the desk in Agnes's room, I went through the remaining case, 'The Case of the Murdered Street Girls' now having been solved. In my notebook I flicked past all my authorly jottings about Miss Giovanna, the sailors and the dark felon. I found a blank page. I rested my head in my hand, thought over all the clues for a while, took up my pen and began to write:

The Case of the Lost Girls

    ★ *Agnes has now been missing for a week. She is unlikely to have run away.*

    ★ *BUT! Everything — especially Ruby Holiday's evidence — points to Agnes having left the British Museum of her own volition, for whatever reason.*

    ★ *Agnes has not been in touch all week. So she is being held captive (or she is dead, and I do not wish to dwell on that).*

Was that all? I stared vacantly at my notes. I who had been such an active unpaid detective for Scotland Yard!

Here were my coffee and cigar. A beautiful fat cigar, its shape perhaps mildly distorted by the modish band round its middle. It had come from a cigar shop nearby. I bit off the top, lit it from the candle and took a deep puff. Ah! There is something about cigar smoke that clarifies the thoughts — and this was a genuine *puro*, grown and rolled in Cuba. The taste was as soft and welcoming as the Cuban sun. With a few gulps of bitterly black French coffee, it soon became much easier to think.

Only now did I realise how much thought I had been expending on the case of the murdered prostitutes. It was as though a whole shelf of books in the detective's library had suddenly become irrelevant. But there were still volume upon volume of mysteries left to study. I dipped my pen afresh and wrote:

    ★ *Three girls have vanished (as far as we know): Agnes (10th September), the lady's maid (name? when? Between 10th and 16th September), Grace (17th September).*

Here I stopped, my pen poised above the paper. When it began to drip ink into my notebook, I laid the pen down, applied the blotting paper and leant back.

As my thoughts wandered, I began blowing smoke rings. I am not a habitual smoker, but I have learnt a few things on my travels. It would not do in the salons of Stockholm – hardly in those of London either – but here in solitude I was free to observe that my smoke rings are almost always impeccable.

Did the disappearances have anything in common? Why, yes! Make way, blotting paper!

> *One thing they have in common is that I was nearby in at least two cases. Could I have been involved without knowing? No! Not unless you believe in magic. But there are other similarities. All three girls disappeared as quietly as mice – the lady's maid and Grace from their homes, Agnes (who was far from home, incidentally) from the Museum. They disappeared entirely without trace. All the girls are good looking. All are, or are perceived as being, the same age: seventeen to eighteen.*

The kidnapped girls and the murdered prostitutes had all been the same age. It is just as I was musing the other day: seventeen is an excellent age. The seventeen-year-old is no longer a child, but well and truly marriageable...perhaps there was some grain of a clue there. Mr Russell had had no moral scruples at all, but anyone a little more particular...or if a man was such that he was attracted to grown women... In short:

> *The three people missing are all YOUNG <u>WOMEN</u>, neither children nor boys. The object must therefore simply be PURE LECHERY!*

I drew an extra line under the word 'women'. Since there was no trace of them, it seemed implausible that they had been victims of sexually motivated murder. That left only one thing...

WHITE SLAVERY!!!

I finished my coffee and took a couple of final puffs at my cigar. There was a thought in there somewhere, trying to get out. I closed my eyes, exhorted the fortifying qualities of the coffee to aid me and tried to lure the thought in my direction, as if it were a shy kitten.

> * *All three have one thing in common. They all encountered Sir Edmund and Lady Margaret at about the time of their disappearance. Agnes went missing when we were visiting the British Museum with them. The lady's maid worked for Lady Margaret and must surely have been known to her husband, too. Grace had been at Sir Edmund's salon the evening before, and according to her mother had 'had her head turned' by the young gentlemen. But what if the gentlemen were not so young? Acc. to Ruby Holiday (and his wife), Sir E. was a dyed-in-the-wool philanderer, and Ruby claims he made up to Agnes.*

> * *Could Sir Edmund's shaky finances have anything to do with the matter?*

I stopped and put down my pen. Here once again was proof of the wisdom of making notes. A new suspicion struck me. I tried to put it out of my mind, and struggled momentarily as a battle fought itself out within me. Then honesty smashed my rose-tinted spectacles. I put an asterisk after Sir Edmund and Lady Margaret and added:

And Professor Devindra.

It was hard, but I had to look the truth in the eye. It was no more sensible to allow my partiality to take over than it was to see people as criminals just because I disliked them. I would have to reserve my challengeable views for my novels. This was real life. And it suddenly came to me where I should be looking.

Has Sir Edmund (or perhaps someone else) carried the girls off and seduced them? Where would he take them? Some den of iniquity in London? Or further afield? NB: WHAT DOES GRACE'S DIARY SAY??? Have the police forgotten about it?

Midnight was approaching, but I could not stay indoors. I would have found it impossible to sleep. I changed quickly into my men's clothes, hung my dress in the wardrobe and looked in on the sleeping policeman. He looked remarkably nice when he was asleep. Before leaving the room, I scribbled a few lines to him. It was important for Owain to know how things stood where the case was concerned. 'Check Grace's diary!' I wrote, and after some deliberation I added a line or two about where I was going. Then I took a sheet of the hotel notepaper, wrote my name and the Inspector's and folded it away in the inside pocket of my jacket. I had taken every precaution. I would have Scotland Yard looking for me if I went missing, and if I were knocked down, the piece of paper would reveal my identity and my sex.

There was something else in the inside pocket. As a lady one is unused to pockets – small items that gentlemen pop in their jacket pockets are carried in reticules or stuffed into corsets or waistbands – so I only use my pockets for matches. The illusion of manliness goes no further than that.

It was an envelope with something thick and rigid inside. 'Miss Bondeson' was written on the front in that neat sort of English handwriting so totally unlike the Inspector's. Ah yes. The

Reverend Amis had given me an envelope just before I stormed out of the wrong door and discovered the yard building.

I tore open the envelope. Inside was a photographic portrait – a rather round face, with an obstinately shaped nose and clear, if slightly swollen, eyes. The face was in shades of brown, but I knew that the eyes were blue. Even so, I scarcely recognised myself in the portrait. My face did not look the same as in the mirror. I would not claim it had ever been beautiful, but the photograph made it look more spiteful and distinct. In the mirror it was softer, sometimes even dreamy. I did not find my appearance in the photograph appealing. I told myself it was the Rector's presence that had spoilt my features. I let the photograph fall onto the desk, took my Spanish walking stick and set off. My destination was Belgravia.

The London night was cold and foggy. My male attire was purchased for mild Parisian nights, and I have no warm overcoat to throw around my shoulders. I therefore walked briskly, with my shoulders hunched and my stick under my arm. There was no cab to be seen. It was almost a relief not to entrust one's life to a cabbie on a night like this. It was not particularly far to Belgravia – the route was much the same as the one I had taken on foot from Hyde Park the day before – and in men's clothes there was no risk of my being molested.

Sir Edmund's house stood in its well-to-do neighbourhood, looking just as elegant as on my previous visit. The hour was late, and even the servants' quarters in the basement were in darkness. I suddenly wondered what I was doing there. The artist was probably asleep, or at any rate in bed, perhaps with his wife or sister-in-law lying beside him. And yet I sensed that the solution lay here, in this house.

Then I saw a light in a window on the first floor. It was shining very gently, in the interior of the room, and the more I looked at it, the more I became convinced it was a nightlight. Someone was lying up there in bed, reading.

Curiosity got the better of me. Maybe I was spurred on by the Inspector's exploits. I went up to the house and tested the drainpipe. It was perfectly solid. Without hesitating, I braced myself against the wall of the house and began to shin up. I am small and light, and enjoyed climbing trees as a girl. There was a tree branch at first-floor level, which I used to manoeuvre myself to the window.

Inside the room, Ruby Holiday lay reading a novel. I could not make out the title, but it was clearly thrilling, for she did not notice my face at the window. It was a standard English sash window, the lower part of which could be raised. I saw that the window was slightly open. I cautiously eased it up further. The house was new and the window did not creak. Then I crawled through and into a sitting position on the window sill. Ruby Holiday noticed me at last and took a breath, ready to scream.

'Shhh,' I whispered, and jumped to the floor. 'It is I, Euthanasia Bondeson.'

'Good heavens!' exclaimed Ruby, dropping her book, which landed open at the title page. I recognised the vignette of *The Young Ladies of Söderbärke*. It warmed my heart that she had been so engrossed in reading it.

'Miss Holiday, I have got to talk to you!'

It says much for Ruby Holiday's intelligence that she did not say a word about my outfit or ask what I was doing in her bedroom. She simply sat up in bed, pulled off her nightcap and twisted her chestnut locks into a knot, which she fastened with a hairpin from her bedside table. I picked up the book and put it on the table.

'I need your help. You have your head screwed on properly. You live in this house and move in the better social circles. Tell me – are you aware of anyone ambushing young girls?

She shook her head. I had expected nothing else.

'Three girls have disappeared from their homes. My companion Agnes, Grace Russell – who attended the salon here yesterday

– and your sister's lady's maid.'

Was the salon really only yesterday? I calculated. Yes, it was. Say what you will about London life – it is not boring.

'Is that so?' said Miss Holiday. 'The little blonde girl disappeared, too?'

'Did you see her?'

'At the salon, yes. A thin, rather pale girl, pretty and attracting plenty of admirers. Not that I know anything of her conversational skills, but... That's the way men are, isn't it? Whenever some new sweetie comes along, they are round her like flies. I was rather amused to see Edmund being so attentive to her.'

'Did you see anything suspicious?'

'She was talking to Professor Devindra as well. And to Ruskin – though I do not think she realised who he was.'

'And the lady's maid. Can you tell me about her? Your sister does not want to contact the police.'

'Afraid the constables will trample mud all over the carpet? It costs to have them cleaned, of course. I saw very little of the girl, actually. She hadn't been here very long. The cook was her aunt, or something like that. The girl at the salon was pretty, but this lady's maid – Elaine, she was called – was a real beauty. Pale, cool – slightly reserved, never flirted with errand boys or anything. We were simply longing to paint her, but Margaret wouldn't hear of it. She didn't like us involving the servants in our activities, Edmund and I.'

'Your activities?'

'Art!' She said the word as if it was in capital letters. 'Margaret used to paint, but she has given it up.'

'Is it only art you share with your brother-in-law, Miss Holiday? I have been given the impression that you have relations of a sexual nature.'

Ruby Holiday lowered her eyes, and I assumed she was blushing.

'That surely has nothing to do with the girls?'

'So you say. But you claim to have warned my companion about Sir Edmund.'

She nodded. I was right – I knew it. Lady Margaret's accusations were altogether too detailed and incredible to be fabricated – at least by a woman like her.

'Does it not trouble your conscience?'

'Oh yes – daily, hourly... But what can I do? You have seen Edmund – he is an appealing man, and when he lets that side of himself show, he has a force of attraction that is purely animal.'

I gave a snort of derision. Ruby Holiday ignored it.

'He painted my portrait. I sat there – quite decently dressed for an artist's model, with a shawl over my shoulders – and his brush was stroking my naked, painted skin. Then he came round to rearrange the shawl, expose more naked flesh – went back to his easel and made my skin and hair look radiant, alluring...with every sitting I was more and more enchanted. I longed for the caresses the painting was getting, I longed for his brush on my skin...'

'I think I understand,' I said. 'I am not actually very interested in your sexual adventures. But the riddles are multiplying around this house. Let us leave aside the girls for a minute. Two questions for now: Who paints Sir Edmund's works of art? And what about his money?'

'Money? His income is from his works, presumably...'

She went quiet and looked at me. I straightened my tie and crossed my legs. It was comfortable to sit like that in trousers, and not at all as repellent as when a woman waves her legs about.

'You are a nasty woman, Miss Bondeson. Don't you know that authors can fall silent? That it suddenly becomes impossible to write?'

'So I have heard,' said I, whose creative flow never seems to dry up. Surely she was not threatening me?

'The same can happen to visual artists. Poor Edmund was a struggling artist – he worked and worked, and no one showed any interest. Then suddenly he was big. Nobility, statesmen and the Queen herself bought his paintings – he earned real money – he had a house built in desirable Belgravia – but one day there were no more paintings. He raised his brush, but could not bring himself to set it to the canvas. He had no trouble with sketches, but paintings...'

'Presumably he had already dipped his brush in too many paintpots,' I said. It was very amusing to see her give a start. Her hairpin began to fall out and her hair slipped down over her shoulders. She was wearing the thinnest and most revealing of nightgowns, and I could well understand her brother in law having succumbed to inappropriate desires.

'That is why I paint his pictures,' Ruby went on. 'The portraits of me and my sister at the Exhibition were the last things he did. Now I am the one who wields the paintbrush. But do not say anything! These high-class people, lords and royalty, would not want to buy pictures by a common Miss Holiday.'

'And what about the money?'

'From sales, of course.'

'I am not that easily duped, Miss Holiday.'

The girl hid her face in her hands, and for a moment I felt genuinely sorry for her. She was a sweet, gifted girl, and it could not be easy to have the family secrets forced out of her. I came along, threw open the closet door, and the skeletons came positively tumbling out.

'I honestly don't know.'

We faced one another – no longer as friends, but as adversaries. She doubtless had some inkling of what I thought of Sir Edmund.

'Three girls have gone missing, Miss Holiday. All three have been in contact with Sir Edmund. You say yourself that he turned the heads of both my Agnes and Miss Russell. You tell me that you both wanted to paint Elaine, the lady's maid. Don't you think your brother-in-law might be involved?'

She opened her eyes wide. Heavens, such eyes! Big and dark – I could feel the brush longing to portray her. My weak pen can never do her justice.

But was her soul as beautiful as her exterior? I was no longer sure about that.

'What tells you Sir Edmund was involved? You are making false accusations, Miss Bondeson! Others have tried to do the same. And you, you are so gullible, so fascinated by everything that does not exist in your mean little country up there in the north!'

'How dare you! Sweden is my native land. I will not stand for it being insulted. What would England have been without the Danelaw?'

'You have never considered that Professor Devindra was in the vicinity when all three girls went missing! He was there when Agnes disappeared, and when little Miss Russell was here. Naturally he knew Elaine. He is always hanging about here. And I can see that you think *him* as handsome a man as Edmund! A man who is...'

'Thank you!' I said. 'I do not doubt your ability to call people from other countries unpleasant names, even those from your own Empire. And I do not give a brass farthing for your accusations!'

The previous afternoon she, too, had made accusations about her brother-in-law. She had alleged that he had shown an interest in Agnes, that she had warned the girl of his tricks. Now she was defending him. I could not believe Professor Devindra was the perpetrator! It was only with the greatest reluctance I had even entertained the thought. I understood even less now that I had before, if that were possible. Miss Holiday really made one appreciate how the female psyche can be seen as utterly inscrutable.

There was nothing for it but to bow – as my outfit bade me – and show myself out through the window. Miss Holiday would not, or could not, say more. I would have preferred to use the door, of course, as it would have been both easier and more convenient, but I was worried that someone, woken by our voices, might be standing waiting on the landing. In particular I was afraid of running into Sir Edmund. I am only a woman, albeit a formidable one.

I was able to reach the ground without difficulty, thank goodness, and quickly made myself scarce. Two streets away, I came to a pavilion I had never seen – turned and retraced my steps. It was actually the first time I had got lost in London. I hurriedly returned to the hotel and crept up to my room unobserved. When I lit the candle I saw the Inspector, whom I had almost forgotten. He was sleeping peacefully on his back, his piercing black eyes closed and the mustard compress on his forehead. I was suddenly uneasy, bent over him and felt his breath. He, at least, had not been murdered. If the compress had the desired effect, he would be restored to health when he awoke in the morning. It would be as well for me to lie down and sleep too, so I would be ready for new adventures when the day dawned.

***

I was awoken by a man leaning over me. My first sensation was one of panic. Men in the bedroom are not something a spinster is accustomed to. I had slept so deeply that I initially had no memory of the previous evening. When I opened my eyes and met Owain Evans's gaze, it all started to come back to me. My anxiety evaporated. He pulled up a chair and sat down by the bed.

Now I could recall Amanda Russell and her husband, the vanished Grace and the hunt for the murderer through Whitechapel, my own nocturnal outing and the conclusions I had drawn from it. A strange calm came over me. Admittedly Agnes was still missing, but perhaps I had discovered enough to find her.

'Whatever have you got on, Euthanasia?' asked my newly

acquired brother, the Inspector.

At first I did not comprehend what he meant. At this early hour his speech was thick and Welsh-sounding, and I thought perhaps he was so unused to female night attire that my nightgown and the nightcap tied under my chin were perfect mysteries to him. Then I looked down and saw that I had not undressed. I had put my hat beside the bed and tossed my boots under the table, but I was still wearing a jacket, tie and gentlemen's trousers.

'Trousers,' I said. 'So I can move around freely at night.'

The Inspector slowly shook his head and smiled at me with his black eyes.

'You're quite right, you know. We are birds of a feather, you and I.'

And he gave me such a tender look that I might almost have fancied he was going to kiss me, were it not for an equally strong feeling that he did not do that sort of thing. My emotions were mixed, but no doubt quite intelligible to my reader. The policeman's brow, on the other hand, was mercifully as smooth as it had been before – not without furrows, it is true, but without swelling. He had removed the mustard compress. The sleep and the treatment seemed to have restored him.

'Can you move your arm?'

He made a few careful movements.

'It seems fine. A little tender, but otherwise back to normal.'

'That was quite a feat, what you did yesterday.'

He smiled reluctantly, and gave me a searching look.

'And what did you get up to yourself, once you had put that stinking bandage on my head?'

I told him about my climb of the night before, and the conclusions I had drawn. He sat listening in silence. When I reached the end, he shook his head.

'Well I'll be damned!'

He had clearly retained his bad habit of swearing in ladies' company even though his head had healed. But I forgave him gladly — because this time he did not say I had an over-fertile imagination and ought to keep to my knitting. Quite the reverse. Owain was totally and utterly convinced by my white slavery theory. He would start by going though Grace Russell's diary — which really had been overlooked in the hullabaloo over her stepfather — and then initiate the search for the girls. It would take a huge number of officers, and the Inspector asked for a piece of paper to jot down how it could be organised. There came a knock at the door.

'Heavens above!' I cried. 'The breakfast.'

At that instant I realised how ravenous I was. Owain Evans slipped out of sight behind the sofa, and I was served that wonderful full English breakfast, perfectly sufficient for two or more. When the waiter had gone, we shared smoked bacon and eggs, sausage and kidney, mushrooms and beans, fried bread and toast — and when I offered my friend Owain my cup, he nobly put his spoon in the milk glass and drank his sugary tea from that.

Now I knew what awaited me. I was to be left alone at the hotel while the police officers did the real work. It pained me to think of it, after I had been in the thick of it for so long.

'So what is left, Owain?'

'Hardly anything,' said the Inspector, surveying the remains of the breakfast. 'We may possibly not have done full justice to the kedgeree.'

'Is that the rice dish? I thought it a little tame for Indian food. But it was not the food I was referring to.'

'What's left is very simple — one might say elementary, Euthanasia. We are simply going to find the girls, and arrest the guilty party. Perhaps it really will turn out to be Sir Edmund, as you believe.'

I am fully aware that the sin of omission is a sin nonetheless, but in my haste I had forgotten to mention Ruby Holiday's accusations concerning Professor Devindra.

'As easy as pie,' I said. 'And what about me — what shall I do?'

Owain Evans took out his pocket watch. Quarter past nine.

'Let's meet at lunchtime up at Scotland Yard. I might have something to tell you by then. Meanwhile – why not devote a bit of time to your new book, which I am so longing to read?'

He bowed on his way out, as if to charm me properly, and I set out paper and pen on the table. Then I rang for a bath, peeled off my male clothes and immersed myself in the hot water. My body was tired after its climb, and although the adventure was not yet over, I felt it was time to cleanse myself and start afresh. I thoughtfully rubbed my hair with my patent mixture, in which rosemary masks the smells of borax and olive. It was pleasant to sink into the tub, dangle my legs over the end, where the soles of my feet were warmed by the fire, and let my hair float free in the water.

After my bath I felt content, fragrant and at least ten years younger. My dressing gown was cool and soft against my skin. I dried my hair with the towel, massaged my own scalp with oil – another of those occasions when I needed Agnes – and sat down in front of the mirror. I would get down to my book very soon. There was not much left to write.

A knock came at the door. I gathered up my hair, thought I would pin it into a simple knot but could not immediately locate my hairpins. No matter. It was probably only a member of staff.

'Come in!'

There I stood with my hair still hanging damp about my shoulders, hair that Sir Edmund could have painted, had it been a little redder and a little thicker. It is certainly long enough. When it is loose and newly washed, I get wet right down to my skirts. And there in the doorway stood Professor Devindra, staring at me.

'Professor Devindra! How nice!' Greeting. Kiss of the hand. Hope my gown is not gaping open. 'I have just taken a bath.' In case he had not realised it from the steam and the scent of rosemary.

We sat down on the sofa and the Professor declined a cup of tea. He had a lecture shortly, but just wanted to look in. We had not seen each other for so long. Not since the day before yesterday, in fact. But how close our encounter had been then.

'We must get to know each other better. What about the theatre one day?'

'That would be lovely!' I said, as foolish as a lovestruck girl. I knew of course that I should be concentrating on the case and on my novel, but the theatre was so tempting. I have always loved dramatic art. Am I being disingenuous? Well, never mind! I was not entirely indifferent to the Professor. With him sitting here, so close to me, I could not imagine that he had ever done anything criminal.

'This evening?'

Even if there were a chase through London, I would not be permitted to join in. I would sit at home, waiting for a man — albeit a very nice man, of whom I was certainly fond, but to whom I was under not the least obligation to administer dabs of extract of lead. There were doctors, after all.

'That sounds an excellent idea.'

'Good!'

We fell silent. I thought of the salon, and wondered how rosy I was looking after my bath. The Professor was finding it hard to keep his eyes off my hair, which was still hanging loose. It was starting to dry, and traces were still visible of it once having been as blonde as Agnes's, before it settled on being what we so generously term 'light brown'. Perhaps loose hair has some special significance in India.

'Professor... I have been thinking about something.'

'Yes, Miss Bondeson?'

He leant forward eagerly, while I gathered up my hair. And just look: there were hairpins in my dressing gown pocket all the time. Thus I instantly became more businesslike.

'Do you recall that letter at Sir Edmund's salon? The one I

opened in error?'

'Yes of course. Or most of it, at least.'

'You mean...you remember what it said?'

The Professor's prodigious memory was not news to me, but there is a difference between remembering rhymes and having total recall of a letter one had only seen for a few seconds. Personally I had seen no more than the word 'nine', and the handwriting had been so illegible that it might easily have been something else.

'Let us see...get a bit of paper and take this down.'

He recited the letter from memory, and I wrote it down. There had been no need for the terrible handwriting: the lines were cryptic enough even in my fair copy:

Eight jewels in the Emperor's crown. 949. Expecting number nine 18 latest.

I read the lines several times. I was none the wiser. The Emperor's crown...the Emperor of Japan or of China? Or Nicholas in Petersburg or Franz Joseph in Vienna?

'The jewels – does that mean the girls?'

'Eight girls, who will become nine.'

I suddenly blanched. Or at least, I felt as if I did. I went cold, especially in the leg region. I had not even had time to put my stockings on.

'Grace Russell! A girl was abducted yesterday!' I cried, and then realised the Professor knew nothing of the mystery. Or rather – I hoped he knew nothing. I therefore gave him a brief summary of events.

'And today is the 18th of September,' he pointed out.

That only left the Emperor's crown, which made no sense to me, and of course the numbers. We agreed that 949 must be some kind of code, which the police would have a better chance of cracking.

After the Professor's departure there was no point in starting to write. I had to put up my hair, and that always takes a good while. Then I had to get dressed, collect my thoughts and, above all, not leave the latest clue behind me at the hotel. By the time I was ready, there was less than half an hour left before my appointment with the Inspector. I slipped the scrap of paper with its enigmatic message inside my corset, where no thieves could reach it. My memory is significantly worse than the Professor's. Then I took a walk. The weather was still autumnal, but I decided it was not raining and swung my furled umbrella in my hand. The leaves had begun to fall, and it was no different from a Swedish autumn. I shivered a little beneath my shawl. My intention was to walk along by the river, but at Waterloo Bridge I saw that London had no riverside promenade. Instead I was faced with a confusion of huts, boats and mud. Perhaps I could have forced some kind of passage and eventually come up near Whitehall, but that did not appeal to Euthanasia Bondeson. Or at any rate, not to the part of me that had just washed its hair and was going to the theatre that evening. I turned and went back along the Strand.

Inspector Evans received me in his office as always – positioned as usual behind his desk, with the London weather spread across his window, and showing little apparent interest in my arrival.

'Miss Bondeson, sir!' announced the same constable who had shown me in once before.

'Behold I bring you good tidings!' he said, like a herald angel. 'We have our proof that the girls were abducted.'

'No!' I cried, delighted. 'Really?' I flopped down into the visitor's armchair and felt the soft upholstery rise to enfold me. All at once I was aware of how little I had slept the previous night. I put the fatigue down to a kind of relief. Despite the terrible news I had received in that chair on occasion, I felt safe in the Inspector's room. I could have taken a nap on the spot.

'Today I have continued what I started yesterday – monopolising far too many officers. It's lucky I am the one in charge of the detective section, otherwise my superior would be very angry.

And the chief of police...well, I shall just have to put up with that. If all goes well, no one will complain.'

'That sounds like my schoolroom rules. My governess only ever punished unsuccessful cheats.'

'My teacher in Wales punished us all, whether we cheated or not. I assume it was original sin he was trying to beat out of us. But my dear Euthanasia – we are forgetting ourselves. We have important work to do. We can't sit here enjoying ourselves.'

I did have my scrap of paper to show him, it is true, and although it was enjoyable exchanging banter with Owain, I wanted to get down to business, too.

We had three items on our agenda. My discovery, his discovery and the police's discovery. We began with the middle one. Inspector Evans had been reading Grace Russell's diary – and what a diary! It was a girl's diary archetypal enough to make me want to cry. First with sadness at the transient nature of girlhood, then with anger at the stupidity of girls. There was a silliness in that diary that one could scarcely believe of the reserved Grace. She had longings, she had dreams. Her heart was adult, but her mind had stayed that of a child. Every other week she fell passionately in love – with a cousin her own age, with a boy at the bathing resort, with a young journalist who had stayed at their house for a while. It was a constant love, chaste and unrequited every time. At least once a week – on Wednesdays – it was compared with her friends' equally maidenly affections for equally various objects. And then, suddenly! One evening, Amanda Russell took her daughter to a salon – an elegant salon, the sort the girl had never dreamt of setting her foot in. Or rather, she had dreamt all too much.

In the diary, she described the Chambers' house and the celebrated guests. Page after page – no spontaneous jumping into the narrative, but a careful survey of the decor and guests. And then, right at the end, a cry of jubilation, straight from her girlish heart:

Oh Diary! You cannot IMAGINE! It is INSANE, I am mad with happiness! Sir Edmund Chambers...oh, you would not BELIEVE, such a MAN!!! So handsome. He looks like a young god...no, a young knight, with long, reddish-blond locks, eyes that...oh! so deep, so expressive... and I would never, ever have believed I would be writing this to you. About a MAN. At last, about a MAN! And not some shabby intellectual, but a REAL ARTIST. And a peer of the realm, what is more. I could tell right away he was unhappy. His wife was so UGLY and WORN and OLD, and he — well, he is older than me of course, but not as old as Mama. He told me — that he was unhappy — and asked if we might not...if I would consider running away with him. Not in earnest, of course, but just as a trial, for a day out. So I said...you know what I said. He is coming tomorrow — or he will send someone for me, he said. I shall be ready.

Haven't I always believed that a knight would come and carry me off on his white charger?

There the entry stopped. I looked up from the notebook.

'I never thought girls could be so easily taken in!'

'But that is just the sort of thing you have written about! I remember in *The Young Ladies of Söderbärke* particularly...'

'Written, yes! But I did not believe it, no indeed.'

The thought of the foolishness of girls overwhelmed me. I had to lower my eyes to the book again, stare at its cover of pale mauve silk and swallow the tears that were welling up inside me. Sir Edmund had beguiled Grace Russell before her mother's very eyes. He had probably leant over Elaine as she dusted the table centrepiece, and investigated whether lady's maids have the same dreams as young demoiselles. And worst of all — he had taken in Agnes. It hurt me to think that she had been prepared to abandon me, albeit 'not in earnest'.

'I have some written proof, too,' I said. 'Shall we take that next?'

'All right,' said Owain Evans. I extracted the slip of paper, showed it to him and explained the background. I had already deciphered most of its meaning. The Inspector dismissed the part about the Emperor's crown as irrelevant – just a 'trifle', he maintained, and I let it pass. Only the numbers remained.

'What does nine hundred and forty-nine stand for, Inspector? Could it be a code? A house number?'

'Well we do have some high house numbers here in London, but I would call this excessive. And wouldn't the street name be there, too?'

'We cannot be sure the Professor remembered it all. This may only be a fragment of the letter.

The Inspector mumbled something about Professor Devindra not necessarily being the most reliable of sources. Meanwhile, he studied the scrap of paper, twisting it this way and that and looking terribly thoughtful.

'It can't be a letter code, unless it stands for a single word or some kind of abbreviation. Nine hundred and forty-nine. Nine four nine...'

Nine four nine. That was what the Inspector actually said. But it also sounded like '*nine for nine*'.

'Nine jewels – that is, nine girls – for nine men. Nine for nine.'

'Ye gods! Now we've got them, the devils!'

If my notion of white slavery really was correct – and how could I be wrong, since Inspector Evans agreed with me for once – the captive girls were intended for a specific number of men. Whether there were nine of them, like the muses, or three, like the graces, the number could be carefully calculated. Maybe they were not to be sold to swarthy foreigners, to spend the rest of their days dancing with emeralds in their navels. Instead, each was intended for some man of note. The Inspector seemed delighted with his conclusion.

When the detectives of Scotland Yard put their sensitive ears to the ground, they can distinguish a series of sounds – of imprisoned souls, of unfortunates, of merry felons. Owain Evans could hear female lamentation from down by the docks, but whether it came from abandoned sailors' wives, or was simply an echo of old woes, one cannot tell.

The constables had searched the docks that day. On the way to Scotland Yard, I had seen for myself what it looked like along the Thames. In Stockholm we are so proud of our water. We think more seldom of the quays. In inner London there are no proper quays. It is like seeing a broad river in a rural village, with muddy banks and barefoot boatmen. Their boats are flat-bottomed and pulled straight up into the dirt.

But London is also a port. The worse the buildings get, the better the docks. The harbour districts are as unpleasant as in most other cities, with dubious taverns and houses of ill repute. Suddenly, every tongue can be heard spoken – even Swedish – and the Thames is bordered with granite and looks like an urban river. Here the docks lie close together – both as little gashes in the line of the river (or that is how they look on the map) and as lakes in the mud of the Thames shore. The first are to be found just beyond the Tower, and then they come one after another, named indiscriminately after saints and parts of the city. Furthest along – nearest the open sea – are the imposing East India Docks.

All along the waterline there are vessels at anchor, and the shore is densely packed with buildings. It is no longer a matter of taverns and brothels. There at the water's edge, marine orderliness prevails. Most of the buildings are warehouses. They exist in Whitechapel and Wapping; they exist in parts of the city whose names I have not even learnt; and they exist of course in Greenwich, of observatory fame.

In the course of the day, the constables of London had combed the warehouses. In front of one disused building they fished out a wine bottle they found floating in the water. Every clue is a potentially important clue. Then they saw that it was empty, yet still corked. In the bottle – prepare to be amazed – was a piece of paper! Someone had sent a message in a bottle.

'I apologise for having started to read the letter. But I didn't understand a bit of it.'

Was Owain being sarcastic? He gave me the piece of paper, and I unfolded it.

It was headed 'The Golden Cross Family Hotel & Tavern, 452 The Strand'. This was the hotel's own notepaper, the printed words large and clear, with a vignette that rather flattered the hotel. Such notepaper has its advantages. If one is a bit of a magpie or needs to write long letters, one can appropriate it from the hotel. There are people who do that.

The letter was in Swedish:

Dear Aunt Euthanasia!

I do not know if this letter will reach you, or what day it is. We are sitting in a gloomy room. Today there are eight of us, yesterday we were only six. They say we are waiting for the last girl.

I realise you must be furious and may have taken on a new girl. You know how fond I am of you, Aunt Euthanasia, like a daughter, if I were one. I was stupid. Sir Edmund gave me charming looks and I, foolish as I was, fell straight in love. Why did I not remember what it says on the sampler at home in Stockholm? 'Love is the wisdom of the fool.' But I believed him. He said such beautiful things, and he soon realised I spoke French. I began to have longings – I know it is wrong – and I thought it would be fun to run away with a man for a while. Miss Holiday encouraged me, she said we were made for each other. You would just think I had got lost, and then hey presto! I would be home and with you again.

But it was not like that. Two hulking brutes came along with a bottle of vitriol, and I have only seen Sir Edmund once and he was not nice.

Nobody has hit me or anything, so you need not worry. Not yet. They want something, no doubt, and we know we are to travel but not where we are going. None of the others want to be here either and they all miss their mothers and employers. All the girls are awfully pretty, so I am sure it is not domestic service they want us for.

Dear, dear Aunt Euthanasia! Forgive me and come and rescue me!

Agnes

My face was hot when I looked up again, and I was aware of tears running down my cheeks. She was alive, as I had thought all along. I wiped away my tears with my sleeve and translated the letter for the Inspector. He nodded in confirmation as he heard how Agnes had been enticed away. A treacherous criminal had caught her in his net, and his thoughtless lover had aided him. It grieved me. Now, every time she cropped up in this investigation, Ruby Holiday sank lower in my estimation.

'So we know who to bring in. We've got constables posted near Sir Edmund's house. But we must find the girls, too.'

'*Absolutely* we must!'

'There's one more thing. Here at Scotland Yard we know a lot of shady types. Some of them are happy to inform on their friends, if we make it worth their while. This abduction of the girls wasn't planned among the usual criminal fraternity. The heavies are hired men, I've no doubt, but they will know even less than Claire knew about the prostitutes. We do have one source, though. A disgusting character who would never set foot in the streets of Spitalfields or Whitechapel. He moves in a higher sphere. His is the sort of indecency that never starves.'

'Not mudlarks who have grown up?'

'No, nor the girls under the street lamps either. The sort of vice he favours is *foie gras* to the street girls' eel pie.'

'I see,' I said, though his I found his imagery unconvincing. 'And what does this gilt-edged villain say?'

'Shall we do this now, or have lunch first?'

'I am still quite full from breakfast.'

Perhaps this was something the Inspector preferred to postpone. No doubt he was ruthless enough in his dealings with the capital's criminals, but he found it hard to broach difficult subjects. He was squirming like a speared eel. I clasped my hands and gave an encouraging nod, trying to appear feminine, almost maternal. There was nothing else for it: he would have to tell me.

The gilt-edged informer knew nothing, not a thing – he alleged. But he had heard – as he put it, so he could not be accused of any involvement – that certain men were actually in the habit of exporting batches of virgins for...

Owain Evans became remarkably terse at that point. It was quite apparent that it was *orgies* that were meant – orgies so unmentionable that the Inspector clammed up when I tried to make him elaborate. He did not seem to know any more. What a waste of police resources. We had learnt more from Agnes's message in a bottle than from the golden gossipmonger.

'The fact that the girls have been moved would seem to indicate they are to be shipped out soon.'

'Where to?'

Owain Evans gave a shrug.

'That's one of the things we must find out. Soon. We're watching the docks, of course.'

I rose from the armchair.

'Then let us make a start!'

'I am happy to – but I don't really know...and what about lunch...?'

'What's wrong with pie?' I asked, and was out of the Inspector's office. He had no choice but to follow me.

We bought a pie apiece, and the Inspector gave me an inspecting look.

'We need something to drink as well. Wait here!'

He popped into the nearest public drinking house and came out with two tankards of ale. Its taste reminded me of small beer, and it was pleasantly tepid in the chilly autumn wind. I munched rapidly through my pie and downed the ale in a few gulps. Now I was ready for anything.

'Euthanasia? There is one more thing.'

'Yes?'

'You said nothing had happened to Agnes yet. You understand, don't you, that there is no need to worry about Agnes's virtue? As long as we catch them before they reach their destination, all will be well. It's apparently part of the ritual for the girls to lose their virginity during the festivities.'

Then I realised the beer had been a lot stronger than Swedish small beer. I threw back my head and guffawed with laughter.

'Virginity? They will be in for a surprise, then!'

'Pardon?'

'Well,' I said, trying as best I could to temper my high spirits. 'You see, Owain.... Agnes is my dearest companion. But you, of course, do not hear the way she speaks. We are both foreigners – to you she probably appears a young lady from a respectable, if poor, family.'

'What do you mean?'

'Dear Owain, can't you guess? Didn't you see how terrified Agnes was in the slums? It was not because she had never seen such things – it was because she never wanted to go back! Agnes was born in the slums of Stockholm. She was not much better than the mudlarks, though we do not have anything quite like them in Sweden. As a little girl, she stole food. There was little profit in it. When she was older, she went on the street. She is more like the girls in the mortuary than you could ever believe.'

Inspector Evans was dumbstruck. He looked very funny,

gasping for breath. If the whole idea had not been so terrible, it would have been hilarious to imagine the depraved Englishmen's astonishment when they discovered Agnes was more experienced in the sexual arts than they were. Agnes had earned a good living in her old profession. It was the promise of a good home and anxiety about disease that saved her, not an abhorrence of vice.

Owain downed the rest of his beer in one.

'That puts my mind at rest on one score, anyway. But we still have eight more to worry about.'

'Thanks for the beer,' I said, passing him my tankard. He returned the tankards to the tavern and offered me his arm.

'You know, Euthanasia, you never cease to amaze me.'

'That is the intention, Owain. Bear in mind that I am an authoress!'

In the midst of all the horror and adventure, I felt a sense of comradely harmony. And on that note one may also end a chapter.

CHAPTER TEN

IN WHICH I PAY SOME CALLS

It was time to uncover the whereabouts of Agnes and the other girls. In my mind's eye I could see a tedious, never-ending hunt through the docks, with Inspector Evans and his policemen charging into building after building, searching boats and pinning recalcitrant sailors against walls for interrogation. But I am not a policeman. Owain Evans had no intention of hazarding my safety in the docklands. So back to the Golden Cross Hotel, and the sight of blank sheets of paper that were wondering if I would ever show any interest in the characters of my novel again. I sneered at them, and did some tidying up instead. If Agnes returned – when Agnes returned – she might not want to stay in London. I packed the portmanteaux with the essentials, and got our trunks ready. After a moment's hesitation I put Three Fingers John's railway carriages in the bottom of my trunk. They would keep flat there until I was back in Sweden. Our rooms were ready to be vacated.

I could do no more. My papers were calling me, as piteously as starveling babes, and I decided my duty lay with them. Had not the novel felt almost finished, a short time ago? I looked through the last chapter I had written. Miss Giovanna had confronted her father, exposed the perpetrator of the crime and given her heart to the man she really loved. The final chapter remained.

Once I got down to it, the writing was child's play. The words snatched me up; Agnes and the police hunt were as far away as a novel, while the fictional world became my reality. After fourteen pages, I prepared to say farewell to the barren coast of my Mediterranean land. I had never really decided if it was France, Spain or Italy. As I wrote, I began to long for that land – for the Mediterranean, where the azure waves break on the shore, where the night is warm and you can sit out on the terrace as long as you like, smoking your cigar as the sun sinks into a blood-red ocean.

As dawn broke the next day, the village was busy again. But everything was different. The sun rose over the bright sea, where the fishing boats lay at anchor. The beach was empty. The villagers were hurrying up the hill, past the church. On its front steps the priest nodded his blessing, took his crucifix and Communion vessels and hastened after the others. Today he was to give extreme unction to the condemned man.

The villagers crowded round the scaffold, where Fernando, the disgraced son of the manor, would soon look his last. Everyone seemed to be there – the public prosecutor, the doctor, the priest who was now sprinkling those assembled with holy water. But two people were missing. The sailor who had survived both the shipwreck and the wreckers' wrath was nowhere to be seen, though he was known to have recovered. There was no sign, either, of Miss Giovanna, who had been the village's good angel in the week gone by.

Miss Giovanna and the sailor – whose name was Owain – went in a different direction. Theirs was not the path of violence, but of love. Before the bell rang for Lauds, they had exchanged their vows at the abbey church in the next village. Through cracks in the ancient vaulted ceiling, they could glimpse the sky. The two young people continued on their way – to the nearest port, where the clipper would take them to new shores. There they would build their own future.

So the novel ended with a wedding, just the way the reader likes it. I had not found it easy to execute the dark Fernando, for whom I had intermittently had warm feelings, but this was supposed to be a good yarn, not real life. The fact that the foreign sailor turned out to be Welsh in that last scene would just have to be interpreted as a tribute to one of my most dedicated readers.

One always has mixed emotions on finishing a novel. In part, it is a relief to be rid of it. Even someone who writes with ease and enjoyment feels the pressure to finish, to give birth to pages as others give birth to babes. And yet it is hard to let the book go. The characters have become one's friends, and one has grown accustomed to wielding power over them. So it was with a smile that I applied the blotting paper to the last page – but also with a tear in my eye. I wiped away the tear, tested the ink to see that it was dry, and tied the manuscript up with string. My only remaining task was to read through the book and check that my inconsistencies were not too obvious. Then the novel would be copied. Back home in Sweden, I would have entrusted it to some woman with neat handwriting – mine is crabbed and careless – but since there were no other Swedish females to be had, I would be obliged to do the copying myself. Agnes would have been no help even if she were there. Her hand was worse than Owain Evans'.

It had grown late while I was writing. There came a knock at the door, which made me jump and take out my watch. Surely it was not time for the theatre already? But no! It was room service, wondering if I would like tea. I should say so! Intellectual work makes me so hungry, and as I was leaving for the theatre at six thirty, there would be no time for an evening meal.

A fire was burning in the grate, and in came scones, dainty sandwiches and a slice of cake. They did me good. I undressed and put on my dressing gown – since I would be changing soon anyway – and warmed my toes by the fire. I sat quietly reading for an hour. I wanted to leave my own book to mature a little before

I went through it, and I was really beginning to enjoy the ghostly tale from Yorkshire.

It was one of those evenings Londoners call 'pea-soupers' when the smoke from the coal fires lies thick over the city, sinks into the streets and reduces visibility almost to nil. The smoke mingled with the yellow-green fog, and the rain set in like a curtain, thin but densely woven. I was quite happy not to have to hunt down criminals out there in the dark. I was able to enjoy a third cup of tea instead. Then I changed into my second best dress, silk, but without a train – and above all, without those bows that are so *à la mode* this year. An abomination, that is what they are!

I was ready just before half past six, my hair newly arranged, my heart expectant, and just as the clock chimed, Professor Devindra knocked at the door.

He was like a breath from elsewhere – from an older time, with other manners and customs. Sir Edmund liked to make his appearance decked out in gaudy waistcoats, but they were nothing to Professor Devindra's. This evening he was more aesthetically attired than on any former occasion, with a lime green cravat and brocade waistcoat of green and black, with silk gloves and tails – gracious me! His tailcoat was green, too, a dark, bottle-green shade I had not seen in a tailcoat for thirty years. He kissed my hand and I followed him out, as oblivious to the world about me as any chit of a girl. But I came to my senses and decided to treat the evening as a test of character – the Professor's, not my own.

It was an extremely pleasant, London-like evening. The Professor had first thought of the music hall, but had changed his mind – either he had a fit of cultural conscience, or could not resist the opportunity to wear his green tailcoat. We went to the Princess's Theatre and saw Charles Kean in *Othello*. The play was important for my English education, and it was a mournful, cautionary tale. See what comes of listening to idle gossip! The ending quite shocked me. We talked it over at length afterwards, in a Turkish restaurant, where it was easy to think about Othello.

The discussion was so fluent and so elevated that I became utterly convinced of Professor Devindra's innocence. This man could not be a criminal!

It was late when the Professor delivered me back to the hotel. He was on night duty at the hospital. In the foyer, the receptionist gave me a telegram, which I opened upstairs in my room.

Bird flown. Usual place, 9 am tomorrow. Owain.

So he liked to be cryptic, the good Inspector! Perhaps it was an occupational hazard. Evidently he wished to see me in his office the next morning and give me the depressing details of his failure. And the bird – who was that? The captive girls? Or Sir Edmund?

Then I had a thought. Had I ever asked Ruby Holiday to keep quiet about our conversation? No, why would I? It was so clearly confidential. But that was before I knew she had aided and abetted Sir Edmund during the abduction. He was her lover, after all. Naturally she would have run straight to him and revealed everything I had said – and I fear I had not been discreet. The money, the girls – I had disclosed it all.

I tore the telegram into a thousand pieces, threw them on the fire and unbuttoned my dress. If Miss Holiday had told her brother-in-law everything, there was no time to lose. And no excuse for sleep. As it happened, I did not feel particularly tired any longer. From outside came the sounds of the London night – shouts, cabs, the singing of some happy soul on their way from the theatre to the tavern. I was brim full of life. Something must be done!

It was decidedly late for paying calls, of course, but sometimes one has to dare to defy convention. I changed into my male evening clothes, piled my hair into my top hat and seized my cane. Then I took a cab to Belgravia.

For the second night in a row, I stood before Sir Edmund

Chambers' house. Yesterday I had been nervous and unsure. Today I could see the house plainly. It was even more elegant than in daylight, its classical facade illuminated by the gaslight from below. I did not intend climbing any walls. As I said, I was not nervous today. I was petrified.

The thought had struck me in the cab. Although this case did not revolve around a ruffian like Mr Russell, Sir Edmund was still a far from appealing character. It was not just my imagination. The fellow was a criminal. What if he became desperate? Perhaps murder would not be beyond him.

So I chose the door. I rang, and there stood a bowing footman, addressing me as 'Sir'.

Sir Edmund was not receiving visitors. He had gone out, the footman said. Then he leant forward and whispered that a number of the other gentlemen had also been enquiring.

'Did he not leave any written message?' I boomed, wondering how the footman could be such a fool. Lady Margaret was indisposed. I wondered if she was intoxicated every night. It might well be a relief to numb one's senses, to see the world in wine red, to let one's sorrows float upwards in fleeting champagne bubbles or sink like the sugar in a toddy. That sort of thing is not in my nature. I prefer to turn and face my disappointments, before hitting back. But perhaps Lady Margaret was suffering more than I ever had. Quite apart from a woman's usual trials, she had a debauched husband, who had moreover taken up with her sister.

'What about Miss Holiday?'

Ruby Holiday was receiving visitors. Clearly, shady types were in the habit of visiting her late at night, and I was shown up to the studio. She stood at the easel, dressed in a becoming velvet smock, her auburn hair tied back with a ribbon of the same material. She was just putting the finishing touches to a painting.

It was a picture of a young woman – evidently a saint – executed in Sir Edmund's neo-medieval style. The saint had a woolly lamb at her side, and was stroking it absent-mindedly with one hand.

Her hair was long and luxuriant, her clothing torn, but dazzling white against her rosy skin.

At first I could not identify the saint. I am not particularly conversant with such symbols. Until I looked at the face. Then I knew. The picture depicted St. Agnes, one of the Christian martyrs of Rome. I recalled that she had been shut up in a whorehouse, where she had repeatedly been violated by heathen men. Yet she had remained a virgin. The woman who had sat for the picture had also experienced incarceration and the whorehouse. Ruby Holiday had painted my Agnes.

I gasped. My heart gave a jump, and I felt my eyes widen involuntarily. There was something not right here – or only too right. Miss Holiday had encouraged Agnes when she only had eyes for Sir Edmund. Perhaps it had not stopped there. Like the keystone that supports an entire Gothic arch, this picture fell into place as the final clue – and explained Agnes's disappearance.

'A Mr Bondeson would like to see you,' the footman said to Ruby Holiday, then bowed and shut the door.

The artist turned. She must have been on her way to bed, for the diaphanous fabric of her nightdress showed under her smock, and she wore a pair of comfortable, fur-lined slippers.

'I think the game is up, Miss Holiday,' I said, with a look in my eyes that I hoped was merciless.

Miss Holiday gave me a smile. Perhaps she found it funny that the footman had mistaken me for a man. She put down her brush and took up her palette knife. Its shape was that of a small trowel, but the point looked sharp, and it struck me as potentially dangerous. I was not smiling. Rage was seething within me. I gripped my walking stick more tightly.

'Why Miss Bondeson! What game is that?'

'I was a donkey not to see it. I was stupid to trust you – just because you are a nice girl and able to tell a touching story, I thought you were innocent.'

'But it is all true!'

'All you said may be true, but all you kept from me – what about that? How can you have used Agnes as a model, when she vanished ten days ago?'

'This? This is not your companion. It is a model we often use.'

'I do not believe you, Miss Holiday. I do not intend to let myself be duped any longer.'

As I said it, I drew myself up several inches and tried to look threatening. Ruby Holiday carefully scraped away a few strokes from the background of her painting.

'Miss Holiday! You are mixed up in the abduction of the young women. Sir Edmund's charm was not the only enticement, it was also your friendship that led them astray. I have liked you from the word go. I could never have believed you as corrupt as Sir Edmund – the seducer.'

Sir Edmund could be as culpable as he liked, as far as I was concerned. I could not have cared less if he sold his soul to the devil. But Miss Holiday had seemed such a formidable person: skilled as an artist, showing solidarity as a sister, and what was more, exploited as a woman. She had truly won me over. As the scales fell from my eyes, I saw a very different sight – a beautiful, ruthless female, who cared nothing for her sisters' misfortune as long as it was to her gain. Money meant more to her than the vile fate of the young girls.

'Where is Sir Edmund? And where are the girls hidden?'

'Do you think I would tell you that?'

Ruby Holiday dropped the palette knife, which was apparently inadequate as a weapon, and picked up something from the floor. It was a long whip, which must have been used for some painting of the torture of Christ.

I gave a scream as the first lash hit home. My cheek felt wet, as if with tears, and I gripped my walking stick with both hands and wished Inspector Evans would turn up. He did not come, and I had no choice but to leap out of range as the whip cracked again. It is lucky I am so nimble. I threw myself aside and tugged at my walking stick. It jammed. Every time I have not had need of it, it has slid smoothly and obediently. This time it was stiff, perhaps suffering from the damp London air.

'Devil's work!' I cried, and hurled myself at Ruby Holiday. I scarcely knew if I was railing at her, or blaspheming. My shoulder rammed into her chin, and she screamed and dropped the whip.

Finally the walking stick yielded. It divided in two, and in my right hand I was suddenly holding a slim, pointed rapier. I do like things that are not what they seem – I have a music box, for example, that is the image of a real-life violin, and a little silver owl that hides four schnapps glasses – and I suppose my writing is like that, too. I had acquired the walking stick in Toledo. It was so delectable that I bought it on the spot, though a concealed rapier is hardly what a lady needs. And the moral of that is: do not avoid nonsensical purchases unless you have to. Because now I had tight hold of Ruby Holiday's dangling tail of hair and had forced her to the floor, my weapon at her throat.

'I'm sure you have no idea how to use that, Miss Bondeson,' she whimpered, but I gave the ferocious laugh that I had learnt from Iago at the theatre:

'Hah! I studied gymnastics with Professor Ling, and he taught me a thing or two about fencing. Maybe you were not aware that Ling was one of our foremost heroic poets?' Here I pressed the point of my rapier a little harder against her neck. 'Never despise the written word, Miss Holiday. Even the dullest of authors – or authoresses, for that matter – may have unsuspected talents.'

'Don't kill me!'

'We will have to see about that,' I said. Tell me where the girls are.'

'You will never get to them! They are already onboard the boat, and there are hundreds of boats in the London docks!'

'You are forgetting that my friend Inspector Evans has hundreds of peelers at his disposal.'

'It will be too late! The boat leaves tomorrow, and then you won't have a chance!'

'Bearing in mind that I am holding a rapier to your throat, I do rather think you could be more cooperative, Miss Holiday. What is the boat's name?'

I shifted the rapier a hair's breadth from her larynx and drew it slowly down her skin. Now we were quits. My opponent was bleeding, too. I noted myself taking a strange pleasure in tormenting her. It was a good thing I so seldom found myself in situations like this.

'*Heliogabalus.*'

Jewels in the Emperor's crown... Ah, so it was the name of the boat that had determined the cryptic wording. Yet the Inspector had dismissed it.

'A fitting name. Where is it heading?'

'To the Riviera... Let me go! Then a chateau in the mountains near Nice.'

I had not the least intention of letting go. The rapier quivered before her eyes, and a drop of Ruby Holiday's blood ran down her throat. Like a viscous, red teardrop.

'And where is Sir Edmund?'

'I don't know. Ow! You're hurting me.'

'That was the idea, actually,' I said, wiping my rapier clean on her velvet smock. In my years of spinsterhood I have learnt to tend wounds, so I knew the scratches I had given Ruby Holiday were most unlikely to do her any great harm. Unless infection or gangrene set in, of course.

'I honestly don't know. Believe me!' She was screaming now, so I put my hand over her mouth and sat astride her soft form. Since I was wearing men's clothes, it was very easy. One has marvellous freedom of movement in trousers.

'Shut up, minx!'

I had a good mind to torment her further, for her duplicity, for pretending to be Agnes's friend and luring her into captivity, for her cruelty to the girls.

'How many girls are there?'

'Nine. One for each of the men. And you know – this is what they always do. They round up girls every year – and enjoy themselves right through October.'

'And what sort of men are they?'

'The better sort. Better than you.'

'That's debatable,' I said, increasing the pressure on her ribs. It was almost as though Ruby Holiday was trying to boast of the men's perversions. There were nine of them – aristocrats, I assumed, or others with sufficient wealth and freedom to be away a whole month every autumn. The rest one could easily imagine. The season was over, but it was still not an unusual time of year to go south for one's health. My sister Eudoxia had spent Christmas on the Riviera several times. And no one would be surprised when the men went off, not even their wives – who possibly did not care for them very much. The upper classes certainly have the gift for avoiding work, and these men were evidently from the highest echelons of English society. But we all know the wheel of Fortune is constantly spinning. In actual fact, these men were the lowest of the low. Folk like Three Fingers John, Mary Smith and Claire were far better people, and knew how to conduct themselves more honourably. Much as I revere our royal family and all other royal families, and respect ancient lineage, I am convinced of the rise of meritocracy and the slow decline of aristocracy.

Ruby Holiday and I clearly had differing opinions on this point.

'I think you had better tell me what happens to the girls.'

'Let me go! I can't breathe!'

I shifted down a few centimetres, so I was sitting on her stomach. Her eyes were acquiring a glaze that looked like anguish. I waved the rapier in her face.

Suddenly the words came pouring out. Maybe confessing felt good; maybe she was trying to impress me with her depravity.

The Inspector's information had been correct: the girls were to reach the chateau intact. There they became one of many components in the orgy. Quite possibly their misery would be valued no more highly than a glass of vintage wine or a mussel-stuffed capon.

The girls were kept incarcerated until their departure. It took some time to collect them all up, when all was said and done, and this year they had been running out of time. Ruby Holiday was not entirely satisfied with Grace Russell. She was too ordinary, and too skinny.

'Do you paint all the girls?'

'Those who deserve it. Edmund and I bring them in here through the back door. No one ever gets suspicious in an area like this! It's funny, isn't it? Morals here are as base as in the slums. Then...we do whatever we feel like, paint their portraits and...'

'Are you implying something I ought not to comprehend?'

'What makes you think that? As I said – the girls have to be untouched when they get to the chateau.'

Miss Holiday was getting rather too insolent for my liking. I showed her the rapier blade. It was so slim, so pliant – and yet so intensely painful.

'What happens to the girls at the chateau, once the men have finished violating them?'

'I don't know.'

'*Tut, tut,*' I said in the English manner. 'That was the wrong answer, Miss Holiday. We will ask that question again: what happens?'

'They are sold to the East – as slave girls and prostitutes.'

'And you feel absolutely no sympathy, of course? So, let us return to my first question: where is Sir Edmund?'

'At his club, I think.'

'A better answer, at any rate.'

I altered my position slightly, so I was sitting on the girl's chest and could keep her under better surveillance. In the heap of instruments of torture there was a thick rope. I needed to get hold of it somehow.

'And why does he do all this? He is not a friend of those big wigs, surely?'

'He has borrowed money from them, lots of money...and this year they were only eight, so he has been allowed to join...'

'So he is both lecherous and dissolute? Why am I not surprised? Who else is involved?'

'I don't know – *ow!*'

From where I was sitting now, it was difficult to use the rapier. So I sank my teeth into her flesh, which was white and inviting.

'Your sister? No? Professor Devindra? I would like a definitive yes or no on the Professor, please.'

'No! No, he's not part of the conspiracy. I only said that to provoke you.'

'Really? Do you have any other names at all, in fact?'

'Edmund dealt with all the contacts.'

I knew this was often the case in criminal circles, so I gave a nod of assent and reached for the rope. Ruby Holiday attempted to wrestle me to the ground, but I had the advantage and was able to hold her down with one knee.

As a frequent traveller, I am well used to tying parcels. I buttoned Miss Holiday's nightgown over her bosom (to spare her blushes), then pulled her artist's smock over her head and tied it at the top. I trussed up her arms and legs with the rope, and rounded it all off by finding a painter's rag that was not too filthy and thrusting it up inside the smock. To judge by her groan, it wedged itself in her mouth, just as I intended. Finally, I made my toilette in front of a mirror presumably used by the models to prepare themselves, put my hat on my head, restored my walking stick to its respectable form, and left.

Out in Belgrave Square I found a peeler. I immediately felt safe.

'Are you familiar with the mystery of the missing girls?' I

asked.

'Certainly, Sir. I was part of the search party today.'

'One of the people involved is lying captive on the top floor of Sir Edmund's house, over there. It is a woman – but be careful! She is a tricky customer.'

'Then I'd better call for reinforcements, Sir.'

'Not Sir. Miss. Miss Euthanasia Bondeson. And I must see your Inspector at once.'

The peeler looked at me in amazement, but he was too used to the mysteries of London to comment on my appearance.

'Inspector Evans has gone home to rest, Miss. But his deputy...'

'The deputy is no use to me!' I snorted. 'I have important information that must reach the Inspector without delay! Where does he live?'

But it was like this: the constable was not prepared to tell me, and I could well understand him. I must have looked pretty suspect myself, with my top hat and high voice. I therefore thanked him for his trouble and left him to pick up Ruby Holiday, who was about to discover what it was like to be a prisoner.

The time was approaching midnight. London had still not settled down for the night. The metropolis seldom rests. It was still dark, sooty and foggy, the gaslights were solitary little flames in the mass of black, grey and white. Nine hours to go until I could see Inspector Evans in his office. I had two options. I chose the first.

London is a manageable city, once you get to know it. I found myself ending up on same streets over and over again. Over the past few days I had moved in two triangles: that of poverty and that of prosperity. The first of these was the smaller. One of its corners was the rectory, another the molly house and the last – if I allow myself to stretch a point – at the Indian restaurant. The other triangle was more extensive, its angles the Great Exhibition in Hyde Park, the Chambers' house in Belgravia, and the Golden

Cross Hotel in the Strand. Only Mrs Russell's house in the suburbs, the theatre and the Museum were left out – and I could have squeezed the last two into my triangle, if I had wanted.

Within the second triangle there was also a hospital, of which I had sometimes thought but never heard much. Professor Devindra was never one to talk about his medical work. I wondered what sort of doctor he was. The hospital was named after the patron saint of England.

I walked round the park in Belgrave Square, past a chapel and past yet another little park. The green parks of London are a delight in daytime but rather terrifying after midnight, as it was now. I gripped my stick more tightly in my hand. To my left towered the hospital, and then I was at the main entrance.

The Professor was a different man from the one he had been earlier that evening. He had changed into a dark suit, a sober outfit more suitable for the hospital. When he saw me he was initially confused, but then he smiled and kissed my bloody cheek.

'You never cease to amaze me, Miss Bondeson!'

It was not the first time I had heard that comment.

'Come up to my room and I will dress that wound,' Professor Devindra went on. I suddenly remembered my damaged cheek and felt it with my hand. The wound was larger than I had thought and still sticky with blood, despite my having wiped it in the studio.

'Do not touch the wound!'

The Professor showed me very plainly what he meant – he put his hand over mine and took it away from my face. I clenched my stick in my other hand. Admittedly I did not think the Professor was part of the criminal gang, but detective work had infected me with a pervasive unease and suspicion.

No room could have been less like Owain Evans's bare and dusty office than the Professor's. Even the ever-changing weather of London was not permitted to hang like a picture on these walls. Thick curtains, deep red with gold threads, were pulled across the windows. The desk was tidy and of that neat size and shape deemed fitting for men by our fathers. By the wall was a sofa covered in red and yellow cotton, and opposite the desk two dainty leather armchairs. The Inspector's office had always made me feel safe, although I had found it unattractive. Professor Devindra's room was beautiful, but it made me tense and uncertain. Perhaps it was the adornments on the walls. The Inspector would never have considered paintings. The Professor's walls were covered in them.

'You have a lovely room here, Professor.'

'I feel at home in it,' said the Professor. 'And the paintings are my own.'

That explained a few things – among others the fact that he dared to hang them at all. I had never seen anything like it! They were lovely, but... I had assumed the Professor and Sir Edmund belonged to the same artistic school. I would have expected pale, auburn-tinted damsels, mournful looks from behind manes of hair, and vaguely Tuscan landscapes in the background. The style was not entirely different, for the paintings were bathed in the same clear, Nordic light, but Professor Devindra's works were populated by semi-naked, orb-breasted ladies. Their skin was of the same dark olive shade as his own, and the blackness of their eyes was enhanced by kohl and half hidden behind gauzy veils. However English Professor Devindra might seem, India was his artistic homeland.

'They are wonderful!' I enthused, fixing my eyes on a crawling, naked girl who had lost her bright red sari and was evidently in thrall to a laughing figure of a god.

'Thank you. My idea is to renew Indian art – to marry the best of West and East, new and old culture.'

As he did in his own person, in other words. But I did not say so. The Professor told me how he would improve medicine, work for the good of mankind and ultimately make his fatherland realise the importance of his art.

'It is my belief that Western art can fundamentally enliven these religious motifs.'

'Are you a heathen?' I asked, shocked, and sat down on the sofa, as he had invited. The Professor avoided my question.

'I am a modern individual. Aren't you?'

'Of course.'

'Do you want a cup of tea? This wound is not serious. Your mother could have seen to this – I will clean it and put on a dressing.'

He opened the door and called for an assistant, who immediately came in with two cups of tea – Assam, naturally – and a bowl of water and bandages. The care of the wound could certainly have been entrusted to my mother or any other woman – the Professor had a light touch and had soon dressed the cut.

'What sort of doctor are you actually, Professor Devindra? You never say much about it.'

The Professor smiled, dried his hands and poured milk into the tea.

'That is because it is a little embarrassing, and not considered gentlemanlike at the older universities. I am a professor of obstetrics.'

'Obst...?' I thought of fruit, but realised my knowledge of German had misled me. My thoughts reorganised themselves, and I felt myself blush. 'Women's medicine? Childbirth? Surely a man cannot...?'

'There are not that many woman doctors, that is the thing.'

I looked down into my teacup. The liquid was almost russet-coloured. The milk ran in to blend with it, swirled round and turned the tea opaque.

'Very true. But conversation is not the reason for my visit!'

'A pause for a cup of tea is always nice.'

'Well yes, Professor...' I said, a little hesitantly. My plan was still not fully formed. 'If I need to get hold of Sir Edmund in a hurry, where should I look?'

'If he is not at home, I should try his club, the Reform Club.

Or, wait...'

The Professor lapsed into silence, took a gulp of tea and seemed to be thinking. Then he resumed:

'Very few people know about this. You are aware, no doubt, that most English gentlemen belong to a whole set of clubs. Edmund does, too. But he keeps pretty quiet about one of them – the Gentlemen's Club in St. James's Street. It is a club where all the members are gentlemen outwardly. But not necessarily inwardly.'

'Can I go there at this time of night?'

The Professor looked at me, making me painfully conscious of my male apparel.

'What would you do if you got hold of him, Miss Bondeson?'

My intention had been to interrogate him, of course, but when Professor Devindra asked, I realised it was a stupid idea. I could assume Sir Edmund would not answer, and even if he did, he would also try to stop me getting to Agnes. As I said – my plan was not really fully formed. I told the Professor the whole story, about Ruby Holiday and Sir Edmund, about Grace Russell's diary and Agnes's letter.

'So good old Edmund is well and truly compromised? *Hmm*!' He fell silent for a moment – a brief moment – and sipped his tea. 'I have to confess I have been keeping something quiet. The letter pointed so clearly to Edmund that I did not want to tell you...'

He stopped, and for once I held my tongue as well. It is sometimes a good idea to let silence do its work. Finally the Professor went on:

'I remember where I saw that giant of a man who delivered the letter.'

'Oh. Where?'

He was at the British Museum just before Miss Björk vanished. How shall I put it – his was not the sort of look I linked with cultivated interests.'

'Do you think...do you think he was involved in the abduction of the girls?'

'I do not know. But Edmund clearly was. And yet he was my friend, even so – perhaps still is, for all I know. That man is a deuced fine painter, you know. I am not easily impressed, but Sir Edmund is truly one of the *greats*. But he has his less attractive side, of course. He despises medicine and is not always tolerant. He has bought some of my paintings, but I am not sure he sees them as Indian culture – probably rather as pornography.'

'There is scope for misinterpretation, it must be said.'

We laughed. The time was coming for me to go, though I would have preferred to stay. Only one question remained.

'The boat the girls are being shipped out on is called the "*Heliogabalus*". Does that mean anything to you?'

'Yes it does, actually...it is a cruise ship. I happen to know that because my publisher is going to the Mediterranean on the *Heliogabalus*...quite soon, in fact. Have I given you a copy of my paper?'

He had not. I was entirely unaware of the Professor having published anything – I might have imagined some kind of academic dissertation, such as one sees in Uppsala. Besides, I was always very careful not to accumulate papers on journeys. They weigh a surprising amount, and if one is unlucky they are also dreadfully badly written.

The Professor produced a slim volume and handed it to me. *Indian and Western Medicine*. It might at least be instructive. Printed in 1851 by Sweet & Sweet, London. Undoubtedly interesting.

I realised there was no more information to be gleaned from the Professor. However sad it felt, it was time to say farewell. I finished my tea, set the cup on the table and got to my feet.

'I have to go now, Professor. Do you know where I can most easily send a telegram?'

'We have a telegraph office in the hospital, so I can help you on that score.'

For a moment I was tempted. Then I thought of how mistaken I had been about people before: Sir Edmund, whom I had admittedly never liked, but been rather impressed by, nonetheless; Ruby Holiday, whom I had taken to my heart but ultimately exposed as an unscrupulous criminal.

'No, I have no wish to intrude into the public sphere. As an author, I have to set a moral example.'

So we were about to part – and I suddenly had the dreadful thought that it was our final leave-taking. Today I had packed our things. If Agnes were found, we would be leaving London without delay.

It pained me to leave Professor Devindra. Men do not interest me greatly, and I have never regretted remaining single, but I would gladly have made this man's closer acquaintance.

'Farewell, Professor. I do not know if we will see each other again'

'Farewell, Miss Bondeson.'

And we stood there staring into each other's eyes, as I had done with a young lieutenant in Medevi, twenty-five years before. Like the lieutenant, the Professor leant down, and as I had done then, I stood on tiptoe and put my arms around his neck. But I cannot recall whether the young lieutenant had the same way of kissing. Wool pressed against wool, and I was aware of the unsettling proximity of a male body. My jacket rubbed on his, our buttons scraped together... In my fight with Ruby Holiday, I had felt the freedom of male attire. Now I felt the trousers pulling tight as I stretched up. Rough fabric encased my legs, rather than caressing silk. It was a strange feeling, but not unpleasant.

'I have often wondered about the morals of lady authors,' said the Professor, coming up for air.

It was a good while before I answered him.

'They are presumably just as good as those of doctors or artists.'

Another pause.

'My friend Edmund chases young women. He does not realise that there are many more advantages to women of our own age...'

Presumably (I thought), advantages like thinking every time

would be the last. But I said nothing, merely kissed him again, not noticing that my tie had come undone.

'Now it really is goodbye, Professor.'

'But surely not forever, Miss Bondeson? You would like India so much! Perhaps we could consider taking a trip there together, one day? There are some wonderful vessels on that route. And such cabins! Port out, starboard home?'

'We shall have to see,' I said to deflect him – but I wrote down my address for him, and received his in return. Then he re-knotted my tie for me, ordered me to leave my wound uncovered overnight, and accompanied me to the hospital entrance. I took a cab to my hotel and made sure a telegram went off to the Inspector immediately. As so often that night, I did not let any of my yearnings show, merely informed him briskly that I would be there at seven-thirty sharp the next morning. Then I was free to sleep well for almost five hours. At my early breakfast, I even tucked into the kedgeree.

CHAPTER ELEVEN

IN WHICH A TOP HAT COMES IN USEFUL

'Well I'll be damned!' said Inspector Evans when I told him of my adventure. 'I was just speculating who the fellow might be who had trussed up Miss Holiday.'

'So now,' I said, 'you can scarcely tell me to wait demurely at the hotel while you go hunting villains. I can do it too.'

'And I spent my evening off writing another ten pages of my slum novel.'

'There is nothing left to astound the human race,' I declared. We were comrades, the Inspector and I, who both came from small, mountainous countries and spoke strange, foreign tongues.

With the camaraderie out of the way, we scraped back our chairs and set off. The constables gave me a few odd looks, but said nothing. In the much-vaunted name of respectability I had dressed in women's clothes, though with minimal corsetry and a skirt I could run in. I had also brought along my walking stick.

So we hailed our cabs and started our day's work, the police force and I. I felt quite dizzy as I climbed up into a hansom cab with Inspector Evans. Excitement, anxiety and fatigue no doubt contributed to my light-headedness. By about midday, Agnes would be gone from this country. The *Heliogabalus* had been searched during the night – ostensibly for customs purposes – but without result. The felons would be cunning enough to get the girls on board, even so. It made no difference how many detectives were standing guard over the vessel.

Geographically speaking, Sir Edmund's club lay within my triangle – in St. James's Street, off Piccadilly, where the clubs were packed as tightly as sardines. They were all discreet on the outside, and presumably grand on the inside. Only the brass plates by the entrances and the uniformed doormen within revealed the existence of the Devonshire Club, University Club and Junior Army & Navy Club. And finally, there at the end – the Gentlemen's Club.

I am a much-travelled woman. I was born in a manor house and, though a commoner, have seen my share of the high life, both in Sweden and abroad. But a gentlemen's club was still a world away from anything I was used to.

It was not the decor that amazed me. The club looked more or less as I would have imagined it to look. It was as elegant as a palace, as cold and impersonal as a government office. There were all the comfortable armchairs one might expect, all the stiff gentlemen and conventional, over-sumptuous breakfasts one might anticipate. It was the atmosphere that was different. All the places I have visited in England – Sir Edmund's salon, the theatre, the molly house, the British Museum – have had a human, sometimes even warm atmosphere. Admittedly there had always been that English reserve, that politeness and good grooming – but even among the friezes, people would burst out into sudden tirades. There was enthusiasm and emotion. Here, all was quiet. It was as cold as the marble slabs in the mortuary, and all wrapped in a net of cool conversation. I stood in the doorway next to Owain Evans and felt the atmosphere. I would not want to spend time here.

Then the first gentleman noticed us. He dropped the kidney fork and stared at us.

Yes, gentlemen. Here we were were. Here I was – a woman – along with my friend Owain Evans and a dozen constables, all in dapper blue tailcoats and top hats. We advanced slowly across the room to the gentleman with light, curly hair who had been peacefully eating his breakfast. As we came in, he was just swallowing a mouthful of kipper. I was pleased to see that he choked on it. I was almost sorry not to be able to draw my walking stick there and then, and personally demand satisfaction.

'Sir Edmund Chambers! I arrest you!'

The artist pushed back his chair, cast a startled look at our company and squeezed himself between the table and the wall. His plate fell to the floor. Trout, veal cutlet, bacon and egg, goose in aspic and *foie gras*, kedgeree and cold cuts spattered in all directions. The gentlemen glared. How dare anybody disturb their elevated, gentlemanly repose? What rabble! What plebs! I could see them appraising us – Owain hardly looks as though he has any connections in the Upper Chamber, and though two of my brothers-in-law sit in the Swedish House of the Nobility, their family lines doubtless do not stretch back far enough. But, gentlemen – merit is the most exclusive coat of arms! I gripped my stick. *En garde*, gentlemen! *En garde*, ye villains and ruffians the world over!

Perhaps it was only fitting for the gentlemen themselves to disturb the order of the place. Sir Edmund cut diagonally across the room as he made a run for the door, pulling off tablecloths as he went, like a naughty child. All round him flew pies of game and beef, poached and scotch eggs, muffins and toast. I ducked as an egg yolk whizzed by. Sir Edmund looked over his shoulder and tugged at chairs as he went, ensuring he left the most corpulent gentlemen blocking our path. How could he imagine he would get away with it? I hitched up my skirts and dashed after the constables and their quarry. Owain Evans surveyed the culinary battlefield, on which cracked salad bowls and upside-down omelettes floated like boats in the puddles of tea. Then he leapt up onto a long table that ran the length of the room and galloped like a Welsh pony over the mountain ridges of flower arrangements and volcanic craters of serving dishes.

The cool conversation had been replaced by cries and protests. Every few steps, something would crunch under one's foot. One had to be careful not to slip on any baked beans. Up on the table, Owain Evans had an easier time of it than the constables and myself – relatively unimpeded, he overtook us at a run, striding over plates and kicking aside the platters that he found in his way. The gentlemen who had been sitting at the table had risen to their feet and were keeping well back.

The chase took us out into the hall, down the stairs and along more corridors. It was emptier here, with fewer obstacles. Though less slippery underfoot than when we emerged from the dining room, it echoed more. We ran, and those around us shouted. Sir Edmund had long legs, and must have been a good runner in his day, but we could clearly hear him panting ahead of us. We were none of us in the first flush of youth – neither I, nor the artist, nor the Inspector. The constables were quick and well trained, of course, but the thick carpets were not that easy to run on, and slowed them down. Owain Evans had a good head start, and as we turned into a basement passage, he was hard on Sir Edmund's heels.

Suddenly, the chase stalled. Sir Edmund slammed a door in the Inspector's face, and I arrived just in time to hear it being bolted from the inside.

'Break down the door!'

Three sturdy peelers hurled their bodies at the door. It was solid, reinforced with wooden crosspieces and evidently barred with a wooden beam, not a standard bolt and hasp. One assumed the door had been there since the building was built, many years before. A substantial gap had opened over time between the door and the lintel.

Owain Evans turned to us.

'Your hat!' he commanded the nearest peeler. The constable removed his hat, and Owain Evans stepped onto it. I was amazed at the Inspector's treatment of his subordinate's uniform – only later did I discover that the constables' stovepipe hats are designed for standing on, and reinforced for the purpose with a framework of wood and iron. That makes one see the peelers' top hats in a very different light – they are not evidence of vanity, and presumably not even comfortable, but terribly useful when the constable (or his superior) finds he lacks height. The question is: what secrets do the blue tailcoats conceal?

'There's a door on the other side! He's gone!'

At that, the whole, snaking line turned and ran back, found another door and issued out into the street, where Sir Edmund was just climbing into a cab. I was now so out of breath that I had to slow my pace.

'Come on!' cried the Inspector, tugging at my arm. Suddenly I was sitting at Owain's side in a hansom cab, and two constables were clinging to the box with the cabbie. Sir Edmund had taken the first vehicle he saw, which happened to be one of the slower, four-wheeled growlers, and we soon gained on him. Our constables shouted from the box:

'Pull over! Police!'

Inside our cab, I gripped tightly onto whatever came to hand, which turned out to be the Inspector's coat tails. Embarrassed, I let go and tried to sit straight and impassive, but we lurched so wildly at every corner that I could hardly breathe. London rattled by like a Diorama – one minute we were at St. James's Park, the next we were swaying through Westminster, and all at once I had the walls of the Tower in front of my nose. There we came to a sudden halt. Our cabbie knew his horses and had driven up alongside the growler, reached out a hand and tugged at the bit to bring the hack to a stop.

We were there before Sir Edmund could open the door – the strong constables, Inspector Evans and I – and each of us did our duty. The constables hauled the culprit out of the cab and twisted his arms up behind his back. Owain Evans told him he was under arrest and recited the caution that always follows a British arrest. The gist of it was that the arrested man had the right to silence, as anything he happened to say could be used against him. As for me, I saw to my own, self-imposed part of the task – I stared contemptuously and spectacularly at Sir Edmund, and thus gathered a crowd of onlookers. The Tower is a popular attraction, and soon visitors from the provinces and abroad were flocking round us, along with street vendors, piemen and pickpockets, all obligingly staring at Sir Edmund. It was a spectacle I appreciated highly – almost more than the *Othello* of the previous evening.

The great artist treated the gawkers with disdain, held his head high and looked down his long, shapely nose at the throng. He treated the policemen in the same manner, though less quietly.

'What do you think you are doing? Do you not know who I am?'

'All too well,' said Inspector Evans, looking Sir Edmund straight in the eye. 'Where are the girls?'

'What girls?'

The Inspector turned to a non-uniformed man who had materialised at his side.

'You'd better make sure you soften up this gallows-bird a bit, Deputy Inspector. Then maybe he'll talk.'

I – and the whole audience – saw the look of terror cross Sir Edmund's face. I suddenly felt sorry for him. He had been so sure of himself – so splendid, so untouchable in his artistic ivory tower. The thought of discovery had never occurred to him.

I stepped forward out of the crowd.

'You!' hissed Sir Edmund.

'I am sure you have some charge of violent conduct and exploitation to add to all the rest, Mr Evans. We must not overlook kidnapping either, in our haste.'

'You are an obnoxious woman, Miss Bondeson! You stick your nose into other people's business, you curry favour with all and sundry and show no judgment in the company you keep! *Unfeminine* – that is what you are!'

'That may be,' I said, 'but at least I am neither debauched nor dishonest. And I am not the one sporting those steel bracelets.'

A detective has to get used to abuse. You could only stand tall, hold your head high and feel that you had actually done something good. The laughter of the crowd felt like a reward, too. They were with me, and against him. I felt I had almost as much of a common touch as in the March uprising of forty-eight.

One of the constables must have twisted the handcuffs, because Sir Edmund cried out, and gave a grimace that I did not find entirely unbecoming on his face.

'Where are the girls? I don't intend allowing you the luxury of going off to prison until you've told me. And that crowd doesn't look very friendly.'

A large fellow behind me sniggered. A moment ago they had seemed good-natured enough, but now they were turning slowly from vendors, country folk, piemen, pickpockets, Germans, Frenchmen and Americans into a mob, which could tear people to pieces like the Mænads of antiquity.

'This man stole away young girls!' I proclaimed to the crowd. A roar went up from their throats – a many-headed howl of vengeance, vengeance on the propertied classes, on the British Empire, on artists, on aesthetes, on all the lecherous men who have ever seduced the young daughters of this world.

'They were taken on board early this morning,' whispered Sir Edmund to Owain Evans, but not so quietly that I could not hear. 'We used the water barge.'

'And you were to sail with them?'

'Yes.'

'With your wife?'

'No, alone.'

'I'll have your ticket, please!' said Owain, and turned to the constables. 'You can take him away.'

So Sir Edmund was marched off under police escort – not only to stop him escaping, but also to stop the public setting on him.

After his ordeal at the Tower, he might appreciate the seclusion of his new lodgings a little better.

It was suddenly very quiet all around us. The constables and the Deputy Inspector disappeared with Sir Edmund, the crowd evaporated as rapidly as it had formed. Owain and I were left standing there in the shadow of the Tower. I took a deep breath, as if I had forgotten to inhale for the duration of the scene.

'What do we do next?' I asked. 'Raid the ship?'

Owain shook his head.

'We can't. The vessel is owned by a French consortium. We suspect one of the nine is a part-owner. Sending customs on board was all right, but I can't send my peelers: the *Heliogabalus* is foreign territory.'

I had been counting on that police raid from the word go. In my mind's eye I had seen Sir Edmund being arrested and a posse of bold peelers rushing on board, flinging open cabin doors and dragging out slimy villains. The girls would swarm ashore, white-clad and innocent, and I would hold out my arms to Agnes...

'We can't? What do we do, then?'

'We put me on board the *Heliogabalus*. I set them free when the appropriate time comes. I've acquired my ticket, as you saw.' Owain looked at the slip of paper he had got from Sir Edmund. 'Damn! It's personalised – and in his own name!'

I eyed the Inspector. They were hardly similar, and Sir Edmund was quite well known, it must be said. His fellow criminals should know him by appearance, too.

'You cannot mean that you intend to board a vessel – alone with those scoundrels, far out to sea?'

'The sea is the least of my worries. What else can I do? If I travelled with a constable, it would attract attention.'

'You will not be travelling with a constable. You will be travelling with your wife.'

'My dear Euthanasia, I am not married – as you full well know!'

'Good grief, Owain! Is your brain completely addled, just because your man is under arrest? You will sail under a false name, of course – and with a false wife! Hail a cab! I know what we shall do.'

Owain protested, I have to admit, but then gave in. It was almost half past nine, and time was short. We jumped into the cab and I gave the address of my publisher. That was also located within the central triangle, thank goodness.

'Euthanasia… I don't understand.'

'You soon will.'

The Sweets' home was in the sort of disorder that always precedes a journey. Mrs Sweet was nagging Mr Sweet, who had not finished his packing, while young Mr Sweet was just having a crisis of self-confidence and declaring over and over again that he could not run the publishing house on his own – and now it was time for Miss Bondeson's troublesome contract, and how could Father even think of leaving him?

The family was somewhat nonplussed by my arrival. The maid had initially refused to let me in, but I took absolutely no notice. Owain Evans – who was perhaps still in a slight daze after the arrest – leant close to her and whispered 'police'. The poor girl subsided onto the front steps and burst into uncontrollable tears. She had once smuggled a whole Victoria sponge home to her mother and feared she was for the gallows.

'Miss Bondeson!' cried my publisher. His tone was not much more amiable than Sir Edmund's had been. 'What do you want?'

'I have a proposal! I had managed to piece one together on the way from the Tower. If the Inspector could do nothing, it was up to me.

'October is not a good month for Nice. It would be considerably better for you to go to Egypt, which has just as much culture, is more exotic, and will give you the chance to see mummies and to bask in a sun that never tires. I admit it costs a little more – let me finish, I am talking as fast as I can – but it so happens that Police

Inspector Evans has an offer for you. The Inspector is the head of Scotland Yard. He and his men are about to intercept a dangerous gang that has been abducting women – my companion and Mrs Russell's daughter, among others. The perpetrators are making off in the *Heliogabalus*. That is to say, *the very same ship* that you are booked on! It will not be very agreeable on board, I can tell you that much. The police are prepared to let you cash in your tickets.'

Owain Evans opened his mouth and shut it again. Mrs Sweet dissolved into floods of tears. Mr Sweet took out a manuscript that he had just thrust into his portmanteau. Young Mr Sweet looked up in relief and exclaimed:

'You are my saviour, Miss Bondeson!'

Mr Sweet senior looked stern, put the bundle of papers down on his desk and said:

'Out of the question. We have been planning this holiday for a long time.'

'Egypt, dear!' ventured Mrs Sweet under her breath. 'I have always wanted to go to Egypt! Perhaps we can find a ship that sails this week...'

'Do you mean to say you do not *want* to go to the Riviera?' said the publisher, giving the lie to his accusing tone by fishing two slim volumes out of his bag. 'I mean to say, you have been on at me about Nice for two years!' Funnily enough, he seemed relieved.

'Abductors of women, my sweet Mr Sweet! How can a respectable woman board a ship like that?'

'I have a proposition,' I said. 'I am prepared to let Sweet & Sweet take all the profits from my next novel...at least...well, let us say the first thousand copies of the first edition!'

'Pardon?'

'...if we can have the tickets.'

Agnes was worth it. I heard Mr and Mrs Sweet conferring in whispers and Owain insisting he be allowed to pay. I was fully prepared to make the sacrifice. My English print runs stretch to at least five thousand.

'You had better make up your minds quickly!' the Inspector said.

'My wife has already made our decision. Here!'

Mr Sweet produced two tickets from his bag. We shook hands on the agreement, but decided to leave signing the contract for the novel until later. This is becoming quite common practice nowadays, and has its advantages, of course.

So Owain and I found ourselves on the front steps, hailing a cab.

'What time is it?'

'A quarter past ten. We've masses of time. I would love a cup of tea.'

'I will definitely need to take some other clothes with me,' said the Inspector, looking at his tweed suit. 'A tailcoat or something. And another waistcoat.'

It had never even occurred to me that the Inspector might own a tailcoat. He was right, of course. It might be to our advantage.

'Fine,' I said. 'My portmanteau is already packed, and I can have my trunk sent on later.'

'You have such foresight, Euthanasia.'

'I hope to get Agnes back – and I find it hard to believe she will want to return to London.'

The cab waited at the Golden Cross Hotel while I paid the bill. There was no problem about storing the trunks. I had been a good guest, who had paid for two rooms for almost two weeks while sleeping and eating for only one. I took two bags with me – my own and Agnes's. It would soon be time for us to be reunited. The Inspector carried out my bag, groaning over the weight of it – it naturally contained the five or six books without which I could not live, the manuscript of *The Wrecker's Revenge* (for copying during the voyage), my writing materials and a few necessities in the way of clothes. I travel light, but I have never learnt to cut down on my reading matter.

It had been an eventful morning, and as I took my seat in the cab, I felt a faintness come over me. A cup of tea would certainly be welcome. I could not even remember when I last slept for a whole night. Not could I recall what date or day of the week it was. Mr Russell had died on Wednesday. That was two days ago, so today must be Friday. I did, on the other hand, know exactly what time it was: ten thirty-five. I had been brisk at the hotel.

The worst part of the day was the one spent sitting in the cab, waiting for Owain Evans. He was not a man to choose his abode for its location. We were far from the stately facades of Belgravia. From here, the view was of the bridges of the city and the masts of ships. The Inspector lived near the docks, but also dangerously near to poverty. A feeling of hopelessness descended on me.

I awoke with a start as the cab door was opened. Owain climbed in and put his portmanteau on his lap. I was still holding my watch. It was ten forty-five. He was quick at packing.

'What do you live in such a hovel, Inspector? Why not marry and get a proper house?'

'I only sleep there. But I am glad you brought it up, Euthanasia.'

I became at once uneasy and expectant. But I had no cause. The fact was, it was just such feelings the Inspector sought to address.

'You are a marvellous woman. But...there is something I must say. When we become Mr and Mrs Sweet...'

He took out the tickets and studied them. The names were correct.

'...anyway...what I wanted to say was that although we will be sharing a cabin, you naturally have nothing to fear from me.'

'Although you always claim *not* to be, I have every confidence that you are a gentleman.' I said, fiddling with my walking stick.

'Nothing is what it appears to be, dear Euthanasia. Nothing.'

He lapsed into silent thought for a moment, and I, having just been roused from sleep, wondered what he actually meant. Then the Inspector went on:

'Certainly I am a gentleman, insofar as anyone can *become* a gentleman and doesn't have to be born to it...but you see, Euthanasia, I am quite simply not a man for the ladies.'

'*Aha*!' I said, and all sorts of odd details fell into place. Owain was as much an adherent of Greek practices as the Reverend Amis and Claire. That might also explain why he was so familiar with the shadier parts of the capital – and why he had helped the Rector clear away all the compromising photographs. I was a little disappointed. But Owain was a good man, I clung to that notion, and a good friend.

'I am more Roman, myself,' I said. 'I am a human being, and nothing human is alien to me.'

The Inspector nodded. We looked at each other for a moment, full of mutual respect. Then all at once, Owain was my superior, giving orders about boarding. I was to go on board with my head down, not indulge my curiosity and look about me until we had put out, and above all not speak too loudly or clearly. Moreover, I was to be careful not to show my face – an engraved portrait of me had, after all, appeared in the *Illustrated London News*. I had not been aware of that. I would have liked to see it, had I known.

I have always been an obedient girl. I wore a veil for boarding, and kept my voice veiled as I answered the few questions that were put to me. No one could have distinguished my face, or my accent. I was sweet and charming, as quiet as a mouse and as decorous as a nun. I lived up to my assumed name in every possible way. I nonetheless managed to see a little of the ship – that it was slender and beautiful, with a splendid, large paddle wheel and short auxiliary masts. There was a deck, inviting one to promenade, the portholes were brass-trimmed and the companion-way to the cabins was panelled in fine wood. Like an impeccable wife, I followed the Inspector and looked away when the steward brought in our luggage.

Then I threw off my hat and veil, hastily pulled out my hairpins, and coughed and spluttered as the mane of hair fell over my face. It took me some time to rein in the rebellious mass, but when I emerged, I met the Inspector's astonished gaze.

'I have not had to keep quiet for that long since the nursemaid put a gag on me!'

'That must have come as a shock.'

More instructions followed: we were to stay quietly in our cabin until the boat was some way out into the Thames, and then the Inspector would reconnoitre. For my part, I was consigned to wifeliness for a while longer.

It is never a mistake to travel with books. I finished off the Yorkshire tale – which has actually proved very good – and turned to an American history of whaling, which Professor Devindra had recommended. I suddenly had the sensation of being aboard a whaler. We were rocking about as if we were in Nantucket. The *Heliogabalus* had put out from the shore, and we were on our way. In the bunk beside me, the Inspector put down his adventure yarn and listened to the sounds of the ship. I could tell from his face that he was thinking about winds and the setting of sails. Perhaps it felt hard to leave old England, perhaps it was a relief to be at sea. I let my own book fall and thought of the country I was leaving behind me – of the green hills, of London's streets and alleyways, of the gas light and the oil lamps, of the Exhibition and the glorious Crystal Palace, and of the fog, swirling in off the sea and settling over the city.

A little while later, the Inspector tiptoed out into the corridor. The book I was reading was detailed and instructive, and I was soon fast asleep. The nights had brought me close to people, but I had entirely foregone bliss in the arms of Morpheus.

When I awoke, there was hardly any daylight coming through the porthole. A single lamp was reflected in the smooth wood of the cabin. There had been a squeak of hinges. A man stood in the doorway. I immediately recognised him as the Inspector. There was a kind of security in having a man to hand, a protector and companion. But I could not quite decide if I was relieved not to need to defend my virtue.

Owain sat down on the other bunk.

'The girls are on board. There's no doubt about it.'

While I was enjoying my beauty sleep, he had gone exploring, as all normally inquisitive people do, up stairs and down stairs (though he called them ladders); he had checked the seaworthiness of the vessel as befitted a former sailor (forgetting in his eagerness that he was supposed to be a landlubberly publisher) and ferreted out details of the cabin layout. Since it was an exclusive vessel, most of the cabins were doubles, but at the far end of the corridor there were some family cabins. Owain had in addition made the acquaintance of both fellow passengers and crew. They chatted about this and that, about the ship, the meals and the Mediterranean.

'I met the most agreeable steward, and told him about my poor, ailing wife, who had felt sick the moment she came aboard. And then of course he couldn't resist telling me that two cabins along there were nine sisters, no less, all keeping themselves to themselves and clearly indisposed, attended by their three servants. "But their father, who we were expecting – that gentleman never came on board!"'

'I can guess what that Papa's name is,' I said, putting aside my book, which had been weighing down my chest as I slept.

'We ought to show ourselves at mealtimes, so no one gets suspicious. But we ought to infiltrate the girls' camp, too, so they know what's going on.'

'Well, we could divide our labours: you show yourself, I'll infiltrate.'

'I was thinking the same thing,' said Owain. 'Presumably the girls have their food sent down to their cabins...'

'...and if I can appear motherly...'

'... then you might be able to ingratiate yourself with the

friendly steward...'

'...and could even the worst scoundrel suspect a little old lady like this?'

I screwed up my face in a manner that used to make my late father exclaim that I really must desist, otherwise I might get stuck like that. The Inspector guffawed with laughter.

Our project became somewhat long-winded. I tried infiltrating for two days, while my 'spouse' complained to all and sundry of his wife's indisposition and her trouble with the weather. The English Channel was as smooth as a millpond, so I soon had a reputation for being a real baby. In between times, we both ingratiated ourselves in our different ways with the friendly steward. The youth was soon calling me 'darling' and the Inspector 'ducks' – a designation I hardly considered appropriate for a man in his position.

On our third day on board, Owain decided it was time to strike. It was a demanding task. While the other passengers tucked into their breakfast, I left my eggs cooling in my cabin. I stood in the corridor, holding my breath. Two cabins along – at the far end of the corridor – that was where the girls were, the steward had revealed. Now it was time to make contact. I crept to the door of one of the cabins and whispered:

'Agnes? Grace? Are you there, Agnes?'

'Aunt Euthanasia!' cried a voice from inside. I shushed her. If only I could still my own heart! It was galloping away in my breast like a herd of Indian mustang, wild and uncontrollable. I felt light-headed, my eyes could not focus and my head ached. In short: I was both agitated and ecstatic, but this task was not about me. It was about nine captive girls.

I tugged at the door handle again. It did not budge. The guards must be somewhere nearby.

'Agnes? Is all well?'

'Yes, they haven't done anything to me – except paint me – dressed almost like Eve, if you understand me, Aunt Euthanasia! And I speak much better English now...'

'Quiet! Be quiet, you silly goose! We are going to rescue you, never fear. Pretend nothing has happened.'

It was taking a great risk, but I crept along to the next door and whispered:

'Grace? Grace Russell?'

'Yes?'

'I am a friend. Are you well?'

'Yes – but I'm so scared! We are being guarded by a *man*, Ma'am!'

'Calm down!' I whispered. 'Just calm down!' All will be well, very soon.'

Yet I wholly understood how she was feeling. Had I not been most indignant when Owain Evans woke me the other morning? I was now getting used to him seeing me while I was asleep, defenceless and unadorned. Never mind that he was not interested in ladies. He was a man, nonetheless. And for a girl such as Grace! Her diary had betrayed how unused to men she was. Girls of that class can hardly speak to a man without a couple of relatives watching over them as energetically as the constables had over Sir Edmund. Men were intimidating – big, hairy and foul smelling. That, at any rate, was how I visualised the fellows who were guarding the girls. I could not imagine them to be in the least like Professor Devindra.

I hurried back to our cabin as fast as I dared and bolted down the eggs before they were completely cold. We had no time to lose.

'You are quite right,' said the Inspector on his return. 'The girls are uneasy, and their guards are getting jittery. With Sir Edmund not having showed up, they could do something over-hasty before long.'

'Has news of his arrest got out?'

The Inspector shook his head and went to the wardrobe for his travelling belt. From it he took a pistol, a little bottle of oil and a rag.

'We have tried to keep the arrest and the whole story quiet. It would be bad for it to get out prematurely. First we must make sure the girls are safe, and then – if all goes to plan – arrest the other eight sinners. If anything were to leak out...'

Owain opened his pocket pistol with a click and studied its interior. Evidently he was satisfied. He began to grease it, slowly and lovingly.

'...if, as I say, the news were to get out, we don't know what repercussions it might have for the girls. Those guards of theirs are no philanthropists.'

'Grace Russell seemed very scared,' I said, observing Owain's activities with fascination. Now he was polishing the pistol, loading it and stroking the short barrel.

'I'd like to put a bullet between the eyes of Sir Edmund and his whole crew!'

Owain gripped the shiny wooden pistol butt and took aim at the porthole. For a moment I was afraid he was going to practise his sharpshooting on our only protection against the fury of the waves. But no. Owain Evans is a sensible man. His anger was evident, but he did not waste bullets unnecessarily.

'You are welcome to go hunting – but be careful how you wave that pistol around.'

'Are you gun-shy?' asked Owain, trying to provoke me, and secreted the pistol in his jacket pocket. I shivered. Now things were serious. The Inspector's hunting instinct was roused. He decided we would strike that evening, after dinner. It would be quiet on the boat then, and both the passengers and the guards dulled by wine.

I had hoped for some peace and quiet that evening. Perhaps I could copy a few chapters of *The Wrecker's Revenge*. But Owain Evans was having none of it. It was time for me to stop hiding myself. That evening we were to dine at the Captain's table. Mrs Sweet was feeling much better, now we were out in the open sea.

To my surprise, I felt a certain anxiety at the prospect of all those unfamiliar fellow guests. I have had experiences aplenty, but this was a new one – being a married woman. Owain Evans kept chivalrously out of the way while I changed. For the Captain's sake I donned a flattering dress, sufficiently well cut to attract the gentlemen's looks. Then, when I was doing my hair, Owain sat in the cabin and commented on the appearance of the other wives.

'Several of them have sort of twisted knots of hair sticking forward round their faces. Quite pretty, I suppose.'

'Undoubtedly, if one happens to be twenty. The Captain and his table will have to content themselves with a chignon, I'm afraid.'

Owain took his pistol from his pocket and fingered it in a particularly annoying manner.

'Just as long as you remember that you are Mrs Sweet and not Euthanasia Bondeson.'

'Does Mrs Sweet have a Christian name, by any chance?'

'Emily.'

'What could be better...but what if anybody recognises me?'

'That's a risk we shall have to take – but I tend to think marriage will be sufficient disguise. No one would expect such a well-known authoress to disguise herself as a publisher's wife. What is more, my identity as Owen Sweet is already well established. I've bored the whole table stiff with my expositions on print runs and types of paper.'

'*Owen* Sweet? My publisher's name is John, just like his son!'

Owain Evans shrugged his shoulders.

'I would never answer to that name. King John Lackland terrorised Wales.'

I sighed. There is something long-sighted about my friend the policeman. Six hundred and fifty years is neither here nor there, if one has suffered an injustice.

'Emily, sweetest...we must go now, if we are not to keep the Captain waiting!'

Owain did not see the face I pulled. He was busy putting away his pistol, opening the door and offering me his arm. I really did hope the pistol would stay in his pocket and not come tumbling out. That would create a very awkward social situation, particularly for one who has had no training in wifehood. My accented English was enough of a problem, as it was. If anyone asked, I was going to put it down to my years in the colonies.

The Captain's table was magnificent, and the Captain himself an impressive figure. He had the bushiest mutton-chop whiskers I have ever seen – except on a baboon in London Zoo – and folded himself in the middle like a razor to kiss my hand.

'Mrs Sweet...what an honour!'

Then we took our places and helped ourselves to the calf's head broth and stewed eels. Owain Evans immediately struck up a conversation with one of the other gentlemen about the hunting season, and the Captain enquired sympathetically how I was feeling.

'I think I have found my sea legs, Captain.'

'I am delighted to hear it, Mrs Sweet!'

We drank our sherry without a toast, and went on with an entrée of braised lamb's kidneys. The lady diagonally opposite began to talk animatedly to me. Had we children? How old were they? I gaily invented two fairly young children. I did not wish to admit to any John just then, either. The woman on the other side also had a nine-year old, and we spoke at length of that unruly age, so far removed from the harmoniousness of eight. It is just as well I have nephews and nieces. We continued up through the age groups and were at last able to engage the gentlemen on that most important subject – the Great Exhibition, which we discussed during the roast lamb, swede and carrots. The third main course was a little lighter – just a few partridges served with fruit jelly – and by then we, too, had reached the lighter topics, namely the London theatre. I had to think carefully here, to avoid sounding like a country cousin. For me, it was a revelation to have seen Kean in *Othello*, but the London ladies were off to the theatre every other day. Nor could I, as is my wont, boast of what Stockholm had to offer. I simply had to grit my teeth, say *just* enough – and that was hard, I would like my readers to know – and sip my champagne, which was the fourth wine of the meal.

The dessert consisted of ginger pudding, served with lavish amounts of custard, of course. The champagne was almost all gone, and I realised I should have been a little more abstemious. Above all, I should not have eaten so much swede and carrot.

The ladies were now to leave the gentlemen to their port. We stood up and were about to file out when the boat lurched. I cried out and lost my balance. Owain Evans threw his arm round my waist, and one of my new, married, female acquaintances exclaimed what a charming couple we made. She would never have believed we had been married so long – no, never!

'Now then, my dear Mr Sweet!' I whispered to Owain. 'Don't spend too long hanky-pankying with the boys when you have a hale and hearty wife!'

I kissed him briefly on the cheek – more insinuatingly than I had ever done before, I have to admit – and sailed out with the convoy of ladies.

'Married women first!' I called to one of the young misses who was pushing in front of me for coffee.

Now my anxiety began to make itself felt. Coffee and port tippling are all very pleasant for a change, but this evening we had more pressing business, Owain and I. I left my coffee half drunk on the table, excused myself and hurried off to my cabin.

'She has an assignation with her husband – *how* romantic!' one of the ladies giggled as I went.

Indeed it was romantic, but not in the way she thought. I did not need to wait long for Owain. He was feeling the tension, too, and had hurried away from his social duties.

'Are you ready?'

'Yes.'

He took out his pistol, checked the charge, and inserted it carefully back into his pocket. We sneaked out into the corridor together as if it were the most natural thing in the world. We were going to storm the cabins, and that would require a delightful combination of cunning and pure violence. With my walking stick on my hand, I knocked on the first door, while Owain Evans hid round a corner.

'Excuse me!' I said, when the door opened. I glimpsed a male hand on the handle, but a young girl looked out. 'There's a man after me. Let me come in!'

'No!' said a peremptory voice from the cabin.

'Oh yes! Please let her!' came a girl's voice. I know it was not Agnes. We were saving her cabin for last. The idea of going on, of saving more girls once Agnes was free – that was too much for me. The others must be liberated first.

Small and supple, I slipped past the girl and found myself face to face with a man, who apart from his frock coat resembled nothing so much as a statue of Hercules. He was no doubt the one who had opened the door.

'Get out of here, missus! Don't disturb the girls!'

'Oh, it's quite all right. I shall not disturb...the girls.'

Even as I spoke, I withdrew the rapier from my stick and pressed it to the fellow's chest.

'Back off! Back off you swine, or I shall slit you open and have your guts for garters!'

'That will do!' whispered the Inspector in my ear, placed an atavistic kick right in the man's midriff, and tied him up firmly with a rope.

The first cabin was liberated. The second was captured just as easily. But when we got to the third, we could no longer restrain the rescued girls. They were swarming around us like summer midges, and Grace Russell was hanging on to my bodice and covering me in wet kisses. I was her best friend, her mother's most honourable comrade, the most splendid woman the Lord had created. Her praise distressed me, when I thought of whose fault it was that her stepfather now lay stiff and cold.

Grace Russell was talking too much, and far too loud. It was as if her relief at being set free had loosened her tongue. The guard in the third cabin was prepared for a fight before we even knocked on the door.

'Who's there?' he shouted through the door.

'The avenger!' piped Grace Russell.

I gave a deep sigh and tried to shove the girl aside.

'Out of the way!' bellowed Inspector Evans.

Now his footwork was really put to the test. With a kick he broke the lock – imagine the security on a magnificent ship like this not being better! A woman could be in all manner of danger! – and engaged with the man inside. If the first two had seemed big, this one was a giant. He reached almost to the ceiling. His thighs were the size of girls' waists, his shoulders broad and inflated by muscle. His features were sketchy, as if painted there by an artist in a hurry. The last time I had seen him, he had been in footman's livery at Sir Edmund's. He shook himself free from the Inspector and grabbed Agnes.

With Agnes held in front of him like a shield, he tried to contain the other girls. I ran forward and received a hard blow. My head spinning, I leant against the wall to catch my breath. The Inspector took the next punch, and Agnes cried:

'Don't worry about me! Get the others out!'

She is a noble soul, that girl – either that, or she has read too many novels.

'Never!' I cried, and jabbed my rapier blade into the expanse of male leg. The leg's owner gave a roar, and the man let go of Agnes to tackle me.

'Go on then! Kill me! You daren't! You daren't hit a respectable woman!'

I stared at him fixedly and waited for the attack. Here he came, his hands held ready to wring my neck as if I were a chicken.

Then there was a loud report, and I felt a wet stickiness on my face. Terror swept over me. What had happened?

'Aunt Euthanasia! Oh Aunt! My dear Aunt!'

The grip on my neck was not that of a murderer but Agnes's soft embrace, and kisses were showering over me. I held Agnes close and felt the calm, the assurance, of having someone to be fond of.

Behind the girl, the villain lay dead. His blood and brains stained the floor and were spattered over half the cabin, over my face and lovely dress. But it did not matter. Agnes was free, and so were all the others.

CHAPTER TWELVE

IN WHICH OUR STORY ENDS

Once the criminals had been thwarted, joy, festivity and jubilation should have been the order of the day, as when the heroes of ancient times concluded every successful military operation with a grand sacrifice to the gods. That was not the case here. First came the tears, then the exhaustion, and after that the burial at sea of the deceased felon. Only then could we exult. The girls shouted for joy, and the vessel rejoiced with them. We were nearing lovely France, and there was no limit to the amount of *foie gras*, oysters and champagne we consumed.

There, just off the French coast, Owain Evans and I drank a toast to the successful solution of the Case of the Missing Girls. We raised our glasses, filled with the same fine champagne that I had once drunk in entirely different company in Sir Edmund Chamber's house in Belgravia.

'An interesting case,' said Owain Evans, as all policemen seem to do, 'but it is not over yet.'

'*Skål!*' I toasted. 'Good health and good fortune!'

'*Iechyd da!*' responded Owain Evans in his mother tongue, and we drained our glasses of the sparkling liquid, so ill matched to the Inspector's rough tweed and rustic palate.

Then my friend was gone. He delivered two fit and brawny villains into French custody. His own route took him inland by train – not detouring round the Iberian peninsula as we did –

and up into the Alps, to the Franco–Italian border. There lay the chateau in which eight men, of noble birth but with ignoble hearts, were eagerly awaiting nine fair virgins. The men would wait in vain. A Parisian police officer had been summoned by telegraph, and he and Owain went together to the chateau to carry out a formidable arrest. We counted on being able to read all about it in an impressive, illustrated piece in the coming issue of a London magazine.

Our course continued along the coast – and 'we' now once more comprised just Agnes and myself. On the day of Owain's departure, the other eight girls had been sent back to England, where Amanda Russell and other anxious mothers awaited them. Even Elaine, Lady Margaret's lady's maid, was going back to her own mother – she wanted nothing more to do with her mistress, and especially not with her master. Agnes seemed to have learnt something from her adventure, too. It was not only her English that had improved.

After the celebration came the calm. That night, Agnes's head rested on my breast once more. After the calm came the expectation, for such is human nature – why should we believe things may turn out badly again? Misfortunes should reasonably be expected to come singly. And perhaps that really would be the case.

The days passed. It was evening. Agnes and I were admiring the sunset from the deck of the *Heliogabalus*. I had waxed eloquent on the subject of our Western cultural heritage, of Greece and Rome, the greatness of France and the importance of Italy. We had left Nice that day. That was a milestone on our journey, for now we were beyond the port to which Sir Edmund had tried to transport the girls.

In the setting sun, I thought back to the first time we met, Agnes and I. It was almost five years before. There was a grand firework display in Stockholm to mark – well, I forget what, exactly. Perhaps some new prince or princess had been born, or some battle or hero king was to be commemorated. It might have been Gustaf II Adolf. Anyway, it was autumn, cold and raw, and I was standing on Norrbro Bridge, watching the fireworks. One of my brothers-in-law was with me as a chaperone – he was the only one of my relations willing to venture forth on such an evening.

The sky was full of blazing dragons, lions, stars and royal monograms. I became aware of a skinny girl at my side. In fact, she was ridiculously close. I felt in my reticule, but since my purse was still there, I looked at the girl more closely. She was very beautiful, although she was so thin. Suddenly I realised she was trying to solicit my brother-in-law.

I addressed the girl on the subject of morality – but then I restrained myself, and treated her to a sandwich and some red wine. Something about her appealed to me. She had her head screwed on, and was of an amiable disposition, besides. I secured a place for her in a home for the salvation of fallen women, where she would learn better morals and then be placed as a farm girl in a country family. Agnes had no objection to the morals, but she was not cut out to be a farm girl. I took her in myself, gave her some education and kept her so well that she no longer felt tempted by her old profession. Like the saint whose name she shares, her cheerful disposition has never been crushed by poverty or vice.

These were my thoughts as I sat relaxing in my deckchair. The sun was now visible only as a patch of light astern, and as darkness fell, so the coast of France melted away behind us. We entered waters where the coastal dwellers speak the tongue of Dante, and approached a life of *il dolce far niente*.

'Look, Aunt Euthanasia,' whispered Agnes at my side. 'That must be Italy up ahead!'

I squeezed Agnes's hand, and she leant close to me. Ahead of us lay the lights of Genoa, queen of mariners and mother of Christopher Columbus. She dominated her bay like a goddess enthroned, her gaze turned on the sea, with high mountains at her back. People had journeyed out from here, and travellers had flocked here. Once again I felt the joy of travel. I could hardly call myself of fixed abode any more. I had been in London, I had seen good and evil, I had made friends and enemies. Now Agnes sat at my side once more, with her soft hands and youthful comments. The pendant at her breast sparkled with all the treasures of the North.

'Well, that was an adventure, and no mistake,' she said once she had shaken off thoughts of the gloomy chateaux of France and turned her gaze to countries new. 'Where are we going now, Aunt Euthanasia?'

The pilot came on board, and the deck began to fill with passengers. Some were disembarking, others merely wished to enjoy coming into a new port.

'Absolutely anywhere,' I replied. It delighted me to say it. I felt bold and full of energy. We were free, both of us, after imprisonment and feigned marriage. Maybe we would leave the boat in Genoa, just ahead of us, or go on to La Spezia, Marina di Pisa or Livorno. Maybe we would stay on board until we reached the coast of Latium, and become Romans for the winter, or leave the *Heliogabalus* and continue by land to Venice, where we could spend the cold months among the gilt and decay of centuries.

'We will disembark wherever the fancy takes us, Agnes,' I said, and saw her shiver of expectation. Young people detest plans, and nowadays I was young at heart. I had not reverted to the role of little old lady. In the cabin, my bag stood packed and ready, the walking stick stuck through the handles. At some juncture we would probably send for the trunks, currently in safekeeping at the Golden Cross Hotel in the Strand in London. For now, we could manage very well without them.

Evening came. We dined at the Captain's table, where our placing had been more modest since Owain's departure. Agnes was tired and went to bed early. She had still not got out of the ascetic habits of the captive life.

I accompanied her to the cabin and sat with her until she fell asleep – just as I had recently sat with Owain Evans. They were so different, those two. With Agnes's hand in mine, I thought back over our adventure. It was still September. In less than a month, we had lived through a whole volume of experiences.

Now she was asleep, my little girl. I carefully freed my hand, stroked her cheek – so soft, so anything but rough – and took out my notebook, some sheets of writing paper and my pen case. Then I summoned our nice steward.

'Chianti and a Cuban cigar, please!'

'Will do, dear. Here or up on deck?.'

I peered out through the porthole. The night was as velvety dark as Professor Devindra's eyes.

'On deck, please!'

By the time my stimulants arrived, I was onto my second letter. My sister Aurora had needed a report, and I was just adding some suitably warm concluding phrases to Professor Devindra Sivaramakrishnan, whose full name I had finally mastered. I signed off, sampled the wine and put the cigar to my nose. *Romeo y Julieta*. Well, well – and without a band round its middle this time. The steward set down the box, cut the cigar and helped me light it.

The cigar tasted of adventure. It had the aroma of London: rich, racy, sinful and alluring. I leant back and smoked in silence. The steward vanished, and I allowed my memories to pass me by in single file. The Exhibition, the tour of the slums, the British Museum. The memories increased their pace, flashing before my eyes. The rectory, the curry restaurant, the molly house, the salon – myself in man's clothes – social calls and climbing walls, the theatre, the fight in the studio, kisses at the hospital and the chase at the gentlemen's club. Heavens! This was the stuff of a novel!

I crossed my legs under my skirt. Modern Babylon lay far away. The scents of the balmy Mediterranean night were all around me. From the sea of seas rose the smell of seaweed and salt. The memory of Wyld's Monster Globe came back. I had visited it in such haste and in such a frantic state that I had hardly paid any attention to it at the time. Now I recalled the enormous expanses of water, all the blue between the shapes of khaki and green. And the waters prevailed, and were increased greatly upon the Earth, and the ship *Heliogabalus* went upon the face of the waters. If I decided to take a dip, the water here would be poisonously salty on my tongue, not lightly salty, like ours in the Baltic. The sea here was still warm.

Summer lingered in the Mediterranean. Lights could be seen from the heart of Genoa and I knew people would be sitting out on café terraces and pavements. They would be drinking local wine and eating salty cheeses made from ewes' milk. Perhaps it was my imagination, but I could sense the smells of the shore. Here the lemons grew; here the grapes would soon be harvested for wine. Soon it would be drunk, young and simple, an accompaniment to roast veal stuffed with herbs and the thin breadsticks of the region. The basil of Liguria stretched out its delicate leaves towards the ship. I could feel Italy calling me.

The ash on my cigar was almost an inch long. I tapped it off. The column fell onto the white-scrubbed deck and scattered quickly. The wind was scarcely perceptible, yet within a minute, the ash was gone, as readily dispersed as the troubles of youth.

I took several deep puffs at my cigar and blew out smoke rings, which slowly drifted out across the water and disappeared in towards the town. The night was still, perfumed and saturated with the love that exists in the natural world. Italy was near, and London far, far away. And yet...

I balanced my cigar on the arm of my chair, took a gulp of wine and reached for my notebook. There were jottings about Miss Giovanna and her sailor, but also lists of what we knew about Agnes's disappearance. So long ago. There were no blank pages until after the middle of the book. I licked my pencil, tried to write, and dipped it in my wine to inject some strength into the script. Now I knew what the next novel would be about.

I held the cigar between my lips, inhaled again and started work on the first chapter – about a port, a vessel and some women who, separated, have various adventures in a foreign city. It all takes place in a world like ours – incredible and immense, terrible and alluring.

I decided to call the city Babylon.

Cambridge – Uppsala – Cambridge
July 2003 – January 2004